SO-BNK-691

PRAISE FOR
ENTER THE JANITOR

"A fresh voice in urban fantasy and an original new hero. And after reading this novel, you might never again go to the bathroom alone…."

—Laura Resnick, author of
the *Esther Diamond* series

"It's always a good sign when I close a book with a giggle. Enter the Janitor *by Josh Vogt is a humorous contemporary fantasy that goes places and meets creatures you won't expect and haven't seen before. His protagonists are definitely not your standard fantasy heroes, nor their cause the usual fight between Good and Evil. Just when you think you've figured out the world, it twists again, landing you in a new place with new perils. Clever, well-written and a bunch of fun."*

—Jody Lynn Nye, bestselling fantasy
and science fiction author

The Cleaners
Book 1

ENTER THE JANITOR

The Cleaners
Book 1

ENTER THE JANITOR

To Ashlee—
Careful. This is gonna
get messy!

JOSH VOGT

WordFire Press
Colorado Springs, Colorado

THE CLEANERS: ENTER THE JANITOR

Copyright © 2015 Josh Vogt

All rights reserved. No part of this book may be reproduced or transmitted in any form or by any electronic or mechanical means, including photocopying, recording or by any information storage and retrieval system, without the express written permission of the copyright holder, except where permitted by law. This novel is a work of fiction. Names, characters, places and incidents are either the product of the author's imagination, or, if real, used fictitiously.

ISBN: 978-1-61475-318-6

Cover design by Janet McDonald

Art Director Kevin J. Anderson

Cover artwork images by Jeff Herndon

Book Design by RuneWright, LLC
www.RuneWright.com

Published by
WordFire Press, an imprint of
WordFire, Inc.
PO Box 1840
Monument, CO 80132

Kevin J. Anderson & Rebecca Moesta Publishers

WordFire Press Trade Paperback Edition May 2015
Printed in the USA
wordfirepress.com

CHAPTER ONE

Ben shuffled into the college library, tugging his squeaky janitorial cart along like a coffin-on-wheels. The moment he entered the place, his right arm started aching, adding a small, but significant voice to the chorus of twinges, knotted muscles, and scars that composed his aging body.

Ignoring this as best he could, he took a big whiff of the place. He snorted and shook his head, gray ponytail flapping.

At the noise, heads popped up from textbooks and tablets as students stared his way. Ben gave them his best grumpy grandpa look until they turned back to their books. A study group that had circled up chairs in the center of the room resumed murmuring calculus equations at each other, which might as well have been a foreign language to Ben.

Resisting the urge to massage his arm, he made eye contact with the young man behind the main desk. Jason, the work-study for the evening, flashed a relieved smile as he lurched out of his chair and headed the janitor's way.

Ben tugged at his blue jumpsuit so his name, threaded in red on the left breast, displayed prominently. The spray bottle hanging on his belt quivered as the water sloshed within. Ben scowled and slapped it.

"Shaddup," he whispered. "I can handle this."

Jason arrived, glancing around as if afraid of angering some librarian deity. His combed hair and tucked polo shirt made him look like the chrysalis version of a politician, close to breaking out of the cocoon into full suit-and-smirk mode.

"If I'd known anyone was coming, I would've established quarantine," he said.

Ben cleared his throat with the subtlety of a garbage disposal. "If I'd known any winnin' lotto numbers, I woulda retired years ago. What's your point?"

Flushing, Jason caught the janitor's arm. Ben let himself be guided to one side, but once they got out of earshot, he grumbled at the younger man.

"Leggo of my arm. The suit don't block everythin'."

Jason snatched his hand back. "I—er. Oh."

"Yeah, 'oh.' And here I thought you was one of the smarter recruits."

"Should I ... uh ..." Jason wiped his hand on his shirt.

"If you caught anythin', it wouldn't matter if you stuck it in boilin' water until the skin came off. Just don't grope me again."

"The Board processed my report?" Jason asked.

"Yuppers. Figured it was worth a look."

Jason squinted in doubt. "And they sent you?"

Ben pushed his sagging cheeks up and leaned in. "You wanted someone prettier? Want me to go steal some lipstick from the girls' dorm and get gussied?"

Jason coughed and backed up a step. "Sorry, I just ... I waited a while to call in. You know how HQ gets if you file too many false alarms. Wasn't sure if I actually sensed anything or was just being paranoid."

Ben rolled his bowed shoulders, which crackled like bubble wrap. "What're we dealin' with?"

"The vents keep rumbling," Jason nodded at a nearby grille, "and I've noticed above-average grime buildup. Definitely Corruption of some sort. Could be coming in from the air ducts. Maybe a muttermite infestation."

Ben sniffed. "Naw. You trainees are gettin' sloppy. Muttermites ain't never made this kinda stink."

Jason's nose wrinkled. "I haven't smelled anything."

"That's 'cause you ain't an old hound dog like me. You couldn't sniff out Corruption if bile got pumped straight up your blowholes."

The water in the spray bottle sloshed again.

"Hmm." Ben nodded. "Good idea."

Jason eyed the water as it spun. "Is that ... Carl?"

"You betcha." Ben patted the bottle. "And no. You ain't gonna hold him, pet him, snuggle, or take a sip."

"I wasn't going to—"

"Hush it. Lemme concentrate."

He shut his eyes to fix on his prey. He blanked out the hushed chatter of the students, the hum of air conditioning, and the clack of fingernails over keyboards. He pushed past every distraction until ...

The subtle foulness in the air congealed into an olfactory hook that set in his nose and jerked him toward the source of Corruption. Along with this came the sound of leather being dragged over rusty metal, and a messy snuffling, like a dog gobbling up fresh goose droppings.

Ben cocked his head at the bathrooms. "We got ourselves a blot-hound nested in the pipes."

Jason paled. "But there haven't been any suicides. They leave pretty distinctive trails, too. I'm sure I would've noticed. And if it has a nest, that's even worse. They always fight hardest against threats to claimed territory and—"

Ben sighed. "Are you tryin' to be helpful or just make yourself look smart?"

Jason stuck his chest out. "I've been studying. Almost ready to test for active field duty."

"Studyin'. Heh." Ben smirked. "Lemme fill you in on a company secret, kid. With the Cleaners, you don't learn through information. You learn through action. Gotten any of that lately?"

"I'm ... not sure you mean it that way."

He clapped the trainee on the shoulder. "Don't think about it too hard. After all, I'm just a geezer here to get the job done."

"What should we do?"

"We? Nuh-uh. I got this. You plant your butt back behind that desk and keep clear."

"Sir, I've been ready for this for a year now."

"If you think that, then you sure as shootin' ain't ready yet." Jason's face fell.

Ben scratched his arm, which itched where the kid had grabbed it. "You really wanna be useful?"

"Please. Anything."

"Then go get me a sign that says the bathrooms are closed. That'll give me time to check things out and see if there's somewhere to fit you in. Anyone in either of them now?"

"Don't think so," Jason said. "I'll get a sign up, but—"

A growl wavered out from the women's bathroom, loud enough to perk up several students who glanced about in confusion. Ben's neck hairs prickled, and Jason's eyes widened.

The librarian wiped at a trickle of sweat that escaped a trimmed sideburn. "Uh … are you sure you don't need any help?"

Ben snorted. "Kiddin'? I've been moppin' up Scum since before you started shavin'."

A grimace. "Right. Guess I'll … get that sign and then alert the scrub-team."

"You do that." Ben plodded back to his cart and hefted a plunger. "Ain't gonna take more than ten, mebbe twenty minutes."

The spray bottle gurgled.

Jason scowled at it. "Does he know I understand him?"

"'Course he does," Ben said. "He wouldn't have said it, otherwise."

"Well, he doesn't have to be so insulting."

The water slopped about, making chuckling noises.

After Jason left, Ben nudged the cart into motion with a knee.

As he maneuvered it between a bookshelf and coffee table, a slender female student burst through the double doors of a side hall. She wore black leather gloves and a white headband pinned frizzy red hair behind her ears. Wide-eyed, she peered around the room until she spotted the calculus study group. She raised a finger in the universal *just a minute* sign. Adjusting her backpack, she bolted through the room.

Ben's blood chilled as he realized she was aimed for the women's restroom. He flung the plunger at her back in a desperate attempt to stop her. However, she slipped into the bathroom, and the tool bounced off the door as it slapped closed.

●   ●   ●

Something thumped against the door, but Dani ignored it as she tossed her backpack onto the counter. She fumbled in the main pouch and hauled out her jumbo bottle of sanitation gel.

In her haste to make it to the study group, she'd bumped into two people on the way. Two! Who knew what their hygienic standards were? When had they showered last? Did they even own toothbrushes? One had awful halitosis, and had huffed an apology in her face as she shoved past, trying to control her rising panic.

She tugged her gloves off and pinched them under one arm. Then she pumped double-handfuls of gel and slathered it over her hands and forearms. The cutting odor of alcohol filled the restroom. Her panic subsided as the fumes surrounded her, a protective shield against a filthy world.

As the gel evaporated, she envisioned it taking bacteria and dirt with it. Vapors singed her nose, but she breathed deep. Clean body, clean mind. She had to remain vigilant, otherwise who knew what germs might hitch a ride on her skin and then burrow deep? A shudder rippled through her as she counted off possibilities: *Staphylococcus. Streptococcus. Escherichia coli.* Oh, god! What if she'd contracted *Clostridium difficile?* Should she schedule a doctor's appointment? Should she—

The door banged open behind her. She shrieked and whirled about as a tall, elderly janitor barged in, waving a plunger like a sword.

"Aren't you supposed to knock?" she cried. "I could've been—"

She dodged as his cart almost ran her over. It rammed into a stall and soapy water sloshed out of the bucket.

"Hustle outta here, missy," he said, pursuing his equipment. She pulled back against the sink to avoid touching as he shouldered by. "We're closin' the place down for a lil' maintenance."

"C-close? But—" Dani hadn't finished her self-assessment. "I need a few minutes, okay? I've got an emergency of my own."

She squeezed her thighs together, faking the urgent need to pee. As she did, her bladder alerted her brain that it could actually use some relief. She stifled a groan. Using a public restroom would tack another ten minutes onto her routine, not counting prep-work to make sure the toilet was clean enough. Had she brought enough wet-wipes?

Grabbing her backpack, she edged toward the nearest stall, but balked as he barred the way with an arm.

"Whoa, hey there." His craggy smile accentuated the bags under his dark blue eyes. Oh god, was there *dirt* in his wrinkles? "Lemme rephrase. Nasty case of pipes backin' up in here. Gotta shut 'er down before things go Old Faithful. If you don't wanna flood of piss all over your shoes, you need to leave. Now."

Tasting bile, Dani considered retreating. But she couldn't leave without finishing her routine. She just … couldn't. He had to be exaggerating. If it was that bad, they would've had signs up and cordoned the place off.

"Look, gramps, I'll be quick. Just a minute or two so I don't wet myself."

"Nothin' doin'. Time to build a little character, princess. Get outta here and lemme do my job, a'ight?"

She sniffed. "Riding bikes builds character. I am not getting a bladder infection because you want to get back to reading porn in the janitor's closet."

He eyed her, grinning for some reason. His brown-streaked teeth made her stomach roil, and his breath had a tinge of spoiled meat.

"I ain't gonna argue about this, princess." He snatched a toilet brush off his cart and prodded her stomach. "Outcha go. Shoo."

She yelped and hopped back. What was he doing? He used that thing to clean up after people … after they … She couldn't complete the thought. He kept jabbing at her while she danced and dodged.

"What—hey—stop!"

A cattle prod would've been less of a deterrent. Her gloves fell to the floor as she jumped away from a vicious thrust. She thought of screaming for help, but what good would that do?

At last, she bumped back against the door. How many greasy handprints had she just come in contact with? How many people washed their hands before leaving? Screw study group. She needed a steaming shower and a change of clothes before she lost her mind.

The janitor came on, grinning like a jester monkey. She tried to kick the brush out of his hand, but he pulled away.

"Ah-ah." He flicked the brush in reprimand.

Droplets hit her forehead, and she stiffened. Code Red exposure. She almost wiped the vile liquid off, but then realized her hands remained exposed. Her gloves. Where were her gloves? Her gel remained on the sink, taunting her. She reached for it even as the distance increased.

"No. Wait …"

The janitor closed the gap. "There's more'n one set of bathrooms 'round, ain't there?" A final jab of the brush had her out in the library again. "Or there's some comfy bushes outside, if you got the gumption."

She bristled. "Now hold on—"

The door slammed in her face.

•　　•　　•

Ben shoved his cart against the door and leaned on it, sighing. Where was Jason with those Purity-forsaken signs?

He studied the place while ignoring the shrill voice outside. The women's room had four stalls and three sinks, walls done in blue and white tile, and a frosted glass window at the far end. Halogen lights gleamed off the fixtures.

Making sure the cart jammed the door, he double-checked his inventory. Mop with the metal-tipped handle? Check. Squeegee with a razor edge? Honed and ready. Radio? Charged. After hefting his mop, he walked by each stall, letting the prickling in his right arm escalate into a burning sensation.

Nothing drew him to any of the toilets, so he returned to the sinks and crouched to check under the counter.

The middle sink turned out to be the creature's hidey-hole. The S-shaped pipe had ruptured halfway down, jagged metal poking outward while black-green ooze dribbled from the hole. Ben gripped his mop like a staff as he kicked at the puddle of inky glop spreading beneath the break. The sulfur stink made his nostrils flare.

"I know you're in there, you cruddy little bugger."

He spat into the bucket of soapy water hanging off the cart. The saliva sizzled as it hit the surface, and he glared at the puff of steam. Using the squeegee, he scooped up a dribble of the black muck and dunked it into the water as well. More foul smoke rose from the tool, which emerged clean.

Carl gurgled in his bottle. Ben stuck the squeegee away and grabbed a rag.

"Yeah, well, you gonna be a tattle-tale? Not like they can do anythin'."

The water formed a brief vortex.

Ben flicked the bottle. "Have a little faith, buddy. If it gets any worse, they'll just kill me and burn the corpse. Problem solved. Everybody goes home happy."

He whacked the mop handle against the pipe. A spark leaped from the metal grip and shot an electric spiral down the copper length. A growl reverberated within the wall where the pipe buried itself in the concrete.

"Gotcha."

Without taking his gaze off the hole, Ben unzipped a breast pocket and pulled out a vial of bleach. He soaked the rag with this and wiped around both ends of the broken pipe. The muck clinging to the metal bubbled away in seconds until a shining copper ring capped the edges.

Another dribble of bleach went into the bucket. He plunged the mop into this and stirred. As he pulled it out, the solution sprayed across the black puddle. Wherever drops landed, steam rose and left the floor spotless.

Ben fought the urge to scratch his arm, which now burned up to the shoulder. He eased through several breaths, distancing himself from the pain. He shut out the sweat slicking his back, the electric buzz of the lights, and the raised voices from outside until only he and the broken pipe existed.

Drawing the mop back like a golf club, he prepared to swing.

● ● ●

Dani hugged herself and tried not to move. She'd never felt more exposed—not even on that night when Tim, her first—and last—college boyfriend, had coaxed her into that disastrous attempt at sex. She'd ended up missing classes for a week.

Never. Again.

She tried to ignore the stares of her fellow students. She knew her reputation as the "campus clean freak." So what? She couldn't comprehend how others wallowed in germs all the time. Didn't they know eighty percent of infections spread through personal contact? Didn't they know library desks had more than four hundred times the bacteria of a toilet?

As her thoughts circled back to bathrooms, her fear switched to fury, and she imagined several sensitive places where the janitor could go stick his toilet brush. How dare he treat her that way? He, above all people, should know the importance of sanitation, and yet he'd been the rudest, crudest human being she'd ever encountered. Even the smell of him lingered like a dog fart.

She gritted her teeth as she considered her options. The nearest women's restroom sat on the far end of the building, and her full bladder might not survive the sprint—not to mention the warzone of contamination she'd be running through without protection. Use the guys' restroom here? Women's restrooms were bad enough. But her bladder made the situation clear. Relief first. Then damage control.

She turned to that door right as the librarian locked it and hung a sign on the knob. He didn't meet her eyes as he mumbled, "Sorry. Closed for maintenance."

She stopped just shy of grabbing him. Instead, she tore her headband off and threw it at the librarian, who ducked as it spun over his head.

"Are you kidding?" she asked through clenched teeth. "Come on. I just need, like, ten seconds."

With a rueful shrug, he returned to his desk. Moments later he spoke in low tones on a handheld radio.

Dani raked fingers through her hair, silently cursing as she tugged a few snarls. This couldn't be happening. How had things spiraled out of control so fast?

She forced her spine straight and made fists. No. She refused to let herself be bullied. She needed her gloves. Her gel and wipes. She couldn't go anywhere without them. What was the janitor going to do? Have her arrested for retrieving personal property?

She glowered at the women's room door. The thought of touching the handle set off mental sirens, but it'd be temporary exposure. Once she got her stuff back, everything would be okay. She could do this. She had to.

As she reached out, a screech echoed from within the restroom.

She paused. That didn't sound like any kind of plunging or toilet-scrubbing. Her frown deepened. What was this geezer up to? A push opened the door an inch, but the janitor's cart blocked anything more.

Screw this. With a wince, she lowered her shoulder and shoved.

•   •   •

Another growl shuddered up from the pipe, liquid and menacing. As Ben checked the cleansing ward he'd set up around the exit hole, someone thumped against the door.

"Keep your panties on," he shouted. "Just a few more minutes."

He whacked the pipe with the mop. Every strike sent sparks flying and a musical chime rang out. Each note melded with the others until the pipe and the wall around it vibrated with a pure tone.

Discordant howls rose in chorus to this. Ben tensed, waiting for his quarry to emerge. One hand went to the spray bottle.

The door burst open behind him. His cart skittered to one side and the redhead stumbled in, almost falling on her face.

Ben swore. "For Purity's sake! I toldja to get lost."

She glared at him with bright green eyes as the door swung shut behind her. "Keep your diaper on. I need my backpack."

He moved to shove her back out. "Go! This ain't—" A snarl warned him. He whirled and lashed out with the business end of the mop.

In that instant of spinning and striking, the beast lunged from the six-inch pipe opening. A dark form swelled to the size of a mastiff, looking like a mad scientist's experiment in mating snakes and hounds. Muscled forelegs reached for Ben's face with obsidian claws that dripped venom. Purple and blue scales covered the sinuous body. Fangs extended; nostrils and yellow eyes flared.

The mop connected. Bleach water sizzled against the creature's skin as the impact redirected the beast past the girl's legs. It smacked into the wall and tiles cracked.

The girl shrieked and jumped aside, knocking Ben's cart over. Water sloshed everywhere.

The blot-hound scrabbled upright. After shaking like a wet dog, the beast opened its maw as if to howl. Instead, it vomited a stringy black mass at the redhead. The sputum slapped her against the wall beside the door, where she stuck fast, feet dangling a few inches above the floor.

She writhed, eyes bugging, and keened, "Ohgodohgodohgod-ohgod ..."

The blot-hound hunched, but Ben stepped in as it lunged. He caught it across the spine and slammed it to the ground, where it thrashed. Claws raked the legs of his jumpsuit but failed to shred the material.

Ben plunged the mop into the beast's body, aiming for the core of Corruption that enlivened it. When the mop connected with a hard ball in the blot-hound's chest, he twisted the handle and sent another surge of energy through it. Cloth strands twined around the ball and he wrenched upward, drawing the core out as it trailed black ichor.

The blot-hound screeched and kicked before going limp. Eyes dulled, its form began to ooze into the floor. Ben crushed the core beneath a heel and then waited until the trembling in his arms faded before going to the girl.

She stared, teeth chattering. "Wh ... who are you? What was that ... th-thing? Is it infectious?"

"You're in college and can't even read?" He tapped the name threaded on his uniform. "I'm Ben. And that was somethin' you wouldn't have had to worry about if you'd stayed out like I toldja."

A splash of bleach water dissolved the sludge pinning her to the wall, and she dropped to her knees. Wet blotches stained her pant legs and crotch, but Ben pretended not to notice.

She huddled in on herself, shoulders heaving as she came dangerously close to hyperventilating. Ben sighed and leaned on the mop as the effort of eradicating the blot-hound caught up with his failing body.

"Don'tcha worry. The scrub-team'll get here soon to give your memories a nice hose-down. By the time they're done, you won't even remember me. Ain't that a relief?"

She blinked up at him, and he recognized the distant look people got when events didn't align with their neat and tidy version of reality.

"Are you some sort of ... crazy person?" she asked. "Please tell me it isn't contagious."

Ben grinned. "Crazy is the easiest explanation, ain't it? Run with that and you'll be just fine." He frowned and flexed his right arm, which continued to burn. Why hadn't the pain faded?

Shouts came from out in the library, along with chairs being overturned and feet thumping. The scuffle in the bathroom hadn't gone unnoticed. Jason had better be running interference.

The girl whimpered and dropped to her butt, trembling.

Ben shook his head. "Look, princess, I ain't gonna hurt you. I'm the good type of crazy—"

A scraping noise jerked him around in alarm. Yellow light flared in the blot-hound's eyes as it clawed up, standing twice as tall as before, reformed legs knotted with muscle. The head rose, now as big as Ben's torso and sporting slavering fangs. As the blot-hound fixed on him, a hungry growl made his guts quiver.

"Oh, cleanse my colon." He snatched the radio from his toppled cart and hollered into it. "Francis, I need backup. Now!"

CHAPTER TWO

The radio sputtered and the red power light flickered like a parting wink from the Devil. Cursing, Ben swept the mop along as he ran back and forth as fast as his arthritic knees allowed.

Carl splashed in the spray bottle, making it sway on his belt.

Ben grunted. "Shaddup. This is—" He skidded on a puddle and avoided face-planting by bracing on the mop. The tip jammed into his chest, and he wheezed. "I got it ... under control."

The water made a spitting noise.

"Yes, I'm sure!"

Regaining his balance, he slapped the mop on the floor and activated the quarantine spell. All the spilled water from his cart flowed together and formed an inch-high band from one side of the bathroom to the other. He knelt and pressed a hand into this, infusing it with raw willpower. The effort left him shaking, but he forced himself to straighten and aimed the mop at the blot-hound across the boundary.

"All right, you sorry excuse for an overgrown tar pit. Think you can tussle with me?"

When the blot-hound didn't move right away, Ben worked up a wad of phlegm and hacked it at the creature. It bit the snot out of mid-air. A purple tongue slithered over its lips and it peered curiously at Ben.

He scowled. "That was s'posed to be an insult, not a snack."

The blot-hound slunk forward and tested the barrier with a paw. The water sizzled against its skin, but the beast didn't relent. It pushed its head further, making it flatten like a mime's hand against an invisible pane of glass.

Ben clenched his jaw, readying. Once the beast set a second paw in the water, he stuck the sparking tip of the mop handle into the band and released a charge.

Electric arcs writhed across the hound's body. It howled, a bowel-trembling noise that scraped over Ben's ears. Off to one side, the redhead clamped hands over her ears and writhed, but he kept his hands on the mop, channeling energy down through it.

With a final surge, the blot-hound crashed its bulk over the swath of water. Its size diminished by a quarter as it forced its way across, but the power Ben had invested in the barrier dissipated and only left the blot-beast stunned.

He stared in disbelief. Only when Carl made the spray bottle rock did he snap out of the shock.

"I ain't gettin' paid enough for this."

As he reached for the bottle, the blot-hound shook itself and lurched forward. It knocked him aside like a bulldozer putting a Tonka truck in its place. His head smacked against the wall and the mop flew from his hands.

He dropped flat. The room danced for a moment, but steadied just as the blot-hound's maw yawned above his face. Maybe letting it get a taste of him hadn't been the wisest thing.

The door flew open, and Jason rushed in.

"Sure you don't need any help?" He froze and gaped at the beast.

Students crowded behind the librarian, craning their necks to see inside. As soon as they got a peek at the bathroom monstrosity, however, everyone screamed and bolted. The blot-hound grunted and raised its head, discarding Ben for fresher meat.

Jason kicked the door shut behind him. He grabbed up the plunger from the fallen cart and shook it at the beast. "A-all right … J-just you and … me. I'm n-not going to let you h-hurt anyone!"

The blot-hound roared and charged. Jason stepped forward and swung the tool. The beast ducked the blow. A paw lashed out, raking the man's throat into giblets. The plunger fell from limp fingers as he toppled into the girl's lap, eyes blank, shirt stained crimson.

●　　●　　●

Dani screamed as she shoved the body away. Hot blood on her hands. Her clothes. Oh god. This couldn't be real. As she fought to keep from vomiting, her mind resorted to analyzing potential threats.

Lyme Disease. Creutzfeldt-Jakob Disease. Toxoplasmosis. Too many variables. She had to find out who this guy was. Get his medical records.

Her vision swam as nausea rammed up her throat. When her sight cleared, the bathroom door had splintered off its hinges beneath the beast's charge. Beyond this, the monster pillaged the library, toppling shelves onto students and shattering tables. Screams echoed alongside cracking wood and brick.

Hepatitis B. Hepatitis C. Cryoglobulinemia.

The janitor—whoever and whatever he really was—lay dazed beside her. Blood oozed from a gash in his scalp. He clutched one of his arms and muttered something about restocking toilet paper rolls.

She got to her knees and crawled over to him. He had to stop this … thing. This monster. But she couldn't bring herself to actually touch him, to try and shake him back to awareness.

Malaria. HIV. AIDS.

His mop lay by her, though. She picked it up—god, a *wooden* handle—and reached over to poke him with it.

"Mister … can you … mister, please—"

He jerked upright as if she'd hit him with defibrillator paddles. He grabbed the mop and yanked it over, pulling her with it. She fell forward and planted palms in the brackish water that coated the floor. Her mind cycled to water-borne contaminants.

Giardia. Amoebiasis. Botulism.

The janitor looked all around, as if getting his bearings. He frowned at her, and then the young man's body snagged his attention. His shoulders and face sagged.

"Aw, kid. I toldja to leave it be …" He struggled to his feet, groaning the whole way. "Ready to work some unpaid overtime, buddy?"

Dani stared up at him. "What?"

"Not talkin' to you, princess." He cocked his head. "I know. Probably. But it's our job, ain't it?"

Oh, he was a Grade A lunatic, for sure.

He stepped past and grabbed her bottle of gel off the counter. "Can I borrow this?"

"No!"

"Thanks."

She snatched at it, desperate to pour the contents over her head. Considering all she'd been exposed to—*HGV*. *Chagas diseases*. *HHV-8*—it might already be too late, but her sanity demanded she salvage what she could.

He moved out of reach, though, and unscrewed the cap. Heading to the doorway, he squeezed gobs of gel out to coat the outside of the bottle as well as his hands. Then he leaned over the threshold and shouted.

"Hey, tall, dark, and ugly. Catch!"

He lobbed the bottle. There came a squelch and a yowl of pain. The janitor plodded out, mop at the ready, leaving Dani frozen on all fours.

What the hell was happening? Janitors duking it out with pipe-monsters? It had to be a hallucination. Or she'd died and this was her private hell. Both were preferable options.

She tried to find a clean corner to crawl into, but contamination taunted her everywhere she looked. Only the sink counter remained untouched by the blood, dirty water, and muck.

Her skin buzzed, and she felt as if her mind strained against the confines of her skull. A bubble of energy surrounded her, a crackling field of power fueled by her horror and dismay. Was she going insane?

Even as she fought to regain control, the sensation grew until she felt like a balloon about to burst. She shook as a foreign power took control. Her bones felt aflame. Coherent thought flew apart as her mind seethed with new sensations. Faint air currents cut over her skin like hot razors, while the tiles chilled her as if carved from ice.

An enormous, invisible hand grabbed her by the spine and lifted her out of her body so she viewed it from above. Glowing lines spread out from her hands and into the floor. As they snaked along, her senses followed and formed a vision of what occurred in the next room.

Vibrations rippled out from the janitor's feet as he ran at the beast. She saw through the light bulbs as he yanked the spray bottle off his hip and squeezed the trigger. Water squirted but didn't disperse. Instead, the stream consolidated into a four-foot liquid whip that snapped through the air. More water flowed over the bottle and sealed it to his hand.

The harsh reek of the beast stabbed her sinuses like a rusty blade. She tried to recoil, fearing infection even in this disembodied form, but the possessing energy forced her to watch. A portion of the creature's head looked eaten away as if by acid.

The janitor charged in and lashed the water-whip like a geriatric Indiana Jones. The watery cord wrapped around the beast's hind leg. It tightened, sliced the limb off at the joint, and wrenched it away.

The beast yowled and collapsed mid-lunge. But it dragged itself around and snapped at the janitor with a maw that put a shark to shame.

The janitor lurched aside while grabbing the tip of his whip and bending it to touch itself. The cord blended into a noose which he snapped over the creature's head and cinched tight. When the beast jerked forward, however, it pulled the janitor against its sloppy backside. The hand holding the mop sank an inch into its hide, and steam erupted from the spot.

Bellowing, the man yanked his hand free and stabbed the metal tip of the mop handle into the beast's back. Using the mop and water-whip as leverage, he hauled himself up onto its torso. The creature reared and threw him off.

Dani had the despairing realization that the janitor would lose this struggle—and once he fell, the entire college would be at the beast's mercy. She clutched for anything she could do while trying to make sense of her new perceptions.

To her elevated mind, the creature appeared as a pulsing, infected wound in the center of reality. A corruption to be scrubbed out of existence. This monster caused all this horribleness. It had to be destroyed. Cleansed.

She realized she could sense other elements as well. The water pipes coursing through the walls. The air churning through the ducts. The electricity racing through the wiring. All of it just needing a push.

The unseen hand dropped her back into her body, where serpents of flame and ice coiled around her spine. She writhed with power that demanded to be unleashed, squeezing until she gave in and turned it loose—

Her head snapped back. Her furious scream echoed further than the walls should've allowed. The power rushed out of her to scour the bathroom and library clean.

Every electrical socket in the library spouted fire. Flames raced across the carpet and turned shelves to ash in seconds. They ate up the walls and scorched the ceiling black. Any remaining students fled, some with smoking hair and clothes.

A tremor shook the building. The fire alarm went off, flashing yellow lights around the room. With a grinding noise, the carpeted floor split beneath the beast's remaining legs. It gripped the edges to keep from plummeting into the crevasse Dani had summoned. The cool smell of wet earth wafted up as the ground shook.

The janitor tugged hard on the noose from the side, trying to tumble the beast into the hole.

Energy continued to pour out of Dani. Her body bucked as her eyes turned up in their sockets, yet somehow she remained aware of everything around her.

The ceiling sprinklers broke open and waterspouts curved to strike the beast from every side. The streams hit with the force of a dozen fire hoses and shredded its inky skin. As its size diminished under the blast, the beast made a last desperate lunge to break free. Another tremor shook the ground and widened the crack.

Screeching, the beast was swept into the fissure. The floor snapped closed with a squish, and black ooze traced the crack left behind.

From one heartbeat to the next, the energy vanished. Dani's mind and body floated free for a few precious seconds. Then exhaustion bear-hugged her and squeezed out the last burps of her strength. Her cheek slapped the floor. She maintained just enough presence of mind to keep her mouth clamped tight against the filth she lay in. Out in the library, the ongoing spray from the sprinklers warred with the flames eating up the desks, shelves, and books.

A pop of light, like a camera flash, momentarily blinded her. The bathroom mirror shimmered and brightened into a rectangle of sunlight. Dani shaded her eyes with a heavy arm as a figure strode through the glass.

The glow faded but the newcomer retained a golden aura as he stepped down from the counter. He wore a white three-piece suit with a spotless tie and fedora. Polished white loafers landed inches from her nose, and she couldn't help but notice they remained spotless despite his standing in the same mess that coated her. In fact, the muck had receded from his soles. This seemed entirely unfair.

He looked down at her and shook his head as if she'd been caught out past her curfew. His ebony skin provided a hard contrast to the outfit, but the sharp angles of his face matched the creases in his jacket and suit well enough.

"What have we here?" His words clipped out as if measured by a ruler and compass.

Before Dani could summon the wits to retort, the janitor trudged back in. He stood panting, soaking wet, and with his jumpsuit charred in spots. He stared at Dani for a moment before swinging his gaze to the suit.

"Ascendant Francis. A bit late, ain'tcha?"

Francis showed a tight, perfect smile. "Hail to you, Janitor Benjamin, servant of Purity. Your message was sparse on the details."

"Oh, so I gotta schedule in advance for backup in unexpected emergencies?"

Francis cocked an eyebrow.

"Don't gimme that look." Ben spat at the other's shoes. The spittle struck an invisible barrier and ricocheted over Dani's ear. "I'm filin' for a full review. Ain't never seen anything like what happened here."

The suit remained unmoved. "Save your excuses for Destin."

"Excuses. You use that word a lot when I'm around. Ever consider exercisin' your verbosity, eh?"

"I'm shocked you used such complicated words in proper context. Did you steal them from a crossword puzzle or is Carl tutoring you?"

"Hey, don't be makin' this personal. Even you could learn a few things from Carl."

"I highly doubt that." Francis' flat gaze shifted to Dani. "I see we have a new recruit."

"Just take her feet already. I'll grab her shoulders. Then get the scrub-team in here, pronto."

As they lifted her, she stared up at their faces and tried to comprehend what was happening. Francis' glow expanded to surround the three of them. Through an increasing mental fog, the golden hue and unexpected warmth made her think about being carried to heaven.

"Are you angels?" she whispered.

The janitor hacked a laugh. "Far from it, princess. We're your new employers."

CHAPTER THREE

Ben grumbled at Francis' reflection in the glass wall of the Employee Orientation room. "Only tell me she's not what I think she is if she ain't."

Francis' brow twitched and his lips thinned. They peered through a seamless floor-to-ceiling window to the white-walled room on the other side, complete with padded cot and tiny sink. The new recruit lay on the cot, dressed in a plain cotton robe. Aside from the occasional twitch, she'd remained unconscious since they'd deposited her there twelve hours ago.

The Ascendant consulted his clipboard. "Analysis confirmed the nature of her power. She's a Catalyst. Likely an inherent gifting that remained dormant until her survival instincts and proximity to your energies woke it." He scanned the compiled data. "Danielle Hashelheim. Twenty-two years old. Biology major, junior year, with an admirable GPA. Has a marked history of mysophobia, a variant of OCD."

"Myso-whatsit now?"

"Mysophobia. Germophobic behavior."

"She don't like Germans?"

Francis sighed, and Ben hid a grin.

"Germs, Benjamin. She's afraid of germs and contamination. Despite that, she'd make a fine apprentice, given the proper mentor."

"Maybe." Ben rocked on his heels. "But I sure wanna weep for whoever gets stuck with this precious little cupcake."

Francis frowned and eyed him sidelong. Ben wondered what that look was for, and then recognized it as pity. He gawped in realization.

"You ain't serious."

"Effective immediately, she's your protégée for the next year." Francis' stiff tone made it clear what he thought of the assignment. "Or until the Board decides she's gained enough control over her powers to be an independent contractor."

"You're ribbin' me. That just ain't possible. What about ..." Ben found himself scratching at his right arm and forced his clenched hands to his sides. "You know my last review by the Board. Even if they did give me back training duty, I ain't gonna take it. I refuse."

"Normally I'd echo your sentiment," Francis said. "Yet despite my best efforts, the Chairman convinced the Board you're the best candidate."

"I don't care what he did. Ain't no way I'm doin' this, even if I have to mop the Sewers from one end to the other. You can shove whatever orders they gave back up your puckerhole."

Francis shook his head as he scribbled a note. "Pucker ... hole. Why do you persist in coming up with new vulgarities? You know the Board will simply add them to the censor list."

Ben tapped his temple. "Gotta make sure the ol' lump still has a spark or two left. Now stop tryin' to distract me. I ain't budgin' for nothin'. This girl ain't getting anywhere near me."

"All variables have been considered," said a new voice. *"You were unanimously voted to be her mentor."*

A pale face gleamed in the depths of the glass, matching neither Ben nor Francis' reflection. Ben glared at the projection, wishing he could wipe it away like any other unwanted smudge.

"Destin." He forced his tone to be a shade more respectful. "Chairman. It'd make my day if you told me Francis here is a few feathers short of a duster."

"Ascendant Francis' sensibility remains intact," Destin said. *"You are her caretaker."*

"You do remember what happened to my last apprentice? The one who drowned with his head stuck in a toilet? And that's before—"

"Any danger has been deemed insignificant compared to that which she presents to herself and those around her. You were and, in my opinion, still are one of the most capable janitors we have, despite the unfortunate circumstances."

"That's a real squirmy way of puttin' it."

"Sir," said Francis, "this girl needs careful handling. Janitor Benjamin is hardly known for his subtlety and empathy."

Destin's smile reminded Ben of an alligator's—starting and stopping at the teeth. *"Francis, your last performance review included the highest praise of many attributes. Subtlety and empathy were not among them either. That's not the point here."*

"What is the point?" Ben asked.

"The point is I fought for you on this, Benjamin, and would not appreciate my confidence being misplaced."

"Shoulda figured your reputation would be involved."

"Consider this a qualified apology for the way we once treated you."

"An apology? Somehow it ain't feelin' like one."

"Despite your unorthodox views and position, I know you will provide the firm guidance that few, if any, of the other Cleaners, could give Ms. Hashelheim. If you encounter any truly serious issues in the course of her training, I am making myself available, despite my busy schedule. But I know you won't disappoint."

Destin's visage faded. Ben let his forehead thump against the pane where the Chairman's face had been. "I'm too old for this."

Francis coughed. "I once swore to never doubt the wisdom of the Chairman. In this case, however, I could make an exception. The consequences of fouling a job should never include being given more responsibility."

Ben glowered at him. "You think this is 'cause of what happened in the library? You think I bungled that and this is some sorta punishment? Didn't Destin review the situation?"

"I gave your report all due consideration," Francis said, "and declined to pass it on to the Chairman."

"Meanin' you put it through the shredder."

"The Chairman can't be distracted by every fanciful account of reanimating blot-hounds."

"Fanci—for Purity's sake, Francis, you think I'd let any regular blot-hound get the better of me? That thing not only popped back up after havin' its core shattered, it at least tripled in strength and blasted through my defenses like they was made of soggy newspaper."

The Ascendant looked pointedly at Ben's right arm. "With your current condition, I'm not surprised your measures proved inadequate."

Ben grabbed the man's lapel. "What'd I warn you about makin' this personal?"

A thump made them both jump back. As they'd argued, Dani had woken and rolled off her cot. She'd run full-tilt into the glass in an attempt to flee, but rebounded and fell onto her butt, dazed. Her stunned phase passed quickly, though, and she shoved back up, fists pummel-ready.

"You mother*******!" she shouted. Her face screwed up as her voice failed to complete the curse.

Ben sighed and crossed his arms. "This oughta be fun."

She pounded on the glass. "Let me out, you ******* lunatics! You ****faced ******!" She clapped a hand over her mouth and retreated a step.

Ben grinned. "Well, now. We might just get along after all."

Dani tucked fists under her arms as she inspected the boundaries of the Orientation room. Glancing down, she appeared to notice her bare feet for the first time. With a yelp, she leaped back onto the cot and huddled against the wall. Her eyes clenched shut, and a tremor rippled the air.

"Hoo boy. Is she—"

Water spouted out of the sink and struck the ceiling. Within seconds, a miniature thundercloud formed, complete with tiny flashes of lightning. Sheets of rain blew about, though Dani remained untouched in the midst of it.

"She's triggered," Francis said, as if commenting on the price of milk. "Must be the fright of her unfamiliar environment."

"Ain'tcha gonna neutralize her?"

"That's your job now." The din within the holding room grew. "I suggest you hurry."

Growling, Ben rapped on the glass until Dani peeked with one eye. Even through the storm, her fury shot his way like a sniper bullet. Her lips moved in silent threat, and thunder rumbled in sync.

"I know you can hear me," Ben said, unzipping a large pouch on one pants leg. "So I'm gonna make you a deal. See this?"

He pulled a bottle of gel from the pouch. Not the same one from the library, which had melted into the blot-hound; he'd come bearing a replacement as a peace offering.

She fixed on it like a magpie spotting a piece of tinfoil. Her fingers twitched, and Ben thought she might launch herself against the glass again to try and grab it.

"Thought you might be wantin' this. But the only way you're gettin' it is if I hand it over. And I ain't comin' in there until you settle down." Ben pointed at the thundercloud brewing just below the ceiling. "Which mean that needs to go bye-bye."

"Bye-bye?" Francis echoed. "Benjamin, really …"

"Hush it. If she's my apprentice, I can use baby language if I wanna." He refocused on Dani. "So what's it gonna be?"

He waved the bottle back and forth, and she followed the motion. As her focus anchored on the offered sanitizer, the indoor cloud evaporated and the waterspout trickled off. Drains sucked away whatever liquid had collected on the floor.

While leery of another outburst, Ben stuck his palm to the window. A pane of the glass slid aside and he slipped through. Edging toward her, he held the bottle at arm's length as if offering a hunk of meat to a rabid wolf.

As soon as it came within reach, she snatched the bottle up, popped the top, and squeezed a third of it into her hand. Ben's eyes watered as she slopped the gel onto her arms, head, and feet with gleeful abandon.

After every last visible bit of skin was coated, a great weight seemed to lift from her shoulders.

"See?" He patted her back. "All better."

She spun and screamed. "Don't touch me, you son of a *****!"

The smack sent his ears ringing. He grabbed her wrist to block a second shot. "Now, princess, let's not make this personal."

"You abducted me, you *******! That's pretty ****** personal."

"You burned down and flooded your library. You might wanna say thanks."

"Thanks? Are you ******* me?"

"If we'd left you there, you'd either be locked up in jail or the loony bin."

"What the **** are you talking about?"

Ben ran a hand over his growing bald spot. *Oh, this is gonna be jolly.*

Her nose wrinkled as she checked him over, obviously unimpressed with his janitor outfit and black rubber boots. He had about a foot on her, but her ferocity more than made up for the difference. He scratched his stubbled chin and figured he might've made a better impression if he shaved more than once a week. Or looked forty years younger. No doubt she'd already filed him away as having dentures and wearing diapers. Not too far from the truth.

"Where am I?" she asked at last. "What's going on? And why can't I ******* swear? Did you implant some sort of chip in my brain?"

"You've watched too much sci-fi, princess. Chips in the brain? That's ridiculous. Naw. There's a company-wide spell in place. Called a foul-filter. The Board figured it was ... what's the word? Unbefit-tening?"

"Unbecoming," Francis offered from outside.

Ben snapped his fingers. "That's the one. Unbecomin' of us Cleaners to have dirty mouths. Gotta keep the image as sparkly as possible."

She poured another helping of gel and worked it between her fingers. "What the **** are you talking about?"

"It's a little complicated," Ben said. "To lay it out plain, you tapped into a latent talent during that little fracas at the library. Francis and I," he nodded to the Ascendant, who bowed, "brought you back here to recover and to ... train." He forced that last word out through clenched teeth.

Dani stared at some distant point. "Latent talent?" she echoed, monotone.

"Yup. Latent talent. Power. Magic. Spellwork. Energy manipulation. Supernatural manifestation of willpower. Mega-weird stuff that sends the common folk freakin' and spawns a whole lotta tabloid headlines. Whatever you wanna call it."

"Magic? That's impossible. Utter bull****."

He cupped a hand around an ear. "Wossat? Couldn't rightly hear you. Some impossible magic must've got in my ear." He sighed. "For a student, I figured you'd get past this mental roadblock a little faster. 'Specially figurin' you was the one who just torched and flooded a library."

Her eyes narrowed. "Am I in trouble? Is that it? You guys are cops?"

"Not quite." Ben sat on the edge of the cot, and she pulled back further. "Look, Dani—can I call you Dani?"

"No."

"Thanks. So, Dani, you're what we call a Catalyst. You trigger natural disasters on a minor scale. It's one of the most dangerous and rare junctions of power around these days. Plenty of folks, 'specially Scum, are gonna want to use that. You're lucky we got to you first."

She eyed him as if he spoke in a foreign language. Then she shook her hair out and sat up straighter. "I want to call my parents."

"No, you don't."

She scowled. "Shut up. If this is some sort of prison, I deserve a phone call."

"It ain't a prison," he said. "It's your new home base. At least until you get a handle on that nasty power of yours."

"Give me my phone call!"

Ben looked to Francis, who shrugged and drew a cell phone— white of course—from a jacket pocket. He tossed it to Ben, but Dani snatched it in mid-air. She'd tucked both hands inside their sleeves so she could hold the phone without touching it. As she stabbed at the numbers, Ben walked outside to wait.

"A'ight. But I warned you."

●   ●   ●

Dani barely noticed as the janitor—or whoever he really was— left the cell and a glass panel slid into place behind him. As the line rang, she tried to force her thoughts into a logical order so she could make a coherent plea for help, but nothing made sense. Janitors? Magic? Pipe monsters terrorizing her college? Had someone drugged her coffee?

The connection clicked, and her mother's voice bubbled out of the speaker.

"Hello?"

"Mom? It's—"

"Danielle! I just got your message. So exciting. So wonderful. Of course, I understand you'll have to miss the family reunion, but such is the price of pursuing your dreams."

Dani's mental equilibrium tilted near to capsizing. "Message? Mom, what the **** are you talking about?"

"Oh, don't tease, silly girl. Now, I'm sad too that we can't have a going away party, but considering it's such a rare opportunity, you don't want them rescinding the offer."

"Mom, please—stop—just ******* stop and listen." As with all previous attempts, the curse formed in her head but vanished somewhere between her brainstem and tongue. "Whoever you heard from, it wasn't me. I've been abducted." She looked over to Ben, who waved and smiled. "They're talking about magic and ... and this guy at the college library died. I mean really died and ..."

She swallowed as her mother cooed.

"It is a magical opportunity, isn't it? I'm sure the other students would kill for the chance to study medicine overseas for a semester. Your message was a bit fuzzy, and I missed exactly where you'll be. France? Germany?"

"Mom, are you hearing a ******* thing I'm saying?"

"What's that, dear? I keep getting static on my end."

Dani ground her teeth. "I've been kidnapped. I need help. Police. Lawyers. Something. You've got to get me out of here. They can't do this to me."

A cluck of disapproval interrupted. "Of course you're going, young lady. Do not even consider turning this down."

"Mom, please—"

"No, Danielle. Do not *Mom please* me. You're a big girl and don't need us holding your hand and braiding your pigtails anymore. We have confidence in you. Don't forget how much we've sacrificed for you all these years."

Dani pulled away from the phone and stared at it as her mother chattered on. Suspicion and horror clumped in the back of her throat, blocking further attempts to speak for a minute. At last she returned the phone to her ear.

"You have no idea what I'm saying, do you?" she asked. "They've done something to you. I could talk about flying to the moon on giant grasshoppers and you'd still hear what they want you to."

"That's wonderful, Danielle. I'll let your father know when he gets back from his business trip. I'm very proud of you, and I know he will be too. Just don't forget to take pictures and write."

●   ●   ●

Ben winced as Dani flung the phone at the window, where it shattered. She returned to sulking on the cot, clutching the gel bottle like a teddy bear. At least it hadn't been his phone. It would've taken weeks to requisition a new one from Supplies.

He remembered his own employee orientation—the gradual realization that his life would no longer be the same. That his dreams no longer mattered in the larger scheme. Better to hit them with the hard truths right off. Stringing recruits along did them no favors. The capable ones adapted to their new existence, while the rest ...

He shook his head. At least she didn't seem the fainting flower type, despite the germ thing. He worked his jaw where she'd slapped him. Nope. Definitely not delicate.

He reopened the door pane and stepped back inside.

Dani turned just enough for one bright green eye to glare out at him. "What kind of sick joke is this? Are my folks in on it too?"

"Wish I could say they was," he said. "But they, plus all your classmates and any close friends, don't even think you're in the country anymore. It's kind of an insurance policy on our part."

"What?"

"Aside from bein' an insufferable ✳✳✳✳✳✳✳✳—" He swung around at the Ascendant. "Oh, c'mon. You even reported that one?"

Francis waved in a silent *Get on with it.*

Ben glowered as he turned back to Dani. "Aside from bein' an insufferable *picklehead,* Francis," he pointed back at the man with his middle finger, "heads up our scrub-teams. If he's done his job, your old dorm room is empty, your accounts frozen, and anyone close to you has received a farewell call from someone soundin' an awful lot like you. I'm bettin' your school transcript even shows you've been transferred to some swanky institution, though no one really knows which one." He shrugged at her increasingly disturbed look. "It's the best way. As soon as HQ identifies a new recruit, the scrubbers wipe out any connection to your previous life so we can train employees without worryin' about inconveniences like friends and family tracking you down."

She sat up, taking several deep breaths. "Employees? Recruits? What is this place? Who are you people? Some secret government agency?"

"Gettin' closer. But replace 'secret government agency' with 'supernatural sanitation department.'"

She stared back blankly. "You're, what, magical garbage men?"

Ben coughed and tried again. It had been way too long since his last apprentice. "We're inside Cleaner headquarters. It's the largest and oldest corporation to remain hidden from the rest of the world, and you are the latest employee to grace these fair halls. Though, technically you're still an intern."

"Unpaid, of course," Francis added.

Ben shot him a look. "Not. Helping."

Dani's brow scrunched up. "The Cleaners. Right. So you run a paranormal laundromat?"

"That's one division of our operations, yup."

"I was joking!"

"Actually, you was bein' serious without realizin' it. Happens a lot 'round here. The Cleaners have been the front line in a battle that's been going on ever since the Babylonians invented soap." He held a hand out as she opened her mouth. "Metaphorically speakin', a'ight? Purity and Corruption—capital P and C, mind you—are the two major players tryin' to rule this planet. We're Purity's footsoldiers. We get the dubious honor of keepin' the rest of the blissfully ignorant folks safe from Scum, in whatever form they take, such as the nasty bugger that tried to nibble our faces last night."

Dani's mouth worked, but no sound came out. She wore the slack expression of someone who'd been cold-cocked by a psychic two-by-four.

"It's a lot messier than that," he said, "but you get the idea. Anythin' you wanna ask right now?"

She nodded slowly. "Who's going to feed my lizard?"

Of all the questions he'd expected, this one made it his turn for a slow blink. "Is that one of those ... waddaya call ... euphorisms?"

She tugged at her frazzled hair. "Euphemism. And, no. I have a lizard. Tetris. He's a bearded dragon. I keep ... kept him in my dorm room. If I'm going to be locked up with you all, I need to make sure he's okay until I get back."

Ben looked to Francis, who cocked an eyebrow.

"There's nothing about a lizard in her profile. My team was very thorough." The Ascendant scanned his clipboard. "All of her possessions from the dormitory are currently stored in locker bay twenty-seven. Had a lizard been processed, I would've been notified."

"Orange and red guy," said Dani. Her focus remained distant. "Thorny all over, but loves to cuddle. He only eats grubs and crickets."

"Send someone to check on it," Ben said. He snorted at the Ascendant's glare. "The woman wants someone to feed her lizard. I think we can do that to ease her mind, eh?"

Dani massaged her forehead. "I'm expecting to wake up in a straightjacket any second now. This can't be real. What proof do I have you're not just some crazy old man?"

"I prefer crazy ol' coot. Sounds more fun." Ben hunched to meet her eyes. "Listen, I know it's tough to believe at first, but I needja to try, for your own good. But if you wanna keep playin' say-it-ain't-so, then there's somethin' you gotta see. C'mon." He moved for the exit.

"Wait." At his glance, she wiggled her toes. "I need shoes. No way am I going barefoot. Do you have any idea how many parasites and germs get stuck on your feet?"

"Princess, you're in the Cleaners' headquarters. You could lick this floor all day long and your tongue would come away cleaner for it."

She grimaced, but eased one foot over the edge of the cot, like a questing antennae. However, she pulled back at the last second.

"I ... can't. I just can't."

A pair of white slippers hit the floor beside Ben. He stared back at Francis. Where in tarnation had these come from? Was he planning on visiting the spa later? When the Ascendant offered no comment, Ben nudged the slippers Dani's way.

She poured more gel into her hands. She first wiped the shoes down, especially spots he'd touched, and then redid her feet before slipping them inside.

Ben squinted at the half-empty bottle. "Ever think you're a little overeager to slop that stuff around?"

"No. Why?"

"No particular reason."

Francis snagged his arm as he left the room.

"Where do you think you're taking her?" the Ascendant asked.

Ben eyed the man's hand until it was removed. "She wants real," he said. "I'm gonna show her real. Then she's joinin' me on my rounds. Unless Destin is givin' me paid leave for the rest of the month, I still gotta job to do. 'Sides, ain't field experience the best way to learn?"

"Don't take her training lightly. I'll be keeping a close eye on you both."

Ben looked over to where Dani stood on wobbly legs. She shuffled toward the exit as if afraid a trapdoor might open at any moment and drop her into a snake pit.

"I'll treat her like my own daughter," he said. "Now go check on that lizard."

CHAPTER FOUR

Dani hesitated as the janitor shuffled down the hall, acting as if he didn't care whether she followed or not. For the first time in her life, she felt cut adrift from anything that could help her decide what to do next. The only firm things she had were the bottle he'd given her and the robe she wore.

She checked behind her, making sure the garment didn't flap open like a hospital gown. When had they switched her into this outfit, anyway? More importantly, who'd done it? She shuddered, thinking of grubby hands pawing all over her. A bath. That would set her mind at ease—or at least keep full-blown panic at bay.

The other man, Francis, watched her from the other side of the sliding glass barrier. His unwavering gaze creeped her out more than the idea of tagging along with Grampa, so she hurried by in pursuit of the janitor.

After catching up to Ben, she went on autopilot while looking every-which-way for an exit. The bland hall continued for a stretch before widening and branching off into a maze of paths. Ben led her through several turns, a large room with shelving stacked with silver buckets, and another glass barrier which slid aside at his touch.

Foot traffic crowded the corridor beyond. Everyone wore either a janitorial jumpsuit or other dirty work getup. They all carried assorted cleaning and maintenance tools, though with eye-catching variations from the normal household implement—such as the duster with fiber optic feathers, or the ladder with runes chiseled into its stone steps.

One woman yelled at a bucket of water she carried past. "You want me to flush you? Huh? You want a one-way trip to the Sewers? Then the next time I give you an order, the only answer I expect to hear is *Yes, ma'am.* No more backtalk."

Ben chuckled and patted the bottle hooked onto his belt. "Some people just can't handle workin' with partners."

"What?" Dani asked.

"Wasn't talkin' to you, princess."

"Who, then? Your spray bottle?"

"Yup."

Dani searched his droopy face for any sign of a joke; seeing none, she shook her head. "***, you must be lonely."

He led on without retort. Dani cringed as she followed, trying to not touch anyone. With each bump, she squirted a little gel and rubbed it on the spot and her hands.

A few folks nodded to Ben, while others wrinkled their noses as if he'd forgotten to shower. With his grungy odor, it was no wonder. A pair of white-suited women walked by, and Dani looked over her shoulder at their retreating backs. Did they glow softly?

As if in response to her inspection, the women pivoted on their heels and stared back. Dani flushed, but waved to show she'd meant no harm. They continued staring, unblinking, until she edged as close as she dared to the janitor.

"What're they doing?" she whispered.

Ben glanced back. "The Ascendants? Oh, just readin' your mind and diggin' up all your dirty childhood secrets to add to your company file."

"What?!" Dani clamped a hand over her head.

Ben sighed and continued walking. "Kiddin'. Geez. They's just curious who the new employee is. Honest to goodness."

They turned a corner, putting the glowing women out of sight. With Ben keeping a few feet ahead, Dani tried to organize the few facts she possessed into a plan of action.

Should she make a run for it? If this was all a big setup, some huge practical joke, then if she ran long and hard enough, she'd burst out of whatever extravagant movie set they were on and back into the real world.

But what if it isn't a prank? The traitorous question slipped in.

Ridiculous, she shot back at herself. *No such thing as magic.* And even if there was, it wouldn't be wielded by an organization of janitors. In stories, magic belonged to wizards and mages. Powerful individuals who channeled mystical energy through staves and wands—

Like mops, plungers, and toilet brushes?

Who commanded the elements of nature—

Like the water and lightning gramps here whipped around in the library?

Who fought the forces of evil throughout the land—

Like that sink monster that made you piss yourself?

*******, she swore. *I will not lose a debate with my own brain.*

How else do you explain it, then, smart girl?

Maybe sewage had backed up gas in the bathrooms and caused her to hallucinate. Maybe she'd slipped and whacked her head, and now lingered in a hospital, hooked up to life-support and all this was some allegorical dream-journey to bring her back to the land of the living.

But what if? After all, *something* had happened in the library.

Finally, Ben turned down a side hall that dead-ended twenty feet later. There, another janitor swept what looked like ashen footprints into a dustpan. He paused and leaned on his broom—which had gold threads spiraling along the handle—and eyed the pair.

"Cleaning up or adding to the heap?" he asked.

"She's upright, ain't she?" asked Ben, pointing an elbow Dani's way.

The sweeper grunted and rested the tip of his broom against the wall behind him. A yellow glow coiled up the handle and flashed into the plaster. Dani stepped back as the wall faded and revealed a gray-bricked room beyond, lined with square insets. Cold blue light lent everything a steely glint.

She followed Ben inside while the sweeper went back to work. A few steps later, she glanced back and twitched when the wall rematerialized and sealed them in.

"Adding to the heap?" She winced as her voice echoed. "What's that mean?"

Ben scanned the insets. "Just a saying some like to toss around here. Don't read too much into it."

"A saying? Like a password?" Dani asked. "Do you have secret handshakes too?"

"If I said we did, would you go along with this nice and quiet-like?"

"No."

"Then no. No secret handshakes."

Dani tried to gauge how far the hallway went, but couldn't see an end. "Where are we?"

"Storage."

"For?"

His lips pressed into a wrinkled line as he went to a nearby inset and withdrew a small silver container. Dani craned her neck as he turned around to display …

"A trashcan?"

He spun it to reveal a gold plaque on the front. Engraved words read: *Jason Scottsdale*. With a flourish, he removed the lid of the miniature garbage can and tucked it under one arm. He dipped a hand in and came up, fingers pinched around a clump of gray dust.

Dani shifted back. "What is that?"

"Ashes." Ben lifted his hand. "Welcome to reality."

Before she could dodge, he blew the ash into her face. His foul breath hit her along with a cloud of particles. She gasped in shock and sucked in a mouthful. Bending over, she retched, trying to expel every last grain that coated her tongue. No matter how much she spat and hacked, the stuff clung to the back of her throat. Her hands shook, bile surged up her throat, and she wondered if gulping sanitation gel might be overkill.

At last, desperate for breath, she straightened and prepared to shriek at the janitor for—

Her knees locked. Ben had vanished. A younger man stood in his place, sporting combed hair and a tie. He appeared transparent except for his facial features and faint body outline.

Grinning, he held his hand out. "Er … hello. I'm Jason. You must be the new recruit."

Eyes widening, Dani backed up until she bumped into the opposite wall. Cold brick pressed against her thin robe, and she shivered.

This was ... this was ... the man in the library. The one who had ...

Died.

He withdrew his hand and smiled sheepishly. "I wish I'd lived long enough to meet you properly, Miss Hashelheim."

She blinked. "Wha—you know me?"

"In a fashion. Once a Cleaner, always a Cleaner, even after we retire. We stay tapped into the company newsletters and memos."

"This," She waved at the hall, which had taken on a foggy blue texture, "is retirement?"

"Not exactly sipping beers on a tropical island, huh? But it lets us stay in the fight, if in a small way. Like helping with Employee Orientation. That's why Ben brought you here, isn't it? To give you the chance to clear up any doubts and confusion." He crossed his arms. "So go ahead. Ask me anything."

Dani chewed her lip. "Were you ... clean?"

"Clean?"

"You know. Herpes. Syphilis. That sort of thing."

"You summoned my ghost to find out if I had any STDs?"

"It's important!"

He sighed heavily, but shook his head. "I was a virgin, okay? Never had any health issues beyond a couple broken bones. Satisfied?"

A small knot of tension loosened inside her stomach, but her relief proved short-lived. "Is this supposed to guilt me into believing?"

His brow wrinkled. "Guilt?"

"Like Scrooge seeing the three ghosts. Aren't you going to blame me for your death or something?"

"Blame you? Hardly." He smiled. "Lady, you saved a lot of people from getting killed. If your talent hadn't awakened like it did, things would've been a lot messier before the end. That beast you destroyed was called a blot-hound. Ben got called in because it was infecting the water supply on campus. Unchecked, it would've caused widespread manic depression, illness, and not a small number of suicides by the end of the semester. That's partly why we're here." His voice turned wistful. "Well, I guess, why *you're there* is more accurate. I had my time, short as it was. Now it's yours."

"Mine? I don't want this."

"You sure? Think about it, Miss Hashelheim. The Cleaners are dedicated to wiping out all forms of Scum throughout the world. All sources of filth and disease. We stand against everything that wants to drag humanity down into the muck of Corruption." He winked. "Germs, too. Doesn't that line up with how you've lived all along?"

"I ... I guess. But I'm supposed to become a doctor. I don't want to just be a janitor, even a magical one." Dani, the Magic Janitor? Sounded like a cheesy cartoon series.

"It may seem odd at first, but trust me. This is so much more than being *just* a janitor. Give it a chance. I think you'll find you have more in common with us than you think. What division are you assigned to, anyways? Janitorial? House-cleaning? Plumbing?"

"They said I'm a Catalyst."

"Oh."

"Oh? What's *oh* mean?"

He raised his hands in a placating gesture. "Er ... well, just try not to kill any coworkers, okay? Doesn't look good on annual reviews."

"Swell. Any other advice?"

"Uh ... oh! Meatloaf Tuesdays in the cafeteria. Avoid it. Good luck!"

Jason faded away, and Ben popped back into view. Before she could say anything, he held out a small cup filled with a purple liquid that smelled of bubblegum.

"Rinse."

The grainy texture in her mouth convinced her to snatch the cup and toss the contents back. She swished vigorously, gargled, and then looked around for someplace to expel the foulness.

He held out his empty hand, fingers curled as if holding an invisible cup. "Spit."

No hesitation this time. She spat into his hand—*That's for blowing ash into my face!*—but after a tiny flushing noise, he uncurled his fingers to reveal a dry palm.

She crumpled the cup and threw it at him. "Do you bring everyone here on a first date?"

He caught the cup and tucked it into a pocket. Then he licked a thumb and polished a smudge on Jason's trashcan urn, set back into its cubby-hole.

"The dead got a lotta hindsight," he said. "I figured you two could use a chat. Purity knows, I've visited here plenty of times for a bit of perspective."

Ben made a circular motion with his hands. The overhead lights brightened and revealed rows of insets stretching down to a distant infinitesimal point. As she watched, each inset brightened from within, revealing countless trashcans with gold nameplates.

She swallowed. Hard.

This was a cemetery. One that testified to innumerable sacrifices to the cause these people upheld. If she followed along so far, this included keeping the world clean and safe. And they wanted her to join them.

That was kind of cool.

As much as her rational mind struggled, she had yet to come up with a better explanation for all she'd experienced. She could opt for the "this-is-all-a-hallucination-or-coma-dream" path, but the practical side of her voted that she start treating this situation as real until evidence proved otherwise.

Besides, the ghost had given her one anchoring truth. If these people, this company opposed filth and contamination, like she had all her life, then why didn't she embrace them despite the ignoble workers they masqueraded as? If they fought disease on a large scale, as she'd dreamed of in pursuing her medical degree, then perhaps they could equip her to do the same.

She needed to accept her world had changed.

No. Not the world.

She had changed. Something impossible had manifested within her. She could feel it, a ball of energy thrumming deep in her chest. She wanted to chalk it up to anxiety or fear, but even the purest, strongest emotion couldn't summon earthquakes, fire, and floods.

And if she denied all this and escaped, then what? There'd always be the knowledge that something lurked behind the curtain of normalcy. Could her sanitation routines protect her? Could she fight pipe monsters with hand wipes and a UV wand?

Yesterday, all had been neat and orderly and clean. Now she couldn't even depend on going to the bathroom without something trying to kill her. She hugged herself and shuddered.

The floor quivered.

Ben spoke in a warning tone. "Hey, now ..."

She realized she'd shut her eyes at some point, but still saw the room clearly. The core of power had lit within her again and sent tendrils probing the elements. Metal. Glass. Earth, far below. All of them waiting to crack and rupture and crumble. The more she tried to rein in the energies, the more her fear spiked and the power swelled in response.

Ben's voice sounded far away. "C'mon, now. You can stop this. Just try."

Dani tried to say she *was* trying, but it came out as a snarl. The floor rumbled, and the power started to peak—

Cold liquid struck Dani's face and splashed over her arms and chest. She gasped and shook her head to clear the water from her eyes. Her cheeks heated as she glared at Ben. He held his spray bottle poised for another dousing, the top in his other hand.

"What was that for?"

"Sorry, but it's the best way," Ben said. "Most talents get stronger through focused willpower. Kick the focus in the nuts and you scatter the energy."

Warily, Dani quested toward the power. The energies had indeed subsided, though a knot of it slumbered in her chest like a swallowed stone.

Ben held the spray bottle her way. "Okay. C'mon back."

"Excuse me?" She jumped as the water soaking her hair and robe splashed to the floor, leaving her dry. The animated liquid formed a platter-sized bubble which rolled Ben's way and flowed back into the bottle.

Dani didn't blink until her eyes started to burn. After he scooped up the rest of the water, Ben sealed the bottle and offered it for inspection.

"Meet my partner, Carl." He swished the contents. "He's a water elemental. I did his folks a big favor a while back and he was their thank you gift. Was gonna introduce you earlier but this all needed sortin' out first."

Dani remembered how to operate her tongue. "A water elemental."

"Yup."

"Named Carl?"

"Well, people can't rightly pronounce his real name, and he seems fine with it."

She edged over and flicked the bottle. The water swirled, forming cavities and geometric patterns too fast for her to identify.

"Was that him talking? What'd he say?"

Ben harrumphed. "Well, the whole of it means he thinks you're attractive. For a human."

A giggle escaped Dani. It rose into a few hiccups of near-hysterical laughter, and she came close to hyperventilating again before regaining control. Ben kept an eye on her, likely making sure she didn't trigger another earthquake.

"I know it's a lot to take in at once," he said, "but don'tcha worry. You've already been assigned an instructor to teach you to control your abilities."

That cut off any lingering mirth. "Who? That Francis stiff?"

Ben cleared his throat and tapped his chest.

"You're. Kidding."

"Wish I was."

"Look, it's not that I don't appreciate the whole bonding-in-a-morgue shtick, but I'm a big girl." She set her jaw and raised a fist. "I can accept all this because I don't have any other options, but I don't want to be chaperoned by someone old enough to be my grampa; especially one who looks and smells like he hasn't showered for a week."

Ben wrapped his hand over her knuckles and forced her arm down. She jerked away and applied a liberal amount of gel to where he'd touched.

"Let's not make this personal, princess. First off, I'm the furthest thing from your granddaddy. I ain't gonna dole out candies and tell the same joke six times in a row. Second, I got as much choice in this as you do. And third, I'm doin' this for your own good. I may not like being saddled with your diaper bag, and you may not like havin' to put up with my handsome mug, but I don't think either of us wanna see the Board hunt you down and scrub you out quicker than you can spit on their shiny shoes."

"What?"

"Oh, did Jason skip that part? Lemme clue you in. If the Board thinks you might go over to the other side, to Corruption, they'd rather wipe you out before lettin' Scum get a hold of your power. Francis would be delighted to do it himself."

The blood drained from her face. "He ... they wouldn't dare. I'll ..."

"You'll what? Reality is, you're a ... what's the word? Libation?"

Her scowl returned. "I think you mean *liability*."

He snapped his fingers. "Right. I'm here to teach you how to be dangerous to Scum and whatnot, instead of coworkers and innocent bystanders. So whaddya say? Wanna learn how to put the fear of Dani into all things foul and nasty?"

She had to admit, she liked the sound of that. It'd be a nice reversal of the role she'd played most of her life. Maybe someday she wouldn't need her sanitation kit. Germs would flee at the sight of her.

"I'll go along with it. For now."

"Glad to hear. Employee orientation is now officially concluded. Welcome to the team. The sooner we start your trainin', the better. Your powers ain't gonna lie dormant for convenience's sake."

He headed for the exit. As the wall faded away again, admitting them back into the main facility, Ben urged her to catch up with a jerk of his head.

"C'mon. You've got toilet duty."

CHAPTER FIVE

en pushed his squeaky-wheeled cart out of the elevator and into the underground lot of HQ's office complex. Dani walked by his side, her gaze darting to every dark corner as if checking for monsters.

They ambled between rows of identical white vans until they came across one which might've been white in a previous lifetime. Mud splatters, rust, and flaking paint covered the paneling, and it wouldn't have looked out of place on someone's front lawn alongside plastic flamingos and beer cans.

Dani stared at it in faint horror. "I thought we were supposed to maintain a clean image."

He patted the side. "Mebbe all the rest like to waste time sprayin' their vans down every time it gets a speck of dust on the bumper. Me? So long as it gets me where I gotta go, it's all the fancy-shmancy wheels I need."

"Still, shouldn't you take better of your company car?" she asked. "I mean, that thing looks half-fossilized. What's Francis' ride? A white stretch limo?"

"When you reach his level, limos are beneath you," Ben said. "So unless your new powers include teleportation, you're gonna just have to enjoy the ride."

She stood back as Ben slid the van's side door open. It rattled aside to reveal built-in metal shelving that held all manner of buckets, cleaning fluid, bottles, extra mops, bundles of rags, and other cleaning paraphernalia. A regular janitorial treasure chest.

She perked up. "Got any gloves in there?"

He scrounged across one shelf until he came up with a pair of yellow rubber gloves and tossed them her way. As she tugged them on, he levered the cart into an open space at the back and locked the wheels in place.

"Why janitors?"

He glanced back. "Eh?"

"Why janitors?" Dani repeated. "If the Cleaners are some big magical society, why not act like it? Why hide behind this corporate front? Wouldn't it be better to take on an image people respect more? Like law enforcement. Or superheroes."

"First off, you really wanna go 'round wearin' tights and capes? Or seein' me in 'em?" He chuckled at her grimace. "Second off, if you think about it, janitors, maids, plumbers ... all sortsa cleanin' folks have been keepin' the world from turnin' into one big ball of mud since people started figurin' out that sleepin' in their own filth ain't exactly the brightest idea. Mebbe politicians and military folk look like they're the ones with all the say-so, but we're the ones that keep things runnin' from the ground up, whether they know it or not."

"Still, isn't it a little on the low end of the totem pole?"

"If you look hard enough, there's plenty to be proud of." He grinned. "You just gotta think like a janitor."

"I wasn't aware janitors did much thinking."

"That sorta mindset is gonna get you in a lotta trouble."

He rummaged around the shelves until he came up with a dusty-brown cleaning jumpsuit which zippered up the front, and a pair of black rubber boots. These he handed to Dani. "Get changed."

She held the suit doubtfully. "These are way too big for me. And I am not changing clothes in a garage."

"Fine. But that piece you're wearin' right now dissolves if taken outta HQ, so I guess you're ridin' shotgun nekkid."

Her eyes narrowed. "You're joking. I know you are."

An engine started in the distance as they stared each other down.

At last, her glare turned pleading. "Please say you're joking." When he remained silent, she stalked around to the other side of the van, calling out, "You try to peek and I'll break your nose."

Ben waited as groans of disgust and shuffling evidenced her attempts to change without falling over. A squeak of surprise was followed by Dani running back around, now wearing a hot pink jumpsuit. She plucked at the waistband and arms, which were just loose enough to give her free range of motion. Otherwise it fit perfectly.

"This thing shrunk! And changed color!"

"One size fits all 'round here."

She craned her neck to study the outfit from all sides. "But why pink?"

"It switches to the wearer's favorite color."

"I don't like pink."

"Accordin' to the suit, you like it a lot."

"How do I change it?"

He briefly shut his eyes. When he opened them again, his dusty blue jumpsuit had turned forest green. "Just a mental command. 'Course if you get too distracted or knocked unconscious, it'll revert back. Pink's nothin' to be ashamed of."

She scrunched her eyes in concentration, and her outfit flickered between silver, cherry, and black before settling on tan. After confirming the absence of pink, she smoothed it down. "It do anything else?"

He pointed to her left shoulder, where red threading had appeared, reading: *Dani*. "Cleaner uniforms are also self-sanitizin'. You could dunk it in a septic tank and it'd be spotless half an hour later."

She looked down in new admiration. "Better than magic armor."

"Plus, it's fire retardant and will keep blot-hound puke and other Scum fluids from dissolvin' your skin if you get hit. And the uniforms help us blend in wherever we're workin'."

"Blend?"

"Yup," he said. "Who pays attention to a janitor or two? We're everywhere. Hospitals, malls, office buildings, schools."

"To fight the forces of Corruption," she said. "Scum?"

"Oh, good. You've been takin' notes."

Ben opened the passenger door and looked to her. She stared at the seat and remained unmoving. Finally he waved and made a mocking bow.

"Well? In you go. Chivalry ain't my strong suit, so take it when you can get it."

She darted to the back and grabbed a clean cloth and bottle of cleaning fluid. She attacked the seat with these until the faux-leather gleamed. Only then did she deign to slip inside and perch herself on the cushion.

Ben muttered to himself as he got in on the driver's side. She sat hunched in her seat, boots tucked up in a full-body cringe.

This won't be no joy ride, that's for sure.

The afternoon Denver sun slanted between the skyscrapers as he navigated the van out of the garage and through the flow of businessmen, tourists, joggers and bikers along the sidewalk.

Astonishment wiped away some of Dani's pensive expression. "We're still in the city?"

"Where'd you think HQ was? The Twilight Zone?"

Her scowl returned. "As if that'd be any weirder than what I've experienced so far."

"Think of this as an education on how the world really works."

"My world was working just fine," Dani said. "One more year and I'd be heading to med school to become a doctor. And now I'm stuck in some smelly van with an old fart for a boss instead of in my dorm, feeding my lizard and learning things that won't give me nightmares. I bet I'm stewing in germs just sitting here."

He straightened, making his neck, shoulders, and spine pop. "A'ight, this is what I don't get, princess. You have these big dreams about bein' a doctor, bein' up to your armpits in sick folk and tellin' people to turn and cough, yet you can't handle a little dirt?"

"Not all doctors deal with patients," she said. "I figured I'd go into research. Lab work where everything's sealed up behind glass. Where I could fight germs from a distance."

"And what makes you hate germs so much, huh? You get bullied by one when you was a kid?"

Her gloves squeaked as she made fists. "They're just … wrong. They get inside you. Invade you. They make you dirty on a cellular level. Make you sick and broken, unless you do everything you can to protect yourself. It's all so messy."

Ben's right arm started itching, but he clamped his hands on the steering wheel. "Life is messy. People are alive; escrow, people are messy."

"You mean *ergo*."

"Whatever. The point is, the more people, the more mess."

"But we don't let things stay messy, do we?"

"'Course not. But you don't gotta go all ninja on a germ and kill it and its whole extended family. Sometimes fightin' Corruption is as simple as not lettin' it get a big foothold in the first place. Preventative maintenance."

"You make it sound easy."

"Then you ain't listenin'. This ain't no cakewalk. You're gonna sweat and bleed and curse your parents' first kiss—and that's just while pickin' litter off a sidewalk. And in the rare instances where people are keeping tidy, there's plenty of Scum happy to chuck muck around. It's our job to keep things as clean as possible and help the innocent folks go on livin' without bein' overwhelmed by the mess."

She stiffened. "Oh my ***. I just realized this explains things."

"What does?"

"This! All of this. It explains everything about me! Why I've always hated dirt and germs. It's because they really are evil."

"Er. No." He tapped the side of his head. "That's just you bein' a little off your rocker."

"But—"

"It's complicated. Don't start slappin' labels like good and evil on everything just yet. It's not that tidy."

He changed lanes, heading for the next off-ramp. Dani looked around.

"Where are we going?"

"I wasn't kiddin' earlier. We gotta clean some mall bathrooms."

"That's disgusting. I'm not doing that."

He grinned. "Oh, you will."

They endured a silent ride south to the Park Meadows Mall. With its mingling of large wooden beams, huge windows, and trees planted all around the main entrances, it looked like someone had pumped a mountain cabin full of steroids and then plastered it with chain logos.

Dani perked up as they drove past the entrance to the food court. "I'm starving."

"There's some leftover tacos in the glove compartment. Welcome to 'em."

"Okay. Not hungry anymore."

"Wimp. Well, if you ain't gonna, then pass them over."

She hesitated until he waved for the food. With a look of incredulous disgust, she popped the glove case open and pulled out two tacos. Even with the rubber gloves on, she pinched each between thumb and forefinger and tossed them into his lap.

He unwrapped them with one hand and crunched down on the stale shells and a mash of cheese, sour cream, wilted lettuce, and mystery meat. She leaned away as he wolfed the tacos down, spraying crumbs. By the time the last bite plopped into his gullet, she clutched her stomach as if sick.

"I can't believe you just ate those."

He patted his paunch and belched. "Builds up the ol' immune system."

She covered her mouth and nose. "When was the last time you brushed your teeth?"

"Wednesday."

"Of which month?"

"That's personal."

He pulled around the back of the mall and parked by a series of trash bins and employee entrances. Ben muscled his cart free and, after locking up the van, wheeled it to the nearest door. Dani trailed behind as if dragged by a leash.

He shoved the cart into a long white-tiled, gray-walled corridor that ran along behind the stores. The air-conditioned hallway smelled of pine and each step or squeak of the cart wheels echoed loudly. They passed by several mall staff who didn't give them a second glance.

He took them down a side hall, past vending machines and water fountains, and toward the restrooms at the far end. Being the middle of the week, only a few shoppers were present—mothers with strollers, elderly mall walkers, and the occasional security guard on a Segway.

"I don't get it," Dani said, breaking the long silence. "You say good and evil don't apply, but aren't these Scum the bad guys?"

Ben whistled low through his teeth. "It's the name the Board slaps on anyone or anythin' that draws their power from Corruption." He unhooked a yellow plastic *Closed for Cleaning* sign from the side of the cart and set it up in front of the men's restroom. "Then you've got your more neutral factions who just don't care much about our fleshy realm. Interdimensional travelers who come through their portals and don't wipe their feet, trackin' existential muck across my clean tiles. Imps leavin' coffee stains everywhere ..."

Her expression went deadpan. "Coffee."

"Yeah. Never give an imp coffee unless you wanna be scrapin' gooey bits off the ceiling for a week."

Ben handed her a bucket with a bottle of Clorox in it, plus a bristled toilet scrubber, and took her to the first stall.

"Corruption and Purity are in a bit of a balance right now. We just gotta keep things from tippin' too far in Corruption's favor. So ..." He gestured to the waiting stall.

Her face scrunched. "But toilets? Isn't that a bit undignified?"

"Stop stallin' and get a-scrubbin'." He smiled slightly. "'Sides, I ain't doin' it just to play the cruel taskmaster. You've been through a lot, and it helps the mind process things if the body is distracted with some good ol' manual labor."

With a groan, Dani shuffled into the stall. Standing back as far as possible, holding the handle by the tip, she half-heartedly ran the brush around the bowl. As Ben watched, the itching in his right arm flared up again. He sucked a breath in, loud enough to make Dani look over her shoulder.

"What's wrong?"

He clutched the arm close and turned away. "Nothin'. I just forgot somethin' in the van. I'll be right back."

• • •

Dani peeked out of the stall as Ben headed out. Why'd he hold his arm that way? An old injury? She'd have to ask about that.

Once the janitor's footsteps receded, she turned back to stare at the toilet as if it were her arch-nemesis. For most of her life, the bathroom had been enemy territory. She'd had to sneak in, using wipes and gel and gloves to fight her way through if she had any hope of coming out unscathed.

Was she going to let those old fears rule her still? Here she stood, empowered, protected more than ever before against filth, and she still balked at the idea of even coming into this place without a full decontamination routine.

She had to start somewhere. It wasn't an ideal situation, but she could at least enjoy a bit of revenge against something that had kept her living in fear for so many years.

Spreading her feet, she took up a defiant stance.

We meet again, Monsieur Toilet. Except this time, it seems I have you at a disadvantage.

She raised the brush and started whacking the toilet all over. Muted thuds filled the restroom, and she grunted with each connection, chanting to herself.

I.

Don't.

Have.

To Be.

Afraid.

Any more.

Footsteps made her freeze mid-swing. Flushing, she spun and dropped the brush to her side as Ben stepped into view outside the stall.

"I was just—" she began.

Several facts slammed into her mind with paralyzing force. The newcomer wasn't Ben. In fact, it didn't appear to be anyone.

The figure stood a solid six feet tall with muscular proportions, clearly defined hands, and a vague impression of horns on an otherwise bald head. Featureless, it somehow gave the impression of staring at her. And its entire genderless form looked to be made of sand and grit that swirled in yellow, brown, and black eddies. Its feet left dusty patches across the tiles.

Scum. She knew it instinctively, as if she'd gained a mental radar that detected the beings the Cleaners opposed. Old fear surged through her, that of dirt and grime getting into the cracks of her skin, her eyes, her mouth. Of being caked with filth.

Dani stammered and tried to regain control of herself. Her power welled up, energy filling her to the brim, wanting to be released. Demanding it.

The creature continued staring.

"I ... what do you want?" Dani managed. She had to calm down. But how, when facing a monster?

Its continued silence mocked her—and yet this affront helped her fear switch to anger. As she did, her grip on her power firmed. She refused to be intimidated by an overgrown dust bunny.

Raising the scrub brush like a sword, she eyed the monster over the bristle. "I don't have to be afraid of you."

She threw the brush with all her might. It struck the creature square in the chest and sunk in halfway. The creature showed no sign of pain; it didn't even seem to notice the impaling tool as it raised a hand. Dirt drizzled from its fingers.

Dani flinched. A light bulb exploded overhead. The creature lunged. Its hand gripped her throat and drove her backward. Her hip slammed against the toilet basin, and her head smacked into the wall.

Stunned, her power fled as her vision dimmed.

CHAPTER SIX

en grumbled as he wedged himself between the soda machine and wall, pinning his arm behind him so he couldn't scratch. Scratching only made it worse.

Should he peel back the sleeve and check? No. Last time he did that, he couldn't eat for a couple days.

Carl made concerned burbles in his bottle. Ben started to snap at him to keep his opinions to himself, but bit back the words. Minor irritants flaring his temper so much wasn't a good sign. He'd been grumpier than normal, what with being forced into a Siamese twin act with Dani, but still ... no excuse.

He ran a thumb along the spray trigger. "Sorry, buddy. I know you're just tryin' to help. Do one thing for me, will yah? Lemme know if I ever go overboard with her, eh? Be a bit of a moral compass so I don't steer her too far off the crooked and narrow."

Carl swirled in question.

"Mebbe, but it's the only way I know how. Hit 'em with the truth, hard and fast, and sort out the pieces later. That's all I can do with her. Hard and fast, and hope she can handle it."

Carl slapped tiny waves together, snickering. Ben frowned until comprehension made him scowl. He shoved back out into the open.

"Oh, c'mon. You know I didn't mean that. You really are a dirty little drip of … hang a sec. What's that?"

He sniffed as he scoped the length of the hall. The area appeared undisturbed, but a foul odor threaded the air, and not one of his old-man farts, either. A scent of Corrupt energies made his arm prickle more.

He stiffened as he spotted the dusty footprints. They originated from a floor-level vent and led past the cleaning sign into the restrooms—and they hadn't been there a minute before. The spray bottle on his hip jerked as Carl spouted in alarm.

"Oh, polish my puckerhole," Ben said. "Get ready for a little hoe-down, buddy."

As he sprinted into the restroom, he snatched the bottle up and triggered Carl, who spun out into a water-whip. All the stall doors were closed, but Dani's feet were visible below the one she'd been working in. The heels of her rubber boots drummed the floor while another pair of dirt-colored feet straddled them.

He wrenched the door open and snapped the whip around the thick neck of the creature that pinned Dani. Its hand had deformed into a shapeless mass that covered her mouth and nostrils. She bucked and strained, but it had her butt stuck in the toilet bowl. Her eyes, gleaming with panic, locked onto him. A muffled scream pushed through the gagging muck.

Ben jerked back as hard as he could. With a hiss like poured sand, the creature released Dani and clutched at the whip as it staggered out of the stall. A ragged wheeze broke from Dani, who spat up a wad of mud and scrambled to her feet.

"What—" She gagged and coughed up more dirt as she grasped the top of a stall wall, looking ready to climb over to get away. "What is that thing?"

Ben wrangled the creature up against a mirror. A flurry of tiny scratches appeared on the glass wherever it touched.

"It's a dust devil," he said over his shoulder. "Don't worry. The water should neutralize it long enough for me to—"

The dust devil reached up and snapped the cord from around its neck like a silk thread.

Ben's eyes widened. "Uh—"

The dust devil barreled into him with a hot blast of sand. It ground in, cutting and scratching; its body plastered against his, trying to smother him like it had with Dani. Ben stumbled back into the stall next to Dani's. The dust devil raised an arm, which narrowed into a spike.

"Holy ****." Ben slammed the door shut.

With a screech, the spike punched through the door and jutted an inch away from his ribs. Ben sucked in his gut and pressed back against the toilet to keep from being disemboweled. The spike withdrew, only to spear back in repeatedly. Soon the creature stood visible through the holes. Not much longer and the door would provide as much defense as shredded tinfoil.

Dani yelped as the dust devil started alternating attacks from Ben's door to hers, giving neither of them a chance to escape.

"Ben!"

"Water," he yelled. "Hit it with water!"

"The bucket's out there!"

"Use the toilet."

"No ******* way!"

Ben ducked as the dusty spike shot past his neck.

"Dani …"

"This is so GROSS!"

Splashing combined with disgusted whimpers. Handfuls of water flew over the top of her stall. The first missed, but the second and third splashed against the dust devil's head and shoulders. Muddy chunks broke off and plopped to the floor. Moments later, grit replaced the damaged spots, but it provided enough of a distraction for Ben.

He timed the charge right as a fourth watery missile smacked into the construct. He flung the door open, dodged another stab, and flung himself at the creature. He managed a last breath before clamping his lips shut as grit scoured them.

Dani yelled in the background, but the dust devil's hissing and the scrape of its body drowned out her words.

Gripping the spray bottle with both hands, he bear-hugged the dust devil and squeezed the trigger. Pure energies focused into the water, he mentally directed Carl until liquid encased both hands. Then he dropped the bottle and thrust his hands into the creature's back. The dirt and dust recoiled from his touch. It should've penetrated like a knife through newspaper; instead, it felt like trying to punch hardening cement.

The dust devil stopped trying to thrust its limbs down his windpipe and reached backward with jointless arms. Its hands clamped around his wrists and tried to pull him out.

Even as he dizzied, Ben kept his mouth shut to avoid breathing. His heart pounded and his lungs felt ready to pop. Then his fingers connected with the dust devil's core. With a mental shout, he yanked it out—a crystal-clear orb with thorny tendrils that tried to dig into his hand.

The dust devil shrieked and reeled back, while Ben gaped at what he held.

"Where ... where'dja get this?"

Short hisses drew his gaze to the dust devil.

"Are you laughin' at me?"

Its horned head swung to regard Dani, who peeked out from her stall. She shrank back and moved to shut the door again. The dust devil struck the door off its hinges, and the ruined metal clattered to the floor. Dani raised her hands as she hunched.

"I'm not afraid of you," she cried. "I'm not!"

Ben turned in place, searching for the spray bottle. Hearing the panic in Dani's voice, he held a hand out her way even as the dust devil closed in.

"Focus and control," he said. "Don't let it frighten you."

"I'm not frightened!"

"Just gimme a second ..."

The spray bottle had rolled under the nearest sink. Ben jammed the core into a pocket and lunged for the bottle just as the dust devil went for Dani again.

"You mother******!" she screamed. "You got me *DIRTY!*"

Her voice rose into a keening, and Ben braced himself.

The power burst out of her in uncontrolled shreds of Pure magic. Every light bulb and fixture exploded at once. Jagged forks of lightning shot out from the sockets and arced into metal fixtures and stall walls.

Twin strikes hit his water-encased hands, stinging the fingers. Ben yelled and shook them to release the liquid gloves. They splashed to his feet as the room flashed purple, yellow, and green.

A spear of lightning pierced the dust devil. It split the grainy body and connected with a black orb in the creature's chest.

Two cores? No ...

The body drew back together as the dust devil twitched and jerked. Ben sensed the power flowing into it, like a river refilling a cup. Some outside force maintained the creature's form despite Dani's overwhelming attack.

In another strobe-light flicker, the dust devil's body expanded into a giant face. Each eye as big as Ben's head, it looked like a generic mask with a bland collection of features. The mouth opened, a tongue of sand formed, and a moan reverberated out like constipated cow.

"M*mmmmooommoo* ... "

Ben shielded his eyes from cutting particles. "Who are you?"

Features twisted into an agonized theatre mask.

"P*pammommoo* ... "

The face vanished, the remaining core shattered, and the dust devil flew apart, spattering the walls. Lightning continued streaming from outlets and sockets with increasing fury. A sharp smell of ozone filled the air and singed his nostril hairs.

"Dani, that's enough!"

Her wail cut through the fizzing and cracking. "I can't stop it."

"Try!"

"******, I am!"

Ben dropped to his knees as the electrical storm rose to a peak. With a final sputter, the lightning vanished, leaving the restroom dark except for a faint wash of illumination from the hall.

After he caught his breath, he took a physical inventory. Aside from stinging hands, bruised knees and aching arms, he felt intact. Mostly. The smell of burnt hair wafted through the bathroom, and his knuckles were suspiciously bare.

"Ben?"

"Here." He coughed and struggled to his feet. "You okay?"

A sniffle. "I'm ... fine. What just happened? Why did that thing attack me? What did it want?"

He wiped over his sweaty, grit-plastered face. "I can't rightly say."

Her snort pinged off the walls. "You don't know? Great. How long have you been doing this again?"

"Hush it and lemme think."

Glassy blotches covered the walls where the dust devil's remains had hit. Ben touched one, and then jerked his hand away.

"Hot," he muttered.

Carl wobbled in his version of *Duh*.

"Did you see the face?" he asked Dani. "Did you hear the voice?"

"Um, maybe? I'm not sure. I've seen and heard too many weird things lately. Now I have to add walking piles of murderous dirt to the list."

"They're called dust devils. But it shouldn't have existed. Not like this. It's impossible."

"Why?"

Her hand found his arm, but he knocked it away. He didn't think any of the dust devil's attacks had broken his skin, but he couldn't see well enough to tell.

"Go get cleaned up," he said, waving her to the sink.

She reared back. "No way. Do you know how many infectious microorganisms are in tap water? Coliforms. Clostridium. Giardiasis. That's not even considering all the corroded pipes it runs through, or all the toxic chemicals they pump in, trying to kill the bacteria in the first place. Might as well drink sewage. I need pure water."

"Suit yourself." He plucked the bottle off his belt and started to unscrew the top.

She raised a fist. "Don't you dare hit me with Carl again." She fished a packet of wet wipes out of a pocket and started cleaning muddy streaks off her face and neck.

He walked out into the lit hallway with her a few steps behind. He hated leaving such a mess. It went against all his training and what pride he had left in his work, but something more important had come up.

As they piled the equipment back onto the cart and headed out, Ben let thoughts tumble free.

"Dust devils are Corrupt constructs. They don't just pop out on their own. Someone's gotta create them and send 'em out with a purpose. Plus, they never travel in less than pairs, never attack randomly, and sure-for-shootin' do not—" He retrieved the unbroken core from his pocket, "—have two cores, one Pure and the other Corrupt."

"Cores?" Dani echoed, as she dug a wipe into an ear.

"Yup. Any spell or construct has to have a core of power that the caster makes, usually by channelin' raw energy or with some fancy ceremony. Otherwise they gotta maintain constant focus or the spell puffs away. With constructs, sometimes the core is an actual physical thingamajig. Somethin' you can tear out and smash up. Other times, it's like … like a psychic knot that you gotta find and snip."

"Oh." She plucked at her gloves, pretending to adjust them, but he still noticed the slight shake of her hands. "So if there were two cores, one Pure, one Corrupt, what does that mean?"

"It'd mean somethin's terribly wrong. It'd mean the dust devil was rigged by someone using powers from both sides."

"So? You can't be bi-magical?"

He shook his head. "It's impossible for the opposin' energies to mingle. They destroy each other. I ain't never experienced somethin' like that before. Far as I know, no one has in the history of the Cleaners."

They pushed out into the back lot and trundled the cart over to the van. Dani rubbed a wipe over the back of her neck as she spat on the asphalt.

"Now what?" she asked. "Go clean some grout and get attacked by mutant termites?"

He waved to the cart. "Help me get this secured. We're gonna go see the boss."

CHAPTER SEVEN

ani craned her neck to look up at the building Ben drove toward. They'd come back downtown, a few blocks south of the Sixteenth Street Mall. The skyscraper he navigated underneath sported a national bank logo, windows shimmering in the sunset.

"This isn't where we left earlier," she said as she continued picking dirt out of her hair. Forget a bath. After the dust devil's attack, she needed a blast from a fire hose.

Ben cleared his throat like a cat readying a hairball. "'Course it ain't. There're entrances to HQ all over town. Some are for emergencies only."

"Is that what this is?"

"Princess, there's a fine line between emergency and catastrophe. We ran over that line and left it bleedin' on the pavement about ten miles back."

"Oh." She grabbed the armrest as he took a hard turn. "So this guy we're going to see …"

"I'm goin' to see him," he said. "You will tech'nicly be in his esteemed presence, but be a good girl and keep quiet, okie-dokie? This is way over your head."

"What am I, janitorial eye candy? Give me a break, Gramps. If I can wrap my mind around calculus, I can handle a little office politics."

He grunted, a noncommittal noise that let her chalk up a point for herself.

"Am I supposed to kowtow and kiss his feet?" she asked.

"Don't ask stupid questions."

"There are no stupid questions, especially about things I have no clue about. How else am I going to learn?"

His laughter made her bristle. "Permission is always stupid to ask for."

"Why?"

"'Cause if someone says 'no,' you can't claim ignorance later."

The van rattled to a stop. Trying to show initiative, Dani hopped out, jogged over to the elevators and hit the call button. Right beside the elevators, a large window looked in on an untidy office, dimmed lights, and a Back-In-Twenty-Minutes sign suction-cupped to the other side of the glass. She checked over her shoulder as Ben joined her.

"What floor?" she asked.

He pressed a hand against the window. Dani squawked as a translucent face thrust out of the glass, defined by deep-set eyes, a trimmed beard, and sharp nose. It studied them both before fixing on Ben. When it spoke, its voice sounded far off, as if coming down a long tube.

"Your business?"

Ben pointed at the ceiling. "I'm here to see Destin ... er ... the Chairman."

"You have no appointment."

"Since when do I need an appointment to talk to my own boss?"

"Everyone needs an appointment to meet with the Chairman. Especially you."

Dani heard something pop, and realized it was the knuckles of Ben's fist.

"Step out here and say that, washer-boy. Just 'cause you watch the streets from up high don't mean you get to spit on my bald spot when I walk past. Now you gonna admit me or am I gonna report you to your superior?"

"My superior is Ascendant Francis, who gave specific orders that you were not to be allowed access to the Chairman unless you went through him."

"He said what now?" Ben's voice roughened.

The glossy eyes blinked. *"I'm only acting under orders, Janitor. If you shatter this junction, it will come out of your pay."*

Ben rapped the pointy nose with his knuckles. A sharp chime echoed through the garage.

"What don't come out of my pay these days? Listen, Destin told me he'd be available in case I encountered serious trouble, so unless you wanna be responsible for keepin' vital information from the Chairman, you're gonna go to him lickety-split. You'll tell him I've discovered an imbalance—a big, nasty one, too. And you'll tell him I ain't leavin' until he hears me out."

"I will have to alert Ascendant Francis of your presence."

"Fine. Do that. But see what Destin says first."

The face withdrew and left the window unmarred.

Dani licked dry lips. "What was that?"

Ben's shoulders remained tensed. "Window-watcher. They guard and maintain the glassways. They also wash the windows of buildings in areas of operations. Keeps the paths open."

"Glassways? Paths?"

She hated how tall he was compared to her. It made her feel small and ignorant whenever he looked down at her, especially with his current impatient expression.

"Patience is a virtue, a'ight? You'll learn as we go. You've already been exposed to more in a day than I was in my first month."

The window-watcher's face reappeared. *"Come through."*

Ben stepped forward, leaving Dani to stare as his body passed into the window and vanished without so much as a ripple. She reached out to test the surface. As she did, his wrinkled, knobby hand shoved back out, grabbed her wrist, and pulled her through.

She stumbled into a bright hallway with white walls, ceiling, and floor. She blinked away the glare as Ben entered another set of elevator doors at the far end. He turned to wave her on.

"Will you quit dallyin'? I'll leave you here until I'm done, if that's whatcha want."

She ran and slipped between the doors just before they *snicked* shut. Inside, silver walls gleamed and a golden light shone down on them, pinning their shadows beneath their feet. The cab hummed and shivered as it ... ascended? Descended? She couldn't tell. She kept glimpsing movement out of the corner of her eyes and checked around for more faces and figures until Ben nudged her with an elbow.

"Stop starin'. It's rude."

She opened her mouth to retort, but his distant gaze told her he wouldn't hear or care about any insult she might sling his way. So she frowned at her feet until she grew uncomfortable enough with the long, silent ride to try for small talk.

"This boss we're going to meet ..."

It surprised her when he answered. "Destin. Destin Felsman. He's Chairman of the Board and he's given his life to the cause of Purity." He said the last part the same way one might say, *"He has a fondness for running over kittens."*

"That's bad? I thought everyone here fell into that category."

"Well ..." Ben picked at the grime under his nails. "He takes things a little further than most. For instance, Destin don't shower when he gets up in the mornin'. He has an entire decontamination room with sonic scrubbers and a flash chamber that strips off a layer of skin. Better than coffee, he says."

She felt a rush of eagerness to meet this mysterious Chairman. Maybe they had more in common than she'd anticipated. "Does he ... uh ... ever let anyone else use this room?"

"Kiddin'? He wouldn't dare let any grunts near the place. Wouldn't want us leavin' our sorry stink around, wouldja, Destin?"

She glanced around the elevator again. "Um ... is he listening?"

Ben squinted into the light. "Yup. We'd be there already if he didn't have so much fun givin' visitors full-body scans. Just one more way the upper crust likes to remind us of our place on the food chain. Ain't that right, boss?"

"Always a pleasure, Benjamin." The tinny voice sounded from everywhere at once.

The elevator jolted to a stop. The doors opened on an enormous office, devoid of almost any features beyond white marble walls, floor, and ceiling. An expanse of gold carpet led down to a stainless steel desk topped with a glass slab, with pearly obelisk statues and crystal paperweights spotting the surface.

The window wall behind the desk provided a view of downtown, with an array of pebbled rooftops, gray alleys, asphalt and rusting steel moving up to the horizon where the sun nestled among the mountaintops.

In between the gleaming desk and the gritty city beyond, a white-suited figure sat in a leather chair, head bent over shuffled papers.

"Ever think you guys take the whole white and shiny motif a little too far?" Dani whispered. "I mean, I get the symbolism, but isn't it a little cliché?"

Ben chuckled. "Sure. But it's always easier to reinforce the stereotypes. Problem is, when you work your entire life buildin' an image, you start to believe it whether it's true or not."

Their rubber boots squeaked until they reached the carpet. She couldn't smell a thing—aside from herself, that is. In fact, the absence of all other smells seemed to increase her own odors, making her uncomfortably aware of dried sweat, toilet water, burnt hair, and the lemon scent of the wet wipes. Her nose wrinkled and she itched to get her gel out, though she suspected it'd do no good.

This discomfort grew as they neared the desk, and she suddenly had the urge to fall on her knees and beg to use the fabled decontamination room.

Have some dignity, she told herself.

Dignity? Let's start with getting clean and work up from there, herself replied.

The man she assumed to be Destin looked up as they arrived. He wore a three-piece suit identical to Francis', minus the fedora. His thin blond hair was combed to one side, not a strand out of place. The paleness of his skin made his blue eyes stand out startlingly bright, the only handsome feature in an otherwise plain face. He also wore white gloves, and a white rose stuck out from his lapel. When he spoke, his voice came out clear but colorless, as if any strong emotions had been scrubbed away along with his outer layer of skin that morning.

"Good afternoon, Benjamin. When I said to contact me if you ran into any trouble, I didn't expect to hear from you so soon. Or in person."

Ben made a sarcastic salute. "Heya, boss. I'd give a 'hello' kiss, but I didn't bleach my lips recently." He plunked down on a corner of the desk, ignoring Destin's pointed look at where the grimy jumpsuit smudged the glass. "Wanna tell me what's up with usin' Francis as a guard dog?"

Destin set aside his silver pen. His fingers left no prints on its gleaming surface. "I am unaware of Ascendant Francis taking on any such function."

"That right?" Ben asked. "You didn't tell him to turn me away if I didn't come here without an appointment?"

"I gave no such instruction. Ascendant Francis does understand the value of my time, so perhaps he is being over-zealous in encouraging that same respect in others. What I wish to know now is whether I was wise in allowing you to interrupt my work. You spoke of discovering an imbalance?"

Ben pulled out the clear orb he'd retrieved from the dust devil and rolled it over to Destin, who stopped it with tip of his middle finger.

"What is this?" the Chairman asked.

"I really gotta tell you?"

Destin cupped the orb in his palm. "It appears to be a Pure core. Is there any reason I shouldn't already consider this a waste of my time?"

"It's a Pure core I tore out of a dust devil."

The Chairman's thin, platinum blond eyebrows pinched together. "Impossible."

"And that was right before we cracked a second, Corrupt core in the same creature."

Destin leaned forward and eyed Dani. "We? Is this true, Ms. Hashelheim?"

"Uh, as far as I know." She swallowed against her dry tongue. When had she become so nervous? "This thing attacked me while I was … cleaning toilets. That," she pointed at the crystal orb, "came out of it."

Destin set the core down with a click. "Interesting."

"Interesting?" Ben echoed. "It's enough to make me wish I didn't have an ****** to **** outta. If someone is out messin' with combined energies, then it could be worse than the time Peters lit that gasbloat on fire. And the two cores ain't the only thing. Dust devils are constructs, right? They need someone to kick 'em into gear."

Destin ticked his pen back and forth. "I am aware of that fact."

"Well, whoever was behind this one hijacked it. Turned it into a communication spell, another thing we didn't know was possible. He spoke to me. Or tried to. I think he's in trouble. Maybe bein' tortured, driven insane by his own divided powers, however he got 'em. And that's not figurin' in the blot-hound I had to put down twice last night." At Destin's questioning look, Ben clarified, "The one that jumped back up after I'd already torn out its core. Stronger than before. Like somethin' or someone was fuelin' it."

The Chairman poised his chin over interlaced fingers. "Why wasn't I made aware of that?"

"It was in my report on Dani here."

Destin shook his head. "I reviewed the facts of her recruitment but saw nothing about any blot-hound anomaly."

"Then maybe you and Francis oughta have a little chit-chat. Meantimes, we gotta figure out what's causin' all this twisted business."

"If there is such a threat, then it must be dealt with," the Chairman said. "Yet I admit to hesitation. If both cores were available for comparison, it could be proved that they came from the same construct. Without them, the story is suspect—not that I consider it such. But even Dani's witness can be disregarded as the mistake of a new employee who doesn't yet know what she saw."

"Don't pull this blather, Destin. We need to get everyone on high alert. It's gonna cause a sh … er … spitstorm if someone's figured out a way to combine the energies of both Pantheons."

"I will, of course, notify the necessary parties, but I won't spread unsubstantiated rumors that might cause more chaos and distraction than the actual problem."

Ben stood and made fists. "What happened to the Destin who preferred action over borough cracks?"

"Bureauc—" Dani started to correct. At his look, though, she fell silent.

Ben fixed on the Chairman again. "Huh? What happened to the guy who shattered an entire sheet of blackshards before we could even see our reflections in their panes?"

"He became Chairman of the Cleaners, Benjamin. I've not forgotten our time in the field, but I have a different perspective now. Different priorities."

"Oh, sure. I guess you do get all sortsa new perspectives when your head gets stuck up your—"

"Janitor!" Destin shot to his feet. "You overstep yourself. My position and influence has kept you with this company thus far, and I find your ungracious attitude tiresome. I am responsible not just for my own life and yours, but for all the Cleaners in this country, not to mention coordinating with our global efforts." He riffled the papers on his desk. "Did you think I sort through these just to keep my desk tidy? That I limit our conversation because I might be late for a round of golf? Benjamin, you know me better than that. While I would love nothing more than to hold your hand, I am pressed on a hundred sides. Any decision I make could affect thousands, if not millions of lives. Be glad you do not have that weight on your soul."

Ben looked—not cowed, but sobered. A bull who'd just been reminded of the ring through his nose. His jaw remained jutted in the face of Destin's lecture, but the blaze in his eyes dwindled to a rebellious flicker. After half a minute, he looked aside, breaking the standoff.

"You have my approval to continue searching for the source of this disturbance," Destin said, retaking his seat. "But for now that's all I can offer. As soon as you provide me with evidence that I can use to convince the Board this warrants further attention, I will have a full contingent of Ascendants to back you up." He waved a gloved hand in dismissal. "I give you leave to clear your next week's calendar in order to pursue this concern, but don't barge back in here until you have something concrete."

Ben crossed his arms. "I'm a janitor, Destin. Not a pay-per-day private eye. Francis or Jack are better equipped to check up on this. Plus, neither of them are ..." A glance Dani's way. "Distracted."

Oh, that boosted her confidence a whole ton.

"I don't send Ascendants chasing shadows," Destin said. "That would be a gross abuse of the power invested in them. And the more people we involve, the more chance we take in spreading uncertainty among our ranks. You can more easily maintain a low profile."

"With this chickadee in tow? Ain't likely."

Dani's fists bunched as her blood pressure rose. Chickadee? What era did this moron think they lived in? The next time he threw some sexist comment her way, she'd have to decide whether to bloody his nose or knee his crotch. On second thought, neither of those offered sanitary targets. Maybe she'd just throw something at him. Like one of the Chairman's paperweights.

"Having her at your side will provide the experience she lacks," Destin said. "As you are fond of saying, is not the best teaching found through action?"

"I ain't gonna expose an apprentice to an unknown danger when she's already dealin' with enough as it is. You knew the risk of puttin' her with me in the first place."

That drew Dani's brows and lips down. Risk? What kind of risk could the old man pose? Besides spitting or hacking on her, that is. The way he hobbled around made her afraid he'd break a hip the next time he lifted his cart.

Destin stood and came around the desk, placing himself between them. Despite only being an inch or two taller than her, his nearness made Dani feel like she'd shrunk a foot.

"I am decided, Benjamin. We each do our part in this." He smiled at Dani, revealing clean, straight teeth. His eyes held an electric hue. "And you, my dear? How have you been enjoying your time with us so far?"

She fought to not squirm and wring her hands. She once more became aware of her myriad smells, greasy hair, and sweaty palms. How could he stand being near her? She wanted to tear her skin off and scrub herself down to the bone.

His smile widened. "Don't fear. I appreciate honesty above all else."

Ben snorted, but Destin remained focused on her.

"It's been ..." She swallowed again. "Messy."

Destin's laugh ricocheted through the room. It jolted her, bringing another wave of shame. She'd never be clean. Not on her own. She was sullied to the core, and couldn't do anything about it.

"Is there anything I can do to soothe this difficult transition for you?" he asked.

"She misses her lizard," Ben said.

Destin blinked. "Indeed?"

Through simmering humiliation, Dani murmured, "Just a pet. I take care of him. He's probably really hungry."

"While I sympathize," said Destin, "we do not allow Cleaners to keep pets. They are often sources of pestilence and filth."

"But ..." She despised her whimpering tone. "He's cute. And funny, and smart ... and ..."

Destin placed a hand on her shoulder and she flinched. Not because she disliked the touch, which felt warm even through the gloves and suit, but because she feared his palm might come away soiled.

"There is a reason cleanliness has always been close to godliness." He kept his hand on her, rubbing a few hairs between his fingers, an oddly comforting, yet mortifying gesture. "Soon enough you will come to see the greater purpose the Cleaners can give you, and the honor it is to serve the Pantheon. A creature such as this ... Tetris ... would only serve as a distraction. I'm sure an intelligent woman such as you knows the many bacterial strains reptiles carry. Salmonella. Campylobacter ..."

His litany sounded uncomfortably familiar, and Dani's resistance slowly buckled under it. She bowed her head, feeling like a speck of dirt he could flick off his suit at any second. She was a wretch. How didn't she understand before? The Cleaners had saved her from a worthless life and given her a chance to achieve true significance. They had every right to toss her aside right then, and she'd beg to be given another chance.

A tiny part of her mind raised a hand. *Excuse me? Exactly when did we become this guy's little *****?*

Indignation sliced down her brainstem and stiffened her spine. Sucking a deep breath through her nostrils, she snapped her head up and glared at Destin.

"What kind of **** are you trying to pull? I already feel bad enough, as it is. Who the **** do you think you are?"

Destin's eyes lost their shimmer.

Ben chuckled behind her. "Good on yah, princess." He moved between them, making Dani shuffle back. "Lookee here, Destin. It's been a long day, a'ight? We'll let you get back to signin' all those big, important papers."

Destin stared past Ben, fixing Dani with … not icy eyes, but they definitely had some slush in them. She struggled to meet that gaze, but kept glancing aside, cheeks aflame. So much for asking about the decontamination room.

Then his thin smile returned, and his amiable personality clicked back into place.

"I look forward to hearing that this problem is resolved." He moved back around to his chair and settled in. "I am sure you won't disappoint me."

With that, the Chairman bent back to his papers. Ben blew him a wet kiss and headed for the elevator. Dani followed, and they rode back down to the bright hall. As they stepped out of the window and into the garage, Ben glanced at her appraisingly.

"Anyone toldja you got great people skills?" he asked. "'Cause they lied."

"I didn't … I wasn't …" Her shoulders slumped. "What happened up there?"

His laugh echoed around, full of unexpected warmth. "You did somethin' not many people can. You made Destin remember he ain't got everyone lickin' his shoes clean. Proud of you."

"Proud?"

"Sure for shootin'. In fact, what say we grab a drink to celebrate?"

"A drink?"

"Yeah. Gotta wet this whistle if I'm gonna keep bossin' you 'round. 'Sides, I need time to think."

Dani massaged the back of her neck. Her encounter with the Chairman had left her with a slight headache. Even now she imagined his bright eyes monitoring her from an unseen corner.

A drink might not be a bad idea, after all.

CHAPTER EIGHT

Standing outside the bar, Ben kept one eye on Dani back over by the van. She had raided the shelves for soaps and scrubs and then worked herself into a frenzy, giving herself what amounted to a sponge bath in the parking lot. Ben couldn't count how many wipes and paper towels she'd gone through. At this rate, he'd have to restock by morning.

Though, he supposed he couldn't blame her, especially after a truck in front of them had belched black exhaust out of its pipes, which had wafted in through the air vents. That had nearly sent her leaping out her door into moving traffic.

"Gotta admit," he murmured, "It's kinda nice havin' someone along for the ride."

Carl spun into a testy whirlpool.

Ben patted it absently. "Aw, c'mon, buddy. You know I didn't mean it that way. It's just good to have someone who's willin' to look me in the eyes and share a drink."

Another spritz of discontent.

"Yeah, but we both know what happened last time you tried alcohol. Took forever to get you outta the pool." He drummed fingers on the bottle. "Destin should've given her to someone else, but I'm kinda glad he didn't, despite my better judgment."

A questioning bubbling.

"Why? I dunno. Wait, that ain't true." Ben tugged and pushed at the saggy skin of his cheeks and throat. "I wanna see her safe. See her through this and know she's gonna make out it the other end with everythin' intact. One last good thing finished before I go. One last taste of what it's like to make a difference. For the better, y'know?"

The water elemental gurgled in reprimand, and Ben's grin went lopsided.

"Me? Morbid? Naw. Just gotta be realistic. Ain't you the one always tellin' me to prepare for the worst?" He frowned. "Mebbe Francis is right. Mebbe Destin screwed the pooch on this one. At least she ain't makin' it easy. Gonna go out in glory or flames with this one."

Carl splashed and fizzed.

"Heh. Yeah. She does remind me a bit of—"

"Hey, you okay?"

Ben twitched and straightened so fast his hips crackled. Dani had appeared at his side without warning. Her gloves, suit, and face gleamed like wax in the glare of the bar's buzzing neon signs. At least her eyes had gone from deer-in-the-headlights to deer-ready-to-ram-a-semi.

He braced a hand in the small of his back and forced a grin. "Yup. Carl and I were just remissionin' about the good ol' days."

"You mean reminiscing."

"Ain't that what I said?"

He pushed the bar door open, and a gust of stale alcohol, hot wing sauce, and grease slapped them in the face. Dani reeled, coughing, while Ben inhaled it like the perfume of a long-lost lover. Once he got a good look at the place, however, his eagerness lessened.

A subtle fog of decay spotted the place, visible only to those eyes attuned to such energies. Clumps of it lurked in the corners like sulking cats, while wisps of Corruption writhed around table and chair legs.

Beside him, Dani recovered and planted fists on slim hips as she frowned at the dimly lit interior. Neon blue lights hung over a long mirror which reflected the cherry wood bar and shelved bottles. Booths stretched along the brick walls, most of them empty and yawning like gaps in a row of teeth.

"You really know how to make a girl feel special," she said.

Ben sniffed, trying to detect the cause of the dank odor. Did the lights seem dimmer than usual? The woodwork grimier?

"I assume you're wantin' a drink of your own?" he asked, shuffling in. "'Cause I ain't sharin'."

"Yeah," Dani said. "I can still taste dust on the back of my tongue. But only if you're paying."

"On the house." Ben waved at the bartender, who nodded back. "Did a favor for the owner a few years back. Cleaned a buncha mold outta the cellar."

"Whoa. Mold. Scary."

"This kinda mold ate brain tissue and made folks into hosts before we scrubbed it out. Since then, I check in once a month or so, just in case it tries to make a comeback."

"You're joking."

"Too old to waste time makin' these things up, princess. In exchange, I get a cozy place to come and churn the ol' noggin in peace. The beer ain't half bad either, if you ain't a priss about it."

"No promises."

As they walked over to a booth, the pain in Ben's arm ratcheted up a few notches. At the same time, the disturbance reasserted itself. Stronger now. Almost a presence.

He'd always had a hard time understanding how he sensed Corrupt energies. It was like a foul wind slapping him in the face, or like holding the positive end of a magnet while the Corrupt powers shoved his way with a negative one.

The bar looked normal. A few men mumbled in side booths. A group of leather-clad bikers laughed in a back corner over a game of cards. Solitary drinkers peered into their mugs as if they were scrying pools.

"Something wrong?"

Dani's question made him realize he stood half-crouched, one hand on the bench he'd been sliding into. She already lounged against the red cushioning, arms crossed.

Ben sat opposite her and scanned the room again. Whatever had his instincts raring, it remained outta sight. If it was a smart little bugger, it'd stay that way.

"Mebbe," he said.

"Okay." She drew the word out. "Should we do anything about it?"

"Mebbe."

A roll of her eyes. "Maybe we could try being a little more decisive."

"Nah," he said. "Just … stay alert. Go get yourself a drink and grab me whatever stout they have on tap while you're at it, won'tcha?"

She saluted and murmured. "Aye, aye, cap-i-tan."

"Cute."

•   •   •

She avoided eye contact with the scruffy patrons as she picked her way over to the bar. Despite her heavy boots, she side-stepped puddles of beer, spilled condiments, and a minefield of mysterious splotches on the floor.

For a janitor, Ben sure did pick a rat's nest to hang out in. Of course, it fit his image and personality well enough. Did the higher-ups at the Cleaners know he frequented this place? Would they approve? Maybe he couldn't afford a tab anywhere else. Did the Cleaners offer overtime or hazard pay? She doubted it.

As she studied the place, the bartender came over and plunked his elbows down.

"What'll it be?" His peppy tone contrasted with the rundown atmosphere.

Golden hair had been slicked back over his ears, and he wore a t-shirt printed to look like a tuxedo jacket. He had long, bare arms—shaved, she noticed—and black leather gloves on his hands. Tattered jeans and tennis shoes completed the look. Attractive in a stray puppy sort-of way. The gloves caught her attention more than anything else. Might she have a kindred spirit here, or was it just some rocker fashion statement? The thought warmed her to him a bit, and she returned his smile.

"A pint of your cheapest stout and another of your most expensive pale ale," she said. "Put it on Ben's tab."

He nodded. "Saw you come in with the old man."

"You're the owner?"

He laughed softly, and she found herself enjoying the velvety sound. A subtle invitation lurked in there. "Sadly, no. Just a new hire. Why would you think I own this crumb-hole?" He had an odd accent, as if he'd just come from an acting class where they practiced Shakespearian theatre.

"You know Ben," she said.

"Everybody knows Ben. At least, everybody who knows him does."

He went to pour her drink, and she waited until he returned and slid two overflowing pint glasses her way. After cleaning off her glass with a wet wipe, she took a sip of the brew. A tingle of discomfort ran down her back as his eyes remained on her, not wavering as she set the drink down.

"What? Did I grow a third boob?"

A sheepish grin dimpled his features. "It's simply rare for a beautiful woman to slum around here. A pity you have to share your good times with that grump."

Dani sniffed. "Do I look dressed for a good time?"

"Sadly, no. Truth is, Dani, you look more like you just got off a rough day of work."

Her gloved fingers tensed on the glass. "How'd you know my name?"

He looked at her left breast. Just before she backhanded him, she glanced down and remembered the name threaded on the outfit.

"Oh. Right." She took another swig. "Yeah, really long day."

"Want to talk about it? Bartenders are supposed to be maestros of listening."

"Not really. Besides, it's crap that'd make you think I was either lying, crazy, or both."

"You don't seem the lying, crazy type."

"Really. What type do I seem?"

"The type who has lived her entire life behind walls and barriers—many of them you've erected around yourself. The type who lives in fear, worried that the smallest threat will slip past her defenses."

She stared, drink unheeded. This had to be a practical joke. Some new employee hazing the Cleaners did. Whatever it was, she refused to let it get a rise out of her.

He grinned. "Listen to me prattle on about things I have no idea about. If I can't help you unburden, perhaps I can provide a pleasant distraction." He tugged off his gloves and set them behind the counter. When his hands came back up, he held a frayed deck of playing cards, which he fanned and offered to her. "Pick a card."

"You're a magician?"

His grin widened. "Of sorts. I promise you won't be disappointed. Give me a chance to bring a smile to your lips."

She squinted at him. Her earlier interest faded as his fawning comments raised more than a few warning flags. But, not wanting to go back to grousing with Ben right away, she drew a card and glanced at it. Ace of Spades.

"Now what?"

He set the deck on the bar and held out a hand. "Place it here, face down. I promise I won't peek."

She did so, and he sandwiched the card between both hands. A moment later, he parted them like a book to reveal empty palms. Wiggling his fingers, he drew them apart and waved them around. The card hadn't left even a speck of dust behind.

Dani frowned. He hadn't so much as twitched once she returned the card. Plus, he wore short sleeves, so he couldn't have slipped it up there.

"Neat trick," she said. "But aren't you supposed to tell me which one I picked? Or make it reappear?"

He spread his arms and bowed, a practiced move that showed off defined muscles. "I haven't mastered that part yet. For now, I just excel at making things disappear." He held out his hand again. "And I'm here to offer this service to you, should you wish."

The chill of the beer seeped through Dani's gloves and made her shoulders tighten. "What are you talking about?"

He smirked as if it were obvious. "A woman like you hanging out with someone like that broken-down janitor? Intuition tells me this is hardly a career path you picked. You have far too much intelligence and spirit for you to willingly lower yourself to this lot in life. If you want to be free of it, I can help."

He'd continued leaning toward her as he spoke, voice lowering, inviting her to come closer. Dani put her glass on the counter between them. A pathetic barrier, but a welcome one. His intuition told him she wanted help? Well, hers screamed for her to drop the conversation, grind it under her heel, and walk away.

"I don't … I mean this isn't …" She flicked her gaze to the mirror. Ben remained slouched in his seat, frowning at the rest of the bar.

The bartender chuckled. "Don't worry about saying too much. I know all about the Cleaners and Scum. Their simplistic concepts of Purity and Corruption. The Pantheons they would delude you into worshipping as gods." He nodded at her raised brows. "Oh, yes. I see they didn't get to that part of the Sunday School lesson yet."

"Like you said, I'm pretty new. But you're not an employee, are you?"

"Hardly. You see, Dani, just because they tell you there are two sides to an issue doesn't mean they're right."

"And you just so happen to know the truth."

"I'd like to think of myself as more enlightened, yes."

"What does your exalted wisdom have to do with me? Why—"

"Dani? What's goin' on?"

Ben's call from behind made Dani realize how long she'd been talking. The bartender grinned, naked hunger in his eyes, like a wolf watching a cornered rabbit.

"I have to go." She grabbed the pint glasses.

"Before you do," he said, "I have one last trick I'd like to demonstrate. A conjuration of sorts, and a token of my good intentions."

He reached behind the counter and she expected him to retrieve the card deck. Instead, Dani almost dropped the glasses when he offered her a squirming lizard. The size of her forearm, with red and orange scales, its wide belly had rows of tiny spikes down either side. It cocked one golden-brown eye at her as it wriggled in the man's hand.

She raised her voice. "Ben? Why does the bartender have Tetris?"

"What?" came Ben's confused reply.

"He has my lizard. Tetris!"

Scuffling indicated the janitor rushing to get out of the booth. The bartender's face shifted slightly, as if a wax mask had melted away. While the overall features remained the same, he wasn't the exact man she'd been talking to.

"You!" Ben shouted, not in warning, but recognition. "Get away from her!"

In a swift motion, the bartender lobbed Tetris past Dani's head. She cried out and turned to try and catch him. She must've dropped the pint glasses at some point, for they cracked on the floor and splashed beer over her boots.

Tail whirling, the lizard smacked into Ben's chest. He caught it by reflex, and it was hard to tell which of the two was most stunned.

A hand grabbed Dani's wrist and yanked her back against the bar. The bartender twisted her arm around and locked it painfully behind her. His other hand clutched the soft skin of her throat.

CHAPTER NINE

A choked cry escaped Dani. Not just from the unexpected pain, but the fact that he was *touching* her. Skin to skin. She could almost feel germs crawling over from him to her.

Mycosis. Shingles. Scabies.

In another moment of shock, she realized the rest of the bar now stood empty of any patrons. Where had they gone?

Warts. Ringworm.

Ben cupped Tetris against his chest, where the lizard clawed at the janitor's suit. Dani could tell he wanted to throw the reptile aside even as he struggled to contain it. Despite circumstances, she felt ridiculously relieved to see Tetris alive. The lizard was the one remnant of her former life; so long as he survived, so did a flicker of hope that she might stay sane.

Ben finally got the lizard held firm in one hand, and then stepped their way.

"Keep your distance, Janitor," the bartender said. "I'd prefer you don't take her back to HQ in a dustpan."

Ben halted. Fear brightened his eyes. Fear for her, Dani realized, and that spiked her already-escalating panic.

Leprosy!

Her power swelled with the burgeoning emotions, rising to her defense. Before it could break loose, however, the bartender's fingers flexed. Dani twitched as something cold shot through her. Her power recoiled from the invading energy and then ... died off.

"Ah-ah," he whispered. "Let's keep calm. Despite what you might think, I'm here to help."

Ben raised his free hand in a comforting gesture, but his face remained strained. "It's gonna be all right, Dani."

After sucking in a slow breath, she managed to speak without vomiting. "Ben? Who?"

His jaw clenched. "His name's Sydney. He's a handyman, or used to be. Now he's Scum." Ben's empty fist clenched. "What'dja do with the real bartender?"

"Dust to dust," Sydney said.

"He was innocent."

Sydney chuckled. "Innocence. What a quaint notion. Now, Dani and I were having a chat. Let me finish what I came to say, and we can all go out for tea and cookies afterward."

"I swear," Ben said, "if you turn so much as a hair on her head gray—"

Dani whispered, "Ben."

His attention snapped to her. "What?"

"You're squeezing Tetris."

Ben looked down to the writhing lizard, which hissed against the pressure the janitor unconsciously applied. He relaxed somewhat and Tetris' struggle abated.

"It's always the violent threats with him, isn't it?" The warmth of Sydney's breath tickled Dani's ear, and she fought a shudder.

Influenza. Nasopharyngitis.

"You got a thing against violence?" she asked through gritted teeth. "How about letting go of my arm before you break it?"

"Hear me out first."

She choked a laugh. "Why should I listen to anything you say? You stole my lizard."

"Actually, I saved him," Sydney said. "If Ascendant Francis' team had gotten to him first, they would've simply disposed of him to remove another tie to your old life, just as they cut you off from your family and friends. You must wonder, if their cause is so pure, their authority so just, why do they force people into their service in such a brutish manner?"

"We ain't forced," said Ben. "We got choices—"

"Like the ones you've given this poor girl?" Sydney shot back. "To do whatever you say or be scrubbed out so her power won't fall into—what you claim to be—the wrong hands? Oh, yes. I can see how that'd be a difficult one to make."

He dropped back to a confiding whisper. "I'm here to save you, Dani. To give you a way out. My methods may be a bit extreme, but I can help you avoid wasting so much … potential." He made a purring noise, and nausea washed through her. "Even my most drastic techniques are a mercy compared to what the Cleaners do. Their slow leeching of your power, your very existence, all for some thankless job scrubbing out the gutters of the world—a fight they'll lose in the end, no matter how hard they struggle."

"What are you talking about?" she asked.

The hand at her throat slipped away and reappeared, holding an empty pint glass before her eyes. The veins on that hand pulsed purple-green. Before Dani could blink, the glass crumbled into dust. And then not even dust remained.

"Entropy is at my command," he said. "I could annihilate you with a touch. Often, when I cross paths with poor, misguided recruits the Cleaners have suckered in, I ease their torment by simply removing them from existence. I came here planning to do so with you." He must've felt her breath catch, for he hastened on. "But fear not. If it were my desire to have you meet their fate, I would've done so already."

"Why haven't you?"

"I confess, there's something about you that stays my hand."

"Got a thing for redheads?"

"While I won't deny the allure of your mane—"

"Did you really just call it a mane?"

"—there's far more to you than physical beauty and strength, dearest."

"Did you really just call me dearest?"

He cleared his throat, and she sensed herself edging out to the brink of his patience. Even Ben's wide eyes clearly communicated, *Quit being a smart-aleck, princess.*

"Dani, you're an infant in our world," Sydney said. "Yet I've exposed myself in order to do you a great service."

"What do you want then? A kiss on the cheek?"

"I want you to recognize that I've spared your life—even that of your scaly friend—while the Cleaners plan to drain you of the marvelous power you wield. Just look at Ben. Do you think the Board truly appreciates what he's given for their cause? Everything he's sacrificed in the name of Purity?" He sounded truly distressed. "You'll become the same sort of husk, Dani, and it breaks my heart to imagine you so."

Ben shuffled in place, eyebrows twitching. "Sydney, just let her go. She don't wanna sign up for your loony bin."

Sydney's weight shifted along with his attention. "Why don't we let her make up her own mind? And while we wait for her to do so, let's discuss the other matter that brought us together today."

"What other matter?"

"Now, don't be disingenuous. It's a waste of both our times. We're already searching for the same thing, old man. Why not pool our resources and avoid any further unpleasantness?"

Wariness and confusion edged onto Ben's face. "What're we searchin' for?"

A chortle. "The second lie is no better than the first. But I can tell you're determined to be the stubborn mule. As for you, sweet one," Sydney's voice lowered, "will you show a bit more sense than your mentor and come with me? I won't force it, as they have. Your choice."

Dani coughed. "I have to go with *no*. Next time you want to seduce someone, try not assaulting them."

"I'm the first to decry violence against women," Sydney said, "but I have to consider my own safety. Without you, dear old Ben might've given himself a heart attack trying to kill me. We wouldn't want that. You're sure you won't change your mind?"

"Uh ... yeah."

A sigh. "No matter. This is just the beginning of what I expect to be a long and satisfying relationship. We'll bump into each other again soon enough. Perhaps you'll reconsider in different circumstances."

Sydney slapped a hand atop the bar. Dani's eyes widened as the wood crumbled beneath his touch. Gray lines of decay shot down to the floor, across to the walls, and ate up the stone to ceiling. A chunk of brick dislodged and plummeted toward Ben's head.

The janitor leaped just clear of the falling debris. The impact shook the floor and Ben lost his footing. Dani's heart skipped, as she feared he would squash Tetris. He rolled, surprisingly agile, and came up into a crouch.

Another shudder shook the building, and Sydney released her. Hacking, both from Sydney's chokehold and the dust filling the bar, she pushed away from the counter right before it collapsed. Lines of decay spread, connected, and ate away the majority of the bar's infrastructure within seconds. And still it spread.

Dani covered her mouth and nose as the walls disintegrated. The mirror turned to slag. The floorboards rotted and, in the back, the floor fell into a gaping basement. Chairs, tables and light fixtures puffed away in a blink.

"Look out!"

Ben barreled into her side and knocked them both clear as a brick pillar toppled over where she'd stood. Even as it fell, the red brick faded to brown, then gray. By the time it would've crushed her, it had crumbled to the last speck of mortar and wafted away.

In their fall, Dani bruised an elbow on the packed earth where there'd once been concrete. Ben lay at an awkward angle, Tetris cradled in the crook of his raised elbow.

"Mind takin' it?" he asked.

Dani sat up and accepted her pet with near reverence. Unspooked by all the chaos and destruction, he angled his head this way and that, no doubt keeping an eye out for the nearest cricket. She took what comfort she could from the familiar bump and prick of his scales, the way his claws dug in, even through her rubber gloves.

Ben grunted and groaned as he stood. A dust cloud obscured their view beyond five feet. Dani held Tetris in one arm while covering her mouth and nose in a sad attempt to filter out the floating particles.

Bronchitis. Pneumonia. Lung cancer.

Ben coughed while trying to wave some of it away. Sydney was nowhere to be seen.

He glanced at Dani. "Are you okay?"

She scowled behind her hand. "Okay? Are you ******* kidding me?"

"I ain't one to judge, but you might wanna get a better handle on the cussin'. Too much of it and the Board shuts down your ability to talk for a couple days. Trust me. It's a bit more effective than washin' your mouth out with soap."

"Yeah? Well, guess what? My mouth was perfectly clean not five minutes ago, and now who knows what I'm sucking down?"

"I got some dust masks in the van."

"A little late for that."

He stuck hands in his pockets. "Guess so. But it's like I toldja, bein' a Cleaner comes with some perks. Our link to Purity buffers us against all the normal dirty business."

She swiped hair out of her face. "That might work for you. You might be fine going around looking like you just had sex with a garbage truck, but guess what? I don't *feel* clean. And that's what matters."

After staring at her a moment longer, he looked around and shook his head. "Cleanse me. I liked this place." He smiled wryly. "At least the lizard's safe, right?"

Dani felt a prick of regret for her harshness. He could've tossed Tetris aside in the face of Sydney's attack, but he'd kept him safe for her sake.

As they trudged out through the rubble to the van, something Sydney mentioned wriggled back into her mind. Unable to shake her curiosity, she edged closer and spoke softly.

"Ben?" He paused with a hand on the driver's door. "He— Sydney—said you've sacrificed. For the Cleaners. For Purity. What have you given up?"

He grimaced and yanked the door open, mumbling as he hauled himself inside.

"A lifetime."

CHAPTER TEN

With Dani cuddling with Tetris in the passenger seat beside him, Ben got out his handheld radio and tuned it to a private channel.

"HQ, this is Janitor Ben. I gotta priority report to make."

Several seconds of static passed before a voice broke through.

"Janitor, please state the nature of your situation."

Ben pulled the radio away from his mouth. He shared a glance with Dani, who asked, "Is that …?"

He brought the radio back up and triggered the speaker. "Francis, what're you doin' on this channel? Since when do you—"

"This is not the channel for comparing job descriptions, Janitor. That's what Human Resources is for. Please state the nature of your situation or sign off."

Ben chewed on a lip, debating whether it'd be worth cramming anything into Francis' ear. Grumbling for Destin's attention wouldn't get results, and another visit to HQ would waste time. He belonged in the field, and if Francis wanted to wrap what he gave them in red tape, then the ensuing sticky mess belonged to him.

"We just had a run-in with Sydney. A scrub-team needs to check out Matt's bar over on Tenth and Garnet—what's left of it.

I wanna to know why this snake reared his scaly head and if it has anythin' to do with the earlier disturbances we bumped into."

Silence. Ben imagined Francis' raised eyebrows and his fist tightened around the radio. If he heard so much as a single chuckle ...

"We've had no reports of Sydney's presence in this region for almost eight years."

"Well you're gettin' one now, ain'tcha? I've done my job, Francis. Now get out here and do yours. Something's goin' on, and I'm steppin' in cow patties no matter which way I go. We're done for the night. I got a new apprentice who needs a shower, food, and sleep if anyone's gonna expect her to work tomorrow."

Dani's eyes narrowed. "I need a shower? You're one to talk."

"Nothin to be ashamed of, princess. Fear does that to a body. Sours everythin' up."

She opened her mouth to retort, but the radio cut her off.

"I've received your report and will follow up on it. If there's any evidence of Sydney's presence, I'll handle it, rest assured. In the meantime, I suggest you return your focus to the assignment already given to you by the Chairman."

Ben bellowed into the speaker. "Don't you sign off on—"

A click signaled Francis' going off-channel. Ben slammed the radio against the dashboard and barely resisted flinging it out the window and driving over it. He only stopped at Dani's alarmed look, and forced himself slump back and breathe evenly.

They sat that way for a few minutes, his arm itching, her silence cautious until she cleared her throat.

"I take it you and this Francis guy weren't bunk-buddies at summer camp."

Ben snorted. "Ever since he got promoted, Ascendant Francis has been one of the most straight-laced, clean-nosed, boot-polished Cleaners our company has ever known. He's been Destin's right hand man for years."

"And you hate his guts."

That prodded a laugh. "Not as much as you might guess. He's just ... too young to be in his position."

"Too young? That applies to pretty much anyone around you."

Another dry chuckle. "I mean he's makin' a lotta mistakes but is just too caught up in his own big britches to ever accept a little advice that might save him from trouble down the road. I've tried to give him some perspective, but that ain't exactly been taken kindly."

"I can't imagine why, seeing how charming and diplomatic you are." Dani leaned back, tapping the spikes on Tetris' head. "You think he's watching to catch you screwing up? Make you look bad so he can look better?"

"Naw," Ben said. "He's not the kinda guy who needs to prove himself. He's already convinced he's better. He just don't agree with the Board's decision to stick you with me. But don't break a sweat over him. I've handled bigger pricks in my day."

She snorted and giggled. "Oh really?"

He squinted at her. "What'd I say this time?"

She waved it away. "Forget it. I'm less concerned about a few ****fights …" She went cross-eyed for a second. "Are you serious? I can't even say that?"

Ben grunted. "Francis maintains a long list of naughty words and phrases he submits to the Board each week to add to the foul-filter. I've contributed a lil' bit."

"Guh. Fine. I'm less concerned about a few *rooster*fights and more about the two attempts on my life before dinnertime."

"It ain't like this for everyone," he said. "Some new recruits go months before buttin' heads with their first Scum."

"Is that supposed to make me feel lucky? I understand I'm supposed to be learning things, figuring out what it's like to be a Cleaner, but I feel like I've walked into my first class and got handed the final exam. Aren't you supposed to help me be better prepared?"

He knuckled his forehead. "I didn't think it'd hit the fan this fast. I'm all for puttin' you on the advanced track. You just gotta realize I got some mucky history stickin' to my boots, and I don't want you steppin' in it. So let's keep the questions to the business at hand."

"All right. Start with Sydney. Who is he?"

"Mucky history."

"Uh, no. Not since he went all Gropey McGroperson on me and stuck his tongue in my ear. Whatever's happened between you two before, I'm involved, whether you like it or not."

Ben stared out the windshield, wrestling with the emotions and memories her question summoned. He'd conquered the flashbacks years ago, but that didn't mean every ghost had been exorcised. *Focus on the facts,* he told himself. *Facts are simple, and don't involve punchin' out the window.*

"Sydney used to be a handyman in the Cleaners," he said. "Handymen are all sortsa gifted in healing—our version of puttin' on Band-Aids and kissin' booboos. When he went over to the Scum, his powers got all twisted. He's an entropy mage now."

"Entropy mage?"

"Yup. He can accelerate the entropic forces around any object or person he gets his hands on."

"And you knew him? Why didn't you recognize him right away?"

"There was an ol' muddy spell on the bar. Some call it a murk, like an oily film on the surface of a puddle. Confused me long enough for him to get us by the short hairs. The other customers never existed, either. They were part of the murk."

"I thought you said he dealt with entropy. Isn't illusion a bit different than turning things to dust?" She smiled at his sharp look. "What? I read some fantasy books as a kid."

He allowed himself to smile back. "Well, I guess you're right. He ain't known to muck around with that kinda whim-wham. So he had help."

"Or he's more powerful now than he used to be. Does he … does he really go around killing new recruits?"

"We ain't really sure what he's been up to, but we got our share of folks who go missin' on the job. Not a lotta Scum take prisoners. For most, the best Cleaner's a dead one."

"Then why'd he spare me? I can't believe he really thought I'd see it as being saved."

"You're new. Mebbe he figures you're vulnerable. Plus he's always had a thing for younger women. And with all your power, I warned you others might try to get'cha to switch sides. Do you know how many Catalysts are actually alive today?"

She shook her head.

"Six, not countin' you," Ben said. "Two are in locked up in loony-bins. One's been missin' for a decade, and everyone figures she's long gone. One's over with our Europe division, and the last two are twins that can only control their power s'long as they're within a hundred paces of each other. So we need to figure out how to control your powers before someone else does it for you."

Huffing, she glowered at the floor. "Okay. Yeah. I get it."

"I don't think you do, princess, but you're gettin' there. And I gotta apologize."

She shot a suspicious look his way. "Apologize?"

He drummed on the dash, avoiding her eyes. "I'm your trainer. That means my main duty is keepin' you safe until you learn to handle things on your own. I shoulda never let Sydney get to you. I won't let it happen again."

Her voice softened. "Are you sure?"

"No. But I'll die tryin'. I swear it on my mop and plunger."

Surprise slapped away her usual sulk. She tilted her head as if seeing him for the first time.

"Okay then," she said.

"So why a lizard?"

She looked to the scaly rascal in her lap. "What? Him?"

"Yeah. Why on earth does a spooked-by-her-own-spit princess have a crawl-in-the-dirt pet like him? Woulda pegged you for somethin' lower maintenance and lots cleaner. Like mebbe a set of collectible spoons."

Dani cupped her hands around Tetris. "My parents made me get him, actually. Said they wouldn't pay for med school until I proved I could get over my fears enough to keep something alive."

"So why not go with a kitty or pup?"

"Fur creeps me out. But something about him living in a desert environment—especially a contained one—appealed. I just kept my gloves on, cleaned his terrarium each day, and got through feeding times as quickly as possible. Eventually, I realized I could handle it. After a while, the little routines I built up around him helped steady me in the face of everything else. Most of the time. I figured I could start small and then work my way up the food chain."

He snorted as he started the van. "Food chain, eh? Here's a tip. With us, it ain't so much a chain as it is a big tangled ball of yarn. You don't work your way up or down. You just gotta try to avoid gettin' strangled by it."

"Oh, *that's* comforting."

• • •

Ben walked out of the motel lobby and rapped on the passenger window. Dani, her face lit pink by the vacancy sign, rolled it down and frowned at the room key he offered.

"Why a motel?" she asked. The small glass aquarium in her lap held Tetris, who lounged on a square of plastic grass, content after having gobbled several mealworms. Dani had tucked away a plastic container full of the insects into one of her uniform pockets. Ben had paid for it all at a pet store they'd driven by on the way.

"You need somewhere to sleep, don'tcha?"

"Yeah, but motels are so … dirty. Did you know thirty-five percent of surfaces in a motel room have some contagious virus? Most places don't even wash bedspreads between each guest."

"I had no idea. But look. They got cable. And here. I gotcha somethin'." He handed her a plastic bag through the window. "Consider it a little *Welcome to the Team* present."

She took it and inspected the contents. "Mini toothpaste? Mouthwash? Hand wipes?" Her green eyes flashed with mirth. "You got all this from the front desk, didn't you?"

He hemmed and hawed until she smiled, though still a shade nervously.

"Thanks. But if you think I'm sharing a room with you—"

He threw his hands up. "For Purity's sake, you really think I'm that much of a dirty old man? You gotta room to yourself. This is just until we can set you up with somethin' more permanent."

"Where do you sleep then? Behind the garbage bins? Don't you have an apartment or something?"

Ben thumbed at the storage section of the van. "If you'd paid attention, you mighta noticed there's a fold-out cot behind the shelves."

She turned to look, and her eyes widened as she spotted the canvas bundle. "You sleep in your van? Ben, that can't be healthy. The fumes from all those cleaning products alone …"

"We're immune to any side effects," he said. "Another perk of the job. Regular cleanin' chemicals don't affect us like normal folk. We can gargle bleach and come out smilin'."

"Really?" An uncomfortably eager gleam lit her eyes.

Boy, he really needed to learn when to shut his gob. "Yeah, but I ain't recommendin' it. Still painful and takes forever to get the taste outta your mouth."

"But still," she said, "you mean this is literally all you do? Drive from job to job, cleaning places and scrubbing out any Scum you run across? That's your life? Don't you do anything for fun?"

He scratched the back of his head. "Have I already mentioned what happens when you give coffee to imps?"

"Yeah. That doesn't fit my definition of 'fun.'"

"Gettin' a job done and done well is enough for me."

"I'm sure."

The needle of his gaze deflated further personal questions. She shoved the door open, forcing him back as she got out with Tetris' cage tucked under one arm.

"That's your room there." He pointed to the closest motel door. "I'll be parked right outside. If you need anythin', just kick the bumper."

Dani alternated between looking at the door and him until impatience got the better of him. He spread his arms.

"Well?"

"I ... I'm not sure I can do this. Can't we go back to Head-quarters?"

"Even if we did, you really wanna sleep with Francis and the Board watchin' you all night? C'mon, princess. You can beat this."

She let out a quavering breath, eyeing the door as if it was a portal to Hell.

Ben raised a finger. "Let's figure this as a lesson in controllin' your power. If you can spend the night here without freakin' out and levelin' the place, we'll chalk today up as a success and go meet a friend of mine in the mornin'."

She brushed her ponytail over a shoulder. "You have friends? Good. I was worried everyone you knew either wanted to kill or shun you."

"Go on. Stop dallyin' and get some sleep."

"Fine. I can do this. I can."

After she marched inside her room and the door clicked shut behind her, Ben parked the van out front and killed the engine. He waited half an hour before slipping out and up to the room door.

After unscrewing the spray bottle top, he hunkered down and poured Carl onto the concrete. The water sprite puddled and reflected his face.

"Keep anythin' or anyone but me away from her, a'ight?"

A burbling noise, like a stream trickling over a boulder.

Ben flicked the puddle. "I know, but she's a more long-term investment than me, you gotta admit. Consider this a favor. I'll owe you. Oh, and make sure she doesn't try garglin' bleach."

A tiny wave splashed his hand. Carl drained uphill and through the crack beneath the doorframe where he soaked into the carpet.

Satisfied, Ben climbed back into the van, unfolded the cot, and shut the door behind him. After settling into the creaking bed, he took down a metal-edged squeegee and laid it beside him. Rubber gloves went onto both hands, a dust mask over his face, and finally, some construction goggles that had black paint obscuring the lenses.

He lay back and wriggled until he got comfortable. No noise but thumping heartbeats and his breath sounding hollow behind the mask. The pain in his right arm throbbed in a separate rhythm to his pulse, a distant ache, but growing stronger.

He wasn't worried about Dani waking up with night terrors. Despite her finicky habits, she was a tough kid, able to process the weirdness she'd experienced without any mental cracks showing. Having her sleeping separate didn't provide him relief from being woken by her midnight screaming.

It would keep her from hearing his.

CHAPTER ELEVEN

Dani stood just inside the motel room, feeling as if she'd walked into a torture chamber. The bed might as well have been a rack, the closet an iron maiden, and the bathroom a cauldron of boiling oil. The shower might've provided some respite, but the thought of so many other bare feet having contaminated the tub raised goosebumps on her arms. All of it stewing with germs.

Norovirus. Diptheria. Rhinovirus.

And that wasn't considering …

Bedbugs. Lice.

Her stomach clenched, and her power flickered awake, eager to seek and destroy all possible threats. She closed her eyes and tried to wrestle the energy into submission. Cords of power latched onto the wood framing and concrete foundation, testing for weaknesses that could send it tumbling down with a small quake. Lights flickered and sockets sparked as the bottled lightning within offered itself to her. The harder she fought it, the quicker it escalated, until she teetered on the edge of unleashing another miniature disaster.

Think like a janitor, Ben had said. What would a janitor do in this situation?

Dani had no idea. She ground her teeth as the magic writhed within her. *I will not burn down a motel room. I will not endanger anyone sleeping around here. I am not Dani the Human Disaster.*

Better to retreat. To convince Ben to let her sleep in the passenger seat. Anything other than spending a night in this pit, battling this rebellious power.

She took a squishing step backward and reached for the doorknob ...

Wait. Squishing?

She eyed the floor. A dark blotch stained the area in a Rorschach pattern, centering on where she stood. Great. Of all the available rooms, they gave her one with leaky pipes. At least it gave her an excuse to vacate the place.

Before she could leave, though, the water swept up into a melon-sized glob. She jumped to the side and raised the plastic bag as if to swat the thing. Only then did she realize this must be the water elemental Ben carried around.

Once her heart rate slowed, she squatted to inspect the creature. Despite its lack of features, she suspected it scrutinized her in turn. When she reached out with a gloved hand, it didn't roll away, but a hand-sized indentation formed on its surface.

"Carl, right?" She glanced at the door. "Ben sent you to keep an eye on me?"

Carl flattened into a splotch again, as if embarrassed to have been found out.

"I'll take that as a yes." As she rose, it reformed into a rippling liquid dome. "I'm surprised. I thought you two were joined at the hip."

The water stilled, and Dani got the sense of being glared at. She flushed.

"Yes. You're right. That was terrible. I apologize."

She went over and set Tetris' cage on the dresser. After digging out a couple more mealworms, she dropped them in with him and watched as he gobbled them one by one.

When she looked down, Carl had burbled up beside her boots. She smiled hesitantly, oddly comforted by its presence. The immediate threat of losing control had receded, though her germ-radar still pinged plenty of warnings anytime she glanced around. She focused on Carl, instead.

"So what's it like being a portable puddle?"

The elemental burped at her.

Sighing, she leaned a hip against the dresser. "Okay. Confession time. I'm not sure I can do this."

Carl's dome tilted, like someone cocking their head.

"I mean this." She waved at her janitorial uniform. "Being a Cleaner. It was an exciting idea, at first, but how am I supposed to protect others when I can't even control myself? I'd like to avoid summoning a tornado every time I go to flush a toilet."

She bumped an elbow at her lizard. "I feel like him. Like Tetris. Suddenly realizing I've been living in a glass box all my life, thinking I could see everything there was to see. Then I get picked up by my tail and plopped into a way bigger world than I ever imagined." She lifted the lizard from the aquarium and set him on the carpet near Carl. "I bet even he has the brains to dart back in to where it's all comfy and safe."

She let Tetris go, and the lizard scurried for the elemental, stubby tongue aimed to lap up the water. Carl spouted and rolled away, Tetris in hot pursuit. Dani snatched her pet back up before he got too far.

"You brat," she said. "Stop ruining my example."

He continued moving his legs, raring to explore every corner of the room. Dani laughed and tickled the softer scales under his neck.

"All right. I get the point. If you can do it, so can I." She glanced at Carl, who had shifted closer, though keeping a bit more distance this time. "What do you think? Want to be a cheerleader for Team Dani?"

A tiny wave slapped her boot. She hoped this was intended as an encouraging pat, versus a reprimanding slap for getting her hopes up.

She returned Tetris to chasing down dinner and then kissed the side of the terrarium, leaving lip prints. Keeping her lips pursed, she hastily opened the tiny bottle of mouthwash and took a swig. The sacrifices she made to show a little affection....

As she swished, Carl washed up the side of the dresser like a reverse waterfall. It rolled over to Tetris' cage, and then pressed against the spot she'd kissed. Water slid around the sides, thinning until it covered every panel. Then Carl retracted into a glob, leaving the cage sparkling, not a smudge to be seen.

Eyes widening, Dani ran over to the sink and spat out the mouthwash. She returned to stare at the pristine terrarium, and then at the elemental that brimmed with obvious pride.

"You can clean surfaces, too?"

An agreeable gurgle.

Dani laid a hand on top of the dresser. After a moment, Carl rolled onto her palm and she raised him to eye-level.

"Tell you what. You help me clean this place up enough that I can sleep, and I'll give this job another day. Deal?"

Carl wobbled, which Dani decided to take as a nod.

"Fantastic."

She turned and flung the elemental across the room, where it splattered across the bathroom mirror.

•   •   •

Dani woke as a sliver of sunlight pried between the curtains and cut through her eyelids. She was sitting in a chair. Had she fallen asleep studying again? *Oh ***, I hope I didn't drool on myself.*

Groaning, she leaned away from the glare and fumbled for the alarm clock to see how much time she had before class. Her hand slapped a lamp, which thumped to the floor. The noise sent her bolting upright, twisting to orient herself in the otherwise dark room.

Where? What?

Oh. Right.

She hadn't actually made it to bed last night, but Carl had wiped down a chair enough for her to settle in. Her lower back and shoulders were strained from sleeping in the awkward position, but at least she'd managed a few hours of shut-eye.

She set the lamp back on the nightstand and turned it on, illuminating what once had been a dingy motel room. Now the walls gleamed and every tile and wooden surface looked freshly waxed. Carl puddled beside Tetris' cage, a silent, watchful presence.

Despite having slept in her uniform, she didn't feel grungy at all. Still, needs had to be met. She peeled her gloves off and dug through the grab bag of cleaning goodies for the wipes, gel, and soap that would suffice for her morning sanitization routine. As she worked gel into her scalp, a knock made her jump.

"Dani?" Ben's voice came through muffled. "Up and at 'em. We got a full day."

She hesitated, wanting a few more minutes of privacy, but another knock denied that luxury. Scowling, she scooped Carl up, stomped to the door and yanked it open. She flung the elemental into the janitor's face, where it struck with the sound of a giant pancake hitting pavement.

"That's for setting him to spy on me!"

Grimacing through the dribbles, Ben held up a paper bag. "I got breakfast. Can I at least come in and use the bathroom?"

"I figured you used a bucket in the van." Dani studied him in the harsh morning light. The circles under his eyes were black and blue while the lines on his face looked etched down to the bone. "You look awful."

"Good mornin' to you too." He handed her the bag, which she tossed onto the dresser. "Got a sesame and a plain. Figured you might be some kinda health nut, so the cream cheese is that disgustin' no-fat kind."

He pushed by and ducked into the restroom. She thanked the gods of bathroom design that the fan turned on and hid most noises within.

Once he emerged, Carl perched on the janitor's shoulder, leaving his face dry. Ben held up his spray bottle with the top off and the living puddle glided down inside. He screwed the spray top back on and reattached it at his hip.

Dani tugged her gloves on and pointed at the elemental. "Why'd you try to slip him in here?"

"Ain't anyone near as good at guardin' the pipelines as Carl."

"Pipelines?"

Ben tossed her the plain bagel along with a plastic container of cream cheese. She considered wiping the bread down with gel. Did being a Cleaner make sanitation chemicals edible as well? That might require some experimenting. For now, she just held the bagel and ignored her rumbling stomach.

"Some Scum," Ben said, spraying seeds as he devoured the sesame, "use sewage lines to truck around. Kinda like a subway system for 'em."

"Like you ... we ... use windows?"

"Sorta. It's one reason we work our tushes off keepin' sinks, toilets, and other outlets clean. Discourages any unwanted visitors."

"Like the blot-hound?"

He nodded, licking his fingers clean. "Plenty of critters live in pipe networks. Lots of 'em come from what the bigwigs at HQ call flouritic realms."

"I think you mean *fluidic*."

"Whatever. They figure they're more comfortable in contained systems. Easier for 'em to mingle and reproduce. Carl's more tuned into that sorta thing."

She huffed. "At least ask next time. I've got enough to deal with without having to worry about getting a drink in the middle of the night and slurping down your partner."

"But if I ask, you might say no. Besides, wouldn't be the first time Carl took that ride." He went to the door and opened it, waving for her to join him. "Let's go. Stewart ain't a patient fella. You can eat on the way."

She followed, picking up Tetris' cage as she did. "Stewart is this friend of yours?" She stressed a doubtful tone on *friend*. "What's he do?"

Ben grinned as he headed for the van. "You might call him a collector."

CHAPTER TWELVE

Admit it," Dani said. "You're just ****** with me, aren't you? Trying to see how far I'll go before I snap."

Ben got back into the driver's seat after pushing open the metal gate the van idled in front of. He raised an eyebrow at her. "Aw, c'mon, princess. You gotta expand your horizons. Embrace new experiences."

"You know the nice thing about horizons? They're far away. And I'm not about to embrace anything here."

As he drove through the gate, she scanned the area with rising trepidation. Garbage mounds formed a miniature mountain range inside the privately owned and operated dump. A few compactor trucks sat in a line against the nearest part of the chain-link fence that bordered the property, and a gravel road cut through the heaps before branching off into various routes. A wisp of black smoke rose to the north. Magpies lived up to their reputation as rats with wings as they swarmed the ground and sky, scouring for anything edible.

Tetanus. Shigella.

Ben eased the van between stacks of tires and rusting barrels. Dani sat up straighter as they entered a bumpy stretch devoted to trash sculptures. Half a dozen humanoid figures, composed of steel beams, car engines and random debris lined the road. Each stood ten feet high, and their heads, made up of anything from welded chairs to old bathtubs, gazed down at the van as it passed.

Ben grunted as he looked up at them through the windshield. "Hoo boy. Stewart's moved up in the world. These suckers weren't here last time."

"You mean the statues? He collects trash art? Classy."

"Those ain't art. They're golems. Stewart upgraded his security."

A rumble shook the area as two of the statues animated and fell into a teeth-chattering walk behind them, keeping pace as the van lumbered deeper into the dump.

Dani gripped her armrest and watched their sudden escort in the rear-view mirror. "Trash golems?" Her voice squeaked.

"Better'n Rottweilers in keepin' folks away, don'tcha think?"

"But. They're. Following. Us. Why?"

"In case we cause trouble or make a mess."

The road ended in a circular pit, fifty feet across. Ben braked and turned off the van, then hopped out on his side. Dani scrunched her nose as the first real whiff of the dump smacked her in the face—burning rubber, rotten eggs, mold and … bacon? She did not want to know where that came from.

The golems creaked to a halt, blocking the way out, and Dani couldn't help but imagine their jagged fists pounding the van—and the two of them—into scrap. She wished she knew what would provoke them.

"A mess?" she echoed as Ben slid the side door open and rummaged in the back for his mop. "This place couldn't be more disgusting. I'll wait in the van while you talk to this guy."

"First you can barely stand the ride, now you wanna camp out in there? Nothin doin'. C'mon." He rapped on the side of the van. "No whining."

She double-checked the back, where Tetris' cage had been secured on one of the shelves. Reassuring herself that he'd be fine—and praying she would be—she eased out.

Something crunched under a boot. She danced away to find an enormous cockroach mashed into the gravel, feelers and legs twitching. She bit her tongue to contain a dismayed squeal.

Typhoid. Rabies. Dysentery.

As she edged around the dying insect, she noticed the shack set against a mound on the side of the clearing. Though "shack" was an exaggeration; more of an outhouse, with a sheet of rusted steel as a roof and rotting plywood walls. A hole had been cut through the front door, with a rubber tire rimming it. No door handle, so one would have to stick a finger into a knothole to yank it open, risking splinters or bites from anything waiting inside.

She'd let Ben handle that.

Ben went to the middle of the clearing and faced the door, mop in hand. Grateful for the heavy rubber boots and jumpsuit, Dani minced her way over as rubbish cracked, crunched, and squished beneath her feet. After a minute, Ben made an impatient noise and cupped his hands around his mouth.

"Stewart," he shouted, "get out here, or I'm gonna call the Sanitation Department and let 'em know I caught you huffin' diapers!"

Dani gagged and clutched her stomach. Then she jumped back as a rat scurried up to them. A second later, she realized it wasn't a real rodent, but one glued together from a toy car chassis, with red LED lights for eyes and a rubber tube for a tail. It squeaked—not an animal noise, but that of rusty hinges opening—as its lower jaw dropped, revealing a metal grille.

"Whaddya want?" The harsh voice made her wince.

"A red carpet and gold-engraved invitation," Ben said, scowling down at the fake rodent. "Do you gotta be so paranoid?"

"Since we's agreed you'd never turn up here again after what you did last time, yes. I's a mite suspectin'. Besides, you gots company."

Ben tilted his head her way. "This is Dani. She's my apprentice."

"I don't be carin' if she's the Pope's daughter. She don't be welcome."

Ben leaned over to look the rat in one shiny red eye. "You're bein' a grouch, Stewart. I even brought that Babe Ruth you've been lookin' for, but now I think I might just keep it for myself."

"Boston Store number 147? 1916? You found it?"

"Sure for shootin'. But I'm only givin' it to you face-to-face. And you're gonna say thanks, all polite-like."

The rat's rubber tail twitched, though Dani couldn't see any mechanism to make it do so.

"Gimme a sec."

The mechanical rat scampered away while thumping and rattling came from the mound ahead of them, like numerous gates and doors being opened and then shut again.

"I thought you said this guy was a friend," she said.

He sighed and stuck hands in his pockets. "It's been a while."

"What'd you do last time?"

A wince. "Tell you later."

The outhouse door opened with a crunch and crack, revealing a tunnel deeper into the mound. Stewart shuffled out and shut the door before making his way over to them.

Hunched and withered, he wore a sports coat made of yellowed newspapers. A candy bar wrapper had been pinched into the shape of a bow tie by a rubber band and pinned beneath his prominent Adam's apple. The green, plastic St. Paddy's day bowler cap on his head had several cracks in it, and he walked barefoot over the old nails, broken bottles and metal scrap that littered the ground without so much as a spot of blood in his wake.

"Card," he said, by way of hello.

Ben reached into his breast pocket and drew out a plastic-sealed baseball card, which he handed over. Stewart smacked his lips as he examined it.

"Oh, yessirree. My scissors will be havin' a bloomin' feast soon enough." The card vanished into his paper jacket. "All righty. What ya wantin'?"

Ben raised hands to both of them once they faced each other. "Dani, meet Stewart. Stewart, this is my new apprentice, Dani."

Stewart plucked the cap from his head. "Charmed," he said, in a tone usually reserved for threatening trespassers with a loaded shotgun.

He bowed and kissed her hand. Even with the glove, it took all her self-control to not jerk away. The stink of sulfur hung around him as if he'd eaten rotten eggs for breakfast.

"Stewart's a garbage man," Ben said. "A trash mage."

She looked over to the animated statues guarding the van. "That explains the golems."

Half of Stewart's mouth rose in a self-satisfied smile. "Righto, missy. Don't you know how much power's all pent up, waitin' to go s'plodey in trash?"

"Stewart," Ben waved to get his attention. "We need information, not lectures."

The garbage man blew a raspberry. "And here's me, t'inkin' you's come for tea. Got a fresh pot on." He winked at Dani, catching her grimace. "Don't worry. T'ain't all brewed rat livers. I's partial to a nice herbal m'self."

Dani shuddered to imagine where he got the herbs.

"We need anythin' you can dig up on manifestations with two cores of power," Ben said.

Stewart chortled. "That's simple. Just last week—"

"Two cores from opposite Pantheons. One Pure. One Corrupt."

That popped the mage's eyebrows up. "You's kiddin'."

Ben crossed his arms. Stewart looked to Dani, who shrugged.

"Don't look at me," she said. "I'm just here for college credit."

"All right, all right," he said. "Lessee what we can scrounge up." He wiped his nose and flicked the results Ben's way. "Scratch out a proper circle while the missy and I gather the components, aye?"

Dani turned to Ben to protest, but he already moved away, kicking debris aside to clear a patch of dirt.

"Go on," he said over his shoulder. "Earn those credits."

She smiled weakly at the mage, who rubbed his hands together, drizzling grit from his palms.

"Now, now," he said, "you's safe as ever with me. Come inside the ol' homestead and help an old man drag out a load."

He took her hand and led her to the rickety door, which opened by itself. Dani tried not to breathe in the mulch-and-bile stench as they entered. She tried to sip air until her lungs demanded she let them do their job properly. At last, she relented and gulped a breath, which tasted of dirty socks.

She had to duck to keep from scraping her head on the ceiling. The walls were packed garbage and earth, reinforced with steel and wooden beams. A running string of dangling bulbs illuminated the way into the first room, little bigger than the back of Ben's van. A rotting chair provided the only furniture, surrounded by haphazard piles of scrap metal, blasted-out computer monitors, and moldy paper.

"You live here?" She looked back out the tunnel to where she could see Ben, who drew the butt-end of the mop through the dirt. "Don't any of you have real homes?"

"Real homes?" Stewart crouched over a pile and started picking through it. "You mean those finicky little snot-boxes you call houses and apartments? You silly folk put so much effort into keepin' them clean it makes me laugh, it does. Always scrubbin' the same bathrooms, or makin' the same bed over and over. Don't it tire you a wee bit?"

"Yeah, but it's worth it. Otherwise we'd be neck deep in ..." She waved around. "Garbage."

He rose with a pile of odds and ends that he shoved into her hands. She pulled her arms as far away from her body as she could without dislocating her shoulders.

"Sure'n it's filthy work," he went on, "but hey, if I t'weren't the one to take in the trash and put it to use, somebody else would. And if'n you's had to choose between me and that unknown else, I's thinkin' you's safer with ol' Bogey Rat here."

"Safer? What's safe about this place?"

He piled more trash into her arms, while she tried not to let the growing nausea wobble her legs too much. Hell existed, and she'd just checked in.

"Folks're tossin' stuff aside all the time," he said, "never realizin' that every bit o' crap they've held in their hands, even for the wee'est moment, becomes a part o' them. Their touch leaves echoes of possession, lines that can be followed back to their source, or twisted 'round and pulled like puppet strings." He plucked the air to demonstrate, showing off yellow nails, crusted with what she hoped was only mud. "Some folks realize how important trash is, and that's why they can never force themselves to get rid o' things. Others call 'em pack rats, but I call 'em smart little squirrels, keepin' all their belongin's close."

He continued digging through the piles, choosing certain items, tossing others back. Dani struggled to keep from flinging the trash aside and sprinting for freedom. Finally, with a last dump of junk, Stewart patted her butt and nodded to the exit. "Righto. Let's go see if ol' Benny's finished."

Only her relief at stumbling out into relatively fresher air kept him from getting a bloody nose. She fumed as they rejoined Ben, who'd drawn a wavering circle in the earth, surrounded by arcane glyphs, one of which Dani thought looked suspiciously like a trash can, and another the three-arrowed recycling symbol.

Stewart hummed as he checked over the drawing, then nodded and pointed at the middle. "Drop it all there, lass. Then you's two gimme a few minutes to prepare the ritual. We'll get those answers for ya, sure as snot dribbles."

Dani tossed the trash into the circle, perhaps with more enthusiasm than necessary. She drew a clean towel from a pocket and attacked the smears on her sleeves and gloves. Stewart bent over and muttered to himself as he arranged items at points along the circumference. Dani and Ben stood aside, watching until she whispered to him.

"I don't understand. Isn't he Scum? I mean, he works with garbage. That can't be Pure magic."

Ben frowned. "He's a friend. Just 'cause the higher-ups wanna paint the fight between Purity and Corruption in black and white doesn't mean a few shades of gray ain't gonna slip in."

"Do the suits know you two are buddies?"

"Oh, I'm sure someone's got a file on him back at HQ," Ben said. "But he ain't no threat. He just likes spendin' his time here with his collection. The Board cares more about Scum crazies like Sydney who get out in the world and preach the sweet song of obliviation."

"Oblivion."

"Whatever."

Stewart rose. "Righto. Here's we go. All set for a good 'n proper divination."

Dani studied the pile of debris Stewart had arranged. It looked like a hairball hacked up by a giant robot cat. Seeing her dubious look, he nudged the heap with a toe.

"Old newspapers are key. Teemin' with information and oracular potential. People's fingerprints, all their worries, fears, right here in ink. Magic older 'n the Rosetta stone." Stewart looked between them. "I's sure as not gonna ask for your blood," he said to Ben. "And it'd be a crime to flaw the lady's lovely skin, righto?"

Ben frowned. "Didn't think of that. Mebbe—"

"Never bother," said Stewart. He stepped around the circle, spitting at intervals. Dani cringed to see blood flecking his spittle. Then he moved into the circle and put his palms flat toward the ground.

Dani gasped as static teased her hair and sparked over her lips.

Ben glanced at her. "Feel it too? That's good. Just don't let it yank your chain much, a'ight?"

She frowned, then realized she felt what he meant. The core of her that unleashed those awful spells had awakened with Stewart's enacting of his own spell. The chaotic power rose within her, like a cobra flaring its hood.

Ben must've sensed it as well, for he leaned in to murmur. "Hold steady. This ain't gonna take long."

A sudden blue aura infused Stewart, as if he'd been hit by a spotlight. At the same time, the tension on Dani's energies lessened and her power slumbered once more. She realized her teeth were grinding, and forced herself to relax.

The mage's eyes opened, and Dani was alarmed to see his eyes glowing bright blue, pupils washed out. As he took up a monologue, flashes of light sparked between his crooked teeth.

"Lessee here. Dual cores. Manifestations. Pure and Corrupt? Nutters, I's say. Waste of time. Mine, specific'ly."

Dani whispered to Ben. "This is divination?"

"This is you yappin' and distractin' me," Stewart barked, making her jump. "Shut it!"

They stood listening to Stewart's grumbling as the minutes stretched from five, to ten, to twenty. Dani shifted from one foot to the other, trying to keep herself awake by seeing how many items she could identify buried in the surrounding mounds. Ben kept his eyes locked on the trash mage, face serious, eyes troubled.

Just as Dani counted her fifth Barbie doll—headless—Stewart stiffened.

"Bloody balls, you's right, Benny. All's over ... got sightin's of a hydra with a mix of Pure and Corrupt heads. It died attackin' itself. T'was a window-watcher who summoned a glasskin and got mauled by a blackshard instead. There be somethin' new makin' itself known."

"Got that part figured out," Ben said. "Since we ain't never seen anythin' like this before."

Stewart's head rotated Ben's way while the rest of his body remained stiff. "I's meanin' new, as in ... newborn." He closed his eyes.

"What Pantheon is it hooked up to?"

"Both. Neither." Stewart's eyes popped open again. "Bats and bitches, Benny, what'd you's get mixed up in?"

The janitor made fists, voice going hoarse. "C'mon. Keep talkin'. Give me all you got."

"It's … afraid. Hunted. So much power. S'like a baby with a nuke in its diaper." Stewart's voice rose until it scraped like razor blades down Dani's spine. "It's noticed me! No!"

Ben stepped forward, shouting. "Release the spell. Don't—"

The trash mage choked as his blue aura brightened until only a glowing humanoid figure remained visible. Raising a hand against the heatless blaze, Dani stumbled back as Stewart stepped out of the circle, reaching for her. A hot-white glow emanated from his eyes, mouth and nostrils. It looked like he was screaming, but from such a distance that she couldn't hear.

Ben thrust himself between them, mop raised to bar the way. "Get back. It's a Scouring. Don't let him touch you."

She looked around him as Stewart staggered forward, arms outstretched like an extra in a zombie movie. "A Scouring?"

Ben's backpedaling forced her further away. "One of the Purest spells you can cast. It cleanses anyone and anything the caster touches, violent-like."

Stewart fell to all fours. When he rose to his feet again, the areas his arms and hands had hit left shining clear streaks in the dirt, like sand heat-blasted into glass. His footprints left the same results.

"Why's he coming after us?" Dani asked, hearing fear in her voice. "What'd we do?"

"I ain't thinkin' he's in control anymore."

"Well, get him back in control!"

Ben scowled, first at her, then at the advancing mage. With growl, he triggered the electric end of his mop and thrust the sparking tip into Stewart's chest.

The blast threw Ben off his feet. His bony frame hit Dani's shoulder a glancing blow and spun her down. Gasping for breath, she looked up as Ben rolled to a stop against one of the van tires, the mop still in his hands. Smoke rose from the metal tip. He didn't move.

Dani turned as Stewart neared, just a few steps away. His eyes and mouth were wide in silent agony as he reached for her face.

She crawled backward, barely feeling rocks and metal slice through her gloves and into her palms. Desperation clutched her heart and squeezed, the quicksilver pulse of magic waking inside her.

"Please ..." she begged Stewart's glowing form. "Don't make me ..."

Her power flared and reached into the surrounding elements. A gust of wind kicked up, blasting dirt over and past her. Then another, until sheets of grit struck the possessed trash mage in a miniature sandstorm. The first few hits blew by harmlessly. But as the wind increased and the severity of each blast heightened, his steps slowed, then stopped, half a foot from touching her nose.

Dani dug fingers into the ground to anchor herself beneath the storm she'd conjured. The energy writhed through her bones. She tasted blood and realized she'd bitten her tongue. Her power wanted full release, to obliterate any threat. But she refused. She gripped it in her mind and imagined herself choking a greased eel into submission. As much as she feared for her life, she couldn't forgive herself if she killed the garbage man.

Stewart staggered, but the blue glow had yet to fade.

Dani screamed against the power's burning insistence. "Just give me a break, already!"

A last blast struck the mage, flipped him heels-over-head across the clearing, and slammed him into the side of a trash heap. The aura winked out, leaving him squished between a refrigerator and a stack of old televisions.

Collapsing, Dani heaved for breath as her power subsided. It left her feeling empty, cored out. Yet the smallest seed of triumph planted itself in her chest.

She'd fought back this time and won.

CHAPTER THIRTEEN

The business end of a mop planted itself by her face.

She frowned at it. *Wooden handle. Doesn't Ben know wood is porous? It soaks up all sorts of germs and bacteria. It rots.*

With a groan, she rolled onto her back. Ben looked down at her, cheeks creased in concern.

"Dani?"

"You really should use a stainless steel mop handle," she said.

A small grin cracked his wrinkles. "You wanna carry a metal mop around all day, be my guest." He checked around. "You actually throttled it down. I'm impressed."

"Didn't feel like control." She waited for the ground to stop tilting. "Felt like wrestling a nest of snakes. And a bull. And a charging elephant. Don't know how I did it."

"I'm just glad you didn't level the place. Let's hope it wasn't a fluke, eh?"

"Thanks for the vote of confidence."

"Well? Whatcha lyin' around for? Might wanna see if you killed the old goat."

"Don't offer a hand or anything." Her limbs quivered as she made it to her feet and joined him in tugging Stewart from the hole she'd knocked him into. She and Ben each grabbed an arm and slowly pulled the mage free. He appeared intact, if woozy. As they steadied him, he blinked and looked down at himself. Then he wrenched free and started hopping around, arms waving.

"What'd you do? What'd you do? I's clean! Look at me."

Dani squinted at the mage and realized he spoke true. All the grit and grime on his hands and anywhere skin peeked through his outfit had been washed away. As he raved, his teeth flashed a brilliant white and his fingernails gleamed as if manicured.

"Side effect of the Scouring," Ben said. "Coulda been worse."

Stewart shook his newspaper sports coat. The pages looked like they'd been printed yesterday. "Worse? What could be worse 'n this?"

"For starters, your mind coulda been wiped and you'd be blubberin' like a baby right now. Or your bones mighta been boiled clean."

The mage licked his lips. "Righto. Guess I's lucky. No thanks to you draggin' me into all this trouble. I's not carin' if you offer a whole deck o' Baby Ruths. I ain't peekin' that way again."

"Not gonna ask it," Ben said. "Wasn't thinkin' we'd get such a direct response."

"You's stickin' your fingers in the Pantheon's pie," Stewart said, poking Ben's stomach. "Both sides are tryin' to keep their business private until things get sorted out."

"I keep hearing people talk about the Pantheon," Dani said. "What is it?"

Stewart goggled at Ben. "She don't know yet? What you been teachin' her?"

"Hold your horses," Ben said. "This is only her second day."

A rumble shook the ground. He glanced at Dani, who raised her hands.

"Not me! Honest. I'm perfectly in control right now. No earthquakes."

"Stewart?"

"All my sentries just popped their tops," said the trash mage, eyes closed and nose lifted as if scenting the wind. "Somethin' nasty just busted through the main gate. One golem's already down. The others be strugglin'. Gettin' some rats into position to see what's happenin'."

Dani met Ben's eyes in unspoken question.

He nodded. "Sydney. He musta followed us."

"And now my beauties are gone! All's of 'em." Stewart shook a fist at a far mound, toward the entrance. "Rot and piss! Don't you know how long it takes to animate one of those? Pieces of art, and you ruined 'em!"

"Thanks for telling him exactly where we are," Dani said.

A wad of phlegm flew past her face. "Don't get snooty, lass. This is my home we's talkin' about. You all leastaways had the decency to respect the paths. He's bargin' straight toward us."

In the distance, a mound shuddered and collapsed, raising a cloud of dust and birds that scattered into the sky. This sent Stewart into another spasm of hopping and fist shaking.

"No! M'kitchen!"

"We gotta get outta here," Ben said, rubbing his right elbow. "We ain't nearly ready to face him."

Dani waved at the van. "Can't we drive out? Is there another exit?"

Stewart shook his head. "M'scouts are seein' half a dozen mudmen at every gate. You'd be crackin' your skulls tryin' to plow through."

Mudmen? Dani frowned and looked to Ben for clarification, but he paid her no attention just then.

"Stewart, I'm gonna owe you a big one if you get us into the Sewers. I know you got a junction under here."

The mage's face wrinkled, reminding Dani of a prune. "And just how're you knowin' that? You been spyin'?"

Ben matched the man's scowl. "You know better'n that."

"Says who now? Sure'n no spy's gonna give himself away."

"Stewart, I promised I'd never—"

"And what's your word worth these days? You've gone old on me, Benny. What's to keep those whitey-tighties up top from pokin' around in that soft brain o' yours?"

"You know me!" Ben waved his arms, almost striking Dani under the chin. "You knew us. When did we … I ever go back on my word?"

Stewart stamped a foot and his prodigious nose looked ready to peck Ben's eye out. "That was then! The both of ya runnin' off, always heelin' to your masters' call. Like I was wantin' no compn'y but the ones I's made. Now you know what it's like bein' alone, huh?"

Dani clapped between their faces. "Hey! Do we really have time to be arguing?"

The men matched glares for another second, and then blew out and looked aside in identical embarrassed gestures. Stewart took his hat off and ran fingers through the few hairs clinging to his scalp.

"She's the one showin' sense. But we's havin' words later, lad."

Ben glowered, but gestured for Stewart to lead the way. As they headed for the door into the mound, Dani looked over her shoulder.

"What about the van?" she asked. "He'll know we've been here."

"Got it covered, lass."

Stewart's fingers twitched, and the two remaining golems animated. They leaned over, scooped up massive armfuls of garbage, and dropped them on the van.

Remembering Tetris, Dani cried out and started to run that way. "Wait! I've got to—"

Ben caught her arm. "Leave the lizard, already."

"Lizard?" Stewart asked, still focused on directing his golems. "What's you blatherin' about?"

Dani tried to wrench free from Ben. "I just got him back. And all my stuff …"

"We're gonna come back, a'ight? But ain't gonna be no good either way if we get caught here. And where we're goin', he's just gonna be a distraction."

Dani tugged once more before giving up. She winced at the clatter as more trash poured onto the van, and hoped Tetris wouldn't be too frightened. After two more such dumpings, the vehicle had been buried.

Finished, Stewart led them back into the mound, past the first room and through a winding maze of dank, oppressive tunnels dug through earth and muck. They passed through black curtains of garbage bags, rotting netting, and sheets of stained gauze. Dani tried to breathe through her mouth, but this made her taste the smells instead, and soon it felt like slime coated her throat.

Ben must've noticed her struggling against her upchuck reflex, for he fished a dust mask out of a pocket and handed it over.

"Figured you might be wantin' this."

She took it with a look of silent blessing and snapped the band over her head. It didn't reduce the smell, but at least she could breathe without wanting to disgorge her own stomach.

After several minutes of ducking and weaving, they came into a passage with luminescent fungal growths dotting the walls and ceiling instead of the usual bulb strings. Stewart led down this until it branched off to the right into a dead end. He stuck his hand into the wall with a squishing noise that Dani would have nightmares about for weeks. Muck spiraled outwards and revealed a steep downward slope into darkness. The bitter drafts that wafted up from it made the rest of the dump smell like a field of daisies by comparison.

"Through here." Stewart stepped aside. "I's be keepin' my guests runnin' in circles as long as I can."

Dani eyed the black path waiting for them with growing worry, while Ben nodded to the mage.

"Thanks, Stewart. Sorry for the bother."

The trash mage shrugged. "Still t'weren't as bad as last time." He winked at Dani and then shuffled out into the passage.

"Exactly what did you do the last time you were here?" Dani asked.

"Later." He nudged her forward and down. "Hoof it."

CHAPTER FOURTEEN

The damp air under the garbage mound changed into a cold rankness that drove its fist into Ben's stomach with every breath. He took a flashlight from a hip pocket and flicked it on, illuminating a rusted steel walkway that ended in a lip twenty strides further.

Dani kept close as he moved to the edge, trying to walk silently so he might hear any pursuers. He had to brace on his mop more than usual. Not even lunchtime yet and his joints already ached as if someone had used them for an extended drum solo.

Stewart had closed the way behind them, and they stood deep enough within the mound to block out everything but their own footsteps. A glance over the side showed rungs leading down to a concrete platform, walled-in except for a narrow brick tunnel leading into darkness.

"Follow me," he told Dani, gesturing at the ladder.

"Where are we going?" she whispered.

"Someplace that makes Stewart's dump look like paradise. Can you handle it?"

After chewing her lip a bit, she nodded. It encouraged him to see determination in her eyes, rather than fear. Though she did adjust her gloves and take a quick swig of mouthwash.

"I won't enjoy it," she said through a mouthful of spearmint. "But I'll survive."

They climbed down the ladder to the grate below, rubber boots thudding against the grille. A short walkway cut through a wall and into the passage beyond. Ben emerged and shone his light up and down the way, breathing soft, alert for anything out of place.

It looked like a normal stretch of sewer—concrete walkways on either side of a channel of flowing muck and debris. Slimy brick walls curved into the distance, with only a few sputtering maintenance lights pushing back the darkness.

Normal ... except for the graffiti decorating the walls. Arcane scribbles, circles and glyphs marked the brick at random. Ben closed his eyes and stretched his senses out, detecting all manner of Scum wards—alarms, traps, charged circles that would summon Corrupt manifestations, and a few portals. Stewart's landfill sat on top of a veritable hub of Scum traffic. Fortunately, most of them were touch-activated; with the others, he'd be able to mask their presence long enough to pass by without activating them.

Carl splashed in his bottle. Ben opened his eyes and suppressed a deep sigh.

"I know. I hate tuckin' tail and runnin', too, but we ain't got many options right now." An insistent gurgle made him frown. "Thanks for the encouragement."

"What'd he say?" Dani asked. She stood as far as she could from the sewage without touching the moldy walls. Half-hidden in the gloom, her face took on a spectral quality, as if she might fade away if kept underground too long.

"Just reminded me of a promise I made way back when. If he falls on the job, I gotta scatter his ashes and tell his family he died a hero."

"Scatter his ... is that even possible?"

"Dunno. And I ain't gonna find out." He thumped the spray bottle. "Don't mind him. He just gets a bit antsy around sewage."

"I can relate." She flinched as something dripped from the ceiling and plopped into the sluggish current. "Where are we?"

"Remember me sayin' how Stewart was kinda in-between Purity and Corruption? A border between both sides?"

She flicked her ponytail over a shoulder. "Sure."

"Well, we just crossed behind enemy lines. Welcome to the Sewers."

Her widening eyes tracked the length of the tunnel, noting the elements he'd been studying. She wouldn't know what they meant, but no doubt she'd picked up on all the volatile, destructive energy the graffiti contained.

"Are we in danger?"

"Assume we are and go from there."

"That's comforting."

"Really? Musta said it wrong."

"Where are we going?"

"Destin needs evidence, yeah? Well, we got a few juicy bits from Stewart, but the Board ain't about to act on the word of a trash mage. We need to get someone more reputable to confirm those reports and link 'em to ours. That way we got somethin' a bit more concrete to toss in their laps." He popped his neck on either side. "But first things first—gettin' outta here with our gizzards intact. If I remember the maps to this junction right, there's an exit hatch a few miles north."

She made a full-body cringe. "A few miles? Through this?"

"We go quick and quiet and we shouldn't stir up anythin' too nasty. Walk where I do, and don't touch the walls, a'ight? Don't even let your clothes brush the brick."

"No problem there." Doubt shaded her gaze as she squinted down the sewer line. She squared her shoulders and took a deep breath. "Let's do this."

"Atta girl."

He raised a hand to pat her back, then caught himself and dropped it again. Before she could question the gesture, he edged out into the tunnel proper and, after mentally orienting himself, headed north.

Gurgles, trickles, and drips masked their steps. The walkway was wide enough for them to avoid the walls, though Ben's right arm erupted into needling tingles whenever he got close. Dani stayed a step behind him and he kept checking over his shoulder to make sure she was still there. Whenever they made eye contact, she gave a shaky thumbs-up and re-secured her dust mask.

After half a mile of skulking, passing by numerous junctions and taking several turns, they came to a larger chamber with a foul pool churning in the middle. Four concrete platforms occupied each corner, connected by footbridges. The ceiling was lost in blackness overhead; not a single grate present to let in sunlight. The air hung heavy and hot, stinking with refuse and—Ben sniffed—yes, blood. Fresh. Used in painting some of the glyphs, perhaps.

He paused just outside the entrance, studying the layout and trying to decide which of the three offered passages to take.

"Ben?"

He looked back to Dani, who dabbed at her face with a towelette. "Eh?"

"How'd Sydney know we were at the garbage dump?"

He frowned at the path. "Good question. Tryin' to figure it out m'self."

"Could Stewart have told him we were there?"

A shake of his head, even while similar suspicions squirmed in his gut. "No. He wouldn't have done that. We've worked together for too long."

"Are you sure?"

A scraping noise spared Ben from answering. He flicked his light off and turned to press Dani into a crouch with him, careful to touch her protected shoulder with his left hand. They'd paused in a deep patch of shadows. He used his mop to balance himself on the balls of his feet and watched.

A band of figures shuffled into view at the corner fifty paces down and moved to the near platform—close enough to hear their hissing and snarls. Dani's breath caught. He squeezed her shoulder, trying to appear confident for her sake even as sweat trickled down his ribs.

The new arrivals paused on the lip of the walkway, long necks stretched as they eyed the river of sewage. Their elongated, flattened heads were covered in virulent green and red scales. Gold, ovoid eyes glittered with the barest flicker of light, revealing slit pupils. Brown robes covered their bodies, unnaturally thin and sinuous, and clawed hands dangled from the sleeves, talons clicking.

After snuffling around for a minute, the first of the creatures slid head-first into the channel. The others slithered after it with quiet plops, flicking barbed tails before disappearing beneath the surface. After the last one swam off, Ben breathed easier. He remained crouching for a few minutes more, just in case.

As he waited, Dani put her lips uncomfortably close to his ear and whispered, "What were those?"

He leaned away. "Ever heard of alligators in the sewers?"

"You're joking."

He shrugged and went back to observing the channel for any sign that the creatures remained. "They're called urmoch. Only good thing is they eat Scum and Cleaners alike. If there's a nest around, it'd explain why this junction is so quiet. We're lucky."

Her expression showed how much she trusted in luck. After another minute, Ben rose slowly and paced into the chamber, mop at the ready. The urmochs' musky odor lingered in the air. Fortunately, that seemed the only thing to remain. The pack had likely gone off to hunt down small dogs standing too close to sewer grates.

Dani emerged from the tunnel after Ben didn't get eaten right away. She groaned as she stretched her arms and back. "Much further?"

Ben nodded to the tunnel on their right. "We're close. Soon as we get outta here, we're high-tailin' it to a nice quiet spot where we can take the next steps."

"We're not going back to Headquarters?"

"Not yet. Destin'll only get his rear in gear when kicked into action by someone even higher up than him."

Her brow wrinkled. "Higher? I thought he was in charge of the whole company."

"That's what he likes people to think. But even the Chairman and Board answer to the Pantheon. And that's who we're gonna give a call to."

"And they are? Give me an answer this time, not a brush-off."

Ben eased around the corner, checking to make sure the tunnel he'd chosen stood empty. "Basically, they're the incarcerations of Purity and Corruption."

"You mean incarnations."

"Wouldja stop doin' that? Look, each Pantheon is ruled over by two Primals, with three Petties fillin' in some of the lesser roles—doin' the laundry, mowin' the lawn, that kinda thing. They're the ones who gave humanity the powers that created the Cleaners ... as well as the Scum."

"So they're what? Gods?"

Ben chuckled darkly. "Some might think so. Destin's certainly willing to pucker up and plant one on their glowing butts. But there ain't no religion for 'em and you ain't gonna ever catch me prayin' their way. They're just high-and-mighty pies in the sky who got too much power for their own good. Purity can't go toe-to-toe with Corruption or vicey-versy without both sides coming up the loser, so that's where we come in. We bust our humps to maintain the balance. Or just to get a paycheck and live to see tomorrow." He shrugged. "Whatever perspective you wanna take. There's plenty of wackos out there who'll sell you a hundred different things to believe."

"What are we going to do?"

"Somethin' I ain't done in years." He gave her a rueful grin. "We gotta summon a member of the Pantheon."

"Indeed you must. And, while it may be impolite to say so, you look like lost little lambs in this place. Might I provide an escort? Or at least some tea?"

Ben spun and his light flashed over Sydney, who stood on the walkway ahead of them. He held a saucer and tea cup, from which he sipped an aromatic brew. The mage grinned and bowed even as Ben thrust his mop out like a spear to ward him off. Neither it nor Carl would last long against the entropy-wielder, but it might give Dani time to escape, though her chances of getting through the sewers alone were slim.

Sydney straightened. "I come to you gloved, offering help, and this is my welcome?" He did indeed wear his leather gloves, along with his tuxedo t-shirt from before, and had added a black cape for, Ben assumed, dramatic effect. The entropy mage took another slurp from his cup and smacked his lips in satisfaction.

"How'dja get ahead of us?" Ben asked.

"By coming here and waiting." Sydney's smile glinted white, even in the gloom. "How else?"

"Then who was bustin' down the gate and golems up top?" Ben thumbed at the ceiling of the tunnel.

Sydney pursed his lips and pretended to think, then brightened in mock revelation. "Yes! A few friends of mine whom I persuaded to plant mudmen around the premises." He raised the cup. "Oh, and a scrub-team from HQ, headed up by one Francis Levaigne. Somehow he got an anonymous tip suggesting the old garbage man has been stealing corpses from city morgues and experimenting on them. Such activity is rarely tolerated, so I've heard."

Ben resisted the urge to look back the way they'd come. "Aww, crap-on-a-stick. Stewart."

Sydney's smile took on a knife edge. "I doubt your associates will be as understanding with him as you've been. Let's hope they don't kill him outright."

Dani clutched Ben's elbow. "They wouldn't do that, would they?"

"Dearest Dani, you have yet to comprehend the ruthlessness the Cleaners possess." Sydney winked Ben's way.

Ben tried to swallow the sour-milk taste coating his tongue. "Whatcha want?"

Sydney swept the tea cup about without spilling a drop. "Simply to guide you through this place. The urmoch and I have something of an arrangement. They don't attack me and I don't wipe out their species. Quite a pleasant folk once you get past the teeth and claws."

"Us willingly go with you?" asked Dani.

"What choice do you have? Fight me here and die, or come with me and live."

"And then die after you use us for whatever you got in mind," Ben said.

"That is dissimilar to your working for the Cleaners ... how?"

They matched each other in stubborn silence for a long minute. Then Ben grunted and tilted his head at the tunnel behind Sydney.

"You first. Keep five paces between us and face forward. I'm gonna be followin' right behind, and the moment you twitch in a way I don't like, I'm shovin' this through your spine." He shook the mop for emphasis.

Sydney smiled over the edge of his cup. "Actually. I'm enjoying this little chat right here. What say we continue it a bit before we so hastily run ahead?"

Dani came up beside Ben, scowling with hands on hips. "You just said you were going to guide us out."

Sydney's little laugh grated on Ben's ears. "Oh, well, it's embarrassing, really." He set his cup onto the saucer with a click. "I lied. It was a necessary delay tactic so they could get into position."

Hissing figures lunged out of the channel, slopping filthy water. Ben had time enough to see a clawed hand strike Dani on the back of the head. She toppled.

Then something bony and wet struck his temple, and shadows rushed up to swallow him.

CHAPTER FIFTEEN

Dani woke to warm lips brushing her forehead. She tried to jerk away, but something constrained her arms, legs, and torso. Blinking the haze from her eyes, she mentally recoiled from Sydney, who gazed adoringly.

"Easy," he murmured. "You're safe."

"Safe?" Her skin burned where he'd kissed. "Do you know how many diseases get transferred orally? Streptococcus. Mononucleosis. Herpes! You think I want to walk around the rest of my life with a cold sore?"

As he smirked, she looked around, trying to see past his looming face. She lay strapped to a marble platform, twin to the one next to her, on which Ben also lay, uselessly straining against his bonds. Shadows flickered around them, teased into motion by the brass lamp hanging from the ceiling. The room had a single red door. No windows. No vents. A mini-fridge sat humming in one corner.

Sydney cupped her cheeks in his hands and forced her to look at him. She didn't know which was worse: the slight dampness of his hands and all the potential bacteria swarming over them, or knowing his touch could turn her to dust with a thought. Either option brought bile to the back of her throat. Instead of kissing her again, he massaged the tender knot on her skull.

"No permanent damage. I'm sorry for the hard knock, but I doubt you'd have come so quietly otherwise."

She swallowed a few times to wet her tongue. "Get your filthy hands off me."

He chuckled and raised a hand. "I assure you, filth is an element I avoid dabbling in as much as possible. One such benefit of my talent is the ability to annihilate any unwanted organisms on my person. My hands are perfectly sterile."

She narrowed her eyes. "What are you going to do with us?"

Stroking her hair, he smiled gently. "Free you, for starters. Just to emphasize that you've nothing to fear from me."

He dissolved the clasps one at a time and helped ease her off the platform onto wobbly legs. The room tilted for a second, and she clutched the side of the slab until things righted. Sydney held her arm, providing an anchor to her reeling senses. She'd never let herself be touched so much by anyone since she'd first learned to walk on her own.

Dani looked to Ben, who glared over at them. His mouth had been strapped shut, and his nostrils flared with each breath.

"Aren't you going to free him too?"

A shadow fluttered behind Sydney's eyes. "I'm merciful, not stupid."

Ben growled through his gag. Sydney released Dani and went over to remove the strap so Ben could speak.

"Beg your pardon?" he asked. "Do recount the various threats you've no doubt been compiling in that gray lump of a brain you have. I could use a laugh."

Ben spat at Sydney, but the entropy mage blocked the spittle with one hand, and the missile vanished on contact.

"You bat rastard," Ben rasped.

Sydney affected a swoon, back of a hand to his forehead. "Oh! He mocks my parentage. Truly, I am *wounded*."

"Yeah, well, it's one of the few insults Francis hasn't added to the foul-filter yet."

"And how is Francis these days?" Sydney asked. "Still pretending his shit smells of cinnamon and cloves?"

"Why'd you bring us here?" Dani asked. She fought the temptation to jump on Sydney's back and try to drive him to the floor. For all his fluttering and amorous attentions, she didn't doubt he kept ready to incapacitate her with a touch the moment she turned violent or tried to flee.

"Three answers to that," he said. "Foremost, I've brought the janitor here to help me in a particularly sensitive ritual. Second, I brought you here to see if you're willing to reconsider my offer. Third, because I knew you'd still refuse, I brought you here to reveal a truth."

That locked her gaze with his. "Truth about what?"

Sydney wiped Ben's sweating brow. Ben tried to flinch from the touch, but the bindings held him still.

"Why, about your mentor here. About why the Cleaners ignored their own rules to place you with him."

"What rules?"

He steepled his fingers. "One critical rule, to be precise: *Those who have been tainted by Corruption shall never be allowed to train any new servant of Purity.* Simple really. Can't fathom how they forgot it in your case."

Her breath caught, and the first tremors of uncertainty shook her thoughts. "Tainted?"

Ben stiffened. "Sydney, I'm warnin' you. Don't make this personal."

Sydney looked at Ben with amusement. "And do you want to know the worst of it? He's a hypocrite. For the very fact that he remains with the Cleaners, doing their work, obeying their commands, he is impure to the core himself."

"What are you talking about?" Dani asked.

Walking around Ben's platform, Sydney took up position next to the janitor's right arm, which kept tensing and relaxing. Fear and fury mingled in Ben's eyes. She knew she shouldn't let Sydney toy with him, however the mage was doing it, but she didn't know how to stop him.

Ben thrashed as much as the straps allowed, and Dani half-expected him to snap a bone from his efforts.

"Lemme outta here, you coward. Too afraid to face me fair-like? Gotta kick me when I'm down? I'm warnin' you! Don't—"

Sydney touched Ben's right sleeve. The material disintegrated up to the shoulder, baring that arm.

Dani gasped. Ben's arm looked like it had been ripped off a corpse and attached to his body. A black stain radiated out from the inner elbow, and dark veins threaded throughout gray and flaking skin.

Sydney waved for her to examine it closer. Dazed, Dani stared at the limb's bleeding sores and the violent bruises mottling the skin down to the wrist—beyond which his hand looked relatively healthy.

Ben fixed the mage with an icy stare. "You just made this personal. You're gonna regret that."

"You see?" Sydney traced the black veins with a forefinger. "This is the mark of the Ravishing. A vicious infection. It only manifests in those who commit the most *unthinkable* acts of violence and betrayal. It is the giving over of the body, mind, and soul to Corruption … and from then on, they are a lost cause, slowly twisting into further depravity. It saps their power and eats away their life until they are nothing but a husk. This is the path Ben is on as we speak."

Resignation dulled Ben's voice. "That ain't true, and you know it."

"Ben …" Dani reached out to his arm, but didn't quite touch. "What happened to you? What is this? Why didn't you tell me?"

His cheeks sagged. "Aww, princess … you weren't ready …"

"Ben killed his wife, dear one," Sydney said, prowling around the table.

"I ain't never did," Ben growled. "Wasn't me. I'll keep denyin' it, no matter what."

Sydney continued his circuit, talking as he walked, while Dani remained rooted, unable to look away from the hideous sight.

"Benjamin was once one of the most powerful and honored servants of Purity. He and his wife worked as a team, striking down Corruption and Scum wherever they went. Such an example to us all. But who knows quite how insanity begins? Is it a slow, creeping thing? Or does it leap and devour all at once?" He moved out of sight behind her. "Poor Ben couldn't handle all the responsibility. During a job, something went awry. Only Ben returned, raving and infected with the Ravishing. He almost destroyed a full scrub-team before they got him under control." He sighed. "Tragic, really. They thought they were showing mercy by keeping him alive."

"How do you know all this?"

"Dani, he's not tellin' the whole story. My wife … she—"

"Why do you think Destin placed you in his care in the first place?" said Sydney. "To give poor Benjamin a chance to prove himself again?" His barking laughter ricocheted around the tiny room. "Maybe that's what he deluded himself into believing. But deep down he knows they wanted him to infect you. To pass on the Ravishing so it would subdue your true power and potential."

Her eyes finally switched from Ben's arm to his face. She saw the pain there, the helplessness—the guilt.

"Is that true?" she asked. She felt numb and listless. "Are you infectious?"

He chewed at his cheeks. "The uniform keeps it contained, mostly."

"*Mostly?*"

"I didn't have a choice," he said.

"Yes, you did. You could've told me."

"Mebbe. But … I'd hoped I could actually make a last difference before I go. Help you gain control. Get your new life started right."

"But you knew." She stabbed a finger at his face. "You knew I could get infected and you kept me with you. Just so you could feel important again. All this time …"

He shook his head. "I've been tryin' to protect you! Come on, princess, can't you see what he's doing? He's twisted things all up."

"Oh, like you've been straight with me. What happened to your wife, Ben?"

"I … don't rightly remember."

"Uh-huh."

Hurt pinched one side of his face. "Somethin' got into my head that day and I've never been able to get it straightened out. But I ain't ever lied to you, Dani. Not once. And I ain't ever gonna."

"That's quite enough." With a swift place and pull, Sydney replaced the gag strap and tightened it until Ben's jaw creaked. The janitor's glare bored into Sydney, but the mage didn't appear affected by the projected rage. "There. Peace and quiet again. Better than listening to convenient excuses of memory loss, isn't it?"

He left her staring at Ben while he went to the door and pulled it open. Beyond waited a well-lit hallway of gray and white mason stone with doors every ten feet or so on either side. He returned to her and took her unresisting hand.

"There are others you should meet. They'll help you understand what's really at stake here. They can offer you true freedom."

With her mind whirling, she let him put his arm around her shoulders and lead her out. The door clanged shut behind them, cutting off a last glimpse of Ben renewing his struggle against the bonds.

CHAPTER SIXTEEN

As Sydney guided her down the hall, Dani kicked into an internal debate about the revelation of Ben's deceit. Was what Sydney said true? Had the Cleaners placed her with Ben in the hopes of subduing her power? Had they not offered her a new world to explore after all, but tried to throw her into a bigger cage?

And if they had, should she blame Ben for his part in it? Maybe it had been cruel of her to leave him behind so quickly; in the confusion, her instincts had prodded her to get as far away from potential contamination as possible.

Even if he'd truly hoped to help her, it didn't excuse him completely. He hadn't lied, true, but it was a serious omission, especially since he knew her hatred of filth and disease. He could've told her. He *should've* told her.

She could've been infected. Doomed to become a shade of herself. He hadn't denied that. Could he really protect her from himself if he'd been too far Corrupted? And if she couldn't trust him, who else was there? Sydney?

She eyed the entropy mage's back as he silently led the way. "Can you really make yourself sterile? Er, that is, not as far and kids and all go, but with germs and—oh, you know what I mean."

He grinned back at her. "Yes, I do and I can."

"Think you could teach me?"

"Sadly, not all of us share the same giftings. Your skills, while able to impact the world on a much grander scale than my own, are not so precise."

"You're saying I'm clumsy."

"Hardly. We simply wield different instruments. You might imagine me holding tweezers while you wield a club the size of a small island."

Once, she might've thought that a subtle dig at her weight. However, she kept her focus, determined to learn as much as she could.

"Ben said you were a handyman."

"There, at least, his memory does not suffer."

"Why'd you leave the Cleaners?"

He grimaced. "The details are unimportant. Suffice it to say that I grew tired of living according to others' dictums. We could never have a dissenting voice, never stray too far outside procedure without being slapped back into place by the Board and its watchdogs. So long as the proper image was maintained, it never mattered what personnel issues festered."

Dani tried to sort out her impression of him. While he worked for those she was supposed to consider the "other side," at least they shared a distaste for being forced in line. Maybe coming with him wasn't the wisest choice, but he at least seemed less inclined to hurt her if she refused to go along with whatever he had in store—unlike the Cleaners being ready to scrub her out the moment she stopped playing by the rules.

Still, even if she decided to return to the Cleaners, she needed to know what other options existed. If Ben could rationalize cavorting with a garbage man, why couldn't she pal around with an entropy mage? While he walked and talked like a poor man's Phantom of the Opera, at least he made an attempt to be charming and didn't smell like laundry detergent and talcum powder.

She realized they'd been walking for almost five minutes without seeing anyone else.

"Where are we?" she asked.

"In the halls of fiery purification," he said, sweeping an arm.

She glared sideways at him. "Oh, yes, the halls of fiery purification. Dropped by here for summer vacation a few years back."

"I don't mean to confuse you." Arriving at a T-junction, Sydney turned right, into another stretch of identical walls and closed doors. "This is one of my homes, and the abode of a fellowship devoted to bringing true purity to the world."

Dani shoved away a momentary, irrational desire to have Ben at her side. "More entropy mages?"

"More?" Sydney's laughter came out deep this time. "No, no. My kind is as rare as yours. No. The ones we go to meet are … enthusiasts. While not the most open-minded folks, they certainly know how to commit to a cause."

"And that cause is?"

"Better to let them tell you. While I'm a believer in their efforts, they're much more eloquent in explaining their creed."

They walked in silence for several minutes more. At last, Sydney shoved open a door and pulled Dani in after him.

She blinked in the dim yellow light that settled over them. The room appeared to be a miniature chapel with rows of cedar pews before a wooden pulpit. A single torch blazed on the wall behind this, and tiny sconces ringed the room, each holding the barest candle-flickers.

A group knelt before the pulpit, heads bowed and hands folded. All were bald. The women among them wore loose white robes, while the men had white tunics and pants. No shoes or any accessories. It all couldn't have looked more sterile. Even after a few sniffs, she couldn't detect a single odor beyond her sweaty self.

As one, the group rose and turned to the newcomers. None of them had any eyebrows, either, and their eyes looked like glowing beads in the candlelight.

"Hail, brothers and sisters," Sydney called out, moving to meet them with Dani at his side. "I have rescued this one from the lies of the Cleaners and brought her here to take her place among you."

She hissed a whisper. "I haven't agreed to anything. I'm not a free-for-all joiner, got it?"

"Greetings and welcome, young one," said the closest man. Dani guessed that if he'd had any hair, it would have been combed back with a dash of dignified gray. "I am Marcus. We are honored to have one of your power in our midst. We have anticipated this day since the founding of our order."

They lined up before her, soft smiles directed her way. The placid expressions and submissive postures started pinging a mental warning of *cult! cult!*

"Who are you?"

"We are the Cleansers. The true servants of Purity." Marcus spread his arms as if for a group hug. "We are your new family."

"Oh, for ..." She turned and shook a fist at Sydney. "You said you'd help me get free. You didn't say I'd have to join a cult."

Sydney's smile drooped on one side and he made an apologetic bow to the others. "My pardon, brethren. She doesn't realize the foolishness she speaks. I assure you—"

"I know full well what I speaketh of, thank you. And no, I'm not drinking the Kool-Aid and no, I'm not riding the UFO or wearing one of those stupid robes." She plucked at her janitorial uniform. "I am so tired of all this. You and your Pantheons and silly battles over a bit of spit and polish. I'm sick and done with it." Dani turned to go. "I'm leaving. And if any of you try to stop me, I'll—"

Marcus stepped forward and gripped her shoulder. While his hold rooted her, his face remained gentle, even kind.

"Young one, you cannot leave. This is where you have belonged since you were born with the spark of Purity within you."

Dani let out a frustrated shriek, and didn't bother resisting as her power loosed. Its triumphant cry echoed hers as it raged free and latched onto the nearest, strongest element.

The flame of the torch exploded and billowed out, pouring into a river of fire that cascaded through the room. It swelled and flooded the chapel until the cult members stood as dark pillars within the firestorm.

While she rode the wave of energy, in the back of her mind, Dani flailed against the horror of burning these people to ashen skeletons. The tiniest part of her tried to cut off the spell, but it burned on until she was certain she'd be standing alone with a few piles of ash around her.

Then it felt as if someone attached half a dozen funnels to the magic and drained it off all at once. The fire fell away as quick as she'd summoned it, revealing an untouched room. The Cleansers all stood before her, unmoved. Each of them held an aura of flame like living wicks. The fire hadn't so much as singed their white garments. At her side, Sydney sniffed and flicked ash off his shoulder.

Dani stared, aghast at the ineffectiveness of her spell. They smiled back, content and patient.

"We have each been touched by the cleansing flame," Marcus said. "We are the ones chosen to purge the disease of life from the world, just as you are." He looked to Sydney. "She has much potential, but is sullied with doubt and confusion. We shall cleanse her mind and soul so there will be nothing but fire left within her. She will be the Cleanser incarnate, and wherever she walks, Purity will follow."

They pressed in, smiles unwavering. Over one woman's shoulder, Dani saw Sydney bow to Marcus and slip back toward the door.

"Sydney, don't you dare leave me here with these lunatics!"

"Only for a time." He fluttered fingers through the crack he held open in the doorway. "Marcus, please keep her feisty spirit intact. I'd rather not have her mind shattered." He winked at her. "When next I see you, dearest, you will welcome me with open arms."

"I'll welcome you with a kick in the—"

The door clicked shut. She lost her threat in a wordless howl as she lunged to free herself from the many clinging hands.

"Ben!" She wrenched an arm loose and punched backward. Knuckles cracked against cartilage and drew a yelp. "Ben! Help!"

A cloth smelling of mint slapped over her nose and mouth. Surprised, she couldn't stop herself from sucking a deep breath. The room went hazy. The edges turned into snakes that writhed around her feet, and the flames became mocking sprites dancing above her head in a halo that spun ...

... and spun

... and

... extinguished.

CHAPTER SEVENTEEN

Ben almost popped his left shoulder out of joint as he struggled.

Gonna string that boy up like a gutted buzzard. Gonna flip his flapper until he squeals like a side o' bacon.

The slab refused to rock, no matter how he threw his weight around.

Gonna shove his head into a bucket and make him blow bubbles. Gonna replace his spine with a slinky and kick him downstairs!

The leather straps remained tight, and he only succeeded in exhausting himself and inventing half a dozen more insults by the time the door re-opened.

Two urmoch strode in, hunched beneath their filthy robes. They moved to either side of him, speaking in guttural bursts. Claws ticked over his ribs and dug in under his chin.

Ben bit down on the strap. Had Sydney promised them a meal? The entropy mage's control over the reptilian creatures baffled him.

One leaned over him, eyes glowing like dull gold coins in the depths of its hood. Its mouth opened, revealing bloodstained fangs. A glob of saliva plopped onto his face and slid down his cheek like a foul tear. A rough tongue licked it off. Fleshy barbs snagged his skin.

"That's enough," came Sydney's voice from the hallway.

The urmoch retreated to the walls with sullen hisses, claws folded within their sleeves. Sydney strode in with less flair than usual, a more set look in his eyes. A touch disintegrated the strap gagging Ben and left fine dust coating his tongue.

"What'dja do with Dani?" he demanded.

"Such concern," Sydney said. "I'd almost think you were smitten with her." He put a hand to his throat. "Though the idea disgusts me. To think of your wrinkled, odorous self with such a pristine creature as her ..." A shudder. "Fortunate that I came along before you could corrupt her body as much as you tried to with her mind."

"Get off your high horse. What's this really about? Revenge? You gonna try and use me to get back into HQ?"

Sydney chuckled. "I could walk in any time I wish and they know it. I prefer to leave them quivering in fear while I turn my attention to more important matters. Now that the fiery little tart is out of the way, you and I can finish what needs to be achieved."

"Which is ...?"

"Still playing the ignorant?" A sigh. "Even if you truly didn't know before, I refuse to believe your visit to the garbage man was in vain. You know the opportunity we face here."

Ben chewed the inside of his cheek. Pretending to not know wouldn't get him freed from these bonds any more than trying to struggle out of them. His biggest chance would be to go along with Sydney as far as he could—as if he had a choice.

"The new member of the Pantheon," he said.

Sydney punched the air. "Precisely! Like you, I became aware of this being's existence and determined its dual nature. The implications are astounding. We are going to summon it, and then we'll—"

"Get ourselves killed tryin' to control it?"

"Don't be so melodramatic."

Ben cocked an eyebrow at the mage, dressed in his tuxedo t-shirt and cape.

Sydney shrugged. "Assuming this new being shares the personified characteristics of the other Pantheon members, it will have intelligence. It can be communicated with. I intend to negotiate. I will provide guidance for a wandering soul that has yet to choose its place and purpose in the world."

"Guidance counselor to the gods," Ben said. "Not really the career I woulda picked for you."

"Hush, now." Sydney gestured, and the urmoch once more positioned themselves beside Ben. A few touches crumbled the rest of Ben's bonds into nothing. Clawed hands tugged him upright, and he shook his head to fight off a wave of dizziness.

His muscles ached and twitched as he worked feeling back into his limbs. Bloody buckets, he hated being so old. He tried to avoid looking at his exposed right arm, with its black veins and decrepit flesh.

"Come along quietly." Sydney headed for the door without looking back. "They have orders to slash every tendon in your body if you disobey."

Ben glanced at his reptilian escorts. Even with his magically reinforced uniform, they'd likely filet him before he could sneeze. So he sloped along after the mage, though still alert for any opportunity. Without his mop or Carl, he could do little to cause a distraction, but that didn't mean he shouldn't be ready to go after Dani, assuming he could find his way through this warren of tunnels.

And a true maze it proved to be, with featureless walls and random turns that confused his sense of direction within minutes. By the time Sydney stopped at another door, Ben couldn't guess whether they'd made any progress or just gone in a huge circle.

This new chamber had walls of pure silver, scrubbed to a frosty shine that blurred reflections. No furnishings, no obvious source of light for the soft blue illumination. No markings. Just a big, metal box.

The urmoch pushed Ben to the left and shoved him up against the wall, which pressed cold against his back and arm. Sydney stood in the center of the room, a faint smile on his lips. Finally, he nodded, as if satisfied with the blandness of the place.

"This is neutral ground," he said. "Cleansed from all traces of either Pantheon."

Ben's eyes widened as he realized what this meant. "You handed Dani over to the Cleansers? Don'tcha know what they're gonna do to her?"

"Of course. Do you think I brought you here by accident? Now she'll never have to worry about tedious things like controlling her power ever again. She'll know true freedom."

"She could burn the city to the ground!"

"And wouldn't that be such a beautiful thing?"

Ben rubbed his forehead, trying to burrow through the skull and massage the ache in his brain. "I keep forgettin' how barmy you are."

Sydney produced a can of red spray paint and sprayed a six-foot-diameter circle on the floor. He filled this with jagged lines, as if someone had thrown a pentacle to the floor and shattered it. In the spaces between the lines, he drew signs of containment and shielding, and then ground his heel over several glyphs, smudging them just so.

He tossed the paint can over one shoulder, where it struck one of the urmoch in the chest before falling and rolling up against a wall. The entropy mage turned, now holding a gleaming knife. With a wave from their master, the urmoch shoved Ben over.

Ben tilted his chin up. "A'ight, then. Quick and clean, if you got the balls."

Sydney tsked. "While I'd delight in splashing buckets of your vitae across the floor, that might draw the attention of the Primals themselves, and I'd rather not be around when they come to feed. No. A few drops and dribbles will do. What better blood to summon the new Pantheon member than that which mingles Purity and Corruption, hmm?"

After a stinging cut on the meat of each thumb, Sydney yanked Ben's hands over the edge of the circle and let several drops splatter the floor. Those from his left were bright red, while the issue from his right held a dark purple tint.

Once released, with fists squeezed to clot the cuts as quickly as possible, Ben found himself pulled back against the wall by Sydney's reptilian comrades.

Sydney raised his arms, the stained knife poised like a morbid orchestra conductor. "To the one born into the center of all things," he called out. "We invite you into our midst. Bless us with your presence and accept the offering of life I provide."

"And don't kill us, eh?" Ben muttered.

A gust blew into the room from another realm. It brought scents of rotting vegetation, and hot oil. Images flashed through Ben's mind—an infinite golden desert with a sun-bleached skeleton at its center, its tusked and horned skull larger than a cruise ship. A black river pouring over the edge of a cliff and plunging into a green void. A vulture descending, claws and beak aiming for the eyes.

He squinted against the rising wind and banished these glimpses. While Sydney's talent lay in commanding the force of entropy, one didn't need any special power to summon a member of the Pantheon. The trick lay in getting their attention, and offering something worth the time and effort it took them to show up. And the more Pure or Corrupt the offering, the likelier it'd be accepted.

Anticipation knotted in his chest, hard and thorny. The few times he'd interacted with the Pantheon before proved harsh and unwelcome. Nothing he wanted to experience again. Now Sydney wanted to conjure this rogue demigod and treat it like a babe to be coddled and manipulated. Even if he succeeded in drawing its presence, there was no telling how it would react.

Sydney stood stiff, his entire focus on sustaining the summoning. The urmoch remained unmoved on either side of Ben, though a white film had slipped into place over their eyes to protect them from the gritty wind. Ben braced himself for a sudden, violent entrance of the being. It might provide the distraction he needed.

The room shuddered and the air in the middle of the circle warped and bulged, as if something enormous sought to shove into their dimension. Then, with a swirl of black wind, a bag lady appeared within the ring.

Ben blinked in surprised recognition.

She wore mismatched high heels, one leopard-spotted, the other red leather—both with heels snapped off—a ragged pair of camouflage canvas pants with one leg shredded to reveal a knobby, scarred knee, and a muddy jeans jacket five sizes too big, with a garbage bag pulled over like a rain poncho. A cascade of Mardi Gras beads hung about her neck, and strands of oily black hair drooped out from underneath a floppy gardening hat. One mold-green eye had mascara smeared around it, and sloppy lipstick made her mouth look twice as thick as it really was.

"Hail to thee, Filth, daughter of Contaminate, consort of Disease," Sydney said, backing up and bowing. "You honor us."

Filth spoke with a fake Southern Belle accent belied by a screeching undertone.

"Who has the audacity—!" Her shout cut off into a hacking wheeze as she focused on the men. Once she recovered, she spat at their feet. "Oh. You two. I might have known. Whattya want?"

Sydney and Ben exchanged looks, mutually indignant that the other had such a well-known reputation with the Pantheon.

Filth held out a dirt-encrusted hand, which had a piece of barbed wire twisted around the ring finger. Sydney shuffled forward and pressed his lips to this, careful to not step over the ceremonial border. Blood stained his mouth when he straightened, but he smiled, widening the cuts.

"Beautiful Filth, matron of depravity, it was not my intent to impose myself upon you. This humble servant merely sought to speak with the fledgling member of the Pantheon. We mortals have felt its presence, of which you are no doubt aware. I seek your blessing in rooting out its hiding place before the Cleaners and their ilk discover it first."

Filth stared at Sydney as she scratched herself under a sagging breast. Then she snorted. "Bugger off. It's none of your business."

Sydney flinched and the slightest stammer invaded his voice.

"Mistress, if I've offended ..." A cough. "Perhaps I didn't present my intentions clearly enough. Surely you're aware of the consequences if this unique being is not persuaded to join you as soon as possible."

"What of it? You think we can't handle a little competition?" Another snort flicked mucus onto her lips, which she licked off. "The situation is under control."

Despite being sandwiched between the reptilian servants, Ben thoroughly enjoyed seeing Sydney squirm under Filth's half-mad gaze. Just so long as she didn't turn it his way.

"I ... ah ... don't doubt at your capability," said the mage. "However, knowing the Pantheon's ... er ... hesitancy in acting directly against one of their own number, I thought to offer myself as a willing servant in tracking down the newcomer and convincing it to see things our ... your way."

Filth pulled her lips back into a snarl, showing crooked, yellow teeth. "And so you offer unwilling blood? That which is sullied by Purity's stink? You think we're so easily satisfied?"

Sydney stalked over and shoved Ben down, cracking knees against the floor. His head was yanked back and the sticky blade pressed against his throat. He stared up at Sydney's flared nostrils while the mage spoke through clenched teeth.

"I will give you his still-beating heart if that's what it takes."

Ben grunted. "I ain't gonna get a say in this, am I?"

"And what do you think I'd do with him?" she asked. "Feed him to my kittens? I'd rather see you reach into the hollow of yourself and give me your own black muscle."

Sydney's grip on Ben loosened. "That would rather nullify the point of me living to continue serving you."

"Yeah, well, it's the price I require for the information you seek."

Sydney's fist squeezed around the knife hilt and the blade crumbled away. As he stalked around the circle, the urmoch placed their talons on Ben's shoulders, keeping him kneeling. Ben tried breathing again, one quivering inhalation at a time. He'd been certain the next thing he'd feel was the heat of his own blood spilling down his chest.

Sydney glared at Filth, who watched his pacing with a smug expression. "I do this for the furthering of our Pantheon," he shouted. "What reason would you have to keep me from success? I see in your eyes that you have the answer I need. With this newcomer devoted wholly to Corruption, you'd finally have the imbalance necessary to overthrow Purity once and for all."

Filth's bag lady appearance shredded and flew apart like paper mache, leaving a black hole with the vague shape of a woman. White eyes blinked out from the void. Blue lips puckered and sucked at Ben's mind while gray worms wriggled along its edges. Words pounded like shots from a psychic nail gun.

"You do not command me, fleshling. Remember who bestowed your power upon you in the first place. Your request is as foolish and ignorant as your pathetic attempts to bludgeon your way into my favor. Do not think to summon me again without consequences."

Her human illusion drew back together, hiding the vision that had Ben wanting to surgically remove his stomach so it could never contain food again.

Filth sucked on a crumpled cigarette and toyed with a fish hook that pierced her earlobe. "Was there anything else?" she asked sweetly.

Sydney turned and slammed a fist into a wall. The silver lining flaked away. The urmoch guards flinched and hissed at the mage, their talons retracting for a moment.

In that instant, Ben hopped into a crouch and snatched up the spray paint can. He somersaulted forward, muscles wrenching in the effort. As he came up, he spun and triggered a red stream into the urmochs' unblinking eyes as they lunged for him.

A claw batted the can out of his hand, but their other swipes went wild as they yowled in pain. Sydney stepped in Ben's way, surprise giving over to rage. A black aura flared around his fists.

Ben pivoted and sprinted straight at Filth. A claw raked down his back. It snagged on the last inch of the swipe and dug into a hip as he stumbled over the line of the summoning circle. Filth raised her hands, but he collided with her and sent them both toppling.

With the circle broken, the spell dissolved and released the magical bindings that kept the Petty in the room. She fled back into her realm, and Ben clung tight, taking himself along for the ride.

CHAPTER EIGHTEEN

Dani clawed up out of smothering grogginess. Her eyes felt glued shut, and her arms and legs moved as if someone had strapped fifty pound weights to each joint. With a sucking breath, she regained enough clarity to shake awake. It took three slow blinks before her eyes fully opened. Even then, her surroundings blurred in and out of focus, shadows turned to light, and her depth perception refused to cooperate.

She snatched vague details from her wavering vision. A tiny room, no more than six foot square. White walls. Mirrored ceiling. A small ledge that doubled as her bed. No door. No window. Not even a toilet or sink.

Dani sat up. Then she spent several minutes fighting the nausea that simple motion induced. As her stomach settled from its flips and flops, her thoughts leveled enough for her to make further observations.

On the upside, she hadn't been woken by being kissed, licked, groped, or otherwise forced into contact with anyone else. The room didn't offer any visible sources of contamination. Initial sanitation assessment: promising.

On the downside, her janitorial uniform had been replaced by another white robe, and she was once more barefoot. All of her personal cleaning equipment had been taken as well. Not so much as a dollop of gel to clean her hands.

She scrunched into a corner of the cot and tucked her feet under, reducing exposure as much as possible. On her own, then. Not even Tetris would drop in for moral support, and she couldn't depend on being rescued. And it was her fault.

Face it, Dani. You made this choice. Sure, you felt justified, but you put yourself here. She gritted her teeth. *And you don't have the luxury of moping. If anyone is going to get you out, it has to be you as well.*

Another inspection confirmed the absence of any obvious exits. If she guessed right, the Cleansers would want to keep her subdued until they were ready for whatever came next. So they'd be monitoring her. If she'd woken too early, likely someone would be coming to administer another dose.

She had to get free. Fast.

She reached for her power, trying to summon enough emotional distress to trigger whatever disaster she could. But it felt like groping for greased marbles at the bottom of a tub of oil. The energies slipped away no matter how hard she fought to draw them to the surface.

Whatever they'd drugged her with made it hard to focus. Couldn't keep it together long enough to control the power for more than a few seconds. Even when she did manage to send a few tendrils questing through the room, they found nothing to latch onto. It was as if her cell floated in an elemental void.

Anger pricked her. Everyone wanted to use her for something. They considered her little more than a gun to be pointed at one side or the other. They all thought she could be charmed or bullied into submission. That she was some lost little girl who would cling to the skirts of whoever looked the safest and gave her enough treats to quiet her bawling.

She'd teach them to underestimate her.

She coiled up her power in preparation to unleash as much as she could at once. She'd tear the room down around her if she had to. A room had to be built on earth at some level. Earth meant earthquakes. Or there had to be some water source she could divert into a flood to crack the walls. She'd rather die trying than remain a prisoner.

She bundled every ounce of determination and anger, building her power, burning away the drugged sleepiness. Eyes closed, she took a deep breath and let the power boil out from her.

The energies speared up through the mirrored ceiling. To her inner sight, it looked like a hand wreathed in glowing vines, reaching out with destructive purpose. She envisioned it stretching and taking hold of ...

Nothing. Not a single mote of earth, fire, or otherwise to grasp. The energies flailed and sputtered. Despair resurfaced as the magic started to withdraw.

Something grabbed hold.

Dani gasped and arched upward. The violent contact made her try to yank the extended power back into herself, but it snagged and kept her spine taut. She felt like a worm dangling on a line, with an extra-dimensional fisherman inspecting her. Was this the Cleansers' doing? Part of the ceremony they planned?

As she hung there, twitching, trying to free herself, it started to reel her in. Her body remained in place, but her mind drew closer to the monstrous presence that held her. The enormity of it threatened to overwhelm.

"Whoever you are," she huffed through clenched teeth, "ever think about just saying hello?"

The lines of her room blurred and stretched. Dani dug fingers into her thighs, using the pain to anchor herself.

"Does it always have to come down to a magical willy-waving contest? Because that puts me at a big disadv—"

Her mind collided with the presence. Her senses submerged into darkness. Dani groped for direction, floating in a lightless ocean.

Not total darkness, she realized after a few moments. The subtlest purple flames licked the edges of her vision. Massive shapes teased her sense of dimension, like planets carved out of a black void orbiting her. And lurking in it all, a crouched figure. Its unblinking gaze settled on her.

Swallowing, Dani determined to confront this head-on. She couldn't stop it from happening, so might as well face whoever or whatever had brought her here. She willed herself to move closer and felt some small delight when her disembodied self responded accordingly.

Yet the instant she eased toward the figure, it sprang away. The dark heavens reeled. When the twisted space oriented itself once more, the distance between her and her captor had increased. It remained just beyond her ability to pick out any details aside from a general hunched shape.

She scowled. "Hey, you brought me here. Quit playing coy."

Waves of raw emotion thrummed out from her observer and drilled into her. The intensity of the feelings washed through her bones and left her shaking. *Wariness. Hunger. Longing. Despair. Fear.*

This last one had her do a mental double-take. Did it … he … fear her? How could that be possible, when it possessed such strength?

The emotions faded, leaving her more scattered than before. Why had she been pulled into this place?

"Can you talk?" she asked.

The figure vanished. The moment it did, its presence loomed behind her, close enough for its breath to tremble her hair. Heart pounding, she remained perfectly still. Cold fingers brushed her neck.

"Sydney? If this is you, you've earned yourself several swift kicks with a steel-toed boot."

The fingers withdrew, yet the presence remained. She envisioned herself standing in the middle of a midnight jungle while a lion stalked the edges of shadow.

"Who are you? Are you here to help me?"

Emotional waves slapped against her. *Trapped. Confinement. Alone.*

"Yes," she said, trying to separate her thoughts and emotions from its. "I'm trapped. I need help. To get free."

Desperation. Searching. Hopelessness.

Dani tried to buffer herself against the alien feelings, but they slipped in and infected hers nonetheless. Maybe her situation was hopeless. Everyone had abandoned her. She might as well give up and wait for whatever came. Why keep fighting?

"Please stop," she said, fighting tears. "If you can't help, at least let me talk to someone who can."

A hand shoved her forward. The void stripped away and her awareness slammed back into her body. She jerked, lost her balance, and toppled off the ledge. Her back and head slammed into the floor, while her legs remained caught over the edge. As she groaned and rubbed her head, she glanced at the ceiling. She froze.

The mirrored ceiling had changed. It now showed a familiar pristine office, where a white-suited figure sat behind a desk, paging through endless forms. Destin paused in the middle of his note-taking and cocked his head. He looked up and stared straight at her.

"Ms. Hashelheim?" he asked. "How?"

"Uh ... good question." She struggled for breath, thoughts frazzled from the chaotic brush with the ... person ... thing ... whatever. Words came out bumpy, and she had to think things over twice before making sure they made sense. "Need help."

"Where are you?"

"Someplace. With Cleansers. Trapped."

His shoulders tensed. "Cleansers? Did Benjamin take you there?"

"No. Not him. We were ... tricked. Sydney."

Destin jolted, as if physically shocked—the first overt reaction she'd seen on his part.

"Why did Ben not alert us to Sydney's presence?"

"Did," Dani said. "Francis. Reported."

Destin's eyes glittered. "Tell me everything that's happened since we last met. Leave nothing out."

Haltingly, she told of their encounter with Sydney at the bar. She detailed Stewart's divination, of the new, dual-natured member of the Pantheons. Next came their escape into the sewers and abduction by Sydney. With each detail, Destin's face hardened, until it looked carved from alabaster. Fury flashed in his eyes, and she waited for his pen to snap in his grip.

At the end, however, he said only, "I see. Most disturbing."

Destin stood and circuited his desk. When he returned to his chair, he sat with the poise of one ready to sprint out of the room the moment they finished talking.

"I am sorry, Dani. Ascendant Francis has made an error of judgment in this instance."

"Uh ... thanks?" Not exactly what she needed to hear, as it didn't help her current situation.

Destin scratched notes on a pad. "I need to pin your location down. Are there any landmarks or details you can identify for me? Something seen or heard before they deposited you in this prison?"

Dani scrunched her forehead in thought. "Urmoch," she said after a minute. "Near an urmoch nest."

He frowned. "Unfortunately, those are not as uncommon as we would like. It will narrow it some, but is there anything else?"

A headache grabbed the base of Dani's neck and started squeezing. Dani scowled against this, resisting the urge to close her eyes and slip back to sleep.

"Leader. Named Marcus."

In a flicker of motion, Destin had a folder open in his hands and flipped to a page. "Marcus? Now that's a name—"

Destin's image rippled and his voice silenced. The disturbance increased, chopping up the scene into fragments that melted away. His concerned face flashed before her once more, and his voice wavered in and out.

"Stay with—ani. I—need … know … verything that—"

Her reflection slapped back into place. A second later, the ceiling evaporated into glimmering steam, revealing a level above her cell. Robed Cleansers stood on the edges, staring down at her. Marcus stepped into view, and the white wall he stood atop melted into a series of sloped steps, like a limestone cave formation. Marcus descended this, steam rising from each footstep.

As he entered the room, Dani struggled to her feet and braced against the slab she'd been sleeping on. Once he reached the bottom, Marcus spreads his arms as if expecting a hug.

"All is prepared," he said. "It is time."

She raised a fist for a feeble strike. He caught her arm and pulled her into his embrace. The mint smell from before rose about her as if he'd bathed in it. Just a sniff of it sent her thoughts fluttering into the distance, and she sagged against his chest.

"Rest, sister," he whispered. "What comes next will require all of your strength."

Dani opened her mouth to retort, but drew in another lungful of vapor.

Her consciousness puffed away before she remembered exhaling.

CHAPTER NINETEEN

Ben's mind exploded with incomprehensible shapes. Inverted faces watched him speed by as he held onto the cold knot of power that was Filth. Unearthly winds buffeted him, threatening to scrape the skin from his bones. Whole worlds whipped past, too quickly for him to do anything but sense their immensity before they vanished into the distance.

Then a sudden lurch and tearing sensation, as if he struck a filmy barrier that ripped beneath his weight. Gravity, noise, and sight reintroduced themselves as he tumbled several yards and sprawled flat. Splashing ebbed away while an oily substance dribbled down his collar and up his sleeves and pant legs.

Filth crouched over him, her bag lady facade making him feel like he was a trash bin she wanted to rummage through. Jagged fingernails punctured the rotted flesh of his right arm. He gritted his teeth against the agony of it.

Her corpse-breath huffed in his face. "That ... was ... foolish. I could kill you with a thought for the impertinence."

This close, staring into her eyes was like seeing the spinning blades of a garbage disposal, waiting for him to be shoved in head-first.

"Was gonna be dead here or dead there," he managed. "There was borin' me, so I figured a change of scenery might at least keep things interestin'."

As she studied him, figures moved nearby, slinking through whatever muck Ben lay in. Without moving his head, Ben watched the newcomers from the corners of his eyes. They were feline in general shape, the same way chainsaws were shaped like butter knives. They appeared to have clown masks over their muzzles with pointed ears twitching above painted faces. Slime dripped from elongated paws, and they mewled to each other in a garbled language that teased the edges of comprehension—though he hardly wanted to know what they said.

Filth shoved him down to push herself up. As she moved away, Ben sat up, holding his wounded arm to his stomach. He got his first good look at the realm they'd landed in.

This pocket reality—what he assumed it to be, at least—had been shaped into a facsimile of a homeless camp, with one side bordered by an oil-slick ocean full of flotsam, and the other a crumbling wall that jutted with sewer pipes and rusted grates. Reeking puddles, like the one Ben sprawled in, dotted the ground in between mounds of burning dung heaps, where humanoid forms huddled and shivered together.

Filth's kittens prowled around him. Their paws slurped with each step. Not true cats, he realized with a sour burp. The knees bent in the wrong direction, and the front paws were hands, though with red-stained curling fingernails. Their visages weren't masks but distorted human faces that stretched into various expressions, switching between taut grins, exaggerated frowns, and bared fangs that glistened with green ichor.

Filth hobbled over to the nearest pipe and cupped a hand under the purple flow chugging from it. After lapping up a few swallows, she licked her lips and eyed Ben sidelong. Smirking, she came back over and offered him the full bowl of her palm. Pale worms wriggled in the ooze.

"Thirsty?" she asked.

Her kittens mewled louder, as if they craved the drink she offered.

He patted his paunch. "Got any diet sody-pop? I'm tryin' to watch the weight."

She flung the liquid into his face. As he knuckled a worm off an eyelid, he wondered if having women douse him twice in one day was a sign he needed to work on his etiquetteness. *Naw. Must be a fluke.*

"It's a pity," Filth said, licking her fingers clean. "You once could've put up a decent fight and made my blood simmer. That's something lacking in your world these days—true passion. Even you've lost the old fire. I can see it in your eyes. Gray as ash."

"Mebbe I am a bit chipped and cracked," he said as goop dripped off his chin. "But just 'cause I've gone gray don't mean there ain't a sharp edge or two left."

She gripped his hair and bent his neck back painfully. "Tell me one thing you care about." Once more, her eyes sucked him in, promising death in reward for a false answer.

Ben grunted. "Dani. My apprentice."

Her eyes flashed with black depths. Ben suppressed a shiver. Getting into a staring contest with a Pantheon member was as productive as trying to stop an avalanche with a scolding finger wag.

Filth backed up, and two of her pets flanked her, rubbing against her thighs. They purred as she scratched the folds of their necks, her barbed wire rings gouging flesh that bled green and white. Their too-human faces squeezed and stretched like putty.

"If this girl is so important to you, why did you allow her to be taken from your care?"

"Don't everybody have the occasional bad day at work?" Ben asked. "I'm gonna fix the mess I've made, sure-for-shootin'."

Filth's laughter jabbed his ears like a jagged blade. "You think you're going to escape this place?"

"You kiddin'? Me try to escape after you was so nice to invite me over for some neighborly chit-chat? That'd be downright impolite, don't'cha think?"

"Then how do you intend to return to the world to, as you so eloquently put it, fix your mess?"

Ben forced himself to meet her eyes. "You're gonna let me go."

She bent over double in mirth, clutching her stomach while her kittens nuzzled her, sniffing about as if wondering what strange fit had possessed their mistress. Her cackling went on for a full minute. When she straightened, black tears streaked her cheeks. She wiped at these and sucked the residue from her fingers.

"Oh, you do amuse me, fleshling. Perhaps I'll paint your face and make you my jester to prance and sing for my pleasure. Why, in all the realms, would I let you go?"

"Well, that's what I'm tryin' to figure out."

Her lips curled into a lopsided grin, and Ben's stomach flip-flopped at the lust he saw there.

"Perhaps you do have some spark not yet smothered in those ashes," she said. "Perhaps I should quench it."

"Naw. Wouldn't recommend it."

"And why not?"

"Gimme a few. I'm workin' on that too. Things ain't makin' much sense right now."

Filth shook her head, flinging stringy hair about. "This is such entertainment. However, the moment you cease to make me smile, my pets will feast."

As one, all her kittens swung round to face Ben, faces stretched into demonic snarls. Their purring deepened into growls.

Filth smiled. "So. Tell me more funny things, janitor."

"Funny, eh? I'm bettin' you've heard the one about the chicken crossin' the road. But mebbe there's plenty of other funny business lately." Joints popping, he eased to his knees, and then his feet. As he thought furiously, he kept one eye on Filth, the other on her kittens. Part of his mind had been fiddling with the tangled knot of events, and a few of the snarls loosened as he mentally tugged at them.

"See, while I ain't ever gonna know calculus like Dani does, I got enough marbles rollin' around in this noggin to add things up, so long as I don't gotta count past ten. Then the shoes come off."

Filth's amused look faltered at the poor joke, but Ben blundered on before she could unleash her beasts.

"Funny thing numero uno. Lotsa weird thingamajigs have been poppin' up in the past couple of days, all of 'em split between Purity and Corruption, which ain't ever happened before. Point B: We learn of a new Pantheon member, somehow pullin' double-duty."

He watched Filth's expression, which became more wooden with each word. He sped up.

"And number four: Sydney, your lapdog—"

Filth swiped a hand. "He swears no allegiance to me, nor does he draw a single drop of power from my realm. Such a fawning sycophant."

"All righty. Then he's the bootlickin', butt-kissin' servant of the rest of the Corrupt Pantheon. Whatever his deal, he shows up, ready to plop this new demigod into your lap, and you tell him to stick it where the sun don't shine. You coulda tipped the whole battle in your favor thisaway, but you acted like he'd called you durin' dinner to see if you wanted to sign up for a subscription to Playboy. Almost like you ain't wantin' the new guy to be found."

She crossed her arms beneath her breasts. "And what does it all mean, fleshling?"

Ben let a crazy thought bounce around for a few breaths. If he was wrong, it couldn't worsen his fate at this point. But if he was right …

"While two wrongs ain't gonna make a right, I'd say a buncha impossible facts can sure add up to an impossible sum."

She glared, hands raised to gesture her kittens to the feast.

Ben pointed back at her. "You're its mother."

Filth stared at him, raised hands now shaking. The kittens' growling heightened into a whine. Filth stepped forward until she and Ben stood nose to nose, and the stench of her enveloped him. Her lips twitched, reminding him of the worms that infested the water she'd offered earlier.

Then she collapsed against him and started sobbing.

CHAPTER TWENTY

en staggered beneath the sudden burden of a weeping goddess. He tried to hold her upright, but she weighed far heavier than she looked. He resorted to squatting and then a quick drop onto his butt where he could brace her without throwing his back out.

He patted his pockets. "You want, I might got some tissues."

She curled up like an overgrown child, arms around his neck, legs across his thighs. The kittens sat on their haunches and joined in with howls and screeches that turned Ben's bones to jelly, heightened by relieved trembling. The notion of Filth being a mother sure seemed crazy when he first thought it, but it made some twisted sense. The newcomer was a child, and every child had to come from somewhere, didn't it? While some folks were known to spontaneously combust, there had never been a report of spontaneous conception.

Well, 'cept for that one time …

Filth's oily tears stained his suit, and he prayed they wouldn't eat through the material. He tried patting her back and rocking a bit, a halting lullaby or two, but realized how ridiculous it was. So he sat still and let Filth weep until her sobs turned to breathless hiccups. Her hair pulsed in time with her breaths as words broke through the cries.

"That ... wasn't ... funny..."

Ben cleared his throat as strands of her hair kept knotting around his knuckles. "Ahum. I ain't never been great at this whole consolin' thing."

"Do you know what it's like," she said between sniffles, "to have to stand back and do nothing as your child is hunted down like a wild animal? How scared he must be ..."

"He?"

She raised her face to his, eyes rimmed red, looking ancient and afraid. "I didn't even have time to give him a name. I had to hide him the moment his powers manifested, and even then it wasn't enough, was it? That's why you're here, isn't it?"

"So we're really talkin' 'bout a kid here. A babe in the Pantheon."

"You couldn't have guessed," she said. "You must have known all along. Which means many others know, and he's still in danger. They all want him."

"There's been a lil' news runnin' around, yeah. I was gonna try a summoning on my end, but Sydney beat me to it."

Sighing, Filth pushed away and stood with her back to him. A wave of an arm dissolved the kittens into puddles that soaked into the ground, leaving the surface covered in mossy scum.

"It wouldn't have worked, either way," she said.

Ben rose. "What I don't get is why it ... he mighta targeted Dani or m'self. Seems like lightnin' strikin' the same place twice."

"Oh, that's simple. Your apprentice recently discovered her powers, yes?"

Ben nodded.

"So she's a newborn, similar to my offspring. My guess is the manifestations have happened to those who've most recently come into their abilities. And you," a glance at his decaying arm, "you wield Purity, yet are infected with the Ravishing. Your body contains some traces of each Pantheon and possesses enough dual-affinity to draw his attention. You must understand, he is like us," she drew her hands to her chest, indicating the rest of the Petties. "Powerful. An incarnation of the battle between Purity and

Corruption. Yet he is alone. Afraid. Reacting through pure instinct. I'd thought him contained enough to avoid detection, but he has somehow pushed past the barriers I erected, and is reaching for anything that might provide an anchor, or lashing out at perceived threats."

"Er … hope this ain't too much me pryin' into business that ain't my own, but … how'd he pop into existence, anyhoo?"

"I birthed him."

"A'ight, that sounds way too simple, what with you all being … what's the word? Multi-differential beings?"

"Multi-dimensional."

He snapped his fingers. "Right. That. So, by birthin', are we talkin' like a magical photocopy of yourself? Cuttin' off an arm and lettin' it grow into its own self? Doesn't some kinda sea creature pull that trick?"

She mimed a rounded tummy. "I conceived him. I and another mingled essences much as you fleshlings do."

"You can make more of yourselves?"

"Of course." Her eyes rolled. "Where do you think we Petties came from? You think we just popped out of the aether? We are the Primals' spawn. Their children."

Ben found himself chewing on his thumb, recalled what his hands had been recently slimed with, and yanked it out.

"Then I ain't quite gettin' it," he said after a bit of spitting. "If you can add to your Pantheon just by a little supernatural hokey-pokey, why ain't the realms stuffed full of godling wannabes?"

"The Primals forbid it. A ban was enacted and enforced by the leaders of both Pantheons. Perhaps the one time they've ever worked in concert."

Ben's brow furrowed. "Why? I figure it'd be the easiest way to get the upper hand over each other."

"That's just it. The Primals have come to love the balance too much. The constant war." Her body swelled as she spoke, eyes flashing black, fingers curling into claws. "The endless supply of supplicants and devotees you fleshlings provide. It has defined them for so long that they've forgotten what it means to conquer. To truly subjugate the world." She shrank back to normal and sighed. "It's also a matter of power distribution. With each birth, each addition to the Pantheon, the realms fracture further. Power is divided and effort must be turned inward simply to keep the newborns from causing too much chaos until they are established."

He squinted an eye at her. "So you get it on with your own siblings? That just ain't right."

"We are not human, janitor. There is no such thing as blood relations here." Filth fluttered her fingers. "But those activities are no longer allowed. The last time any offspring joined the Pantheons was in 1346, when Plague was incarnated. Tempestuous times."

It surprised Ben when he knew what she referred to. He'd never paid much attention to his history lessons, but the date stuck out nonetheless.

"The Black Death."

"Mm."

"But this ain't just a new Corrupt Petty we're talkin' about. It's Pure *and* Corrupt. Which means you ..." He stuttered as his guts clenched. Another impossible addition got tossed into the insane lump sum. "Oh, cleanse my colon. You got it on with a Pure Petty, didn't you? You pulled a regular Romeo and Juliet, but without the whole poison and dyin' part."

Filth scowled and tugged at her snarled hair. "It was unintended. A mistake. Neither of us thought it possible."

"You're tellin' me you had unprotected supernatural sex?"

"Shut up."

Shaking his head, he took a deep breath, then regretted it as it provided a deep whiff of this realm's miasma of rotten odors, which would be spoiling his appetite for days to come.

"Who's the proud daddy-o?" he asked.

"I removed that knowledge from myself. It was a most ... disturbing coupling."

"Gotta say, I ain't believin' you let yourself forget that juicy tidbit."

"I don't care what you believe."

They glared at each other for a few seconds, until Filth surprised Ben by averting her eyes first.

"What now?" he asked.

"Now we decide what part you'll play in this."

Ben crossed his arms and planted his feet. "Naw. Now you gotta decide whether you want my help or not. 'Cause if you do, you're gonna help me get Dani back first."

Wrinkles gouged her face. "I've shown you a large mercy by not reducing you to a slopping heap. You already owe me much. Don't be fooled into thinking you're entitled to make demands."

"I ain't gonna do this without Dani. She needs me. And I need her." Seeing the stubborn set of Filth's chin, he held out both hands, trying to appeal to her mothering side. "Look, we've both got a kid out there about to get steamrolled by people who hardly have their best interests in mind. I ain't gonna be able to do this without her help, and you can't do this without mine."

Filth held unnaturally still, as if her body had been put on standby while her mind went into processing mode. Finally, she reached behind her back and drew his mop and spray bottle out from nowhere.

"Carl," Ben cried, overjoyed to see his partner unharmed. "They been givin' you the VIP treatment?"

Carl sloshed in the bottle and sprayed Filth's way.

"Yeah, well, don't forget to leave a tip."

Filth handed his items over, but kept her grip on them, forcing him to look at her. "I'll send you back to your apprentice," she said. "But you must swear you'll do everything you can to keep my child safe."

"I gotta ask, why me?" Ben asked. "I mean, c'mon. You could have your pick of servants the world over."

Her hungry smile returned. "Consider me a secret admirer of your past work. Plus, you are one of few who don't compare us to gods. Not even in the core of yourself. We're just very powerful bosses in a metaphysical office complex. I respect a man who doesn't bow, no matter how many heels press on his back."

"Should I think differently?" He waved away her glare. "Fine. I'll do it, even if I can't imagine how right now. It'd help if I knew how to actually find it … him."

She released his tools to rub her temples. "I removed that knowledge from myself as well. Too much risk. Too many seeking. I am being summoned by a dozen others at this very moment, wishing to have my blessing in the hunt. I'm ignoring them, of course."

"Guess we do it the hard way. I'll figure something out."

Filth closed her eyes for a moment. Then a gasp escaped her. "Janitor, she's much closer to the flames than I anticipated."

That stiffened his spine. "Who? Dani?"

She nodded. "You must hurry. If they succeed in the purging ceremony, it will drive her mad. The Cleansers have never had someone of her power in their grasp before. Not even they realize what she'll unleash should she fall under their sway. The air itself could catch fire across the globe."

"I kinda think that's what they've been hopin' for."

Her eyes opened, having lost all the humanity that once sparked within them. Her voice also fell flat, as if part of herself had departed.

"You will need strength to oppose them all. Are you prepared to accept the cost this task will demand from you?"

"If you haven't noticed, lady, we ain't playin' for the same team. I don't get my power from you."

"Part of you knows our touch. I shall use it."

"Hey, now, I ain't never said you could—"

Her hand clamped onto his infected arm. Icy pain shot up it. A hiss exploded past his lips as her barbed rings carved into the rotting skin, drawing dark blood.

"There is one who I sense draws closest to exposing my child," she said. "Stay close to him, and you might yet find the chance to do as you've promised."

"Who? Sydney?"

A shake of her head. "Destin."

The puddle they stood in swirled up and into a waterspout with them at the center. The foul waters of the realm crashed onto his head and swept him away.

CHAPTER TWENTY-ONE

Ben splashed down onto a hard surface. His nose mashed against stone, and sharp pain jabbed into his side, making him fear a few cracked ribs. He lay there panting, bruised all over from the buffeting current that had washed him here. Normally, he did the flushing. *Not as fun to be on the flipside, no sirree.*

He rolled onto his back and waited until the ache in his side eased. A light touch confirmed his nose wasn't broken; this small relief inspired him to sit up and get his bearings.

He'd arrived in one of the sterile corridors of the Cleanser compound. Silver doors lined the hall. There were no sounds other than water dripping from his clothes and hair. His mop and spray bottle lay a few feet away. Filth had vanished, and he guessed she remained in her realm, waiting to see the results of her gamble.

Groaning, he got to his feet and retrieved his tools. The residue of Filth's realm clung to him, making him squish and squelch. However, as he stood gathering his wits, the oily water drained off him and his suit and gathered into a puddle around his feet. This separated into rivulets that snaked away into the nearest cracks in the stone and grates.

A look at his bared right arm didn't reassure him. The puncture wounds from Filth's nails and rings remained. They oozed and puckered with a life of their own. He felt no pain for the first time in years, but that didn't comfort him either. Pain let him know something was wrong, and the absence of it made him worry and wonder what Filth had done to him before she booted him back to this reality.

Gurgling drew his attention to the water sprite within the bottle. He lifted it and watched as the water formed hollow geometric shapes, flowing from inverted triangles to dizzying Celtic knots between blinks.

"Rough ride, eh, buddy?"

Carl slapped the sides of the bottle. Each impact pinged Ben's fingers in reprimand.

"Missed you too," he said. "But ain't you been moanin' about needin' a vacation for a while?"

A whirlpool of denial collapsed into another sullen gurgle. Ben smiled despite the grim circumstances. Then Carl flowed through another barrage of splashes.

Ben grunted. "I'm worried about her too. Ready to go kick some fire-lickin' butt?"

An affirmative spritz tickled his palm. He sighed and looked up and down the hall.

"Problem is, we're back where I started, no more knowin' where to go than before." He looked at the ceiling. "Fat lotta help this is, Filth, you ol' witch. Coulda at last stuck me back—"

The door nearest to him opened, and a Cleanser in a white robe strode out. He stumbled and stared at Ben with wide eyes.

Ben rushed and shoved him back into the room, an arm against the man's thin throat. A glimpse showed the room bare of everything but the necessities—washbasin, wooden slab for a bed, a locker for what few personal belongings the Cleansers allowed themselves.

He pinned the Cleanser against the wall. A burning aura flickered around him, but he rapped the man's head against the stone and the flames puffed away.

A second look revealed his hostage was little more than a boy. A fresh recruit. Probably one of the street kids they lured in with promises of food and shelter, and then brainwashed into being preachers of their fiery gospel.

Ben thrust his grizzled face at the boy's. "Lookee here. You know who I am?"

Brown eyes glistened with barely contained tears. The boy trembled as he nodded.

"Good. Then you know I make geezers sittin' on their porches with shotguns look like cuddly kittens. Now, I'm gonna ask you a simple question. If you ain't inclined to answer honest-like ..." he squeezed the trigger of the spray bottle. Water flowed out into a six inch blade that shimmered along its razor edge. "This is Carl. He don't like bein' lied to. The first lie gets an eye cut out. The second'll cost you a few jiggly bits. We'll keep going down the list until we get to your tongue, which we're gonna wash out with lots and lotsa soap before dicin' it up into chewy nibbles. Comprendify?"

A fervent nod.

"Where've they taken Dani? My apprentice. The Catalyst."

"She ..." The boy licked dry lips and rasped, his throat bumping under Ben's hand. "Taken to t-the womb. Holy rebirth."

"Where's that?"

The boy rambled off a series of directions through the halls. Ben had him repeat it three times, making sure he said the same thing each go.

"Thank ya kindly," he said, after deciding the boy spoke true. "Word to the wise. These people are real violent whackjobs. Get outta here while you have a choice, eh?"

Another crack of skull to stone sent the boy sliding into a heap. Ben scowled and looked around for anything that might help. Slipping into a white robe wouldn't provide any useful disguise unless he shaved bald. And any costume would only get him so close. Best to take a frontal assault and hope the element of surprise lasted long enough.

But Dani's purging ceremony would be heavily attended, likely by some of the most powerful Cleansers in the compound. Before the Ravishing, he might've been able to subdue them all, but now ... working alone ... he didn't feel so confident.

His gaze went to the washbasin, and the plain faucet curving over it. He brought the spray bottle up to eye level.

"Buddy? We gotta talk."

• • •

Dani's eyes opened in another series of heavy blinks. She was being jostled, yet felt as if she floated along, arms dangling in midair. As the numbness withdrew and her blurred vision cleared, she realized she lay in Marcus' arms as he carried her down a long, torch-lit hall. Granite columns supported an arched ceiling, with swaths of red and orange light sweeping aside the shadows.

She tried to roll out of his hold. Even though sleeves covered his arms, who knew how long it'd been since he'd washed his robe? And he breathed heavily with each step, huffing over her face as he exhaled. It was enough to get her stomach roiling again.

They hadn't restrained her in any way, but her body refused to respond to her brain's commands to escape. She might as well have been a hay-filled scarecrow.

She stared past Marcus' chin at the ceiling, which had been painted with saintly figures, reminiscent of the Sistine Chapel. Except here, the people writhed in fiery torment—or perhaps they danced. Blue skies were clouded with ash and rivers of flame swept along the landscape. Like a church devoted to bringing about the fiery apocalypse the street-corner prophets always warned about. One that wanted to plunge its followers into Hell, rather than rescue them from it.

After mustering up the scraps of her strength, she forced a single word out, paper-thin.

"Where ..."

Marcus kept his eyes forward, looking peaceful, though Dani sensed excitement in the way his jaw kept flexing and the tensing of his arms. In any other situation, he might have been handsome, a reassuring presence. Now he trod along with the inevitable gait of one carrying a garbage bag to the curb.

"This is the hall of rebirth," he said in a hushed voice. "Here, your old life will be burned away, allowing your true self to rise from the ashes and claim the glory you are meant to have."

"Don't ... want ... glory, you ... idiot..."

His thick forehead rumpled. "You'd rather remain the enslaved minion of a feeble old janitor?"

She tried to respond, but he drew her closer, pressing her mouth against his broad chest.

"You will see. You will be our goddess, and bless us."

"Doubt ... that ..."

A thrumming sensation crept into Dani's awareness. Not so much a sound, but a vibration infusing everything around her, even the Cleanser who carried her along. The robe stuck to her sweaty body in the heat of the chapel. The temperature increased with each step Marcus took, as did the thrumming until she could barely think past the vibrations.

Marcus swung her around, so she got her first look at her destination. The end of the chapel was taken up by an enormous metal wall. Pipes jutted from this and fed into the ceiling. Near the ground, numerous levers, wheels, and dials covered the metal barrier.

Other Cleansers stood around a long marble slab which jutted up against the center of the gleaming wall. A wheeled tray rested on the slab, set into tracks.

Dani's breaths quickened. The tray looked large enough for someone to lie down on.

A female Cleanser pulled a lever and a door rattled upward at the far end of the slab, revealing the machine's interior. A ball of flame roared out. Dani tried to cringe back, but her traitorous body wouldn't even twitch in self-preservation. None of the others flinched as the fiery spout receded, revealing the hellscape within what she now recognized as an enormous furnace.

"No ..." Her denial puffed away.

Marcus stopped beside the trolley and laid her upon it. The others stepped up on either side and crossed her arms over her chest, straightened her legs, and fanned her hair out, as if preparing her for a burial ritual.

In some sense, Dani realized, they were. Her thoughts and heart raced, the two things not numbed by the soporific. They wanted a fire goddess. They wanted her to become like them, except exponentially more powerful. She would be shoved into the furnace, forced to be transformed into whatever vengeful creature they craved to worship.

Her tears dried the instant they leaked free.

If not, she would be burned alive.

•   •   •

Ben crouched behind a pillar at the end of the hall, trying to ignore his achy knees. As feared, he knew these Cleansers, especially Marcus. All of them were infamous for acts of arson the world over, often blamed on terrorist groups or ecological activists. They'd created plenty of messes the Cleaners had been brought in to mop up.

Wincing, he pressed a hand to his stomach, swollen near to bursting.

The muscled leader of the cult smoothed Dani's hair and bent to whisper something in her ear, like a father comforting a frightened child. Ben bristled, seeing her weak movements which subsided a second later. Drugged, most likely. He couldn't believe she'd go along willingly with this madness. Of course, his hiding the Ravishing from her hadn't helped. If he'd told her from the start, maybe none of this would've happened. She might not have felt betrayed and gone with Sydney. He hoped she could forgive him, but for that to happen, she needed to be rescued first.

Ben swallowed against the increasing urge to vomit. *Not yet. Hold it together, bucko. Almost time.* He took a steadying breath, fully believing he might be racing to his death. But he'd made a promise.

"Ready?" he asked, tapping the spray bottle at his hip.

Carl's responding splish-splash didn't instill him with the bravado he craved. His mop lay by his feet, discarded for this fight in exchange for another weapon.

Squeaking jerked his attention back to the ceremony. A Cleanser turned one of the wheels along the furnace wall. One of the pipes shuddered as fuel swept through it, feeding the flames so they roared higher. Renewed heat washed out the open door, strong enough for Ben to feel it where he squatted.

There were no prayers. No chanting or calling upon the Pantheon. The Cleansers were, if anything, efficient. Realizing the moment had come, Ben rose and charged toward the gathering just as they pushed Dani into the furnace.

"No!"

His shout was drowned out as the door slammed shut behind her.

While the rest of the Cleansers stared at the furnace, Marcus looked Ben's way. With an impassive expression, he gestured to the others. The Cleansers turned as one. Their fiery auras erupted into being and burning lances soared from upraised hands straight for him.

CHAPTER
TWENTY-TWO

Dani tried to scream, but the heat sucked the air from her lungs. Amazingly, she felt no pain. She realized a small part of her had clung to the hope of being rescued up to this moment—the fantasy that Ben might come charging in and vanquish her captors. That she'd wake up from this nightmare, clutching her pillow in her dorm room.

The furnace door clamped shut behind her. The tray reverberated.

It took her several moments to register the lack of searing pain. The heat remained, but as a distant presence, licking around the edges rather than consuming her.

The numbness suppressing her sizzled into nothing. Dani stood and hugged herself in confusion. The tray should be blistering her feet. The crackling air should've melted her skin. Thorns of fire curled and thrust, but didn't pierce her.

The furnace walls remained unseen through the firestorm raging all around. Dani turned in a circle, afraid to move lest she nullify whatever spell kept her safe.

All right. So, think like a janitor. A bucket of water might be a good start in dousing this inferno, but that'd kind of be trying to put out a volcano by spitting on it.

Her train of thought puffed away like smoke as a figure stepped forward. At first, the newcomer appeared like a mannequin set on fire. Its featureless face reminded Dani of the dust devil from the mall bathrooms. As it approached, however, it reshaped until, when it stopped half an arm's reach away, she faced herself mirrored in blistering red, orange, and white.

The fire-Dani smiled, its teeth and eyes blue flames. Then it recoiled, and its light dimmed slightly. Words were branded into Dani's thoughts.

Oh, god. You're *the one they want me to manifest through? You've got to be fucking kidding.*

Dani's eyes narrowed. How come this copycat got to swear when she didn't? Not fair in the slightest.

"Who are you?" she asked.

Who are you?

"Dani."

Then I'm Dani.

Dani backed up. "No! I'm me! You're some kind of elemental ... thing. A monster."

It stalked forward, footprints glowing. *Is that so? Let's compare notes. Here I am, born of Pure fire, free from all the trappings of decay. And there you are, sweaty, stinking, full of mucus and blood and shit. A disgusting pile of flesh infested with who knows what sort of rot.*

"Hey! There's nothing wrong with my flesh."

The creature swept its hair over one shoulder in an uncomfortably familiar gesture. *Please. You humans are little more than sentient mold. I mean, look at you. You're bags of mud on two legs. You even have pores. Ugh.* It crossed its arms and sulked. *This is not what I had in mind.*

"What are you?" she asked, fascinated despite herself.

A higher order of life, it said. *I've tried for so long to keep away from your mucky little realm. To keep your grubby fingers off my essence. And the one time I poke my head up to take a look, see where I end up? Getting bonded to one of* you. It shuddered. *Fuck. Just the thought makes me want to take a long lava bath.*

Dani shifted toward the grate. "So you don't want me? That's cool. I'll just be going."

A wall of flame whisked up and blocked off that path.

Now, I didn't say that, did I?

The power emanating from the creature swept over Dani, and cold sweat prickled despite the furnace's blaze. She tried to reach for her power, to summon a monsoon or earthquake and banish the manifestation. But the firestorm engulfed her senses, blocking out any other elements.

The alter-Dani's smile turned pitying. *The sad fact is we're both stuck with this arrangement. Might as well make it easy on each other. You be a good little fleshbag, let me take control, and I'll keep things neat and tidy. I'll cleanse us, inside and out. What do you say?*

Dani looked around, wondering how a brightness that rivaled the core of Sun didn't blind her. It would be dishonest to say some teensy part of her didn't want to jump at the offer. To fuse with a being of pure fire? To be rid of all filth and freed from the constant struggle for sanitation? Why not?

But as she considered it, the offer became far less appealing. This wasn't life. This was sterility. This was destruction. She'd be giving up too much of herself in exchange for indulging in a single facet of her personality. It wouldn't be freedom, but just another sort of prison—one she'd have even less control over.

Fists clenched, Dani matched glares with herself. "No. I don't want this."

Are you shitting me? I can give you the life you've always wanted. You'll never have to worry about being contaminated by your lesser nature.

"Lesser?" A snap of flame matched her laugh. "If I'm such a lesser creature, how come you're trapped in here with me? You're just as much a slave as they want me to be."

Her fiery self waved a hand, molten globs dribbling from the fingertips. *The Cleansers are a passing fancy. Perhaps they hold the upper hand for now, but even they won't be able to control us for long.*

"And in the meantime, they'll use us to get rid of anything and anyone who stands in their way."

Don't cling to such a transient reality. The other's face melted into a sneer. *Fire is the fate of all life. The sun burns to sustain this world, but eventually all will be consumed, melted away like so much dross so the true beauty can emerge. The longer you fight it, the more painful the purification is. I'm giving you the chance to go along willingly.* It crossed its arms again.

Trust me, I won't enjoy the process any more than you.

Dani dropped her eyes as the hem of her white robe began to char. The heat had risen subtly, parching her throat, tightening the skin on her arms and face. Panic fluttered in her chest, but she stamped it down. She would fight this until the last ember of her sanity snuffed out.

Her answer croaked out.

"No."

Then, as your mentor might say, this ain't gonna be pleasant, princess.

Her mirrored self lunged. Dani stumbled back, but slammed against the metal furnace wall. She smelled burning hair, and her vision filled with the blue flickers of her twin's eyes.

White-hot lips pressed against hers. In shock, her mouth opened and the flames poured in. The creature shot a final thought her way as it burrowed deep.

Oh, ick.

●　　●　　●

Ben surrendered to the pressure building inside him. With a choking noise, water spewed from his mouth. It spurted out a few inches, then wrapped backward and around his head. His vision blurred for a second as water gushed up his throat, into the air, and then down his body.

In moments, Carl's kin, drunk straight from the spout, coated him from head to toe. The liquid barrier flowed with his motions, covering every inch, yet allowing breaths. Better than Kevlar when it came to janitorial body armor.

Ben braced himself as his vision cleared enough to see the incoming flames. But the water armor turned aside the burning spears like toothpicks chucked at a brick wall.

He barreled into the nearest Cleanser, cracked a knee into the man's crotch, then trampled over him and rammed a shoulder into the next's sternum. He hoped the loud crackle came from his opponent's chest and not his own joints.

Burning hands grabbed his arms. He planted a foot and threw himself to one knee, yanking his attackers down and off balance. As they stumbled, he rose. Water balled around his fists, forming liquid maces which he slammed under their chins. They flew backward, senseless.

A woman stepped into his way, holding a metal staff in both hands. She grinned as the metal became a bar of fire.

Ben snapped a hand out. A portion of living water flung across and slapped onto her face. The Cleanser dropped to their knees, scrabbling at the smothering liquid mask. The staff rolled away, extinguished once it left her grasp.

He spun and eyed his remaining opponents. Two Cleansers remained standing, the youngest-looking of the group. They stepped back. Their auras extinguished.

A scream shook the air.

Dani.

Ben dove for the lever to reopen the furnace. His hands steamed as he gripped it, and the encasing water elementals squirmed in pain. Ben grunted in sympathy. The sprites couldn't be destroyed so easily, but they could evaporate and be sent floating into the atmosphere until they regained enough strength to re-condense. Too long within the furnace or subjected to the Cleansers' attacks, and he'd be exposed.

"Just a little longer," he promised. "Drinks for all after this, I swear."

He yanked on the lever, but it had been locked into position. As he searched frantically for a way to release it, a flicker of white warned him too late.

The punch sent him staggering. Ben groaned and worked his throbbing jaw. The bitter flavor of blood infused his mouth. When he spat, a yellowed tooth hit the floor. One step closer to dentures.

Marcus advanced on the janitor, fists wreathed in flame. "This is a holy place. Your sin has no place here."

Ben threw a wad of water at the man. Marcus slapped it out of the air, turning it to vapor. The Cleanser surged forward, grabbed his throat to shove him against a pillar. The water armor hardened under his touch to keep Ben from being choked, but it couldn't repel the attack.

Ben's brief hope dimmed as he looked over the man's broad shoulders and saw a dozen more Cleansers race into the hall. The alarm had been raised. His window of opportunity had closed. He'd be kickin' the metaphorical bucket, soon enough.

Sorry, princess. I tried.

In the other direction, holes burned through the furnace wall, red-hot on the edges, flame clawing the openings. The roar of the furnace thundered to new heights. Metal slag poured down in gray rivers that scorched the white marble.

Marcus gazed, looking peaceful despite the chaos raging to break free. "She comes," he whispered.

Ben's infected arm raised of its own accord. The watery gauntlet receded, baring his hand. Jagged needles broke through his fingers and pierced Marcus's throat and face. The Cleanser gagged as Ben's arm pulsed, feeding into the other man's flesh.

Dismayed by the Corruption pouring from him, Ben tried to pull away but the limb no longer responded to his control. It continued pumping toxins into Marcus as the man's grip weakened until he fell to the floor, spasming.

Ben stood stunned. The Cleanser smiled in bliss, despite the black veins etching his body.

"You are too late," he said. "Our goddess is born."

He shuddered once more before his eyes glazed. Even in death, his skin writhed as the Corruption ate through him.

Cleansers ringed Ben, looking furious and horrified, while the furnace continued to melt from the inside out. He shifted from side to side, trying to spot a chink in their barricade. As his arms and legs trembled, he reconsidered the wisdom of leaving his mop behind. Of course, if they saw him using it as a crutch, they might attack faster.

Another group surged into the hall. Ben feared even more Cleansers—but the commotion resolved into Francis and two dozen Ascendants. Their Pure auras repelled the smoke billowing through the chapel.

The fire-worshippers turned to face the new threat. Voices rose as the Cleaners spread out in teams of threes and twos, weaving through the pillars to attack on all sides.

The Cleansers scattered to meet this new threat, leaving a lone girl to face Ben. He glowered at her, noting her pale face and trembling lips. When he feinted a grab, she shrieked and bolted.

Ben hurried back to the lever and started punching and flipping every dial and switch around it. When he hit the tenth button along a row, a clunk indicated an inner clamp had been released. He grabbed the lever and shoved it down. The door ground open.

Hissing drew his eyes up as an enormous slab of metal fall away from the wall and tumbled toward him. It plummeted, while his own sense of time slowed to let him contemplate his demise. Even if he dove, his legs would be crushed beneath the debris.

Someone grabbed him from behind and a white aura surrounded them both. Molten fragments spattered against the aura and dropped away into steaming clumps.

Ben turned to see Francis step back, wiping his hands as if sullied by touching the janitor. He glanced at Ben's exposed arm, finger-needles dripping venom. Francis scowled, but pointed at the furnace door.

"Go! Get her out!"

Ben raced for the opening. The watery armor quivered as the heat soared with each step, but he pressed on. His knees popped as he leapt onto the marble slab. Icy pain knifed up his thighs, but he kept his balance and ducked his head to enter.

A dragon's blast of fire shot out of the opening and flung him back to the floor. His liquid armor absorbed much of the blow, but he still lay stunned.

He raised his head as Dani emerged, striding forward like the Queen of Hell.

CHAPTER
TWENTY-THREE

ani's red hair had burned away, replaced by tongues of fire that settled on her brow like a crown. Curtains of flame curled around her body, replacing the white robe she'd worn.

Much of the fighting stopped at her appearance. The Cleansers abased themselves. Francis' team froze in their positions, while the lead Ascendant glared at Dani as if she were a mustard stain on a favorite tie.

She stepped off the marble slab, leaving footprints charred into the stone. She moved with a royal grace, hips swaying, head erect.

Ben's attack on the Cleansers had wearied him to the core, and the liquid armor had gone bubble-thin. His joints clamored for relief as he stood and stared at his apprentice.

"Dani?"

"Hello, Ben." An echo overlaid her voice and each word flashed light in her mouth, as if she held a glowing coal on her tongue. *"What do you think of your princess now?"* She spun around, like a girl showing off her ballet tutu.

Ben eased closer. "I'm thinkin' you oughta take a few deep breaths, kiddo. The Cleansers don't gotcha anymore. You ain't in danger." Trying to make it a comforting gesture, he reached out with his water-covered hand. Her eyes lit like miniature torches, and he jerked back as the hair singed off the back of his hands.

His Corrupted arm rose in disembodied self-defense. Ben roared as her hand clamped around that arm. The flesh sizzled, and he dropped to his knees, gasping.

"Dani," he spat about between waves of pain, "this ain't you."

Her fingers tightened. The stink of scorched skin filled his nostrils.

"Oh, it is, Ben. My true self."

She put a foot to his chest and kicked, which skidded him back several yards. He curled up around his throbbing arm, where a black handprint scarred him.

As he recovered, Francis ran up behind Dani, face set, aura bright. Ben thrust his good arm out.

"Hold on a sec—!"

Dani glanced over her shoulder and made a bored gesture. The Ascendant cried out as flames engulfed him. He spun through the air and slapped to the floor, white suit marred by ashen streaks. He tried to rise, but collapsed, wheezing.

Ben got to his feet again, hands on his knees. "You don't wanna hurt these folks."

Her eyes blazed at him. *"Why not? They've stripped me of everything I had. Denied me any choice except to be a good girl and do as I'm told."* Her chin tilted up. *"Why do you heel to their whistle, Ben? Is it because you've lost all other purpose in life? Because you're too afraid to stop begging for whatever handouts they toss your way?"*

Motion from the corner of Ben's eyes told him the scrub-team was positioning itself to advance from all sides. He had to keep her distracted.

He held his arms out, exposing himself to any further attacks. "I'm with them 'cause … 'cause I'm dyin'. This …" He raised his infected arm, wincing as the skin split along the elbow joint. "The Ravishing's gonna kill me in a year. Two if I'm lucky—not that anyone would call that luck, eh? I keep workin' for the Cleaners 'cause I figured it gave me the best chance of figurin' out what happened to my wife. Maybe find a way to make … what's the word? Amenities for what I let happen."

Her eyes narrowed into molten slits. *"You mean amends."*

He brushed his forefinger and thumb together, too tired to make them snap. "That's the one. Thank ya."

The glow in her eyes dimmed, and her voice lost its rasp as she trembled. "Ben ... please ... help me ..."

He reached for her again, but then shielded his face as her power flared again. She dropped to her knees, face pressed to palms as waves of heat rolled off her.

"Get away from me! All of you, just leave me alone!"

"What are you waiting for, Benjamin?" Francis' shout cut through the smoky hall. "Restrain her."

Ben's right arm burned, both from her touch and the Corruption within it. A single scratch would be enough. As it did with him, the Ravishing would subdue her power, making her manageable—according to the Board's idea of management. It might even work if her power hadn't already escalated too far.

Dani punched the floor. Stone cracked beneath the blow.

"Let me go," she cried, though Ben sensed she didn't shout it at any of them. "I'm me. I control this." A shudder passed through her, and she regained some of her earlier poise. *"I'll torch you all. You're filth! You're nothing. Nothing!"*

He clenched his hand, snapping off the brittle needles. "You got this. I bet my bucket on it."

Her responding sob made him want to rush in and hug her tight, but the heat kept him at bay. That's when Francis signaled the teams, and the Ascendants closed in.

Dani reared up, arms raised, hands clutching. *"I can hear your heartbeats! I can feel your breaths. I can taste your ******* footsteps! You fleshbags disgust me."*

Miniature volcanoes erupted through the floor and surrounded her and Ben. Lava spouted through the buckled marble, cutting off the encroaching Cleaners. Cries echoed as the mounds grew twice as high as Ben.

He dropped to the floor beside her, as close as he could bear without frying his face off. Fiery missiles soared overhead, and the two of them knelt within the ring of fire as the earth shook. Ben cupped his hands around his mouth and shouted.

"You gotta let it go. I promise everythin's gonna be all right. I'll tell you everythin'. No more secrets, or I'll eat my mop."

Molten tears streaked her face as she looked to him. Her mouth moved, the words too quiet for him to hear, but he read her lips well enough.

I'm afraid.

He smiled sadly as he mouthed back. *Yeah. Me too.*

Her eyes squeezed shut. The cloaking fires burned all the brighter, as if resisting her attempts to extinguish them. She slammed her fists to the floor over and over, striking out at an unseen target.

The flames turned white and blue, too bright for him to look at directly. The rest of his water armor evaporated, and he huddled as the heat threatened to turn him into a side of bacon.

As if pinched out by a giant forefinger and thumb, the flames vanished. As they did, the cauldron of fire pouring from the furnace subsided and the miniature volcanoes stopped chugging lava. The heat seeped away unnaturally fast, leaving black rock, pumice trails, and ash drifting from the ceiling. Blessed silence and coolness settled over the room.

Shouts started up around what was left of the hall. Ascendants scrambled over the tiny mountain range she'd conjured. As they did, Ben and Dani lay there, too weak to do anything other than stare at each other. Her arms covered her body as best they could, as the banishment of the fire hadn't returned her white robe. But Ben was too old and too exhausted for her nakedness to make him even slightly uncomfortable.

She managed a lopsided smile. "I did it."

His chuckle split his cracked and burnt lips. "That you did. Proud of you."

"Ben … I'm sorry …"

"Aw, shucks. Ain't nothin' to be ashamed of. We all gotta let ourselves throw a temper tantrum or two. You shoulda been there when I hit puberty."

She propped up on an elbow. "Did you really mean it? About telling me everything?"

"Sure for shootin'. Let's start off with somethin' that's gonna work up a tizzy. I ain't really—"

A black garbage bag snapped down over Dani's head. She cried out and started to struggle, but a trio of Ascendants strapped her hands behind her back and zip-tied her wrists together. She writhed on the floor, screams muffled.

Ben shouted and lurched up to help her, but arms hooked around his elbows and a knee jammed into the small of his back and pinned him in place.

CHAPTER
TWENTY-FOUR

Dani's feeble kicks stopped as her panicked adrenaline rush drained away. Her breathing was loud in her ears, and the bag stuck to her sweat, smelling of plastic.

While blind, at least she didn't suffocate. Every time she drew an unsteady breath, fresh air swirled into the bag and then whisked away with her exhalation. A magical ventilation system? More Cleaner tricks, she guessed. But a garbage bag? They were treating her like trash. Like Scum.

"Lemme go! You idiots. She controlled it. It's over. There's gotta be hundreds of Cleansers runnin' around here. Get on them and stop hasslin' us."

Ben's distant voice was punctuated by scuffling. What were they doing to him?

Her captors dragged her upright and marched her over the barrier she'd erected. The ruptured stone cut her feet, and she stumbled. They lifted and carried her along like a bundle of soggy newspaper. Ben coughed and groaned beside her, and she wondered how badly the old janitor had been hurt.

When they halted, she sensed a crowd of people around them, and cringed. She stood naked and bound, unable to even cover herself. The shame burned almost as hot as the power she'd wielded. Words hissed inside her, sounding like water thrown on live coals.

You see? This is how your life will always be. Leashed like a bitch trained to beg for her treats.

Dani scowled inside the bag and shoved down on the rising presence. *You won't control me again. And cut out the cursing. If I can't, then you get to zip it.*

Laughter flared deep in her mind, but the voice didn't return.

"Is she secured?"

Francis' footsteps clicked across the stones as he approached. The Ascendant holding her right arm answered.

"Yes, sir. Completely neutralized."

Ben spoke on her right. "Francis! Whatcha think you're doin'? You gone a few kicks short of a can-can?"

"This is procedure, Janitor Benjamin. I'm cleaning up yet another mess you've made."

"Dani ain't responsible for what happened. You got no right to truss her up."

Dani bristled at the Ascendant's weary sigh.

"She's dangerous, Benjamin. In fact, she seems even more out of control now than she did when first given to your care. I knew from the start it was a mistake. I'm saddened it took this much death and destruction to prove me right."

"You're gonna blame her for what the Cleansers started?" Ben said. "If you didn't have slop for brains, you mighta noticed the only reason we ain't all charred bone right now is 'cause she pushed through a purgin' ceremony that woulda driven anyone else crazy."

Dani shivered at the fresh memory of the possession. It had been like looking out through another's eyes, except ... it had still been her. A version of herself surrendered to the seductive power, apathetic toward anyone else. That part of Dani hadn't given a flea's nipple about who would live or die, so long as she got her way. Everyone and everything had been expendable. Was that what a sociopath felt like?

"The Cleansers will be dealt with," Francis said. "My scrub-team is sweeping this compound."

Someone called from the far end of the hall. "It's good to see things under control. However, I am still tempted to let my temper get the better of me."

Dani rejoiced as she recognized Destin's voice—a feeling she'd never expected to associate with him. By the multitude of approaching footsteps, she figured the Chairman had brought his own team. Finally, a break. Things would get cleared up and this bag would be taken off her head.

"Chairman," Ben said, relief clear in his voice. "Glad you hustled on over. Would you mind tellin' Francis to get his paws off my apprentice?"

Dani rolled her shoulders, ready to give the Francis a nasty glare once she could see again. However, shock shoved her indignation aside when Destin replied.

"No. I am afraid I cannot allow that. Ascendant Francis, nullify Janitor Benjamin as well."

"What?" Ben's roar would've sent an angry bear scrambling back into hibernation.

"Sir?" For the first time, Dani detected doubt in Francis' voice. "I don't see the necessity of—"

"Are you refusing a direct order?" Destin's chilly tone raised goosebumps on Dani's arms.

Silence. Then Ben snarled and shouts erupted. An elbow bruised her shoulder, and her guards struggled to keep her upright as bodies jostled them.

Ben grunted as if struck, and his threats became a smothered string of unintelligible growls. Fear spiked through Dani's chest as she realized he'd been restrained too. However, the emotional surge didn't cause any reaction from her power. Something negated it, whether the garbage bag or the Ascendants' auras.

People muttered around her until Francis silenced them with a cough.

"Chairman, I in no way debate your authority, but can you enlighten me as to why this is necessary?"

"I read your report," Destin said.

"My report? But, sir, I—"

"Just because you didn't deliver it to me does not mean I lack access to it. You remain thorough in recording events and observations, but your perception failed you in this instance. Specifically, you have underestimated exactly how far Janitor Benjamin has fallen, and how effective he is at manipulating our perceptions, including using the girl to divert attention from himself."

"Destin," Ben sounded as if he stood in another room, "I'm this close to—"

More shuffling by Dani's side, and then a harsh whisper from Francis. *"Benjamin, for Purity's sake, be quiet and let me handle this."* He cleared his throat. "Sir, I'm not sure I understand."

"In just the past day," Destin said, "Janitor Benjamin was witnessed associating with a garbage man, something he has been forbidden from doing numerous times. He also was the first to report Sydney's presence, which you neglected to inform me of. Speaking of which, how did you learn of this location, Ascendant Francis? I was only made aware of the situation through chance and followed you here."

"Sir, perhaps if we waited until we are back at Headquarters, I could—"

Heat slapped against Dani, and a flaring aura stung her eyes, even through the bag.

Destin's voice boomed throughout the chamber. "Ascendant Francis, might I remind you that there is a chain of authority within the Cleaners for a reason? You seem to have forgotten your place in it. When I ask, you answer. When I command, you obey. The effectiveness of my position is entirely based on the information I receive, how I decide to act on it, and the people I trust to carry out my will. If this situation had been ignored much longer, it might have gone beyond any hope of containment. As it stands, we have little time to fix the damage. No more delays. No more excuses, otherwise you will be suspended without pay until further notice, if not demoted to bucket work."

Feet shuffled, and Dani imagined she heard Francis' spine pop as he came to attention.

"My apologies, Chairman," he said. "These oversights will not happen again."

"Correct, because I am now in direct control of this cleanup operation. Do you wish to know what else I gleaned from your report?"

"Gladly, Chairman."

"Janitor Benjamin's meeting with Sydney was not coincidence or accidental. As horrible as it is for me to comprehend, I cannot think of any other purpose for it than to seduce Ms. Hashelheim to Corruption, rather than being the antagonistic encounter Benjamin might have you believe."

"What?" Ben and Dani spouted in muffled unison.

"The destruction of the bar lends credibility to the story of an attack," Destin continued, "but if Sydney had confronted them with murderous intent, we all know they would not have escaped unharmed."

"Spit on your soul, Destin," Ben cried. "I ain't got a clue what you think this is gonna get you, but Sydney's still out there, and—"

"Sydney has been captured," said Francis. "I interrogated him myself. That's how I knew where to find the Cleansers. He directed us here."

A few heartbeats thudded by. Ben's voice rumbled with suspicion. "When?"

"A few hours after we finished cleaning out the dump," Francis said. "He was discovered spying on our scrub-team and is being held in an isolation chamber, thoroughly neutralized."

"Now that's a plain ol' trick if I ever heard of one," Ben said.

"Perhaps he intended it as such," Francis replied. "But he underestimated our capacity to counter his entropic power. I intended to alert you to this development, Chairman, but our time to act was limited."

Dani strained to get a sense of Destin's mood. He couldn't actually believe what he was saying, could he? It was all wrong. He should be rescuing them.

"I will deal with Sydney later," Destin said. "For now, observe how the condition of Benjamin's Ravishing is significantly worse than last observed. What does this evidence? Few things would accelerate the decay this much—in fact, I believe it comes from nothing less than direct contact with an entity from the Corrupt Pantheon. Janitor? What do you say to this?"

"You wanna know the truth? Sydney hustled us here against our will," Ben said. "He handed Dani over to the Cleansers as part of some deal, and then had a little kumbaya time with Filth, offerin' her tea and biscuits in exchange for tidbits on whatever's churnin' up all the muck we've been wadin' through."

"Filth?" Destin's voice went low and hard. "You spoke to her? You allowed her to infect your mind with deceit?"

"No," Ben said, frustration burred his words. "For Purity's sake, lemme explain."

"I'm sorry, Benjamin," Destin said. "As much as it pains me to say, you are too Corrupted to be trusted further. Has the Ravishing finally reached your heart? Perhaps your mind?"

"I ain't Corrupted," Ben said. "Purity still signs my paychecks."

"Then explain the Cleanser lying dead with his brains rotted out of his skull and his blood turned to bile."

"That's—"

"Yes?"

Ben curdled phlegm in the back of his throat and then hocked a wad. "I'm done talkin' to you, Destin. You got things all nice and twisted-like." He shifted beside Dani, and she caught a whiff of bleach through the bag. "Francis, use your noggin. Do the right thing."

"He will do what is necessary," the Chairman said. "You, on the other hand, will be dealt with as the Board sees fit. I'll argue for a merciful sentence." Ben started to protest, but Destin spoke over him. "I wanted to trust you in this, but the time has come to remove you from service. Ascendant Francis, prepare your team."

"As you say, Chairman."

Ben asked, "Whatcha gonna do with Dani?"

"Her fate is no longer your concern," Destin said. "Her place among us will have to be reevaluated, given the circumstances. I can only hope she is salvageable."

"Destin ..."

"Hm?"

"You are one maggoty, mud-rakin', pus-drinkin', son of a motherless billy goat!" Ben grunted in satisfaction. "There you go, Francis. Have fun convincin' the Board to add any of those to the list."

Footsteps echoed as the Chairman moved away. "Take them back to Headquarters. Use all precautions. Should they resist in any manner, apply lethal force."

CHAPTER TWENTY-FIVE

Already blinded, Dani lost any sense of sound as soon as Destin condemned them to whatever constituted a prison in the Cleaners' facilities. Only touch remained.

Rough hands forced her to walk and kept her up when she stumbled. The floor turned from broken stone to smooth marble. A single act of decency came when they lifted her legs one at a time and untied her arms to maneuver her into a full-body jumpsuit that zipped up the back. She never thought she'd feel relieved at being stuffed into one of the Cleaner uniforms again, even though they didn't provide gloves this time. She tried to peek out from under the bag without success.

The suit better not have turned pink on her.

Her arms were resecured, and they shoved her along again. After another few minutes of walking, there came a brief pause, followed by several measured steps forward. A chilly, liquid sensation passed over her. Where it touched the exposed part of her neck, it left it feeling numb for a moment. She recognized it as the same sensation from when Ben took her through the window portal on the way to see Destin. So they'd been transported back to HQ through one of their glassways.

They strode onward, the floor now cold tile, the air dry in contrast to her increasingly damp skin. What was it with her sweat glands lately? She didn't need them to let her know she was nervous.

Anxiety rose with each step until she felt she might drown in it, give way to the panic and make a fruitless attempt to escape. This would accomplish nothing but exhaust her further and perhaps give them reason to switch her over to a straitjacket. Still, the dread kept notching up, heightened by the almost complete sensory deprivation. She tried to reel her thoughts in, to give herself an anchoring focus.

She just had to think like a janitor, right? What would a janitor do in this situation? First of all, a janitor wouldn't have stuck her head inside a garbage bag. Health hazard, that. So that was one step backward …

A spot of wetness worked up her back, beneath the suit, tickling like an ant as it went. Or a spider. This thought sent her thrashing. She almost popped her shoulder out of its socket trying to grab at her back.

Her escorts shook her in warning, but kept moving her along. Gritting her teeth, she forced herself to bear its presence. Whatever it was, she had no way to stop it.

The tiny intruder paused where the trash bag circled her neck. Then it bumped beneath it, continued up her neck and plopped inside her ear before Dani could squeal. She started to jerk her shoulder against the side of her head to dislodge the lump, but a voice buzzed in her head.

"Chill, princess."

Startled recognition made her stop walking, but the Cleaners dragged her on. She scrambled to get her feet back under her as she whispered in reply.

"Ben?" Her voice sounded flat within the trash bag.

"Trottin' along right beside you. Sorry for this whole mess. For what it's worth, I figure that show back at the furnace is a sure sign you can handle your power well enough."

Dani turned her head from side to side, but the blackness remained. "How are we communicating?"

"Oh, right. I left a bit of Carl in my stomach. He's got this spiffy little trick where he transfers vibrations through the jawbone and eardrums."

"Carl? Did he cook up that weird armor you were wearing?"

A cough. *"Well, him and a few hundred of his pals. The bindin's they've slapped on us cut off any outside energy, but they can't fiddle with what's already inside us. You learn to be ready for these kinds of situations."*

She smiled wryly, even though he couldn't see. "Including your own boss deciding you've gone crazy and been Corrupted?"

"Eh. After seein' enough of my coworkers bounce their sanity checks, I figured it pays to be prepared. Was only a matter of time for me."

Her mind's eye conjured images of Ben's Corrupted arm, all black and green and gray. A shudder passed through her.

"Ben, what really caused the Ravishing?"

"Wanna worry about gettin' free first?"

She bit her lower lip, not liking the feeling that he was brushing her off. But arguing would waste time she suspected they didn't have. "Does that mean you have a plan?"

"I've been workin' with this kinda equipment for years. You'd think I'd have figured out a few tricks around it by now."

"Have you?"

"Here's hopin' so. Now, hang on. This next part might sting a bit."

"Sting?"

A pair of droplets trickled through the bag lining and up her cheeks, where they zipped into her eyes before she could shut them. She blinked against the smarting and started bending over, an instinctual hunch against the invasion.

"Don't be so squirmy. Our walkin' buddies might get cranky."

Dani straightened, eyelids fluttering as light blossomed.

"Howzat?"

She shook her head, trying to overcome the urge to knuckle her eyes. The world reappeared through a blue, glistening film; if she turned her head too fast, the edges of the hall swirled before settling back to true. The bag remained over her head, but the sprite projected a semblance of vision straight to her eyes, the same as it slipped Ben's voice into her ears.

"Thanks," she said as she took in their surroundings. Two Ascendants marched her and Ben—looking like a cheap scarecrow with his lanky frame and a trash bag for a head—down a wide hall, glass walls on either side. Through these, she glimpsed sunken rooms crowded with iron cages, dark figures chained within, crystal balls full of writhing smoke, glass doors rimmed with frost, and steel grates bolted over black pits. Every dozen yards, padlocked doors stood above stairs that led to the lower level. Dani wondered if the bag were taken off, would she hear screams and shouts of whoever and whatever was imprisoned here? Or would it remain unearthly silent?

"What is this place?" she asked.

Ben didn't give any indication of their secret conversation. His infected arm had also been wrapped tight in black plastic bags and bound behind him.

"The Recycling Center. It's where we bring Scum that we don't wipe out right away. Sometimes, if they're human—and we get to 'em in time—the Corruption can be removed. Other times, we study constructs or lost causes to figure out ways to fight 'em better next time."

"And ... what will they do to us?"

"Depends."

"They're going to put us in diapers?"

"That's good. Keep a'hold of that humor. Helps keep the heebie-jeebies at bay." He cleared his throat. *"For me, they're probably gonna stick me in containment until the Ravishing really does start gnawin' on my brain. For you, I'm thinkin' they'll be druggin' you up ten ways to Tuesday, or ... well ..."*

Dani bit her lip. "Or what, Ben?"

"Ever see Ol' Yeller?" He hastened to continue. *"But don't worry, kiddo. It ain't gonna come to that."*

"How do you know?"

"'Cause I ain't dead yet."

At that moment, they came within sight of a set of steel double-doors at the far end of the hall. They stopped before these, and one of their escorts placed a hand on the metal, face cast in shadow below his fedora.

Ben preempted her question by half a second.

"Quarantine," he said. *"It's where we stick the really naughty kids who stay up past bedtime and refuse to brush their teeth."*

Dani felt rather than heard the doors open. The rumbling shook her from ankles to shoulders as the entrance slid apart. They were pushed into an oversized elevator, large enough to hold at least twenty people. Dani glanced at her captors, gauging their alertness. Was this where they made their escape? It gave them a confined space to fight in, but still ... an elderly janitor and her against four muscled and possibly armed men? Dani didn't want to know the odds on that brawl.

"Ben? What do we do?"

A shock jolted the chamber, and she twitched before she realized the doors had slammed shut behind them. As the elevator shook and descended, Ben's silence gnawed at her. Did he really have a plan?

The elevator shuddered to a stop and the opposite wall split into another pair of doors, revealing a dark hallway lined with more assorted prisons. Rows of them stretched into the distance, light spearing the shadows between each cell.

"Get ready."

Without a huff to betray him, Ben lunged forward, tearing away from his captors.

"Ben!"

She imagined shouts as two suits chased Ben, who careened from side to side, bashing his shoulders against pedestal bases, toppling globes and cracking glass doors. He pounded down the hall like a pinball, ricocheting from wall to wall, surrendering momentum to slam into frosted panes or kick at locking mechanisms.

Then an Ascendant threw himself forward. Arms wrapped around Ben's legs, and the two fell flat. Ben's laughter crackled in her ears, and for a moment she feared he'd lost his sanity after all. The guards dragged him to his feet as she was marched down to him.

She snorted. "That worked well."

As she said this, their escort shuffled in place, looking this way and that. One drew out a radio and yelled into it, while the others formed a perimeter around the prisoners. Dani looked back along the hall and saw the results of Ben's dash.

Black smoke poured out from a cracked globe, while sludge writhed out of a broken door and flowed toward their feet. Jagged claws cut through a dissipating curtain of light and dug into the floor. Dozens of eyes gleamed as they focused on the nearest prey.

"This here's the problem with bringin' an old hound like me home to be put down." She could almost see Ben's grin through the bag. *"I know what we got chained up down here."*

In another second, the hallway crowded with hunched, winged, and fanged figures. Others strained to shake of their restraints, the bonds disrupted enough for them to bull through the rest.

"Duck and cover, princess!"

She dropped to her knees as something winged overhead and snatched up a guard. The man flailed, and his aura snapped into being around him. Smoke rose from the creature's talons, and it dropped its prey. However, he'd already been taken to such a height that the landing left him stunned.

The other three spread out, auras bright, trying to push the escapees back into their cages. One woman disappeared under a wave of dark mud, which congealed into an egg shape. Handprints appeared from within, stretching the webbed skin like rubber. Another guard lashed whips of light at what appeared to be a cadaverous bear, and the third continued shouting into his radio while throttling an imp that gnashed at him with shark teeth.

Ben elbowed her. *"Hustle thisaway! Don't get lost."*

Still hooded, and with their hands bound, they raced into the maze of prisons.

CHAPTER TWENTY-SIX

Dani focused on not tripping. Despite fleeing for her life, she felt ridiculous as they sprinted between rows of pillars, heads bent and arms tied behind their backs. She couldn't help the thought that they ran through an amusement park haunted house. The Janitor's Gauntlet of Soapy Horrors.

Ben seemed to turn at random. He cut down dark halls, taking them through empty rooms and past stretches of glass doors where motionless figures stood backlit by the glow of containment spells. Some of them were humanoid, while others had far too many limbs and heads, or none at all.

Ben and her breaths filled her ears as they ran, making it sound like a huffing competition. None of the walls were marked or sectioned off in any way she could see, and the blue film over her eyes cast everything into the same pallor, making it impossible to tell one corridor or room from another. Sweat ran down her face, unimpeded by eyebrows any longer, but the water lenses blocked any salt sting.

As they turned down the umpteenth hallway, Ben stopped so suddenly she smacked her face against his back. As she stumbled, he turned and tilted his head apologetically.

"This oughta be far enough. No sense keepin' on if we're just gonna trip over our own feet."

Dani eyed the way they'd come. Lights flashed along it. Emergency alarms? She had no sense of how far they'd run. She flexed her arms, but the zip-tie still dug into her skin.

"How do we get out? Open sesame?"

He turned sideways, displaying his arms. *"You mighta noticed I've got a bit of a way with water, yeah?"*

"So?"

"So, with all them school smarts, I'm sure you've learned that we're … what? Sixty or seventy percent water?"

"That's something kids learn in kindergarten, Ben. What's it—whoa."

Ben's arms withered as she spoke. The sleeve of his left and the trash-bag wrappings of his right hung loose over bone-thin appendages, while other spots in his body filled out until he had a padded waist and triple chin sagging out from under the bag.

The zip-tie slid over his wrists, and he sighed in relief as he tossed the binding away. After another moment, his bony hands swelled back to normal and the rest of his body thinned down. Flexing his fingers, he peeled the garbage bags away from his right hand, but left the arm covered.

"It ain't that hard," he said as he stretched and popped his knuckles. *"You just gotta clench the bladder until things get back to normal."*

"I didn't need to know that."

A tug drew the bag off his head, revealing his haggard features. The stubble on his cheeks and chin made him look ten years older, though his eyes gleamed with energy. Dani thought he might be having a little too much fun showing off.

He released her bound hands, and she relaxed slightly as the bag whiffed off her head. Water dribbled out of her eyes and ears to splatter on the floor. She shook her head as normal senses returned, bringing with them a smell of lemon and pine. Cold air made her scalp prickle. She rubbed her bald head and where her eyebrows used to be, silently bemoaning the loss of her hair. Though, on the upside, it'd be much easier to keep her scalp clean.

Sirens wailed in the distance, warning them not to stay in one spot for too long. Warning lights sliced yellow and red beams across gray walls. Distant yelling was followed by howls, snaps, and splashes. These died off, and Dani glanced at Ben, who nodded for her to follow as he walked the way they'd been heading.

"Ain't nothing to worry 'bout," he said. "The Ascendants can handle themselves." He trotted along, not quite as fast as before, but not wasting time either. Dani jogged to catch up, swinging her arms wide to enjoy being free.

"What are Ascendants, anyways?" she asked as they loped down the hall.

Ben grimaced and kept his eyes forward. "Well, you got the Chairman and the Board. So think of Ascendants as upper management. They're the ones Purity gives a bit more *oomph* to."

"Oomph? Do they get a little *sproing* and *whizzbang* too?"

"Their glow ain't just for show, is what I'm sayin'. Those auras repel pretty much all but the cruddiest Corruption. They don't ever gotta shower, use the bathroom, or all that other daily maintenance. They stay spit-shined twenty-four-seven. Plus they get better benefit packages, company cars, and gold watches when they … uh … what's wrong?"

Dani went stock still in the middle of the hall and threw her hands up. "Why didn't anyone tell me this from the start? I would've signed on without a second thought!" She shook her head. "I swear, if we live through this, I'm applying for the Ascendant fast-track."

One side of his face scrunched up. "I wouldn't aim that high, kiddo."

She glared. "What? Don't tell me this place has a glass ceiling. I saw plenty of women wearing those zoot suits."

His frown deepened. "It ain't that. It's just most people don't know that bein' an Ascendant grinds down the soul, little by little, until all you've got left is a nice pile of white powder, with barely any humanity left to be worth a snort."

He resumed jogging ahead, and, after a huff of disbelief, she followed suit.

"What do you mean?" she asked, once she caught up.

He eyed her sidewise, obviously displeased with her continuing the discussion. "Bein' human means havin' a little bit of dirt under the fingernails, princess. Ain't none of us perfect or pure, no matter how much we wanna be. It ain't in our nature. So when you get Purity's little nightlight followin' you 'round, forcing that kinda state on you ... well ..." He shrugged. "It might be fun at first. Never havin' to shower or brush your teeth. Always smellin' fresh-like, never havin' to comb your hair. But all those little things ground us. They remind us of who we are. Strip that away, and you start thinkin' all sortsa unhealthy things. You start thinkin' you're better than everyone else who ain't Ascended. You wall yourself off from everythin' and anyone that ever mattered. You get cocky. Anyone not at your level might as well be yesterday's lunch—even other Cleaners who put as much sweat and blood into the job as anyone else."

Dani pondered this as they ran along. It didn't seem fair. Ever since seeing Francis in the library bathroom, she'd wanted to tap into the secret that kept him spotless. And now Ben was telling her it might have a cost higher than she was willing to pay.

"So that's why Francis and the others always act like we're something nasty they just stepped in."

He nodded. "It takes a hard knee to the balls to make any of 'em realize they're just as vulnerable as the rest of us."

"Is that what we're doing now?"

"Sorta. Except instead of a knee, we're gonna use a sledgehammer."

After another minute, a previous statement snagged on her mind and dragged a question out. "Ben?"

"Eh?"

"You said 'most people don't know' about what it's really like to be an Ascendant. How do you?"

He slowed to a walk, and Dani backpedaled to stay at his side.

"I was one," he said.

"What?"

Ben hugged his right arm to his side. "I was an Ascendant when this happened." He flashed a ragged grin. "Hard to believe, huh? One of the youngest the Board ever approved, ain't that the truth. You think Francis is a prick? You shoulda seen me. Why Karen ever stuck with me, I ain't never guessed."

"Your wife."

Pain cracked Ben's face into a hundred fragments. "Yeah."

"Will you tell me what happened now?"

He hunched, his earlier willingness to explain spooked by her pursuit of the topic.

She reached out, not quite laying a hand on his shoulder. "Please, Ben."

"Dani, this ain't—"

"The right time? I don't think there's ever going to be a right time, if you have your way." She stepped around and blocked the way, arms crossed. "You promised an explanation, and I'd like to hear it before we meet up with more goons who will try to scour us out of existence."

Ben lowered his head, giving her an eyeful of gray ponytail and bald patch. Dani didn't budge. She kept one ear attuned for sounds of pursuit, but didn't think a chase party had come close to cornering them, or else Ben would've shown more need for haste.

He looked up, but didn't meet her eyes. "A'ight. First thing you gotta know is that I'm thirty-two years old."

CHAPTER TWENTY-SEVEN

Ben watched Dani as his words settled in. He felt funny admitting it, a mix of shame and relief he couldn't sort right away.

"You're ... what?" she asked.

He chuckled. "Thirty-two. What? I don't look it? And no, before you ask, I ain't jokin', and I ain't crazy. Leastaways, not that much." He bent his right arm around. "It's been five years since the Ravishing latched onto me. I was twenty-seven then. See? I can do math." He grinned briefly. "It clogged up my power somethin' fierce, but it also has some other nasty side effects. Like shuttlin' me to the grave a might bit faster. I figure I got the body of a seventy-five-year-old now, and I'm gonna be dead in another year or two."

She looked him over, gauging him in light of this new information. Likely guessing what he used to look like, imagining what it would be like if she'd contracted the infection from him.

"How did it happen?" she asked.

"Sydney fed you a slice of the truth. Karen and I worked together, cleanin' up some of the nastiest Scum around. We loved our work. It ... brought us together." He ran a hand through his hair, pangs of memory tightening his chest. "I ain't even got the foggiest of what the original assignment was. We went in ready to wipe the place clean. Next thing I know, I'm wakin' up back in HQ, Karen's dead, and the Ravishing is gnawin' up my arm. But ..." His voice lowered into a growl and his teeth ground together. "I ain't never killed her. Never. I woulda died before raisin' a hand against Karen."

Each word clawed at the old wounds. He tasted bitterness, and his hands trembled until he clenched them, resisting the desire to strike out against the ghosts of a not-so-ancient past.

"Destin stuck me in quarantine for months to make sure I weren't no threat. When the Board finally let me out, I'd been stripped of my position, bounced back to janitor, and given side jobs to keep me busy. Whatever or whoever did this to Karen and myself ain't never been caught. I don't even know if they tried to hunt it down. Any reports got locked away from my pryin' eyes, and I ain't got the clout anymore to dig 'em back up."

His rising fury sputtered as weariness overtook him. He sagged against the wall and hid his face behind a hand, keenly aware of Dani watching him. These days, as his body continued to fail, it was hard even for him to remember himself as a young man. A lifetime shed in a matter of years. No chance to avenge Karen. Not a single friend left—if they'd ever been such—who trusted him, what with a Corrupt disease eating his flesh away. He'd kept doing his job because it was the only thing left. It provided a false hope that he might uncover something that would cure him, or reveal a clue about what happened. Some way to gain closure.

But nothing ever did.

Dani moved his way, hesitated, and then stepped back. "I'm sorry," she whispered.

He closed his eyes. "Yeah. Me too."

They stayed that way for another minute as he struggled to collect himself.

"What'd Karen do here?" Dani asked. "Was she a janitor too?"

Ben pushed away from the wall. "Naw. She was a maid. A Handmaiden of Purity, as they're rightly known. You mighta called her a witch."

"A witch?"

"Yuppers." He mimed sweeping. "Witches have always worked for the Cleaners. Why d'ya think they're pictured carryin' brooms? They're some of the tidiest folk you'll come across. I've always been partial to mops, m'self. Somethin' she and I never agreed on."

She squinted. "I still can't tell when you're being serious or not."

He rolled his shoulders, forcing himself to focus on their situation. "We've wasted enough time. C'mon. It's just around the corner."

Dani looked around as they started jogging again. "What is? A back entrance to this place?"

"Naw. Only exit is that elevator we came down."

"Then shouldn't we have cut loose before we got locked in here?"

"Mebbe. But then we'd be stuck tryin' to get through HQ by ourselves."

"By ourselves? Are we here to get backup?"

Ben turned the corner in question, where the hall dead-ended in a steel door. He strode up to it, grabbed the handle and yanked it open to reveal an unlit room. At his side, Dani eyed the darkness.

"Why isn't this one locked?"

"'Cause if whoever is kept in here gets loose, a locked door ain't gonna stop 'em." He stepped inside. Motion sensors detected his presence and illuminated the room.

Dani gasped.

A man sat in a chair that had been bolted to the floor in the middle of the room. Two metal rods extended from the ceiling on either side of him, with iron tubes held parallel to the ground. His arms had been locked into the tubes, and his bare hands stuck out from the far ends, unable to touch anything. A garbage bag had been tied over his head.

No one could mistake the tuxedo t-shirt, however.

"No way." She stared at the imprisoned Sydney while Ben did a quick circuit of the room. "How'd you know where they stashed him?"

"We built this room specifically to put entropy mages into a time-out." Careful not to brush against Sydney's fingers, Ben undid the first clamp holding the mage in place. Before he could remove it, however, Dani planted herself in the way.

"What are you doing?"

He looked from the locks to her and back. "You got eyes, don'tcha?"

Her green eyes darkened. "Ben, give me a single reason we should free this lunatic."

"Don'tcha trust me, princess?"

She glowered up at him, an expression he found himself growing far too fond of.

"I do, but I still want to know why. I'm done running blind. I want to help, but I can't unless you tell me what to expect."

"Fair 'nuff." He brushed himself off. "We need his help to get outta here. I ain't strong enough to do what needs doing, and your powers—"

"I can control them now!"

"—are still a might bit too cranky. I want us grabbin' what we need and walkin' out without killin' anyone. These are still coworkers we're gonna go up against. If we got him backing us up, mebbe they'll get smart and stand down."

She frowned at the floor, then at the entropy mage. "What's to keep him from killing us?"

"Ain't no entropy mage ever been caught before. They've all gone down fightin', or offed themselves before we could bag 'em. That means Sydney …" he nudged the man's ankle with a toe. The mage didn't twitch. "He's here 'cause he wants to be. He's got somethin' planned, and I'll bet a month's pay he'll work with us so long as we got the same goals in mind. That and I'm countin' on a healthy dose of sibling rivalry."

"Sibling … what are you talking about?"

"You ain't noticed the family resemblance?" Ben bent back to the clamps. "This here's Destin's baby brother."

CHAPTER
TWENTY-EIGHT

ani stared as Ben continued undoing Sydney's prison. Where he touched the metal, blue glyphs flashed and then faded. After he freed the legs and torso, Sydney's arms remained in the bars as Ben tugged the bag off the man's head.

She saw it then, and was pissed that Ben had to point it out to her. Sydney and Destin sported the same blond hair, the same fine-boned features, the same self-assured look to the eyes, though Sydney radiated cockiness in place of Destin's managerial authority. If the two men had stood side-by-side, or if Sydney had worn a white suit, she'd have noticed earlier.

The mage beamed at the two. "I wondered how long I'd have to languish here. You took your time."

She slapped him hard enough her palm stung. His head snapped to the side, and a red mark painted his cheek. She wiped her hand off on her jumpsuit and knew it'd take several bottles of gel before it'd feel clean again. *Worth it. Totally worth it.*

"Not quite the welcome I was hoping for." He worked his jaw. "But from you, a slap is practically a kiss." He looked her over. "By the missing hair and smell of smoke, I take it the ceremony didn't go as planned. Don't worry. I can appreciate the sensuality of a bald scalp as much as flowing curls."

Ben stepped in, forcing Dani back as he glared down at Sydney.

"Right, then," said the mage. "To business?"

"Pleasure first."

Ben's fist cracked across Sydney's opposite cheek. The mage slumped with a groan.

"That's for makin' it personal earlier," the janitor said. "Mess with my past again, and you'll get worse comin', hear?"

Sydney coughed a chuckle, and his words came out slurred, "Roger. Loud and clear. Over."

"Now, we've all made nice, so listen up, pretty boy." Ben scratched at his right arm. "Your big brother is dippin' his toes into a deep muck pond. I know there ain't nothin' more you'd love to see than him drown, but we both know he's got an annoyin' habit of spinnin' these situations to his advantage. Now, we either get your help stoppin' him, or you can rot here. What's it gonna be?"

Sydney stretched, arching his back as much as his arm-bindings allowed. "It's worse than you think. Destin never did learn the value of humility, and being appointed Chairman of the Board only exacerbated things. He thinks he has to control everything. If a single element goes beyond his authority, he fears his world will come tumbling down. Now that he's alerted to the existence of the fledgling, my guess is he'll take it as opportunity to elevate his power all the more."

"What'cha mean?" Ben asked.

"I realized, in the many quiet hours of contemplation this place allowed me, that until a place is found for the newborn within either Pantheon, it remains exposed to outside manipulation. It has no realm to fall back to for strength, no sense of identity or purpose within the balance. It will be searching for some way to anchor itself. Destin might well offer himself and leash its power in the process."

"Is that possible?" Dani asked.

Ben scowled, not taking his eyes off the mage. "Destin's got a little trick where he can make others submit to him," he said. "A little perk as Chairman. With some, he can totally take 'em over. You felt a touch of it when you met him, 'member? He gets his hands on the hybrid, and he might well twist it 'round his pinky finger. I don't wanna imagine Destin with a demigod on his payroll."

Dani shuddered, remembering Destin's touch, how worthless and unclean she'd felt, ready to do anything to raise herself in his estimation.

"Oh, I've given lots of thought to it," Sydney said. "Which is why I'm now determined to destroy it before anyone can sway it to their bidding. Some things shouldn't exist."

Ben rubbed his hands together. "A'ight. We gotta get up to Destin's office. Hopefully find somethin' that'll give us a bead on where he and Francis are headed. Then we're gonna do everythin' we can to stop 'em."

Sydney nodded. "Agreed. It's refreshing to see a spark of intelligence left in you, old man. I suggest we hurry."

Ben spat a wad of water into his hand. He drew this into a cord between both forefingers and thumbs and then strung it around Sydney's neck, where it tightened into a wire-thin collar.

Sydney's nostrils flared. He kept a mask of joviality on, but his eyes hardened.

Ben crouched to meet his glare. "Before I let'cha go, lemme explain somethin'. You're along for the ride, but only so long as you behave. That means there ain't gonna be any killin'. You're gonna get us out of here with as little fuss as possible. You so much as scratch someone and you're gonna be lookin' up at what's left of yourself, wonderin' where your head got to." He raised a finger. "Oh, and if you're thinkin' about trying to dissolve the collar, get a hand within an inch of it and Carl will decapitate you faster than you can sneeze."

"Executed by a water sprite named Carl." Sydney sighed. "How mundane *that* would be. But you've made your point. You have my word, however far you trust it. I'll stand the indignity, if only to see my brother thwarted."

Ben swiftly removed the remaining clamps. Dani's breath caught as Sydney stood and rubbed his bruised arms, but he made no aggressive moves. The mage and janitor eyed each other, until Ben nodded.

"Let's get going."

He took the lead, leaving Dani to jog alongside Sydney as they left the cell.

"How'd you get caught?" she asked as they re-entered the hall. He turned his head enough for her to see an inflamed bump, like a mosquito bite, just below his ear.

"Soporific dart," he said. "Fear not. I only allowed it to touch me because I knew my capture would reunite me with you. Otherwise their efforts would've been useless. Over the years I've learned to be ..." he winked, "... very talented with my hands."

She rolled her eyes. "Men. No matter how fancy your vocabularies are, you always resort to sex jokes."

They rounded the first corner into a larger, empty room, and then stopped. A barrier of janitorial carts blockaded the entrance to the adjoining hall. Five Cleaners stood in front of the barrier, all in orange jumpsuits. Mops. Brooms. Squeegees. They spun and hefted the tools like barbarians preparing to launch themselves onto a battlefield to fight for their independence.

Ben took point, nodding at them in turn. "Lucy. Gabe. Raoul. Tim. Aaliyah. Good to see y'all."

Lucy, a heavyset Hispanic brunette with a plain face and serious eyes, shook her head at them.

"Ben, your little stunt got us pulled off our coffee breaks."

Ben winced. "Ooh. Sorry 'bout that. You can head on back." He looked over their shoulders. "Where's the team that brought us in? I figured they'd be here by now."

"Still cleaning up the mess you left by the elevator," Lucy said. "You let a *gorgrum* loose, you know."

Ben's eyes widened. "I thought all of them were in the eastern facility."

The Cleaners glowered at the would-be-escapees.

"C'mon." Ben spread his hands. "Be smart about this. Trot on back to your coffee while it's still warm."

Lucy held a mop over one shoulder, though Dani noted the woman's white-knuckled grip.

"Reports are you've been Corrupted," she said. "And you've freed an entropy mage. You know the rules. We can't believe a word you say. Even if you're telling the truth, you'd do the same in our position."

Ben shrugged. "Eh. Probably. So, the hard way?"

"You could surrender and save us the trouble."

"Naw. I gotta stop Destin before he enslaves a demigod."

Lucy sighed. "And here I was, hoping you'd at least try to pretend to be sane." The mop swung off her shoulder, and she planted it in front of her, both hands on the pole.

The smell of ammonia stung Dani's nose, making her gasp. Her eyes watered as the opposing janitors drew spray bottles in unison and triggered them. Watery missiles, spears, and whips soared across the room.

Sydney stepped forward, hands raised. As each attack struck, no matter the angle or speed, he touched it in midair. The water vanished as soon as it hit his fingers. His arms blurred as he spun, ducked, and jumped in an intricate dance that had Dani staring in grudging admiration. He moved gracefully, always balanced, nearly precognizant of where the next attack would come from. She and Ben stood a few feet away, but remained untouched by a single drop.

After half a minute of the barrage, the janitors tossed the bottles aside, their reservoirs depleted. A few exchanged worried glances, but none retreated.

"Shall we continue with this tiresome game?" Sydney asked.

A janitor wielding dual squeegees sprinted at the mage, weapons raised. He slashed down. Sydney dodged and snapped a kick into the man's near elbow. The janitor cried out, and the squeegee flew from his hand and spun past Dani's ear. She turned and her heart hiccupped as the edge sliced into the wall and stuck there.

Why didn't anyone warn her about this sort of thing?

The janitor recovered and struck out again. Sydney swiveled on a heel and snatched the remaining tool from his attacker. The squeegee crumbled into black dust.

Sydney grabbed the man's collar as he staggered off balance. The jumpsuit puffed away and left him standing in nothing but his boots. His eyes widened and he hunched to cover himself. Sydney smiled in apology before laying the man out with an uppercut.

Dani almost clapped, impressed despite herself. As if sensing her approval, however, Sydney glanced back and grinned, which cooled her enthusiasm immediately.

Ben put a hand on Sydney's shoulder and drew him back.

"C'mon, Lu," he said. "It don't gotta be like this."

The woman shuffled forward, mop raised. "Ascendants will be here soon."

"So stop wastin' our time. Just stand aside and no one gets hurt."

She yelled and motioned for the others to attack as she did. Ben lunged to intercept. He caught the striking mop on a raised arm. The cloth tendrils of the mop coiled around his forearm and tightened. However, he braced and used the connection to yank Lucy his way. The woman stumbled into his arms. She started to rear back, but Ben grabbed her around the back and hugged her to him. As her face rose, he kissed her hard.

Dani stood dumbstruck. The other charging Cleaners all stopped as well to stare at the lip-locked janitors.

When Ben released her, Lucy clutched at her throat, face pale and strained. She sank to her knees. Gurgling noises bubbled out of her wide mouth and froth spotted her lips. Her chest heaved. Her eyes rolled up in their sockets and she slumped over.

A watery blob flowed out of her lips and back over to Ben. It crawled up to his left hand, where it reformed into a transparent glove.

They looked at the remaining janitors, who drew back after seeing two of their number dropped so quickly.

Ben glanced her way. "Dani? Showtime."

Dani showed off her meanest, most sadistic grin as she strode forward. The janitors stumbled over their own carts in their haste to escape.

She pouted at their scramble. "I don't know whether to be relieved or insulted."

"They was just delayin' us," Ben said. "The real fight's waitin'."

"How many should we expect?" Sydney asked.

Ben grabbed the nearest cart and shoved it ahead as they left the room. As Dani snagged a pair of gloves off the cart, she noticed he winced with each step and favored his right arm.

"Except for our escort back here," he said, "Destin and Francis took most of the local Ascendants along for the fun. Even if they got the message out, reinforcements are gonna take time to arrive."

They ran into the main hall leading up to the elevator. Dani paused in the process of tugging the gloves on.

"Uh … Ben? There's nobody here."

Ben's eyes narrowed. The mess he'd made by releasing the imprisoned creatures had been cleaned up except for a few scorch marks along one wall and an inky blotch dripping from the ceiling. The elevator stood open, inviting them in.

"Up we go, then."

"Tally-ho," Sydney murmured. "The windmills await."

Dani shot him a glare, but received a charming smile in return.

They rode the elevator in silence, each tensed for what waited above. As the doors opened, Dani took in the scene in a glance.

The white-tiled hall stretched out wide before them. The glass panels on either side had frosted over, blocking sight of the cells and cages on the lower levels. Halfway down, another blockade had been set up, consisting of plastic yellow Wet Floor signs strung together by red-hot bands of crackling energy that Dani guessed weren't healthy to touch. Cleaners crouched behind this barrier, spray bottles, pressure hoses, and soap dispensers readied like a firing squad.

The four Ascendants who'd brought them to the Recycling Center stood in front. They were battered, their formerly spotless suits now torn and stained, their faces bruised, and one sported a bloody nose. However, they looked determined as their bright auras cast the hall into stark relief. The janitors Dani had sent running had joined with ten other Cleaners, all of whom wielded the usual array of tools. She got the impression of a mob with torches and pitchforks preparing to storm the castle—though in this case, the roles were somewhat reversed.

"Impressive," Sydney said. "I'll never fault this company its efficiency. But all in vain, as I said before."

He knelt and punched the floor. Cracks raced out from his fist and, before any Cleaners could react, four of them dropped through pits that opened beneath them. Their yells cut off with clatters, bangs, and groans.

The path of Corruption, however, diverted around where the Ascendants stood.

Ben put a hand out before Dani could move by him. "Get back. Let Sydney and me handle this, eh?"

"Like h—" she started to say.

"Zip it," he said. "You're strong, but you ain't trained for this. I don't want any deaths on your conscience." With that, he stalked forward, attention locked on his coworkers.

"He's right," Sydney said. "Let us keep you an unsullied flower for now, shall we?"

Dani snarled as the mage left her behind as well. She hated to admit that Ben might be right. While her power didn't threaten to take over her mind and body anymore, she didn't know how far she could trust it. The very nature of natural disasters, minor or large scale, assumed plenty of violence and chaos would be involved. So she fumed as the men engaged the line.

Ben waded in first. His motions were stiff and guarded, but he kept his back straight, trying to defy his aged body. He swatted the mop at anyone who came within range. The Cleaners behind the barrier loosed a variety of missiles. He slapped some aside, while others were absorbed into the mop brush. One janitor threw a giant soap bubble his way. When the mop handle popped it, the resulting shockwave knocked him back a few feet.

While he kept the remaining Cleaners occupied, Sydney raised his hands and advanced on the Ascendants. Their auras mingled and expanded into a field that walled off their section of the hall.

The entropy mage set his palms against this glowing field and leaned against it. The light dimmed where he touched, but didn't vanish. A high-pitched whine started up, and Dani imagined it came from the air molecules trapped between the opposing powers. Sydney pushed closer to the suits, erasing their auras an inch at a time.

A pair of Cleaners slipped around the sign barrier and flanked Ben without him noticing. One man held a plunger like a battle mace, while the other, a tall, thin woman, readied a broom.

Dani looked around for something to distract them with. She spotted the cart Ben had brought with them. Grabbing the handle, she jumped behind it and raced down the hall like a manic child in a supermarket.

"Hey!" she called.

The man spun her way and raised the plunger. Dani let the cart go, and it rammed into his hips. He shouted as he twisted down. An audible pop came from his knee and ankle. Dani winced, but couldn't hide a satisfied smile.

The woman shoved the cart back past her prone companion. Dani easily sidestepped it and cocked an eyebrow as it rattled away behind her.

"Copycat."

The man propped up on one arm, still holding the plunger. He glared at her even as his face twitched in pain. Then he suctioned the plunger to the floor. When he pulled up, it tore a head-sized portion of tile and concrete up with it. He lifted the chunk and flung it and the plunger her way.

Dani threw herself to the side. The concrete block crunched into the elevator doors behind her. Pebbles sprayed everywhere.

"Dani," Ben shouted as he intercepted a soap-water javelin. "I toldja to stay back."

"They started it!"

The woman swung her broom over her head. Air whipped up until she stood in the center of a small whirlwind. When she snapped the broom out in front of her, the whirlwind launched Dani's way.

Disregarding Ben's order, Dani reached for her power for the first time since being shoved into the furnace. Her lack of fear surprised her. Perhaps that aspect of her personality had been left behind during the purging ceremony. Whatever the case, she felt fully in control. Centered.

However, the magic within her recoiled, as if disliking being summoned rather than overwhelming her whenever it chose. Dani imagined it as a miniature of herself hiding in the dark corners of her soul, and shook a mental fist at it.

Don't make me spank you.

Power surged through her and into the surrounding elements. Her senses expanded along with it, discerning all the potential storms she could brew in the confined space. But the maid had already done the work for her.

She latched onto the whirlwind and dove into it until she grasped the Pure core energizing the spell. Her enhanced sight traced the tendrils of power trailing back to the maid, like a leash on an attack dog. A snip and snatch had the leash in her grasp, and she sent the wind roaring back in their faces.

The maid slashed the broom down. It cut through the whirlwind and chopped it into swirling bits that fluttered aside harmlessly. The women faced off. Dani waved for her to come closer.

"I can take anything you throw my way," she said.

The maid smiled. "Very well."

A cushion of air picked the woman up and launched her forward.

CHAPTER
TWENTY-NINE

Dani had an instant to think, *Nice trick*, before the maid hit. The collision sent them both tumbling. They slammed onto the cart, which rolled into the nearest pane of glass. The floor-to-ceiling window shattered, and they flew out over the edge.

The cart plummeted, scattering tools, rags and buckets, while the two women remained aloft on the conjured wind. They spun and grappled for control. Dani grabbed the broom handle and yanked the maid into a head butt.

The hit almost broke Dani's nose, and she cried out as pain lanced through her face. It still got the reaction she wanted, for the maid's eyes crossed and she released her grip. They flipped and fell with Dani on top. At the last second, the maid conjured another gust of air to cushion the drop—except Dani's added weight smacked the maid hard to the tiles, and her eyes fluttered shut.

The maid's body softened the hit, though it left Dani breathless for a few seconds. Light cuts stung her face, but she didn't sense any major injury. All this personal contact though was ratcheting up her contamination alert into the red zone. She wiped her forehead and was relieved to see less blood than she'd expect from a paper cut. Still, exposure was exposure and—

Deep breathing and slurping noises tore her away from the sanitation assessment. She'd landed near a row of dark pits with metal grilles over the tops. Gleaming eyes stared at her from between the bars, where the hungry noises also came from.

This large roomed housed at least fifty other cages, cells, and pits, each with misshapen occupants peering out. Some paced on hind legs. Others slithered. A few bashed themselves against their glassy walls in an effort to get at her. Only by chance had her fall not broken open any of their prisons.

She looked up to the ongoing fight beyond the shattered glass. Ben had knocked out the janitor Dani had lamed, and now blocked another barrage of watery spears. Sydney tore portions of aura away like tissue paper. He glanced over, and looked stricken at seeing her cast down.

"Dearest!" He turned from the Ascendants and made to run down to her. "Fear not. I'll protect you."

"Idiot," Ben cried. "Don't stop—"

As Sydney ceased pushing back their auras, the Ascendants' energy pulsed in a single combined attack. Their golden light flared into a white nova that encompassed the hall.

Dani flung her hands over her face and squeezed her eyes shut. While the explosion of Pure energies was silent, the aftershock was not.

A wave of power threw her to the floor and skidded her along until she bumped up against a wall. Lights danced outside her eyelids. Glass shattered, the floor quaked, and the whole roomed tilted around her. But the wave washed over as if she were a rock in a riverbed. A distant part of her mind realized that she wielded Pure energy as well, and as such wouldn't be negatively affected by the blast.

Ben and Sydney, however …

She opened her eyes as the last rumbles faded. Her head pounded, and all noise sounded distant, as if she wore earmuffs. She groaned as she staggered to her feet. With a hand on the aching small of her back, she got her bearings.

All the glass along the upper hall had been blown out and strewn across the floors. Ben had fallen to one knee and used the mop to prop himself up, while Sydney had disappeared. Only three Ascendants remained, and a few Cleaners slumped over their barrier, dazed. Dani pressed a hand to her stomach as nausea cramped it. Had one of the Ascendants actually destroyed himself to defeat the entropy mage?

In the brief lull, the elevator from the lower level opened again. The Cleaner Sydney had denuded stumbled out, an unconscious Lucy draped over his bare shoulders. He gaped at the scene until an Ascendant yelled something. Then he staggered past a rousing Ben and vanished through the exit portal.

One Ascendant moved toward the nearest stairs, while the other two came at Ben from both sides. Ben lurched upright. He'd grabbed a dropped spray bottle and blasted one of them in the face with a stream of water. The other he warded off with the mop, which writhed and snatched at their eyes.

A curdling hiss made Dani turn. She'd bumped up against the base of an iron cage, where a complicated network of chains kept its occupant bound in the center of the bars. The creature had three leathery wings, albino skin with red tattoos writhing across it, and rusted nails instead of teeth. Its eyes were positioned along its throat, rather than on its blank face, and it stared out at her with clear hunger.

Its voice sounded like cats being skinned alive. *"Free the gnash, and it will aid you."*

"I ... don't think so," she said.

It shifted. Chains clinked. *"The gnash does not break its word. The gnash promises to only eat your heart after it has stopped beating. Such is the gnash's mercy."*

Dani shook her head, trying to clear her fuzzy thoughts.

"The gnash thinks you will taste delicious."

She turned to rejoin the fight, but paused as her gaze slid past the creature and fixed on the occupant of the next cell over. She cried out.

"Ben!"

"Kinda busy!"

"Ben, it's Stewart! Stewart's in this cage!"

"What?" Another yell, and the sound of a body hitting the floor. "Where's Sydney? He got knocked down there with yah."

"Uh …"

She whipped her head around and finally spotted the mage lying twenty feet away. He still breathed, though blood trickled from a cut on his scalp. When she knelt beside him and grabbed his shirt, his eyes opened but remained unfocused.

"Has the Valkyrie come for me?" he whispered. "Am I finally to ascend to the feast of the gods?"

Dani sighed. "All that bragging, and a few Ascendants get the better of you because you got distracted?"

She grabbed his arm and dragged him up and stumbling over to Stewart's cage. He clutched her shoulder and a few other spots that would've had her punching him back down if not for the urgent circumstances. Once they got back to the cage, she pushed him up against it and took his chin to make him look at her.

"Sydney, I need your help."

The entropy mage's eyes brightened and he roused from the last of his daze. "What ails the fair maiden?"

She pointed to where Stewart stared out at them. Dressed in a gray robe, the trash mage had been curled in a fetal position when Dani first saw him. Now he'd noticed the commotion going on and had risen to pound at the glass containing him. Stripped of his garbage regalia, he looked like a bald old souse, uncertain of his whereabouts after emerging from a drunken stupor.

"Get him out," she told Sydney.

Sydney's nose wrinkled as he looked over the trash mage. "This bumpkin? Hardly worth your affections."

"Sydney, please. He's …" She stumbled as she started to say *He's Scum too.* "He's a friend. We've got to get him out."

"My actions have already balanced any debt I owe. What would compel me to add another to our number? What token could you offer that would convince me?"

Dani barely kept herself from knocking him cold. This was not the time to bargain.

"What do you want?" she asked.

"A passionate kiss."

"No. No way. Forget it."

He turned his face aside and wiped a hand across the cheek. "Very well. Then a simple peck here, where I have just now sterilized the flesh. The merest balm to soothe my wounded soul. The slightest show—"

"Oh, shut up."

She leaned in, brushed her lips over the smooth skin, and then stepped back, wanting nothing more than to take some steel wool and acid to her mouth. Grinning as if she'd just accepted a marriage proposal, Sydney tapped the glass, which vanished liked a popped bubble.

"And now, to avenge my honor and prove myself worthy of your affection." Miming a swirl of a cape, he ran back to the stairs, where the Ascendant had reached the bottom. They clashed once more in a flare of light.

She caught the trash mage as Stewart weaved out of his prison. He sagged into her arms and almost dragged her to the floor. Inwardly cursing at all these men fainting on her, Dani patted his crusty cheeks—thank the heavens for gloves—and jostled him.

"Stewart. Stewart, wake up. We need your help."

The man's face screwed up, and he weakly pushed her away. "No. Please. Not another bath. I's beggin'…"

A less gentle slap. "Stewart!"

"Eh? Lass?" He blinked around. "Oh. This place still. Was hopin' t'was a nasty dream."

She helped him stand and then oriented him so he noticed Ben taking on the two Ascendants on the upper hall.

Stewart chuckled. "The ol' boy gots himself clenched in a mighty tight sphincter, don't he? Always his way."

"Can you help him?"

Stewart perked up. He pointed at the janitor cart that had crashed down with Dani. A garbage bag hung off one corner, weighed down by whatever trash it contained.

"Just get me over t'that beautie, and we'll see if we can't be workin' up a ruckus."

•   •   •

Ben tried to not faint. It had been too long since he'd channeled so much power for such a long time. The Ravishing clawed through his arm, and each time he had to snatch at another ounce of energy, it throbbed, trying to deny him access to the magic.

The two Ascendants fought in tandem. One darted in to throw a punch or kick while the other diverted his defense or struck his Corrupted arm with their aura, blazing the pain higher. He tried to keep that arm angled away, with little success.

Throwing Pure energies against Corrupt often had destructive results, but Pure against Pure felt like two battering rams repeatedly slamming into each other. The weaker one would eventually collapse, but neither had a distinct advantage.

He triggered another spray of water from the bottle he'd requisitioned. The Ascendant on his left bulled through it and struck his ribs with an elbow. Ben wheezed and tried to block with the mop. A foot stomped it down and it tore from his hands. A kick caught him in the jaw.

Strategy fled. Ben scrambled on all fours to get out of range. The Ascendants closed, ready to beat him flat.

Mebbe I shoulda retired when I had the chance.

Then a surge of energy enervated him. Not questioning its source, he lunged upward and caught the nearest Ascendant under the chin. As he stumbled back, Ben kicked the mop at the other's feet, who jumped to avoid tripping over it.

As the Ascendants came at him again, he intercepted each hit and landed a few of his own. They backed up, frowns replacing their confident smiles. Ben rolled his shoulders, for once in five years not feeling the fiery aches in his knees or the knot of muscles down his back. His limbs felt lighter. His thoughts raced.

He spared a glance over his shoulder. Stewart stood near with Dani at his side. The trash mage clutched a soda can in one hand and waved at Ben with the other.

"Get on then, lad. Don't be wastin' the effort."

With renewed strength, Ben turned to finish with the Ascendants. He hesitated in surprise as the Ascendants—and any Cleaners left standing—sprinted away. They fled through the window portal at the far end of the hall, as if called to retreat by some unheard signal.

Ben watched them flee, dumbfounded for a moment. Then an awful realization seared into his mind. Destin must have anticipated Ben making to free Sydney. He'd also counted on Ben not being willing to kill any other Cleaners in their efforts to escape. How better to get them all together where they could be disposed of in a single blow? The man had probably even put together a flowchart for the whole operation.

Feet stamped up one of the side stairs. Sydney chased a third Ascendant out into the hall. Ben lowered his head and raced to intercept.

"No, you don't!" he cried.

He grabbed the Ascendant's jacket a few feet from the portal. The man slipped out of the sleeves and bolted through the glass. The window melted away a heartbeat later, leaving solid stone in its place. Ben barely stopped before he smacked headfirst into the wall.

"Dagnabbit!"

He pounded a fist against the wall, raving at the Chairman and cursing himself for his lack of foresight. Another stall tactic. Long enough for them to activate the Recycling Center's more drastic security measures. He had to warn the others. They had to ... to ...

Dizziness made his head spin in one direction while his body went the other. He couldn't feel his right arm anymore. He staggered back toward Dani and Stewart. He had to warn them about something. What had it been?

Dani and Stewart stood further away the faster he walked. Blood pounded in his ears, and his sight grayed around the edges. Dani's lips moved, but no sound came from them.

Stewart dropped the soda can. Ben watched it tumble in slow motion. The dull aluminum gleam. A last brown drop on the tab. Greasy fingerprints on the side.

His focus narrowed to the instant it hit the floor. When it did, his awareness dropped away with it.

CHAPTER THIRTY

Dani hollered for Sydney as Ben collapsed into her arms. He weighed far heavier than she'd expected, and she nearly sprained her back trying to keep him up. Sydney appeared and added his support. They laid the janitor flat. Ben looked pale and his breaths came shallow. His arms and legs twitched.

"What's wrong with him?" Dani asked, crouched over him. Had the spell Stewart cast been too much? Had he suffered a heart attack or brain aneurysm?

"Wrong?" Sydney echoed. "He's an aged man who took himself beyond his limits in this fool's escapade. He needs a chance to recuperate."

She looked up. "We need to get him out of here. Find a place for him to rest."

He tilted his head to where the portal had vanished. "It seems the exit has been closed. Permanently."

Dani stood and frowned at the wall. Stewart had gone back to picking through the garbage bag contents, while Sydney watched her expectantly.

"If all they wanted to do was trap us in here," she said, "why'd they stick around to trade bruises?"

"That was the single way in and out of this portion of HQ," Sydney said. "Closing such an established portal is not as simple as flipping a switch. It requires considerable strength; with the more practiced Ascendants off on their mission with Destin, my assumption is the ones we faced here were tasked to delay us until they could cut the connection."

Dani swiped her hair back in frustration, only remembering her baldness when she touched bare skin. Great. Now she'd transferred whatever germs she'd picked up on her gloves to her head. She dropped her hand and glowered.

"Can't you just break open a hole in one of these walls and keep busting through them until we get outside or into another section of the building?"

"Dani, Headquarters isn't a cohesive structure. Didn't Ben mention?"

"He said something about various entrances once, but didn't elaborate."

Sydney tapped fingertips. "Each stretch of offices, supply depots, and containment centers is a separate entity unto itself, confined within a pocket reality and connected through the window-watchers' glassways. If we broke through far enough, we'd end up falling into the cracks between our realm and that of the Pantheons. The Gutters. Not a pleasant place to visit, assuming you survive the first step."

"We can't just sit here and wait until they come back. We need to think of something."

"Let me know when you do."

Ignoring her scowl, Sydney retrieved the white jacket Ben had torn off the Ascendant and held it up for inspection. His nose scrunched.

"Not exactly my style, but beggars mustn't choose, and all that blather." The white material faded to gray and turned tattered and threadbare. Sydney slipped into this and adjusted it about his shoulders. "Better. They do say the vagabond style is all the rage these days."

Not a bad look, she silently admitted. With his close-cut hair, boyish features and mismatched clothes, he held the air of a down-on-his-luck street magician. She kept this opinion to herself. Didn't want him to think she actually noticed his appearance.

She stomped over to one of the carts left behind in the evacuation. There, she retrieved wipes, all-purpose cleaner, and a sponge. So armed, she went to work restoring a semblance of personal sanitation. It was all she could do until they came up with a plan.

As she polished her scalp, she glared around. Wonderful. Trapped in a magical prison with hundreds of Scum creatures wanting to chew on her vital organs. This made studying for semester finals seem like a vacation.

Plastic and cloth rustled as Stewart sat next to her. She glanced at him. He didn't look as silly without his newspaper jacket and plastic bowler hat, but he didn't exactly boost her confidence, either. Maybe if he had one of those trash golems around …

"I don't suppose you've got some whizmajig spell that can transport us back to your dump, huh?"

He tugged an ear. "Lass, if'n I did, you think I'd still be here, waitin' for you to come pop me free?"

"Good point."

"What's you doin' here, anyhoo? Thought you'd be far and away by now."

She explained what had happened after they escaped the dump. She added everything Ben had told her about the hybrid Petty being born, plus Destin removing her and Ben so he could go after it himself. As she started in on the prison break, Stewart cut her off with a tongue-click of disapproval.

"What?" she asked.

He tilted his head to where Sydney stood, craning his neck to try and admire himself in the new jacket. "Now, lass, I's not one to be judgin' your pick o' beaus, but—"

Dani tossed a used wipe back onto the cart. "I tell you all that and you're worried about me hooking up with an overgrown brat?"

The floor shuddered. Stewart's spine stiffened.

"Oh dear," he said.

"What?" She snatched up a squeegee. "What's wrong?"

Sydney hurried over. He and the trash mage exchanged a look, and the entropy mage grimaced.

"I don't think Ben expected them to go this far. Nothing we can do to stop it now. Do you have any protective measures in that bag of tricks?"

Stewart plunged a hand into the trash bag, concentration etched on his face.

"What's happening?" Dani asked.

"Consider it a dead man's switch in case a portion of HQ is compromised," Sydney said. "Or, say, if a janitor decides to start freeing Corrupt prisoners."

Stewart held up a ball of crumpled bubble wrap.

Sydney nodded. "That'll do."

The trash mage bent over the plastic clump and began muttering as he traced sigils around it. Dani jabbed the squeegee at Sydney's chest.

"Tell me—"

He tapped the edge, and the tool crumbled into nothingness. "They're going to collapse this portion of HQ."

The blood drained from her face. "Collapse?"

"The entirety of the Recycling Center will implode, purging everything and everyone it contains. The option remains for us to break out into the Gutters. I suggest we take it."

"But you said—"

"When presented with the complete certainty of a horrible death and the mere possibility of a horrible death, which would you choose?" He pointed to Ben. "You and Stewart carry the old man. I'll need both hands to open the way. Unless you wish to leave him behind."

Dani tried to stare him down. Even with Carl still threatening to decapitate him, how could she trust what he said? For all she knew, he could take them back to the Cleansers, or deliver them to the urmoch to be eaten alive.

His gaze didn't waver, and finally she huffed and waved for Stewart to join her by Ben.

"I got his arms," she said. "You get his feet."

They hauled the janitor up between them. Sweat beaded Dani's forehead as they trudged over to Sydney, who had moved to the wall where the portal had been. He rapped on it as if testing for studs behind the stone.

Another tremor shook the chamber. Stewart squawked and almost dropped Ben's feet. As Dani struggled to compensate, she looked to Sydney, wondering why he hadn't opened the way out yet. Then she noticed the thin line of his mouth, the twitch of a cheek, and the slightest tremble to his hands.

He was frightened. And for someone who could erase objects and people from existence with a touch, realizing he feared what waited in the Gutters unsettled Dani more than anything.

Then he placed his hands on the wall and closed his eyes. The wall disintegrated into a square hole. Wind howled into their faces, bringing with it scents of mulch, ice, and another sharp smell that, oddly, made Dani remember visiting elephants at a zoo as a child.

Darkness waited beyond.

Sydney's smile wavered, then firmed as he turned to her and extended a hand. "Trust me."

She stepped up beside him, Ben a heavy weight on her shoulders. A horrendous metallic shrieking started behind them, along with an eruption of heat that struck her back.

Sydney shouted, "Jump!"

They leapt through. The moment she crossed the threshold, Ben's weight vanished. An odd momentum caught her and spun her around. Stewart, Sydney, and Ben fell alongside her, flailing in the void. The light of the Recycling Center dwindled fast, but the opening remained large enough for her to see what came next.

As the pocket reality containing the Recycling Center shrank and twisted in on itself. Dani's eyes strained to make sense of the warped dimensions.

The walls rippled like waves, picking up fragments of the collapsing chamber and flinging it all toward the hole Sydney had created. Dani realized that normally it would've all shrunk into a homogenous, lifeless mass, but they'd given some of it a way to escape the pressure.

A last twist and scrunch, as if a giant fist clenched around it. Glittering debris and bodies spewed into the space overhead and fell after them. The light winked out.

They plummeted into darkness.

CHAPTER
THIRTY-ONE

ani didn't feel the ground when she hit. With a loud pop, the fall just ceased, as if the laws of inertia and momentum had wandered off to check the pantry for a snack. She lay on a gritty surface which felt neither hot nor cold. Its rough texture scraped her cheek as she stirred, fearing a broken neck, snapped knees, or other hideous injury.

A quick self-analysis proved her body responded as she commanded it. She had her share of aches and bruises from the brawl in the Recycling Center, but otherwise her arms and legs moved fine, and she could think clearly. But what about the others?

Fingers dug into gray dirt as she gathered herself.

Dirt?

She jerked upright, but dust stung her eyes and made them water. Her hands trembled as she fought the urge to knuckle at the pain. It would just grind the particles in more. Possible eye and skin infections shot through her mind.

Conjunctivitis. Septic shock.

Her breaths quickened as panic stirred.

Cellulitis. Gangrene. Osteomye—

She mentally snapped at herself. *Stop already. You just fell through some interdimensional hole and you're worried about infections? Do you really think that's what's important right now?*

You sure about this? the jittery part of herself asked. *Because I'm just getting started on this list. Got some nice necrotizing skin disease we could fixate on.*

If she'd been exposed to anything, there was no undoing it. She could have a hissy fit or she could put on her big girl panties and deal with the situation at hand.

She took a slow breath, and this time the exhale came out calmer. Right. Perhaps it was time to figure out where her companions had gotten off to.

Blinking away the dirt, she tried to make sense of where she'd landed. The sky was a black, starless expanse dropping to a colorless horizon. Craters pockmarked the ground around her, with stark shadows and gray boulders reminding her of photos she'd seen of the moon's surface.

"Anyone?" Her call came out hoarse—probably from all the screaming she did during the fall.

Someone moved by her side. A pale hand reached for her. Dani almost took it, until tattooed wings quivered in her peripheral vision.

The gnash—whatever a gnash was—had been thrown free in the collapse of the Recycling Center, and lay in its chains a few feet away. The iron bands had tangled around its legs and neck, but one arm had gotten loose, and it used this to drag itself toward her. Its albino form almost shone in contrast to the surrounding bleakness.

"Come to the gnash, pretty thing," it said. *"The gnash will protect you."*

She crab-crawled a few feet away, then stood on shaky legs. "I'd rather not get eaten," she said, holding a hand to her chest.

"The gnash does not eat helpless little girls."

She swallowed. "What does the gnash eat?"

"Little girls who fight back. The gnash savors the clawing and screaming and kicking and—"

"Well, I'm not going to fight right now, okay? So, no munching."

Its throat-eyes brimmed with yellow tears. *"No fighting for the gnash? No fleeing?"*

She turned her back on the creature to scan the area for the others. A hand settled on her shoulder. She screamed, spun, and punched with all her strength. Knuckles connected with a flat stomach.

Sydney gasped and fell back, clutching his abdomen.

Dani stood over him, fists shaking. "Don't do that!"

He managed a weak smile. "I deserved that. Bad manners to sneak up on a lady."

"Be glad I didn't break your nose. Where are we?"

With a hand twirl, he invited her to look for herself. Concrete slabs, shattered tiles and rebar lay all about, either half-buried in the colorless earth or forming miniature craters of their own. Stewart sat dejectedly on a pile of cinder blocks, with Ben's sprawled form at his feet. The janitor remained unconscious. Neither looked hurt by however far they'd fallen, nor had any of the following debris proven deadly.

Her gaze shifted to the surrounding landscape and her breath caught as she realized the scope of the place.

They stood at the base of a low range of ashen mountain peaks. A stretch of gray earth ran a few hundred feet out from the mountain roots until it broke off into the jagged edge of a ravine. Dani tracked the length of the canyon, which ran out of sight in both directions and appeared to have no opposing edge—simply a place where the world fell away into nothingness.

Okay. We aren't going that way.

"Where are we?" she asked.

"I believe you're repeating yourself," Sydney said as he stood.

"Yeah. You didn't answer, so I asked again."

He patted dust off his shoulders, which improved the state of his jacket not at all. "We're in the Gutters. A realm of dead worlds and little else. Closest thing you'll come to Limbo outside of some questionable religious beliefs."

She snorted, and then glanced at him in suspicion. A decent joke and a straight answer all at once? What prompted that?

"But where in the Gutters? Where do we go from here?"

"Unfortunately, your first question doesn't have a real answer. The Gutters aren't a place you can map out. There are intersections between this realm and ours, but I'm unfamiliar with the one we came through. As for the second, I didn't have the luxury of planning much beyond keeping us from being impacted into our own bowels."

Dani adjusted her gloves as she tried to figure out the best course of action. With Ben still out of commission and Sydney being anything but optimistic, it looked like she needed to take the lead.

"We obviously can't stay here," she said. "We need to move. Try and find some shelter, maybe see if we can scrounge up anything to eat and drink." Not that she'd trust anything unless it was boiled for a few hours.

Giardia. Dracunculiasis. Bilhar—

"Shut up," she growled under her breath. "Not helping."

Sydney frowned, perhaps thinking the mutter aimed at him. "When I say this is a realm of dead worlds, I mean it in the utmost sense. Nothing grows here. No water either. The only living things you'll encounter in the Gutters are trapped here, passing through, or hiding out—and you rarely want to meet up with something that considers this realm a decent hiding place."

"Speaking of encountering things," she said, "we've got another problem. Something came through with us. Calls itself a gnash."

Sydney looked over at where the creature lay in its bonds. "Indeed."

"So, uh, what exactly is it?"

Sydney chuckled. "A gnash is a manifestation of Corrupt hunger. So long as you don't tempt it with what it wants, it will remain relatively docile. Show fear or attempt to run, however, and it will attack."

The creature screeched through its nail-teeth. *"The gnash knows this place. The safe places. The hungry places. Do not leave the gnash alone."*

It looked up at them, and Dani had the impression it was trying to make puppy eyes. The fact that its eyes were situated along its throat made the attempt all the more disturbing.

She went over and crouched by the gnash, though not too close. "You know where we are?"

"The gnash travels far," it said. *"The gnash knows the darkness of this realm-not-realm as well as the void always in the gnash's stomach. Places to go between and back and forward. Will none feed the gnash?"*

"You're talking about intersections. Ways we can get back to our realm."

"*Yes. Gnash knows. One is near, but the gnash's legs are weak from hunger. Give the gnash strength to walk, and it will show the path.*"

It reached for her with its free hand, but she stood and returned to Sydney, who looked at her with alarm.

"Dani? Surely you don't mean to—"

She snapped a hand up. "I don't plan on moping around here until we starve or die of thirst. He's not my first pick for a tour guide, but unless you're lying about not knowing where we are, we don't have many other options."

His voice lowered. "I've dealt with such creatures before. Given the first opportunity, you'll be halfway down its maw before you can scream."

"Only if I tempt it first, like you said. And if it turns violent, I'm sure you can protect me." She smiled at the liquid band dimpling his neck. "Carl isn't going to decapitate you for killing Scum."

"Therein lies … a problem." Sydney cleared his throat. Despite the surrounding gloom, Dani thought he flushed. "Entropy does not exist within this place. Many of the natural laws do not apply here."

Her brows rose. "You're powerless?"

He made a shushing motion. "In essence. Until Ben awakes, we are reliant on you and any muckwork he," he pointed an elbow at Stewart, "can summon. Can we keep from shouting that fact?"

She briefly shut her eyes. No wonder he'd feared entering this place. If it nullified his ability, he must be feeling vulnerable, something she doubted his ego suffered well. While a small part of her gloated at this, she also knew they might need his skill, the gnash being one of many unknown threats.

Dani woke her power just enough to search the area for elements she could whip into a disaster.

"Okay." She opened her eyes. "There's air here, and I can sense earth, so my powers aren't out of the question. But so long as the gnash doesn't know you can't hurt it, you can still act like a threat. Now go get that beast freed enough to walk, but leave the chains on its neck."

Sydney peered at her. "You've changed since we first met."

He bowed and, to Dani's pleasant surprise, went to do as told without further argument. Mulling over what he meant by her having changed, she joined Stewart in his vigil by Ben.

"Sorry for the mess," she said. "I'd say something about frying pans and fires, but it'd just sound stupid."

Stewart squinted up at her. "Lass, if you hadn't come along, I'd be smaller'n a pea's spit right about now. I owes you my life."

"You don't owe me anything," she said. "Good thing is, I think we might have a way out of here."

He sucked through his teeth as he nodded. "Nasty place, the Gutters. Heard o' it. Never thought I's be seein' it with me own eyes."

She eyed the garbage bag he'd somehow held on to during their tumble. "Anything else useful in there?"

Stewart rummaged through the bag. "Aha." He held up a used matchbook. "This may help."

A wave of his hand, and the matchbook vanished. Dani wondered what this was supposed to accomplish until she took a second look at his hand. His fingers had become five giant matches. He struck the thumb-match off the ground and it blazed to life. This returned some color to their faces and clothes, but didn't illuminate anything more than a few yards away.

Sydney came over with the gnash trailing him on a chain leash. It looked mournful as it hunched along, as if expecting a swat on the nose for peeing on the carpet. Dani stood between it and Ben, making sure it didn't get any ideas about snacking on what it might assume was a helpless victim. She took the chain from the mage and tried to not think too hard about what the other end connected to. Like the blot-hound, this creature made her think of an oversized germ, a virus given monstrous proportions that needed to be destroyed. For now, though, it might prove useful.

"You can carry Ben," she told Sydney.

He sighed. "From prisoner to pack mule. Have I not suffered enough?"

"I'll let you know when you have." A rattle of the leash brought the gnash's attention to her. "Take us to the nearest intersection. No funny business."

The gnash's throat-eyes glistened. *"Hunger is never funny."* It trotted toward the gray mountains and pulled her behind.

CHAPTER
THIRTY-TWO

Dani kept trying to blink her eyes clear as they walked, but finally decided the light of this realm, not her eyes, was the problem. The finger-flames Stewart conjured didn't illuminate far enough to imbue her with any confidence. The darkness seemed physical, like the world had been wrapped in black curtains.

They passed by other piles of rubble from the Recycling Center at odd intervals. When Dani remarked at how far some of the debris had scattered, Sydney explained there was no correlation of distance between this realm and theirs.

"People can take advantage of this," he said. "If you know the ways and have the means to open them, you can sometimes control the entry and exit points. It's tricky, however, and there are no guarantees you'll make it back out the same route."

"So when we reach the intersection," she asked, "how do we open it?"

He fell silent again and, after a few unsuccessful attempts to force an answer, she gave up and let him sulk.

They discovered no buildings. No paths. Just the bland mountains ahead, looking no nearer for all the time they'd walked.

She looked to the creature she'd nicknamed Gnashy. It kept up a steady clip, its hairless, muscled body bunching and pulling in ways that had nothing to do with muscle or bone. Every so often, it dropped to all fours and knuckled along before rising on hind legs again.

Some of her biology studies kicked in, and she wondered what one might discover if they got a gnash on the dissecting table. Did all manifestations and constructs contain nothing but energy and spell cores, or were some of these creatures organic cryptoids that hadn't been discovered by modern science?

"Where are we headed?" she asked it.

"Place the gnash knows. Hole in tall rock. Keeps non-food from biting off naked heads." It pointed a claw. *"There."*

She strained her eyes but failed to pick out any distinctive features along the foot of the mountains. With Stewart and Sydney on either side, tasked to keep a watch for any threats, she focused on making sure Gnashy didn't get any bright ideas.

Its three wings turned out to be non-functional as far as she could tell. Three thin bones jutted from its shoulders and spine. Flaps of translucent flesh hung down from these and quivered with each step. Were they for heat dispersion? Some sort of sensory organ?

Gnashy's mouth hung open and it panted with a purple tongue flopped over its rusty teeth. She couldn't stop comparing it to a puppy. An evil, ravenous, bite-your-face-off puppy, true, but still. She prided herself on using the resources she'd been stuck with, betting Ben would've done no different.

She resisted the impulse to giggle as she imagined the reactions of her classmates, or better yet, her family, should she return with such a creature in tow.

Look what followed me home, Ma. Can I keep him?

Gnashy stopped, and she almost bumped into its back fronds.

"The gnash smells food."

She shook its chain to urge it onward. "Does Gnashy ever stop smelling food?"

Its oversized nostrils flared. *"This is living food. Angry food. Frightened food. Hunt with the gnash?"*

"No. No hunting. Bad Gnashy." She waved to catch the men's attention. They edged closer while keeping their eyes on the surrounding area.

"What's wrong?" Sydney asked, setting Ben down to give his arms a rest.

"Gnashy says he smells something nearby."

Stewart raised his hand. The first match had extinguished, leaving his normal thumb with a blackened nail. Now his forefinger lit the area. Gnashy turned a slow circle, sniffing and licking his bleeding gums. Then he stiffened and stared in a particular direction. The three of them looked that way, and Stewart mumbled something that flared the light a bit higher.

A flash of orange, off that way.

While Sydney might not command entropy for the time, he still proved nimble and fast. Before Dani could call out, he'd sprinted toward the movement.

Someone rose and turned to flee. But Sydney threw himself forward, and the two tumbled together. While the attack looked careless, Sydney rolled through and came up on top. He had a knee on the person's hips and their wrists pinned to the black earth.

"Don't move or you're dust," he said.

The person beneath him went slack and uttered a soft sob. Dani ran up, Gnashy's chains jangling as it followed. With a mix of dismay and relief, she recognized the person as the maid she'd faced. While she didn't enjoy the thought of another body to worry about, at least it meant the woman had escaped the implosion.

"Let her go," she told Sydney. "I can handle her."

When he reluctantly did so, Dani planted herself at the maid's feet. She made sure the woman got a good look at the party surrounding her, and then gestured for her to get up.

"We're not going to hurt you. What's your name?"

The maid pointed to her breast pocket. Dani mentally kicked herself as she spotted the name threaded on the jumpsuit. *Patty.*

Dani smiled grimly. "All right, Patricia. You know what I am and what I can do, right? I'm sure they sent out memos."

Patty's scowl answered that.

"You want to get out of here alive?"

A petulant nod.

"Fine. Then you do as I say, got it? I don't care where you are on the organizational chart. The Chairman just gave us all the pink slip and had security escort us out without a severance package. Are you going to really keep fighting us because of his orders?"

Patty curled her upper lip. "You're Scum."

"They are," Dani said, circling her head at the other three. "I'm not. Neither is he." A nod at Ben's prone form.

"You have a gnash with you!"

"This cuddly fellow?" She couldn't make herself actually pat Gnashy's shoulder, so she waved in its direction. "He's been a good boy so far, and if he keeps it up, he might get a treat later on."

"The gnash will enjoy a meaty treat."

"Quiet," she said under her breath. She beamed at Patty. "We're just companions of convenience until we get out of the Gutters. You can come with us if you want, but that means you play nice. Otherwise, we'll figure out some way to tie you up and leave you here for whatever else comes snuffling by. Got that?"

Patty licked her lips. Fear shone in her eyes, but she nodded and stood slowly, as if fearing another tackle from Sydney. Or perhaps it was the way Gnashy kept drooling her way.

"What's the plan?" she asked.

"Get to an intersection and figure out how to open the way back to our world."

Sandy-brown eyes widened. "You know where one is?"

"I don't, but the gnash does, and he's showing us the way." Dani saw the planned insult rise to Patty's lips. "If you have a better idea, by all means, speak up." They matched glares until the maid looked aside. "Right. Let's keep moving."

Dani kept one eye on their beastly guide and the other on Patty. The maid hung back a few steps, but didn't go beyond the circumference of light Stewart cast. She scowled every time she caught Dani looking.

At last, Gnashy stopped. The peak of the nearest mountain blended into the sky. Only on the furthest edges could they make out the gray blur of an outline. Before them was a cliff wall with an uneven hole cored into the base, large enough for a truck to drive through.

"The gnash has brought you here. Here is a safe way."

"The cave?" Dani asked, pointing to the opening ahead. "That's the intersection?"

"No. Old nest of the gnash, carved near safe way. Once, much feeding. Now, only hunger for the gnash." Despite its scratchy, needling voice, it still communicated sadness in its tone.

Dani saw nothing but the endless ashen landscape and their tracks marking the way they'd come. The others appeared as perplexed as she felt.

"Where is it then?" she asked.

Gnashy stamped its clawed feet, raising a puff of ashen dust. *"Is here. Can you not smell? Can you not taste?"*

Dani raised a hand to her face, preferring to not smell and taste too much of the grit. "You can't open it for us?" Half-fearing an ambush, she stretched her power out into the earth and air to detect anything amiss.

"Never the gnash opens," it said. *"Not the gnash's place or power. The gnash waits as things go in and out, up and through. Sometimes it pounces. Sometimes it follows and drags food back. Never opens."*

She glanced at Sydney, who shook his head and made a pushing motion, warning her to not call him out in front of the others.

On her order, everyone spread out, though not so far as to lose sight of the others, and none straying too close to the cave entrance. They tramped around in circles, trying to spot the intersection the gnash claimed existed. Dani had no idea what to look for, having expected a miniature wormhole, a door in the earth, maybe a flashing light.

She used the gnash as a makeshift dowsing rod, pulling it to different starting points and then letting it tug her back to the area it had first indicated. Once she triangulated a spot thirty feet out from the cave entrance, she used the toe of her boot to scratch an *X* into the dirt, and called Stewart over.

"Can you sense anything?" she asked.

He sniffed the spot. "There's somethin' here, sure 'nuff. Twitchin' m'nose like an old stink, but I's got no firm fix. Sorry, lass. If I had an ol' key or doorknob, mebbe so. Otherwise we ain't goin' nowhere."

"Great." A look Patty's way, as the woman had sidled up to eavesdrop. "Anything you can do?"

The maid tossed her hair back. "Maybe if I had my broom. From what I've heard, you can't exactly pry these things open with your bare hands."

Dani suppressed a groan. Now what? She resisted the urge to flop down and pout, not wanting to show weakness in front of the others—or get herself dirtier than she already was. Instead she kept studying the area until she fixed on the black opening in the base of the mountain. She pointed that way with her chin.

"Let's scope out the cave. At the least, it will keep us from sitting out in the open."

"What if something's in there?" Patty asked, scowling at the gnash. "What if your pet is trying to lure us in so its family can pounce?"

"The gnash does not like to share. No family. Nestlings all gone. All tasty."

"Lovely," said the maid.

"Then you can help us handle whatever pops up." Dani thumbed up at the black sky. "Besides, I don't like this dark sky. Anything could be hiding out above, waiting to swoop down the moment we're off our guard. At least the cave gives us a defensible position."

The group gathered at the threshold until their eyes adjusted to the interior. Dani kept her power poised, ready to shake the rock walls down or whip up a gale. With a look between them and collective tense of their shoulders, they ducked inside.

Nothing clawed their faces off. Nothing tore their hearts out of their chests. The first wind Dani had experienced in this realm patted their faces as it passed by, smelling of mildew and leaving her cheeks feeling skuzzy. She ran her gloved hand along the near wall. The mountain's interior had the glassy, smooth texture of obsidian. The floor of the cave remained the same purple-gray dirt, punctuated by knobby mounds which Dani didn't dare uncover for fear of exposing bones.

They stopped a few strides further. Sydney breathed in relief as he laid Ben down. Stewart jogged along until he hit a dead end twenty feet down, where his finger-lights glinted off the stone.

"None be sneakin' behind our backs 'ere," he said as he returned. "Good a spot as any be."

Dani smiled at him, and then at Gnashy. "Thank you."

The gnash made a sound like a food processor, which Dani guessed was its approximation of purring.

Patty gasped, putting a hand against a wall to steady herself as she stared at the ceiling. Dani frowned at the woman.

"Hey, buck up. If I'm not grabbing my knees, you don't have any excuse."

"Dani," came Sydney's voice. "Look up."

She did.

"Whoa."

Countless black facets composed the roof of the cave. These must've drawn in and magnified what little light existed in this realm, for they projected an image of what hid in the dark heavens.

Planet upon planet hung above them, each gray and unmoving. She stopped counting at fifty. Without any sense of scale, Dani couldn't tell how far away they were, but some appeared as big as Jupiter, while others reminded her of silver moons. Several were frozen in the act of crashing into one another, planet-wide cracks piercing their crusts. None showed any signs of water, orbits, or lights that might indicate a civilization.

"What is all this?" Patty asked in wonder and fear.

"Behold the dead worlds," Sydney said.

Dani shook herself free from the overwhelming view. "The what?"

"Some people think these are all the worlds Corruption has conquered," he said. "They became so thoroughly twisted that their very essence died out. Others think these are all the versions of the Earth that were destroyed in other realities. Quantum castoffs, while our own living world continues on."

"You think differently?"

"I know differently." He raised a hand to the ceiling display. "We are seeing the future. This is the universe as it is fated to be. Lifeless. Dark. Empty." He tilted his head back, as if bathing in the non-light. "Yet there is a harsh beauty to it. A peace in understanding that oblivion comes for us all in the end."

"And that just gets you off, doesn't it?" Patty said. "You entropy mages are sick."

He smirked. "Sickness. Health. Death. Life. Darkness. Light. Corruption. Purity. Ugliness." His hand rose to Dani's cheek. "Beauty."

"Evil and Good," she said, pulling away.

Sydney shook his head. "All the ones I listed are natural aspects of existence, but those two are ones we humans tack on to give our lives meaning. They are the lies we tell ourselves—that this is good and that is evil. That one act of destruction is done with noble reason, while another is thoughtless malice. The distinctions are all in our fickle and easily deceived minds. They have no place in reality."

"I don't have to listen to this." Patty pushed off the wall and headed for the cave entrance.

Sydney sighed as he watched her go. "A pity to see those so thoroughly indoctrinated that they refuse to hear any truth but that which they desperately cling to."

"As if the same couldn't be said of you, Mr. Oblivion-or-Bust."

"Ah, but I once saw all this with a mindset similar to hers."

"How?"

"I've been here before." At her surprised expression, he clarified, "Not this exact spot, but another world, perhaps one of those we gaze upon even now. When I was a handyman with the Cleaners, we followed an *icarusk* as it tried to claw through the realms and destroyed it here.

"When I saw this sight for the first time, it almost broke me. To realize that no matter how much we fought, no matter what we sacrificed, no matter how many gallons of our life's blood we spilled on the stones for the ungrateful bastards who pull our puppet strings—none of it is of any significance. So I spurned my former calling and refused to bow to Purity any longer. Every world eventually ends up here, lifeless and dark. So why fight? Why not hasten the inevitable?"

"You must not get invited to many parties," Dani said.

"Depends on the venue."

With Gnashy in tow, she left him gazing up at the dead worlds and walked out to where Patty slouched against the rock wall just outside the entrance. Patty didn't acknowledge her arrival, and the two of them stared at the horizon for several minutes.

Gnashy's heavy breathing wore on her patience, so she pulled it over to the other side of the entrance and pointed to the ground.

"Sit."

Gnashy plopped to the earth, its back frond-wings quivering.

"Stay."

Its head lifted, so the throat-eyes blinked up at her pleadingly. *"Mistress bring the gnash a snack?"*

Dani hesitated, unsure what to promise the creature. It had proven helpful and placid so far, despite its fearsome appearance and questionable appetite.

"Maybe when we get back to the real world," she said. "Do you like candy? I can probably scrounge up some."

It nodded like a child that had been told it could have a free pony ride. *"Marrow is sweet candy."*

Suppressing a shudder, Dani went back and sat down beside Patty.

"Hi."

The maid glanced at her and sneered. "Go away, Scum."

"Hey, I didn't say, 'let me eat your firstborn child and use your bones as a toothpick.' I said *hello*. Try again."

Patty bowed her head. "What do you want?"

"That's a little better. I just want to talk. You wouldn't believe how much testosterone I've had to put up with ever since the Cleaners snatched me. Is there always this much pit-scratching and chest-bumping going on? Just don't tell me the showers are co-ed back at HQ."

The faintest of smiles twitched Patty's lips.

"So." Dani tucked her knees up to her chest. "How'd they recruit you?"

Patty spoke slowly at first, as if uncertain whether some joke was being played on her. "My family has always been part of the Cleaners. My brother is a plumber. I've got an older sister who's a window washer. My parents are retired."

"Lucky. Must be nice to have been raised for the job. Cuts down on the surprise when something jumps out of the toilet and tries to bite your butt cheeks."

A dry laugh escaped the other woman, and Patty graced her with a sidelong look. "What about your family?"

Dani grimaced. "They apparently think I'm overseas, being the good little tuition investment I've always been. I'll supposedly get to see them again when I finish my training." She blew a raspberry. "As if that's going to happen after this whole fiasco. I guess I should lower my hopes from getting my old life back to coming out alive and sane."

"How'd they find you?"

"Burnt down and flooded my college library—at the same time. Neat trick, huh?"

That drew Patty's full attention. Now that they weren't trying to kill each other, Dani realized how close the two of them were in age. Patty couldn't be more than two or three years older.

"You went to college?"

"Yeah. People do that sort of stuff when they aren't mopping floors and squishing pipe monsters for a living. Didn't you go?"

"Why bother with college when I already knew what I'm supposed to do with my life?"

"Supposed to or wanted to?"

"Is there a difference?"

"There should be."

"Not for me." Patty sighed. "You're the real lucky one. You at least got to know what that kind of life is like. Don't get me wrong, I love my work, but sometimes it's hard when you can never escape it. With my whole family involved, it's the only thing they talk about. All my boyfriends have been other Cleaners, which is never a good idea no matter what company you work for. Plus, I have to constantly lie to any friend I have outside the business about what I really do."

"I'm lucky?" Dani pointed at her bald head. "See this? This is from a bunch of Cleansers trying to turn me into a fire goddess. Before that I was attacked by giant lizards. I got sandblasted by a dust demon—"

"I think you mean dust devil."

"Whatever. And before that, it was a blot monster in the women's bathroom."

"Blot-hound."

"Whatever! I haven't been at this job for a week and I already want to know what the retirement plan is like. You call that lucky?"

Patty scratched the back of her neck, looking confused. "But ... after all you've done and seen, you still want to go back to your old life?"

Dani opened her mouth to say of course she wanted to go back. That she craved a normal life full of textbooks and tuition, of dorm rooms and feeding Tetris in between math lectures and study halls.

The words stalled in her throat. It would be peaceful, yes, though she might struggle with paranoia, knowing some of the things hiding beneath the kitchen floor or in the air ducts. And there'd be the constant struggle to control her powers. But somehow it all seemed so ...

Boring?

"I dunno," she said. "I still want to get a medical degree, but maybe—" She realized the other woman had started quietly crying. She took Patty's near hand and gripped it. "Hey? What's wrong?"

Patty wiped her face on her arm, smearing her tears. Then she flung a hand out at the dead world before them. "What if we're stuck here forever, wandering some wasteland until we drop from hunger or thirst? I don't want to die this way."

"Hunger? The gnash knows hunger. You do not."

Dani shushed the gnash. It muttered and crouched again while she leaned in to whisper.

"We're going to make it out of here, okay? You'll see. I bet you'll even get a ton of overtime pay for this."

"Nope. Overtime pay isn't retroactive, and you wouldn't believe how much paperwork you have to file just to get it approved in the first place."

Dani narrowed her eyes. "What about unexpected emergencies or late-night jobs? We don't get anything tossed our way for the extra effort?"

"All expected sacrifices for the good of the company."

"Let me guess ... the Ascendants don't exactly play by the same rules."

"Of course not. They're salaried, not hourly, for one thing. Get to come and go as they please. Plus, one of my ex-boyfriends was in Accounting and showed me some of their expense budgets. You wouldn't believe—"

Sydney shouted from within the cave. "Dani! Ben's waking up."

With a happy cry, Dani jumped to her feet. Patty's hand slipped out of hers. The maid looked up, lips twisted with the effort of holding back further tears. Dani tried for a reassuring smile.

"Don't worry. Things are already getting better. Come on."

She called out, "Gnashy, heel!" as she ran back into the cave to where Stewart and Sydney knelt beside Ben.

The janitor groaned and shifted as if waking from a bad dream. His eyelids fluttered open. Dani tensed, worried that he might be suffering from something other than exhaustion, like internal bleeding. There'd be no way to treat that here.

He focused on her, looking confused for a moment. Then he smiled.

"Hey, princess."

Dani released the breath she'd been holding. "Ben. Thank ***. I was getting worried."

His gaze flicked over to Sydney and Stewart, who bowed and nodded respectively.

"What happened?" Ben asked. "Where are we?"

"We escaped the Recycling Center," she said. "But we're not exactly better off." She explained Sydney's breaking them into the Gutters and the dead end at the intersection. "We haven't had time to figure out how to open it," she concluded. "And we've got some others with us. I didn't know what to do and wasn't sure when you'd wake up and ..."

He reached up and patted her shoulder. "Good to see you too."

She smiled and squeezed his hand.

A scream rent the moment.

Hot panic burning through her, Dani dashed back outside. Her scream echoed the first.

Patty lay half a dozen yards away, eyes wide and lifeless. One arm had been torn off at the shoulder and thrown aside like a gnawed chicken wing. The rest of her had been slit from sternum to pelvis.

Gnashy raised its muzzle from her flayed torso. Teeth dripped crimson as it offered Dani a handful of kidney.

"Feed with the gnash? Sweet candy."

CHAPTER
THIRTY-THREE

The trio of wing-like flaps on the gnash's back had expanded into translucent bags, each filled with a miasma of fluids and scraps it sucked out of the dead maid.

Snacks for later, a dark part of Dani's mind whispered.

She stared, bug-eyed, while the gnash cocked its head as if confused by her hesitation to join in the meal. Only when it bent down for another bite did she snap out of her shock.

Horror, rage, and disbelief lit up her mind. She cried out in denial and spread her arms, sending her power grasping as far as it could reach. It latched onto dead stone and stirred air unmoved for eons. Her heart pounded treble pace, and the earth shook in time. Her breaths raced, and the air spun about.

The gnash rose into a crouch as it sensed the disturbed elements.

"What ... have ... you ... done?" With each word Dani yelled, gusts buffeted the gnash from all sides. It cowered, hands above its head while its throat-eyes squeezed shut.

The gnash is sorry! The gnash hungered.

"You killed her! Monster!"

Her curses turned into babbling as she let the magic build. It didn't control her, but joined with her fury, both raising each other to new heights of power.

Her mistake. She'd tried to ignore the gnash's true nature. Tried to pretend it was a pet, a toy, when it remained a blight on existence. A splotch to be scoured away. A disease to be cured.

The gnash turned and fell to all fours to lope away. Dani clenched her fists. Two crevices shuddered open beneath its feet. It wailed as it dropped in up to its knees. Another wave slammed the earth back together. The gnash keened and fell over, legs gone below the joints. It dragged itself forward, trailing white ooze.

Dani's final cry shook the mountain. A car-sized chunk of obsidian shattered above her head. As it fell, the wind caught it up and spun the gleaming black shards into a whirlwind. This flew over and stopped above the gnash. Its spinning tightened and sped up until a cone of razor glass narrowed down to needlepoint a bare foot above the creature.

She reached out and visualized her power as a giant hand holding the spike.

She stabbed down.

The explosion tilted the horizon for a moment. Shards sliced her cheeks, forehead and scalp, but she didn't care. The tremors beneath her feet didn't fade for another minute.

Panting, Dani stared at where the gnash had been. Black rubble marred the formerly even horizon. Glass plinked against the mountain and pattered the dirt around her. She strained for a single glimpse of white, any remaining scrap of the beast to wipe away.

Footsteps tread soft behind her. The others had been calling her name all along, but she'd been so taken by the spell that she only heard them in retrospect.

A hand touched her shoulder.

"Dani?"

The strings of tension vibrating through her body snapped. She dropped to her knees and elbows. Her mouth pressed into the dirt as she wailed. The earth muffled her, but the cries reverberated through her mind and heart.

She'd killed someone. Patty was dead because of her. She might as well have gutted the woman herself.

Sobs wracked her. She hugged herself, trying to contain the grief tearing her apart from within.

Ben sat and pulled her head and shoulders into his lap. He stroked her hair as a father might, but said nothing. Eventually the hysterics ebbed and left all her thoughts and feelings hollow. Her vision swam with black and gray, the same colors that painted her soul.

As she let the swirl of numbness drag her down, a last whisper flitted through her mind.

I approve. Perhaps you have potential after all.

• • •

She woke with a start. Yet again, half of her mind tried to leap forward with the assumption that all the recent horrible events were just a bad dream. Then the other half caught up, choked her hope, and threw it into a cage until it learned to behave.

She lay on her back in the cave as grit dug into her scalp and neck. The endless display of dead worlds floated overhead. She watched it, hypnotized by the unnatural stillness. Not a single star winked. Not a single cloud scudded across the faces of the planets.

Shuffling made her turn her head. Ben sat at the cave threshold, a few feet away. Cross-legged, hands on his knees, he stared out at nothing in particular.

"Sydney and Stewart built a little cairn," he said without looking her way. "We can go visit if you want."

Dani expected tears, but only a dry burning came to her eyes. Aside from a twinge in her chest, she remained drained.

"I killed her, Ben." Her voice matched the grayness of the world. She tasted ash … or perhaps that was what the air here tasted like and she hadn't noticed until now.

"Ain't what it looked like to me," he said. "Looked more like she let fear get the better of her and tried to hightail it from a gnash. Once its huntin' instinct got triggered, it went downhill from there." He finally met her gaze. "You didn't kill her, Dani."

Her turn to look away. "I might as well have. If I hadn't kept that beast around, she'd still be alive. She'd still be able to go back to her family. I'm a murderer."

"Naw. You was just on a job where someone died. Big difference. Patty came here on Destin's orders. She chose to tag along with you, if the others tell me right."

Dani snorted. "I chose to bring the gnash with us. I chose to use it as a guide."

"Cleaners are trained to deal with gnashes," he said. "If she'd kept calm, it never woulda attacked." When she didn't respond, he sighed. "Not even a six-eyed oracle coulda said for sure how thing's woulda ended up. You just gotta do whatcha think is right at the time and hope for the best. You ain't ever gonna be prepared for everythin'. And when things get flushed, you gotta learn from the mistake and keep it from happenin' again."

Her fingers clutched the soil. "Is that what Patty was? A learning experience? Is this part of employee orientation? Learn to Lose Someone 101—"

His flinch clipped off her words. The look in his eyes told her he knew exactly how she felt. She knew attacking him to be unfair, that he was only trying to help, but it didn't matter; she needed to vent and he provided the only target. Neither met the other's eyes for a few minutes. Then Dani pushed herself up to lean against the cave wall. Black pebbles drizzled off her outfit.

"So that's it?" She didn't bother disguising the bitterness in her voice. "I rationalize it all and move on?"

He smiled sadly. "There ain't never just a 'that's it.' I ain't gonna promise you won't see her face in your dreams or hear that scream when you wake up. Everyone in the Cleaners has their share of ghosts. We've all been part of a team that got their turds tossed on a griddle. It's part of the business. Part of the job. It's rough and nobody likes it, but you can't beat yourself bloody when it happens.

"And ..." He mimed sucking his thumb. "... if you let this make you curl up and cry for momma the rest of your life, there's gonna be more folks out there who'll end up like Patty 'cause you ain't there to protect 'em."

That snapped her eyes to his. "What?"

His face and voice took on a harder cast. "Time to grow up a little, princess. You wanna be a doctor, right?"

She nodded, confused about what that had to do with this. Was he saying she should've had the medical skills to save the other woman?

"When you get that fancy diploma—and you're gonna—you'll have all sorts of smarty-pants know-how that I ain't even gonna try to pretend I understand. Fancy surgeries and amputatin' heads and stickin' leeches on people to suck out their bad humors. Whatever. But what if you just sat around and whenever a patient came to you, you sent them packin'? You don't treat them 'cause you're too scared of failing?"

"That's not fair, Ben. Setting bones and performing surgery isn't the same as hunting down monsters and scrubbing mystical toilets."

His brows rose. "Ain't it? Corruption's just another disease muckin' up the place. You got the power to clean some of it away and keep a lot of other folks from worryin' about it. No matter whatcha do, you're gonna have lotsa lives in your hands. Being the smart girl you are, you're gonna do the best you can, but sooner or later, someone'll bite it—and there ain't nothin' you'll be able to do. Either it'll be old age or a truck smackin' 'em down in the middle of the street. Sometimes folks just give up and let go.

"You can't make folks choose to live safe. You can't squeeze life into the box you built for it. Look at us here, right now. You think I scheduled this into my calendar to build up some extra vacation time?"

"Oh, so we get vacation days, but not overtime pay?"

His brow rose. "Who toldja that?"

"Patty ... she ... just before ..." Dani waved a hand randomly, not able to complete the sentence.

Ben's demeanor softened, but lost none of the conviction. "Blame's a nasty game to start playin'. It can go on forever. You blame yourself now. Sure. But how far back you gonna go? Is Patty's death my fault 'cause I didn't get us out of the Recycling Bin? Destin's for tossin' you my way as an apprentice? Your parents' for givin' birth to you? See where I'm goin'?"

She scowled. She hated how pat he made it sound when the twin vipers of regret and self-pity twisted inside her. She hadn't even known Patty for more than a few hours, and on opposite teams for most of that time. How could her death hit so hard?

"You are so full of crap," she said. "Telling me all this when you aren't even over your wife's death."

She expected him to snipe back. She wanted the attack, a way to battle out the tension building within her. Instead, he closed his eyes and his shoulders drooped.

"You got that right," he said. "I ain't over it. Plenty of excuses I could use. I never got the chance to say goodbye. No body. No funeral. I got stuck in quarantine most of it, gettin' poked and prodded." His eyes opened, glistening slightly. "But I ain't there now, if you notice. I picked my mop and bucket back up and went to work again. Maybe if there'd been some closure, I coulda let it go, but I ain't ever had that kinda luck." He stood, joints clicking to match his winces. "The truth is, I don't wantcha to give up 'cause I need you with me."

She stared up at him. "Why? I've been nothing but trouble since you got stuck with me."

"I can't do this on my own, Dani. And you're the only one I trust here."

"What about Stewart?"

Ben bumped a shoulder. "That codger will do what he has to to get through this, but he'll scamper at the first chance. I need someone I can depend on."

Dani rubbed the back of her neck as she tried to pacify the emotions head-butting each other in her stomach.

"Promise this isn't about me being a stand-in for Karen."

"Hate to wound you, kiddo, but don't imagine for a second that you'd ever replace her." He offered a hand. "Whaddya say? Help this old fart finish the job?"

Dani gripped it and hauled herself up.

CHAPTER THIRTY-FOUR

Ben led Dani out of the cave and over to where Sydney and Stewart sat on a mound of black rock. Twenty feet behind them, another smaller pile stood where they'd buried Patty.

Ben glanced at Dani as they approached. Her features still twisted every so often, moving to the verge of tears and then back. Sydney looked questioningly to Dani, and she shook her head. To Ben's surprise, the entropy mage appeared truly saddened that she didn't desire his comfort.

Stewart rose and snapped a salute. "What's the plan, boyo? Please tell me we're gonna be movin'. M'butt's gone numb sittin' on this heap, watchin' a whole lotta nothin' go by."

While Dani had been recovering, Ben had been thinking through the situation, taking stock of all that happened, their limited resources, and where they needed to go from here. It felt like raking through mud for precious gems, but he'd unearthed a few gleams of hope; so long as they turned out to be pearls, and not bits of tinfoil, they might stand a chance.

"I got a feelin' that we ain't got much time before Destin finds the hybrid," he said. "The moment he lays a hand on it, ain't nobody gonna be able to face him down."

Dani hugged herself and shivered. "Then can you get us out of here so we can stop him?"

He raised a finger. "Wrong question. The right one is: do we wanna get outta here?"

"Yes," they chorused.

"Good thing this ain't a democracy." Ben waved aside their grumbles and pointed at Dani. "You did a better job than you mighta thought in gettin' us outta the Recycling Center."

"What do you mean?"

He paced a few steps away and then turned so he could eye them all at once. "Stirred my noggin a bit while you were restin' up. And I figured we're right where we need to be. Or close enough."

Sydney sat up straighter. "I believe I see what you're saying."

Ben nodded. "Where else is the hybrid gonna be safe but here in the Gutters? Ain't no native life, and barely anythin' skips between the realms all that often. It's neutral ground, so it ain't gonna react to Pure or Corrupt energies in any tellin' way. And the hybrid's gonna be mostly cut off from our world."

"Except for when it's trying to kill us," Dani groused.

"Now, don't be blamin' it," Ben said. "No more than you'd blame a baby for screamin' when it's hungry or poopin' its diaper full."

"Yeah, but infants don't conjure demons to smother me."

"So it's a baby on magical steroids. Ain't no reason to hold a grudge."

"Even assuming it's somewhere in this realm," Sydney said, "how do we find it? How do we search through an infinite number of dead worlds for a single godling? It could take lifetimes to visit each one, even if we had the ability."

Ben grinned. "We don't gotta search. We get it to come to us."

Dani glared. "This better not be where you say I get used as bait."

"Naw. You're the net."

A roll of her eyes. "Wonderful. I'm the net. Why do I get that dubious honor?"

"You're stronger than any of us. There are still enough elements around that respond to your power, an advantage the hybrid ain't gonna have. It's gotta draw straight from itself for any energy; figurin' how long it's been doin' that already, its tummy is probably growlin' for power. That's how we're gonna get its attention—offer it a source of energy to feed on."

"What source?" Dani frowned when he tapped his chest. "Wait. Why you? How does that work?"

"Think about it," he said. "We know one thing for sure: the hybrid's been drawn to you and me, yeah?" He pointed her way. "Filth said her child took a fancy to you 'cause you're both newborns, so to say. But I got a couple other bits in my favor. First off, I got both Pure," he raised his infected arm, "and Corrupt energies inside me. They ain't exactly gettin' along, but I still match its dual-nature enough to snag its attention. Plus, I got a trump card."

He explained how Filth had invested some of her power into his infested arm. "I think she just wanted to strengthen me, but her taint sweetens the deal. Every babe knows its mother's smell, so ..." He paused, lips pursed. "Well, just think of me as a big ol' bottle of mother's milk."

Their faces screwed up.

"Did not need that mental image," Dani said. "But if you're some supernatural nursemaid, why hasn't it arrived yet? If it's here, it should've sensed you and shown up."

Ben frowned. "Been thinkin' about that too. Best I can figure, the energies and Filth's taint ain't strong enough."

"So how do we make them stronger?" she asked.

Ben faced Sydney and smiled. After a few seconds, comprehension dawned on the mage's face, but he crossed his arms in refusal.

"No, Janitor. You will not ask that of me."

Dani frowned. "What? Say it, already. I hate feeling like I'm the only here who isn't telepathic. Or is that something else you've been keeping secret?"

"The easiest way is gonna be weakening my body until it can't resist the Ravishing no longer," Ben said. "The more it gets a hold on me, the more it oughta magnify the Corrupt energies. Make 'em powerful enough to hook our prize and reel it in."

Alarm sparked through her eyes. "But ... won't that ... kill you?"

"Not if Sydney does his job right. I ain't askin' him to turn me into dust. I gotta stay alive for this to work, but I'm gonna be weaker than a crippled kitten, sure for shootin'. That's why you gotta be the front-woman. I ain't gonna be much help." He turned back to the mage, who had turned subtly away as if to deflect Ben's words. "C'mon, Sydney. You can finally get your hands on me and do some real damage."

"Not this way, Benjamin. It isn't …"

"It ain't what?"

Sydney looked aside and rubbed his brow. "Honorable."

Dani snorted. "Since when do you believe in honor?"

"Despite your preconceived notions on how I operate, I maintain several strict rules of conduct. One of them is to never facilitate suicides. Do you know how many people, once they learn of my ability, come begging to be erased from their miserable existences? It is incredibly tiresome."

Stewart coughed and raised a hand. "Beggin' pardons, but I's seein' a few problems with your plan."

Ben nodded for him to go ahead. Stewart shuffled in place and adjusted the garbage bag thrown over one shoulder.

"As I'm seein', you's needin' him," he pointed to Sydney, "to gets you on death's bed so the muck takes over, right? Raise a big enough stink and Filth's kid comes a-sniffin'."

"Yup."

"Then how's he gonna do it if'n he ain't got no power here? None of his fancy hand wavin' works in this place."

"That's the one knot I ain't untangled yet." Ben nodded to where Dani had scratched the *X* in the dirt. "We gotta figure out how to open the intersection. If we link this world and ours, Sydney can go all jazz-hands on me and everythin' hops from there." He eyed each of them in turn. "Any ideas?"

While Sydney and Stewart frowned at each other, Dani came up and grabbed Ben's good arm. "Can I talk to you for a minute? Alone?"

She dragged him away until they were out of voice range of the others. Then she squared off with him and her eyes glittered with contained anger.

"Get a burr stuck under your saddle?" he asked.

"Ben, I don't like this."

"It's the best chance we got."

"But you'll die!"

"Mebbe. Mebbe not. It ain't the way I planned to go out either, princess, but few folks really get the choice of how or when."

She made fists. "Why? Why are you willing to throw yourself away for this monster? It's tried to kill us. It's not even human! It's done nothing to deserve this kind of sacrifice from you."

He lowered his head. Truth was, he'd been arguing similarly against himself earlier, when the first outline of his plan took shape. But underneath it all lay the convictions that got him involved with the Cleaners from the very beginning. The same ones Karen had shared, and that the two of them had fought so hard to uphold.

"Dani, this hybrid ain't a monster. Sure, it's got plenty of potential to be, but so did you when your power kicked into gear." She winced. "It ain't some fresh power source to be tapped into, neither. That's the way Destin sees it, and I'd like to think I'm a far cry from him. It deserves a chance to live, just like any of us."

"So do you!"

He smiled sadly. "I've had my life, princess. I admit, it was a bit shorter than I woulda guessed, but there've been a few bright spots along the way. I took this job knowin' it was gonna be the death of me someday. If that's what it takes to finish this, then I'm ready. Might as well make it count, eh?"

Tears welled in her eyes. Fearing any outpouring of emotion on her end, which might release the ones he held tightly under control, he drew her into a hug and made his voice gruff.

"Hey, don't start missin' me already, kiddo. I ain't dead yet."

He held her as she silently quaked in his arms. In the distance, Sydney and Stewart had turned their backs to them and conferred with animated gestures.

"You can do this, Dani," he said. "If I ain't there at the end, I'm countin' on you to be. You gotta promise me that much."

After a few more sniffles, she backed up, wiping her face and nodding. Ben grinned, unable to help himself. The earth of this world had stained all their hands and much of their clothes by now, and when she rubbed at her tears, it left dark streaks across her cheeks and beneath her eyes.

She looked suspiciously at his sudden change of mood, then noticed her black hands. Her responding grin was weak, but at least present.

"We're a sight, aren't we?" She puffed a laugh. "What I wouldn't give for a hot bath right now. Does HQ have any whirlpool saunas? You know, the ones with bubble jets?"

Ben started to join in the laughter, then froze. Dani's humor faded.

"What's wrong?"

He ran over to the cairn and began flinging obsidian fragments aside. A few sharp edges made shallow cuts on his fingers and palms, but he didn't slow down.

Dani cried out behind him. "What're you doing?"

After tossing another handful of rocks aside, Patty's blood-spattered jumpsuit became visible. They'd cleaned her up as much as possible and Ben took care not to disturb her remains more than he had to. Brushing aside pebbles and black dust, he found her breast pocket and zipped it open. A quick search retrieved the item he'd hoped to find, and he spent another minute restoring the cairn before returning to his companions.

As he walked up, the three eyed him as if he'd just stepped out of a septic tank. He held up the small bar of soap he'd retrieved.

"We're gonna blow a bubble."

CHAPTER THIRTY-FIVE

They exchanged worried looks.

As if volunteering, Sydney stepped forward. "Being in this business for as long as I have, it pains me to ask: are you serious?"

"Thanks," Dani said. "I'm tired of being that person."

"If you work with soapy water most of your life, you're gonna get pretty good at blowin' bubbles," Ben said, tossing the bar from one hand to the other. "You oughta see some of the illusions the window-watchers whip up with a simple film. But that ain't what I got in mind. The realms don't rightly mix it up with each other, but they do bump shoulders, like a buncha balloons rubbin' against one another. We're inside one, so all we gotta do is punch through to the one we came from."

Dani's brows scrunched. "But if you poke a hole in a balloon, it pops."

"Look, the metaphor ain't perfect, a'ight? Just go with it."

Ben snatched at the water collar on Sydney's neck, drawing the liquid back to himself. An invisible tension left the entropy mage, who breathed in relief.

"Thank you," he said, scratching furiously at the nape of his neck. "I've had this itch for hours."

Ben displayed the water in one hand, the soap in the other. "We poke a hole through the intersection and slap a film over the breach. Goin' with the whole balloon setup, figure that this realm is pretty much deflated, while ours is stuffed full of air. You're gonna get an imbalance, eh? Part of our world oughta spill out over here and make a sorta bubble of life where Sydney's powers'll start workin' again. He does what needs doin' and we snag ourselves a hybrid."

Stewart squinched a craggy eye. "Wot's to keep this hybrid-thingy from slippin' right out through the hole we's makin'? Ain't that what we's tryin' to stop inna first place?"

"Soon as it sticks its head up," Ben said, "Dani stuns the hybrid however she can, you hit it with your best bindin' spell, and we ..." He indicated Sydney and himself. "We hope for the best."

Sydney sighed as he tugged his lapels straight. "Now this is a plan that fills me with confidence."

Ignoring him, Ben pointed at the trash mage. "Stewart, you help in preppin' the bubble and trap. You got a lot more know-how in settin' boundaries and containment spells than any of us combined."

"That's a tough one to pull," Dani said, "considering I have no experience whatsoever."

"Oi. Watch that tongue, lass."

Dani stuck hers out. "Bite me."

Sydney looked put out that he didn't have anything to occupy himself with while the others bustled about. He sat back on the rubble heap while Ben and Stewart drew out the dimensions of the intended bubble in the dirt, forming a circle with Dani's X set on the circumference.

Stewart etched glyphs along the rest of the border. Some of these focused on connecting the intersection to a stable and safe location in their world. Others created the basis for the containment spell. It took him a solid hour, and he finished with a design of three arrows forming the corners of a triangle, set on the opposite side of the circle to the X. When he stepped back with a satisfied nod, Ben surveyed the large circle, at least fifty feet in diameter.

"Looks solid enough." Honestly, half of what Stewart had etched into the ground went beyond his comprehension. Summoning and binding never were his strengths, but what he understood appeared workable. He held an arm out as Dani leaned in. "Careful. Don't wanna mess up the squiggly lines. Any one of them gets broken, and everythin's gonna bust up in our faces."

She took several careful steps back. "Um, Ben?"

"Yeah?"

"What do we use to make the hole? Are we really just going to try and stick our hands through some interdimensional membrane?"

"Naw. We just gotta enchant an object to stick through the boundaries, like a needle."

Dani raised a finger, then sighed and shook her head. "I know. I know. It won't pop. So where's our needle?"

"Oh, I dunno. Where we gonna find something really sharp in a place where a few ginormous chunks of obsidian have been blown to itty bitty shards?"

She whiffed a punch past his shoulder. "Fine. Don't tell me. Be all cryptic." She went to the pile that had buried the gnash and rooted around. When she returned, she carried a six-inch black crystal, thin enough Ben figured it could tickle someone's liver without them noticing.

He nodded approval, and she went back to talk with Stewart. While she did, Ben sat near the border of the circle and pretended to study its construction. In reality, he closed his eyes and forced himself to face the very real possibility that he was about to die.

"Been a good run, ain't it?" he whispered.

Carl gurgled in his stomach.

"I know. Fat lady ain't sung, and all that, but you gotta admit, things ain't lookin' pretty." Ben laid a hand over his gut. "Then again, I guess things wouldn't look all that pretty where you're at, huh?"

Bubbles fizzed and popped, and he stifled a belch.

"Regrets? Less than I woulda figured. Wish I'd gotten the stuff with Karen all sorted out. Told Destin what I really thought of him a lot earlier. Eaten more barbeque before it started givin' me heartburn."

Water shot up and splashed the back of his throat.

Ben grimaced. "Y'know, I prefer these little chats when you're in the bottle."

"Hey."

He opened one eye. Dani crouched beside him, hands on her knees.

"Stewart says the containment circle is charged," she said. "It's a one-off trap, so hopefully it'll hold long enough for us to get the hybrid under control."

"A'ight then." He rose, grunting as his knees popped like miniature firecrackers and sent painful flares through his thighs. "One last bit of business."

"What's that?"

He opened his mouth and hacked. Water shot out of his throat and glommed onto his hand, where it swirled and foamed. He held this out to her. He expected her to recoil in disgust, but she cupped both hands and received the glob.

"You're giving me Carl?" she asked, staring at the water sprite.

"For his own good as much as yours," he said. "If anythin' happens to me—"

That summoned her angry look. "Why'd you have to go get morbid on me?"

"If anythin' happens," he repeated, "take care of him. He's as loyal as they come in the elemental way of things."

Dani eyed Carl, who spun into a series of geometric shapes and then subsided with a gurgle.

"I know, buddy," Ben said. Oddly, handing over his long-time partner affected him more than the thought of his potential death. Of all his associates, only the water sprite had stuck with him after Karen's death.

"I don't like this," Dani said. She looked ready to fling Carl back in his face, but cradled him against her chest.

He smiled ruefully. "Me neither. Now don't figure on keepin' him too long though, if I got anythin' to say about it."

The sprite rolled up to Dani's shoulder, and she tried to lean away.

"Uh, where do I put him?"

"If there ain't a bottle handy, usually I just swallow ... oh ... right. Guess that's a little close to swappin' spit, huh?"

She flushed. "Am I that obvious?"

He pushed up his wrinkled, sagging cheeks. "Ain't ever pretended this face was gonna win beauty contests. Just let him slip into your sweat glands. That way he can pop out wherever you need."

Hearing him, Carl did just that, gliding up to Dani's bare neck and absorbing into the skin. She twitched once, but otherwise handled it fine. Her cheeks filled out a bit, as did her fingers, which she frowned at.

"Great. Now I'm filthy, tired, hungry, *and* bloated."

"You get used to it."

They stared at each other, and Ben searched for final words. Something encouraging, a way to help her get on with her life after this, whatever happened. Dani spoke first, however.

"Ben ..."

Stewart's shout cut between them. "You two done mopin', or is we gonna have to start passin' out hankies?"

Ben and Dani shook themselves from the mutual silence. Anything left unsaid could be interpreted however the other wanted. She pushed him gently back toward the others.

"Let's go blow a bubble, gramps."

CHAPTER
THIRTY-SIX

Dani watched from a few yards back, Sydney by her side, as Ben and Stewart prepared the spell. She'd handed the obsidian needle over to Ben, who coated it with a layer of soapy water he'd mixed up until the shard turned opalescent.

Stewart knelt by the triangular glyph and hovered hands over it. Eyes closed, he took up his muttering chants. Ben glanced back with a weary smile.

"Stay ready, kids."

He stretched a band of water from forefinger to thumb of the same hand. Dani laughed to herself as he placed the glimmering shard in the crook of this and pulled it back, like a pebble in slingshot. He sighted between the fingers and aimed for the X across the circle.

Dani held her breath. She counted each second by the pulse in her ears.

Ben let fly.

The needle shot over the boundary. The instant it did, Stewart pounded a fist into the glyph, and the circle lit up with a wavering blue-green light. So long had they been in this bleak, colorless world that the sight almost made Dani cry out in relief.

Right as it crossed over the X, the needle struck. A third of it disappeared mid-air, and the rest hung there as if hammered into an invisible wall. Dani tensed, ready to run in case anything went violently wrong. After a few breaths, however, nothing changed.

"C'mon," Ben muttered. His hands clenched and unclenched. Dani watched him as he stared at the needle.

The needle trembled as if tugged from the other side.

"C'mon!"

The pearly coating ballooned into the size of a man's head. Ben whooped in triumph as the bubble expanded. It swelled to the borders of the circle and stopped. Stewart raised his hands as if physically keeping it from moving further. The bubble strained against the boundary before it snapped back into a stable dome, twenty feet high.

Once settled, it turned translucent and gave a clear view of what they'd created. Where the X had been, there now stood an arched, two-dimensional hole, big enough for any of them to walk through. The area within the containment circle shone with white light, a stark contrast to the gray earth.

Dani looked closer at the portal and realized blurry shapes were visible within it, as if she looked through a doorway back into their world. She recognized the dark mounds in the distance, with small roads winding between them.

"Isn't that your dump?" she asked the trash mage.

Stewart shrugged without looking her way. "Where else is I's supposed to grab hold? 'S good as any. Holdin' firm," he told Ben. "Should be right 'n ready."

Ben stepped over the boundary. Dani watched nervously as the bubble rippled around him, but it let him pass without injury. He marched around inside the bubble, went up to the portal, stuck his hand through and drew it back. Stewart grimaced as Ben rejoined them on the outside, but otherwise maintained his vigil over the glyphs. Their green-blue glow cast the garbage man's wrinkled face in such a light that Dani thought of mold growing on tree bark.

"It worked." Ben's relieved grin elicited a brief one of her own. He rolled his shoulders like a prize fighter. "My turn."

Dani bit her lip as Ben unwrapped the plastic bags from around his arm. The festering sores looked worse than before, coring deeper into the flesh. From the wrist to the shoulder, all the skin was pallid and gray, glistening with a green sheen. A series of scratch marks dug down from this elbow to inner forearm, crusted with black blood. What made her cringe most was a black handprint where she'd grabbed him while imbued with the essence of fire. How did he stand the pain?

Ben waved for Sydney to join him. "Step on up, pretty boy. Put those magic hands to good use for once."

Sydney cocked a brow. "You forget. I never changed my mind from earlier. I won't harm you, helpless and willing as you are."

Ben scowled. "Don't be wastin' our time. This thing ain't gonna stay open forever."

"Then you shouldn't have opened it," Sydney said. "You simply decided to go ahead with your stellar plan, not considering that perhaps we weren't all in agreement on how to proceed."

Ben's expression darkened. Dani backed up as he stalked over to Sydney. The men squared off, Sydney's calm unwavering in the face of Ben's anger. Then Ben smirked. "What'cha afraid of? Killin' me?"

Dani caught Sydney's quick look her way. The slightest flush tinted his cheeks.

"Oh, I get it," Ben prodded the mage's chest. "You don't wanna look bad in front of your little crush. Cute, but I ain't got the patience for your simperin'."

Two slaps sent Sydney reeling. Ben closed the distance, fists clenched. The veins in his temples and neck pulsed.

"Get over it," he shouted. "You're actin' like a teenager who doesn't know how to stick on a corsage. Need me to chaperone until your balls drop?"

He shoved Sydney, who stumbled again before catching himself. When he righted, Ben grabbed the front of his jacket. The janitor turned and, with a shocking show of strength, threw the mage off his feet and into the bubble. Sydney squawked as he somersaulted, coming up within the circle. Light glittered on his blond hair and accentuated the tattered state of his white jacket. Before he could exit, Ben jumped over and shoved him further in.

"That's right. You think I'm just gonna lie down and let you sap me dry? You're gonna have to work for it. Just try and lay a hand on me. I'll have you cryin' 'grampa' before I'm through."

His hook mashed Sydney's ear. The mage hopped away, hand to his wounded face. His appalled look was so comical Dani almost laughed.

Ben waded in. Sydney took several more hits to tender spots, chuffing and grunting with each. Dani saw the moment when testosterone and adrenaline took over. Sydney stiffened under the barrage of hits. Shoulders flexed. Fingers tensed. Nostrils flared.

Ben's next punch came straight at his nose. With a yell, Sydney latched onto Ben's hand. Darkness pulsed.

Dani cried out as Ben withered. One instant, he stood gray-headed, wiry, and tall. The next, his hair flowed white and coarse. He shuddered and hunched, spine twisted out of true. His skin turned mottled with purple and brown. Each joint poked out, knobbly and swollen.

Ben bent before Sydney, hacking and wheezing. "A'ight. Good start. Hit me again."

Sydney hesitated, still gripping Ben's hand. The janitor reared back, though his arms and legs shook as if he might collapse.

"Do it. Else I'm knockin' between your legs to prove you ain't got a pair."

The fury in Sydney's eyes flared, as did his power. Ben's face contorted in a silent howl. Dani spun away, hands over her eyes, refusing to watch.

Awful silence waited behind her. The softest groan made her turn back. Ben's limbs were as thin as kindling. The jumpsuit hung off him like skin ready to be shed. He was almost unrecognizable, practically a skeletal mannequin with his eyes sunken deep in their sockets. A few scraps of hair clung to his scalp. Warts spotted his neck and his lips had taken on a purple tint.

Sydney dropped the janitor and backed up, disgust writ on his pale face. As he retreated, Dani ran to Ben, fearing he'd been killed outright. His breaths came in fits; his blue eyes had glazed over with thick cataracts. He looked so tiny curled up on the ground. His hands had been reduced to claws, which she gripped, trying to offer her strength.

"Dani?" His voice had faded into a crow's chuckle.

"I'm here," she said. "How do you feel?"

"Oh ... chipper. Figured on doin' a jig." He sputtered. "Guess this is ... what a turd feels like just before ... it gets flushed."

Sydney sat with his head in his hands. Dani didn't give him a second glance, though she knew she was being unfair in ignoring him. Ben had practically forced this on himself, but that couldn't stop her horror at what Sydney had done.

"Unzip me."

She looked down at Ben, who fumbled at his uniform.

"What?" she asked.

A yellow fingernail tapped the zipper. "Open up ... the suit. It's blockin' ... the Corruption."

Dani reached for the tag.

"Careful ... don't be ... touchin' ..."

She tugged it down to his waist and moaned in sympathetic pain as Ben's chest and shoulders were revealed. The Ravishing had spread as planned. The skin across his torso looked ready to slough off, and she kept her hands well away, even gloved as they were, not just to avoid contracting the infection but to keep from hurting him further.

As he'd done earlier, she cradled his head in her lap, trying to provide as much comfort as she could. The back of her mind started screaming about all sorts of germs she might contract, but she ignored it as best she could. He felt too light, as if his bones had been replaced by sawdust. His shallow breaths frightened her, and she listened hard for each one, not knowing if it would come.

While she held him, she woke her power to its slightest degree and let it burrow into the ground around her—the first step in the plan she and Stewart had discussed. Finesse wasn't and likely never would be her specialty. Natural disasters, big or small, weren't known for being discrete events, but she could punch hard on short notice.

Now the hybrid just needed to show up.

As minutes turned to ten, turned to half an hour, Dani feared Ben's sacrifice was for nothing. What if Destin had already found and enslaved the hybrid? What would they do if nothing happened? How could they return to the world with him this weak? The Cleaners would no doubt track them down the moment they showed their faces.

Ben's breathing had steadied and deepened. A small relief. She wondered if he'd fallen asleep. Then he lurched in her arms and gave a soft cry, eyes still closed.

"Dani?"

She bent to his faint words. "Yes?"

He spit up black blood which dribbled down his chin. His whisper wavered through trembling lips.

"It's comin'."

She looked up. The black sky had split open, revealing the dead planets floating overhead in their somber palette. Among them, a purple light winked into being. It blazed brighter as it soared through the heavens straight for them.

CHAPTER
THIRTY-SEVEN

ani tracked the purple flame as it arced toward them. It
enlarged with every second until, with a start, she realized
where it would land.

"Oh, son of a *****."

She scrambled to her feet, trying to be gentle in the rush. She
grabbed Ben's shoulders and dragged him out of the center of the
circle, where the comet aimed. He'd lapsed back into uncon-
sciousness.

The area lit with a violet hue. The air screamed as the hybrid
punched through whatever atmosphere this world still possessed.

Once she reached the edge of the bubble, Dani dropped to her
knees and curled herself over Ben, knowing she provided about as
much protection as wet newspaper against a sniper bullet.

With a wail, the purple comet slammed into the earth. The
shockwave almost pounded her flat onto Ben, and she fought not
to crush him. The ground shook. Thunder clapped. For a moment,
she feared the earth might split and swallow them all.

When the noise and reverberations faded, she raised her head.
Gray dust obscured everything beyond an arm's length. She tried
to call out without opening her lips more than a fraction.

"Stewart? Sydney?"

"Here!" Sydney's voice, off to the left.

"Oi," came Stewart's, from outside the bubble.

Dani stood on shaky legs. "Where is it? Do you guys see it?"

Through the haze, a figure crawled toward her. It moved spider-like on all fours. Dani jumped back, throat tightened so she couldn't call out.

"Now, lass!"

Stewart's shout pushed her into action. Dani unleashed the power she'd been holding in check. The earth bucked with the short, intense earthquake she'd triggered, and the figure flipped backward, out of sight.

A howl cut through the air. An electric charge sizzled in the air as Stewart's trap sprung. Energy crackled around the edge of the circle, snapping like a thousand mousetraps triggering at once. The bubble quivered, but remained intact, as did the portal on the far side.

Further silence.

Dani worked her jaw until her ears popped. "Did we get it?" *And, if not, should we start running?*

The last of the dust settled. Sydney stood a few yards away, wiping at his gray-coated clothes and face. "We captured something." He nodded at a huddled figure halfway between them.

They joined each other in studying what had fallen into their midst, and it took Dani a few seconds to make sense of what she saw. She met Sydney's eyes, noting the same befuddlement there.

"This is a godling?" she asked.

A teenage boy lay in the circle, bare-chested, clad only in tattered jeans and old sneakers. He had buzz-cut black hair, olive skin, and thick lips. When he returned her stare, his pupils were black with a shot of gold. Bands of blue-green energy had lashed around his ankles, waist, and wrists, and strapped him to the ground. Each time he strained against them, sparks coursed across his skin and made him cower once more.

Dani didn't know what she'd been expecting. Something monstrous. Maybe demonic in appearance, or like an oversized slug. Alien. This ... this was a malnourished teenager who looked ready to weep from fear. Not exactly awe-inspiring.

The hybrid groaned and then opened his mouth wide and yowled. They stepped back from the wretched noise which shook the air, like a hundred alley cats coming into heat at once. Dani felt as if the cries reached into her chest and snatched for any scrap of pity she contained.

"What's it doing?" she asked with her hands over her ears.

Something tugged her pants leg. She jerked before realizing Ben had crawled over and snatched at her clothes to get her attention. His lips worked a bit before a couple words creaked out, barely heard over the hybrid's cries.

"Check ... the pulse."

He fell back, exhausted by the effort of speaking. At the same time, the hybrid's howls cut off. The teen's head turned to stare at Ben, his gaze so intense the eyes seemed to glow.

Sydney edged over to him. When no further howls erupted, he knelt and quickly pressed fingers to the throat. He rose moments later, looking disturbed. "Weak, but present."

"So?" Dani asked.

Sydney frowned down at the boy. "Pantheon members don't have pulses. They project human appearances for the sake of interacting with us, but there's no need for them to imitate things like blood flow or other internal fluids and organs."

"What's that mean?"

"This ... it ... he's partly human."

Dani glanced at Ben, but the janitor remained conked out. "I thought it was the offspring of two Petties," she said. "Wouldn't that make it all Petty?"

"Apparently he was mistaken."

She planted hands on hips. "What do we do?"

The teen kept his eyes locked on Ben. His lips pursed as if trying to suck the janitor to him through a straw. Grunts and groans escaped with each heave of his chest.

"Hello?" Dani asked, crouching. "Do you understand us?"

His gaze snapped to her. She wavered as images and feelings shoved into her mind.

Emptiness. Loneliness. The teen had wandered the void, flitting from world to world in search of ... something. Anything. Anyone. He wavered between panic and fury, alternately wanting to lash out at the agony the universe inflicted on him and find someone to just hold him. To whisper in his ear that everything would be okay.

A hand shook her and broke the spell. She blinked up at Sydney, who returned her gaze with concern.

"He's in pain," she whispered. "Terrible pain."

"As Ben guessed, he's likely sustained himself entirely on his Petty nature," Sydney said. "Without food or water, his human elements must be suffering."

"I know him," she said.

He frowned. "Know him?"

"He tried to help me earlier, when the Cleansers had me locked up. We communicated somehow."

Sydney stroked his chin. "Are you sure that was not some drug-induced hallucination?" He waved her glare away. "Even if that's true, how do you know he was trying to help? He could've been toying with you. This is a being unlike anything ever encountered before."

"All the more reason to try and learn who he is. Figure out how we can help."

His smile turned pitying. "You barely know enough to keep yourself from getting killed in this world. What makes you so sure you can perceive his needs?"

"I know enough! I may not be able to tell the difference between a blot-dog and dirt demon—" She leveled a finger as he opened his mouth. "Do. Not. Correct. Me. I may not know everything, but I know when someone needs help. All this time, everyone's been chasing him down and treating him the same way I was when I first got recruited. Like he's an object. A weapon to be controlled or a threat to be wiped out. But he's a person."

"Only partially."

"More than I'd give you credit for. Even partially, it's enough. He's like us. Ben was right; he deserves a chance, and we're the only ones able to help him."

Dani braced herself and met the hybrid's eyes again. No mental barrage hit her. He just stared back, silently pleading. She locked onto her decision, determined nothing could shake her from it.

"Stewart." The mage looked up from where he studied his glyphs. "Can you release the trap?"

"Wot?" cried the trash mage. "After all we's done to snag 'im?"

"Belay that," Sydney shouted. "Dani, you're being reckless."

"We only needed to restrain him until we could figure out what we were dealing with. Now we do, and I'm certain he won't hurt us."

Sydney cocked a brow. "Why is it our responsibility?"

"Uh, besides the fact we lured him down here? It's what Ben would do if he had the strength."

"Ben's no longer in charge. He's given up much for a creature that deserved nothing. A worthless sacrifice."

"So you're in charge? Now that you have your power back, you're Mr. Know-it-all-do-it-all?"

Sydney flushed. "I'm trying to be rational. A simple glance into this boy's eyes and you're convinced he deserves warm milk and a bedtime story. What if this is nothing more than a front? He *is* still half Corrupt Petty."

"But he's human, too."

"Which makes it easier to know what we should do. This kind of union was never meant to be. Humanity is not made to mingle with the Pantheon. The conflicting natures will tear him apart sooner or later. It will be a mercy to stop his suffering now."

Dani stepped between Sydney and the hybrid, who moaned and thrashed behind her.

"Mercy? Just like the mercy you've shown all the recruits you've murdered?"

He winced. "Such a vicious word flung from your tongue."

"What would you call it, then? Huh?"

He looked away for a moment, eyes closed as if seeing his victims parading before him.

"Inevitable," he said at last.

"Uh-uh. You might believe that, but I refuse to. We all have choices, and mine is to help this boy."

"At best, he'll be a simpleton. At worst, a wild animal."

"You don't know that for sure. Look me in the eyes and tell me you can predict exactly how he'll turn out."

He held her gaze for a few moments, and then dropped it. "I can't. Not when you demand the truth from me. But I do know if you take responsibility for him, it will be a terrible burden on you, and that is something I will not allow."

Sydney moved to go around her and she planted herself in his way again. His long-suffering look sharpened with impatience and black auras pulsed around his hands.

"You can't block me forever, Dani. I only need a single touch. This is best for both of you."

She shifted to block him once more. "Think of what you're doing. It shows a lot of what you really believe about me."

The energy faded from his hands. "I don't understand."

"You're not really concerned about the hybrid and what he might or might not do. To you, he's an inconvenience. A tool to keep out of your brother's hands. And when it comes down to it, you don't think I can protect him. You think I'm too weak. That I'll break under the pressure."

Sydney rubbed over his face, and she sensed his defense crumble slightly.

"Do you know what I was studying to be before my power showed up? A doctor. That meant a life dedicated to helping others. Healing them and giving them another chance. I've probably lost any chance of ever going back to that, but I can at least bring some of it with me."

He looked torn but the slightest bit of resolve still hardened his eyes. His pride demanded a compromise of sorts, she realized. What could she offer to break down his last resistance?

"Look, Sydney, if you spare him, I'll … I'll …" She swallowed hard and tried not to choke on the words. "I'll let you take me on a date."

His eyes bugged slightly. "Pardon?"

"A date. I'll do the whole makeup and dress thing. You can get flowers, a violin player, carriage ride, whatever you want. Once this is over, you name the place and time, and I swear to you I'll be there for the whole night. Just let the kid live."

A gleam entered his eyes, a mix of suspicion and desire that made her instantly want to retract the offer. But what could a single date hurt?

He hung his head and the tension seeped out of him. "Very well. But only so you might know the depth of my affection and desire for you."

"Sure," she said. "Let's talk about that later, okay? We've got to figure out a way to get somewhere safe so he and Ben can recover."

He threw an angry look at the hybrid. "It would help if he spoke. Communication abets cooperation."

"Maybe he doesn't know how. Like one of those children raised by wolves."

"Not the most comforting comparison."

Motion over Sydney's shoulder caught her eye. A shadow moved across the portal they'd opened. Dani sucked in a breath.

Sydney turned to see what startled her. A blurry figure slid into place, about to enter from the other side. Sydney must've realized the danger at the same time she did, for he ran to the nearest border of the circle even as she shouted.

"Destroy the bubble!"

Sydney pressed his hands against the film and closed his eyes in concentration. He fell back as if kicked in the stomach. After a few gasps, he looked to her, shocked.

"I can't! Something's keeping it open."

Dani looked to the trash mage, who sat outside the circle, cross-legged, eyes closed. His head tilted upward, as if in communion with something.

"Stewart, can you collapse the spell?"

He didn't answer. Not so much as a twitch to indicate he heard.

"Stewart!"

She turned back to the portal as the first Ascendant stepped through.

CHAPTER
THIRTY-EIGHT

They filed into the bubble, ten in total. As Sydney and Dani took up stances by Ben and the hybrid, the Ascendants formed a shoulder-to-shoulder wall before the portal. Their auras glowed far brighter than the ones they'd faced in the Recycling Center, and they all moved with confidence and authority that would've made a Secret Service detail look like the Three Stooges.

Francis followed the last of them and frowned on seeing the escaped prisoners. He stood a pace ahead of the rest, hands clasped behind his back, fedora tilted at a roguish angle.

Any lingering shadows fled the circle as Destin arrived, and even the Ascendants' auras paled in comparison. A feeling of immense unworthiness slapped over Dani's thoughts, and she found herself cowering, hands raised against the Chairman's glory. How could she even dare to think she might gaze upon him? She was vile. Insignificant.

Flames flickered in her mind and burned away the insidious feelings.

You're not going to let it be that easy for him, are you?

She forced herself to stand tall and glare at Destin. His aura still stung her eyes, but her anger provided enough of a buffer for her to resist surrender.

Sydney moved in front of her and faced off with his older brother. His threadbare jacket, black jeans, and harried look struck a sharp contrast against Destin's immaculate attire and unfazed expression.

The Chairman nodded across the distance. "Sydney."

Sydney returned the gesture. "Destin."

Francis moved toward the entropy mage, but Destin snagged his coat and pulled him back.

"Blood unto blood," he said.

"Is that the Chairman quote-of-the-day?" Sydney asked. "It'd make a great motivational poster."

The brothers lunged at each other. They met halfway, hands smacking into the other's waiting grasp. Locked in mirror stances, they strained in both body and power to overwhelm the other. Perspiration beaded their reddening faces as energy crackled between them.

Destin grinned fiercely. "Always the weaker. Relying so much on your power to protect you." With a judo twist, he threw Sydney up and over one shoulder and slammed him to the earth.

Sydney jumped to his feet and ran in, launching a punch. Destin caught the blow as if Sydney moved in slow motion, his Pure aura repelling his brother's entropic touch. Once more, Sydney flipped and landed, this time with an audible snap. He screamed and clutched a shoulder that flopped loose in its joint.

Destin stood back. With pained huffs, Sydney levered up to his knees. As he lurched to stand, Destin snapped a kick into the side of his head. The mage dropped, arms and legs splayed. Before he could recover, Destin stomped on and shattered his brother's arm. Sydney screamed anew. He rolled onto his back and clutched his ruined arm to his chest.

Blood streamed out of Sydney's nose and ears, and he alternated between hysterical laughter and sobs. The Chairman stepped aside as a pair of Ascendants rushed in and zip-tied Sydney's wrists and ankles.

"Are you going to behave yourself," Destin asked, "or must I lecture you as I did last time? Mother and Father are not pleased with your behavior of late."

Sydney curled his lips into a snarl. "Leave them out of this."

"You guys have parents?" Dani shrugged when the two looked at her. "I just figured you both came pre-packaged."

"Quaint. As for you, Ms. Hashelheim, you've disappointed me."

Another wave of shame slapped over her. She struggled to maintain her poise beneath its weight. So easy to let it drag her down and bury her will. Destin was much wiser, far more confident than she. He knew how to handle this situation, and obviously her past actions showed no reason for her to be trusted any longer.

With a snarl and shake of her head, Dani shed the worst of the attack. She faced the Ascendants and Chairman, despite being thoroughly outnumbered and outmatched.

"Beggin' pardons." Stewart appeared within the bubble. Dani looked at him in silent thanks for not letting her go down alone.

He raised a hand. "Can I be leavin' now? Afore there's any hittin' o' women? I don't got the stomach for it."

Francis inclined his head. "Of course, Mr. Connolly. Your assistance will be rewarded as promised."

Dani's eyes widened as Stewart shuffled through the line of Ascendants unopposed. He only stopped when she cried out, "Stewart, what've you done?"

The trash mage paused on the threshold of the portal, head bowed, back to her.

"Mr. Connolly here has been immensely helpful in keeping track of your location and activities for us," Destin said. "While we could have expended much of our own effort in tracking down this abomination," he gestured to the hybrid, "and would have succeeded in time, this was a much more efficient route. In exchange for opening the way to you, he has been promised that his abode will be considered a safe haven so long as he never oversteps its boundaries again."

"I's your word?" Stewart asked.

"Of course," Destin said. "The contract has already been authorized and filed by the Board."

Dani growled. "Traitor."

"I'm protectin' me home," Stewart said, chin lifting. "You'd be doin' the same if'n your folks was threatened."

"It's trash, Stewart. Not your family."

With a final sad look, Stewart vanished through the portal. The Ascendants closed ranks again.

"Now then, Ms. Hashelheim," Destin said, "if you would stand aside, we'll—"

A hacking noise interrupted them. Their gazes settled on the withered body by Dani's feet.

Ben was laughing. "I ... I ... got it all wrong." He wheezed and blood bubbled out a nostril. "All ... wrong ..."

Destin sneered at him. "I wondered where you'd acquired a corpse from. It's as we feared. Corruption has consumed you fully."

"Dani ..." Ben's rheumy eyes met hers. "You gotta ... let ..."

His head dropped back. Breaths rasped out. Dani shifted in place, torn between keeping them from Ben and shielding the hybrid.

"I won't let you subjugate him," she said, leaning toward the teen.

"Subjugation?" Destin pressed a hand to his chest. "As if I would ever sully myself by even touching such a creature. No. We are here to eliminate it before it can do further harm."

"But he's human too," Dani cried. "Can't you see?"

Destin's look combined pity and disgust. "Corruption can take many deceiving forms meant to lure you into complacency." His gaze turned to the cairn in the distance. "Have you not learned this lesson already?"

Her anger rose, and the wind with it. "I've learned a lot of things."

She'd been letting her power trickle out ever since the first Ascendant arrived. It had wormed its way through the air and earth, locking the elements to her will.

Wind roared into life around the bubble. It picked up the rubble piles and whipped the obsidian fragments into a black tornado. Its tip encircled them while its dark crown reared into the sky.

As Dani poured herself into the spell, two Ascendants sprinted for her.

Her power responded half through her focus, half out of instinct. Obsidian blocks peeled out of the storm, sliced through the bubble and smacked into her attackers' foreheads. They slumped to the ground and stirred no more.

The tornado widened, spinning ever-faster with the bubble at the eye of the storm. It ripped out more chunks of the nearby mountain, adding shards and boulders to its deadly winds.

"Who else?" she shouted. "I'm dicing anyone who comes an inch nearer."

Destin strode forward. A flock of obsidian needles soared his way, but shattered into powder against his aura.

"Ms. Hashelheim," he called. "Impressive as it is, you cannot keep up this effort indefinitely. Already I see you wavering. You've not the training to resist us."

"I'm trained enough."

"Should you collapse this storm, it will kill everyone here," Destin said. "Is that the murderous legacy you wish to leave?" Smiling at her furious silence, he waved to the others. "Take her."

As the Ascendant's marched forward, Dani let her awareness flow out further. It followed the lines of powers she'd threaded through the ground until the earth became part of her body.

Stone walls and columns jutted up around their feet. One Ascendant took the brunt of a sprouting pillar and flew through the air with a shout, while the others jumped over or dodged the extrusions. She tore the ground into a chasm. Two fell into this and vanished.

She swirled her hands and, on their next step, the final three Ascendants plunged hip-deep into black quicksand. They grappled with each other for support as they tried to pull or push each other free.

She planted her feet as she prepared a scouring blast of wind and rock. She could do this. She could stop t—

A blow from behind sent her to her knees. Her vision blurred, and the spell sustaining the winds and churning earth wavered.

Another hit planted her face-first in the dirt. Someone grabbed her arm and rolled her over. Francis crouched above her. One hand gripped her throat with bruising strength while the other reached into his jacket. He came out holding zip-ties and a garbage bag.

"I am sorry it's come to this," he said.

She spat in his eye.

Carl struck true. Francis screamed as the living water burrowed into his socket. He clawed at his face and rolled away, writhing in agony.

Dani sucked in a breath as she sat up. Her head and heart pounded in opposing tempos that made it difficult to concentrate. Wetness trickled down the back of her skull and dripped along her neck.

She looked around at the situation. Sydney remained bound and bagged. While no Ascendants remained to block her, part of the chasm she'd opened had ripped the earth between her and the hybrid. It'd take a mighty leap to cross the distance.

The Chairman had already done so and headed for the hybrid. All the while, his calm had never broken. With so much of her strength invested in the storm, Dani barely had enough to keep herself upright. How could she get to the Chairman in time? How could she face his power?

Ben stirred beside her. "Dani?"

"Ben! What do I do? What do I do?"

His smile had lost several teeth, and the others were rotted in the gums, but his eyes shone with determination. "Free him. The hybrid. Help him get to me."

"To you? Why?"

He hacked and spat into the dirt. "We ... brought it here with my energy. I can still offer that."

"What? I don't understand."

He gripped her hand. "Trust me. You ain't gonna ... stop Destin alone ... but the boy ..." Another tremor shook him. "Give him a chance. Let him use ... my power."

"But Ben—"

"Finish ... the job, princess."

As his eye fluttered closed, he mouthed the words once more. *Free. Him.*

Dani screamed in frustration and helplessness as she cast about desperately for a solution. Free the hybrid. How? Stewart had created the spell that contained the hybrid, and it was fueled by the circle keeping the bubble and portal intact—which the Ascendants now controlled. If Sydney couldn't break it down, how could she?

Then it came to her. She just had to think like a janitor. And what would a janitor do with a messy problem?

Wipe it away.

She reached up to the sky and visualized herself holding the world's largest floor polisher. She slammed her fists into the ground. The tornado drove all of its might down onto the glyphed ring sustaining the bubble. The etchings resisted being worn away, but she applied several hundred years' worth of wind erosion in seconds. No matter the power invested in them, the glyphs couldn't last forever.

The bubble popped, but the portal remained. When the barrier ceased to be, so did the trap that had restrained the hybrid boy. He somersaulted backward and landed on his feet, hands raised like claws.

Destin hesitated a few paces away. With a running start, the hybrid leapt over him. The Chairman shouted and reached up in an attempt to drag him down. His fingers brushed a trailing sneaker. With another bound, the hybrid crossed the chasm and thumped into the dirt beside Dani.

He sniffed at her, nostrils flared. Shaking like a wet dog, he flung himself at Ben. The janitor had woken again and stared up at the half-human teen with feverish expectation.

"Do it," he said.

Dani watched in horror as the hybrid reared back. Fangs and tusks lengthened along his jaws as he chomped the janitor's neck.

CHAPTER
THIRTY-NINE

ani's shock broke her connection with the last fragments of her spell. The swirling rocks rained down with a clatter, leaving the survivors in an empty circle surrounded by obsidian hills.

She stared as Ben accepted the hybrid's bite without resistance. His distant smile remained fixed as the teen gnawed him like an old bone.

"That's it," Ben said. To her surprise, his voice sounded stronger, with the brusque of his former self. "Drink on up."

The hybrid moaned and pressed against the janitor. Dani realized he was feeding on whatever energies Filth had invested Ben with.

Ben's satisfaction faded and twinges of pain rippled over his face. "A'ight. Enough."

The hybrid hugged him tighter. The extended jaw clenched, and Ben started shaking and gagging.

"That's enough. Enough!"

He bucked against the bite, but the kid held on. Dani finally got her feet under her as Ben's skin paled and turned paper-thin. Something was wrong. The light that had returned to his eyes dwindled and extinguished. His limbs went listless.

Refusing to watch him get eaten alive, she ran to wrestle the hybrid away. The hybrid's mule-kick caught her in the sternum. With a croak, she dropped to her knees, lungs seizing. Her vision tunneled until she could only see the teen leeching off her mentor. Her friend.

Something bulled her aside. She wheezed as she fell over. Where was chivalry these days?

Destin rushed by, kicking up black earth in his haste. With a furious cry, he grabbed the hybrid's shoulders and tore him off Ben. As the hybrid released the janitor, Ben's body slumped lifeless. Drained of all color and vitality, he looked like a husk dropped in the dirt.

In contrast, the hybrid was flushed and restored. His gold-shot black pupils flickered in a dozen directions until he focused on Destin. The Chairman's aura burned hot, but the teen didn't so much as blink in the glare.

They circled each other like boxers. Destin feinted right. When the hybrid shifted that way, Destin darted to the left and caught the hybrid's throat in the crook of his arm. He drove him to the ground, then knelt and got his hands around the hybrid's throat. The boy choked and his face purpled as he clawed up at the Chairman's face.

As the two grappled, Dani crawled to Ben, inch by inch. She searched for any sign of life, but he might as well have been a wax figure. When she got close enough to touch, she confirmed her worst fear. Wooden skin. No breath. No pulse. Not a flutter of power left.

She collapsed alongside him, feeling too weary to mourn. She'd failed him. He'd trusted her to protect him in the end, and she'd let him die. She'd let the hybrid kill him, just like she'd let the gnash kill Patty. It didn't matter that he'd told her to do it—she should've been strong enough, smart enough to figure out another way.

Meaty thumps drew her attention back to the fight. The hybrid had rolled Destin onto his back and now laid into him with savage punches. One fist glowed white, the other a knot of darkness. Each strike snapped the Chairman's head from one side to the other. Blood streamed from Destin's eyes, nose, and mouth.

All at once, his aura vanished.

With a triumphant howl, the hybrid stood and grabbed Destin by his jacket and pants. Thin muscles straining with inhuman strength, he raised Destin over his head and threw him at the chasm.

Destin shouted and flailed as he soared over the abyss. He struck the opposite edge and barely grabbed hold in time to keep himself from dropping in. He clung there, struggling to keep his grip, much less pull himself back up.

With him out of the way, the hybrid spun and snarled at Dani. She sat motionless as he approached. Ben's death had stolen the last of her strength. Whatever happened, she hoped it would be quick and painless.

But the teen stopped a yard away, shoulders heaving, eyes wild. Slowly, the manic energy receded, leaving him looking like a normal boy once more. Kneeling, he raised his arms to the sky and bellowed. The power of his first words rocked Dani.

"MAMA! PAPA!"

The echoes raced into the distance, and Dani sensed the call searching for its targets.

A purple-and-green crack split the air, and some*thing* stepped through it. Dani got an instant's impression of a void coiled upon itself like a serpent, with grinding teeth along the edges and a puckered, sucking mouth in the center which opened into churning depths.

It resolved into a bag lady in desperate need of a makeover. The woman's hideous appearance had been uselessly covered by chintzy leopard print pants, bead necklaces, sloppy makeup, and a purple hat with a peacock feather stuck in the brim. She pranced along with the air of a catwalk queen. Greasy hair dripped as she flipped it back from her eyes.

"Hello, dearies," she called. "Mommy's here."

The hybrid clapped in delight and ran to her. She stroked the teen's hair and pressed his head to her chest. Her eyes glittered as she looked over at Dani.

"You're Filth," Dani said. "The Corrupt Petty."

Filth fluttered a crack-nailed hand before her mouth as if embarrassed by the recognition. The barbed-wire rings and bracelet gouged trickles of blood. "And you're Dani, the Catalyst. I've heard so much about you, lovey. We really must have coffee sometime and catch up."

Dani tried to summon rage. She tried to feel sorrow. Anything to shake her stupor. She surveyed the ruin around her, the Ascendants, most of them unconscious or bleeding out. What had been the point of this? It had seemed so clear just a bit ago, but now she found it impossible to grasp why this all had been necessary.

"Something wrong, lovey? You look a tad pale."

When she turned back, she yelped in surprise, for Filth stood inches away, the hybrid still at her side.

"I warned Benny this would end in tears," Filth said, "but all in all, I think you both did a marvelous job. Don't you?"

Dani started to shout to this woman ... this thing ... that Ben was dead. That her son had killed him.

"Shh." Filth laid a finger to Dani's lips. It smelled of sulfur and dung, and the skin rippled against her mouth as something undulated beneath it. She didn't even have the energy to pull away.

Filth made a popping noise with her mouth and looked past Dani to Ben's body. "Now, Benny," she called. "Don't be pretending. T'isn't kind to play possum."

A tearing sound spun Dani around. Something bumped within the shell of Ben's body. The white skin buckled, cracked, and flaked away into powder. Another figure became visible as it wriggled loose from the husk that contained it.

A young man's head shook free and shed the old face like a paper mask. The left arm ripped free. A firm hand gripped the earth and dug in as he sat upright. Blue eyes opened, and Dani's disbelief kept her from recognizing him for ten long heartbeats.

"Ben?"

It was, but the Ben he should have been if the Ravishing had never touched his body. His skin and muscles were toned, his long hair gone black, and not a wrinkle to be seen except for the laugh lines around his eyes and mouth.

He sat up and spread his arms to catch his balance, but fell over onto his right side. Where his Ravished right arm had been was nothing but a fleshy stub.

After floundering upright, Ben stared at the absent limb. He licked his lips.

"Huh. That's a surprise."

"Ben!" She flung herself at him.

He laughed as he caught her in a one-arm hug. "Careful, princess. I'm still a might bit achy."

She held him out to stare at his young face. The large nose, the hooded eyes, and broad forehead. A bit of stubble about the chin and jaw. "What happened to you? How is this possible?"

"He fed my child," Filth said, tousling the teen's hair. "Gave my boy the strength to defend himself."

Ben looked himself over. "The kid sucked the Corruption right outta me. I thought it was gonna kill me, but I guess I'm just more of a wuss than I figured. The pain made me panic a bit."

"But ... you're young!"

He grinned, revealing white teeth. "The Ravishing smothers your power, shovin' your true self aside until it takes over completely—but it don't destroy what's already there. With it gone, my Pure energies put in overtime and managed to undo the damage." He glanced at his missing appendage again. "Though ... not quite all of it, looks like."

He took her arm as she helped him stand. He tottered and regained his balance before nodding to the Petty.

"Filth."

"Janitor."

He wiggled the stub. "I kinda remember you sayin' you couldn't fix it."

"I couldn't, and I still cannot," she said. "Nor did I expect my son to. His powers seem to be in flux as he matures. I truly don't know what he'll end up being capable of."

"Gotcha. Then I ain't gonna bother thankin' you."

Filth perked up. "Ah-ah. I see you trying to sneak away, my love."

Two dark forms flashed out of the portal she'd emerged from. They blurred through the air and landed on top of Destin, driving him to the ground. He'd managed to scramble back onto solid ground and had been making a dash for the portal out of this realm.

The creatures Filth had summoned appeared to be enormous black cats, but with human faces plastered over their skulls. They growled as they squatted on Destin, and their tails whipped in his face.

"Monster," he cried. "Release me!" His frantic attempts to free himself weakened after a minute, and his aura buffeted the oversized cats without avail.

"Well, hello to you too." Filth sauntered toward the lip of the ravine. "Miss me? You never call anymore."

"What's going on?" Dani whispered to Ben.

"Didn'tcha hear? He," Ben nodded at the hybrid, "called for his parents. And now they're both here."

Dani frowned. Then her eyes widened. "What? Him? Mr. Perfect?"

Ben laughed again, a strong, clear sound that lifted her heart from the muddy pit it had wallowed in for far too long.

"We all got our vices, eh?" he said. "I never woulda guessed how deep or dark his ran. Or that he coulda hid it so well."

"You don't understand," Destin cried. "You have no idea what it's like to be in my position. The responsibilities. The people I send to their deaths every day. The constant pressure from the Board." His officious attitude vanished as a whine entered his voice. "No one person should shoulder such a burden. It can't be done."

"He came to me to escape," Filth said. "So lonely. Needing a gentle hand." Lips curled in a clown's smile. "He can be such a dirty boy."

"He was trying to kill his own kid," Dani said wonderingly. "Once he figured out what the hybrid was, he knew it was only a matter of time before someone found out where it came from. All this just to save his reputation."

Destin managed to raise his head beneath one of the cat's rumps. "That thing is not my child!"

"Au contraire," Filth said, raising a mud-caked finger. "Considering Disease and I have not had a good romp for at least ten years, I doubt it'd be anyone else's."

Dani tensed as the teen padded over from Filth to her, but his broad smile elicited a grin of her own. He took her hand and shook it twice in large, pumping motions. Then he squatted in the dirt and started drawing intricate designs with his pinky.

"What's going to happen to him?" Dani asked.

"Mm?" Filth turned from staring at Destin. "Oh. Not my concern. I leave him for you to care for."

"What?" Ben started, still leaning on Dani. "But weren'tcha worried about him?"

"Was I? Your memory must've been enfeebled by that doddering body. No. I only cared that he not be abused before he had the chance to fend for himself. With the strength you've transferred to him, he'll soon come into his own. He must carve out a realm for himself, as I'll not share mine with the little bastard." Her eyes flashed black as she glared at the hybrid. "A warning, from mother to son. Do not think to call upon me again, or I shall stew the flesh off your bones and feed it to my pets."

She flipped back into a sweet smile. Blowing a kiss to Ben and Dani, she turned and flounced toward the portal, bead necklaces jangling.

"Come along, kittens."

Her feline pets jumped off Destin. One snagged his jacket in its maw and tossed him in the air. He landed and rolled up to Filth's feet. She grabbed his arm and yanked him up into a hard, long kiss. When he wrenched away, lipstick smeared his pale face, and terror gleamed in his eyes.

"Ben! Dani! Help me! Don't let her t—"

Filth smacked him back down into the dirt. As he sobbed, she ground a foot onto the back of his neck.

"Do you remember our games?" she asked. "I've thought up some new ones. Have you ever tried Dress Up? Tea Party? No? We'll have to fix that, won't we?"

"Hold your horses," Ben said. "Destin ain't your property. We gotta bring him back with us."

"Are you kidding?" Dani asked. "Let her take him."

"Naw." Ben straightened and rolled his shoulders. "Destin might've dished some pretty nasty muck about, but he's still gotta face the Board and explain things. That's the way things work in the Cleaners."

"A pity I'm not on your employee roster," Filth said. "Your rules bore me, lovey."

"Take him and we're gonna have to come after," Ben said. "You're gonna be dealin' with every Ascendant we can throw your way. Think it over. You ain't wantin' that kinda trouble."

Filth's expression went flat, and Dani glimpsed the creature hiding behind the mask of flesh.

"My kittens and I will be waiting to welcome you," she said.

Destin's cries turned pitiful as she gripped his hair and headed for the portal, dragging him behind like a scrap of toilet paper caught on her heel.

Ben stumbled after, off balance as he tried to adjust to running with one arm. Dani stared, then cursed and joined the chase, passing Ben and closing the gap with each stride. Destin saw her coming and groped for her.

"Please, Dani! I'm sorry. I'll do anything. Just don't let her take me!"

Filth glanced over her shoulder as Dani closed the gap. "Don't worry. I'll let him out to play every now and then."

Dani lunged for the Chairman, arms outstretched.

Ben shouted. "Filth, now don't you—"

Filth stepped through the portal with her prize, and Destin's scream cut off as it snapped shut behind them. Dani grunted as she spread-eagled into the dirt.

Something poked her stomach, and she sat up to find one of Destin's white shoes. She held it up for Ben to see.

His shoulders drooped. "For Purity's sake. The Board ain't gonna be happy 'bout this."

"Mama? Papa?"

As Dani stood, the hybrid tottered over and stared at where Filth's portal had been. Then the kid bear-hugged her waist and nuzzled her stomach as he whimpered. She tried to pry him off, but he might as well have been welded on. At least the jumpsuit protected from direct skin contact for the time being.

"Uh, Ben? What do we do with him?"

Ben sighed, still watching where his old boss had vanished. "I guess we take him back to HQ and pray for some common sense and mercy."

Dani snorted. "Yeah. No bet."

"C'mon. Let's see who's still alive."

●   ●   ●

They went to Francis first. The scrub-team leader lay frozen in a contorted position, his face a rictus of pain with one eyelid puckered shut. When Ben looked to her in question, Dani ducked her head.

"A little Carl got in his eye."

Ben whistled. "Ooch, princess. Smart move, I gotta admit … but ooch." He bent over and tapped the Ascendant's temple. "Hey, buddy, hustle on out."

Francis wept. The tears streamed down his face and congealed into a puddle, which Ben scooped up in his remaining hand.

With the hybrid latched onto her, Dani watched Ben from the side. She detected something off about him still. Despite his restored youth—something she would've rejoiced over—melancholy shaded his expression. Perhaps it was just the lost arm, but she sensed it went deeper than that.

The janitor helped Francis stand, and they exchanged silent looks, forearms clasped.

Ben waved at the hybrid. "You heard."

"All of it," Francis said. "Despite the agony inflicted on me, I believe I'm capable of filling out a detailed report for the Board. It should resolve matters well enough, though they'll still want a full debriefing."

"That's it?" Dani said, scowling at the Ascendant. "No apology? No 'Sorry for almost getting you guys killed'?"

Francis' lips thinned. "I was—"

"Just doin' your job," Ben said. "Followin' orders. I woulda done the same if our roles was reversed. Probably. We all make mistakes, ain't that right, Francis? It's only human."

The Ascendant leveled an icy look at Ben, but then he sighed. His expression thawed, if slightly. "I suppose."

Ben clapped the man's shoulder. "Righto. Now all we gotta do is learn from 'em. So, whaddya think we oughta do with the kid?"

"Not for me to decide."

Ben didn't look satisfied with that answer, but let it lie while they rounded up the surviving Ascendants. As they dug out the three half-buried in the quicksand, Dani realized they still missed one of their number.

"Where's Sydney?" she asked.

Ben and Francis looked around with her. After several minutes of searching, they uncovered no sign of the entropy mage except for scuff marks and a few footprints near where he'd been bound. Francis frowned at the tracks.

"While incapacitated, I glimpsed someone bolting through the portal you opened, but thought it an illusion caused by the water squeezing my eyeballs. If it was Sydney escaping, my guess is he didn't wish to stick around for the aftermath. Wise, since I'd now be forced to take him back into custody."

"He'll be back," Dani said.

"What makes you so sure?" Ben asked.

"I owe him a date." Ben and Francis' brows rose, and she sighed. "Don't give me that. You're just jealous. Oh," she turned to Francis, "I'm going to probably need a night off whenever he gets in touch. Want to run the paperwork on that for me?"

He coughed. "I sincerely doubt taking a comp day to fraternize with an entropy mage will be approved. A bit of conflict with the company's interests, wouldn't you agree?"

"Francis …" Ben shook his head wearily. "Just process it for her, a'ight?"

They finished rousing and retrieving the Ascendants. Dani at first feared some of them might try to finish what they started, but they were too well-trained. A bark from Francis, and they regrouped until further commands were issued. One or two glared at Dani and the hybrid attached at her hip, but none so much as cleared their throats aggressively.

Once the scene had been cleaned up as much as possible, Francis went to the portal. A swipe of his hands, and it blinked out of existence. His aura knifed into the space where the first portal had stood. A new hole appeared, revealing the stark interiors of HQ.

The Ascendants marched through first, Francis on their heels. Dani chewed her bottom lip, wondering at the wisdom of returning to the Cleaners' center of operations. They had no assurances of safety. Whatever authorities took over in Destin's absence could decide to imprison her and Ben all over again, take the hybrid captive, or try to kill them all outright.

Ben put his hand on her shoulder. Confidence brimmed from him, and she took courage from it.

"I'll go first," he said. "Gimme a few minutes to smooth things over, then trot along behind."

"Ben, be careful."

A chuckle. "What're they gonna do? Fire me?"

With a wink, he jogged through and vanished. The teen whimpered again. Dani shushed him and patted his head. "It's okay," she said, trying to make herself believe it. "You're safe with us. We'll take care of you."

He looked up at her with shining gold-and-black eyes, and she hoped his trust in her wasn't about to be proven wrong. After counting off the time, Dani stepped through the portal with the hybrid clinging to her arm. Her vision blurred for a moment. When it cleared, she drew in a sharp breath.

Neither Ben nor Francis greeted her. Instead, a white-masked welcoming committee filled the room before her.

CHAPTER FORTY

The hybrid buried his face in Dani's shoulder. She stood as still as possible while taking in the scene.

The square room offered one door to her right, but with no obvious handle or latch. A dozen people crowded the space before her, each identical to the rest. White masks covered their features and they wore white robes with the hoods up. She couldn't differentiate between male and female, and their eyes all had an odd gloss that hid their true colors.

They stared at her, unmoving, silent. Sweat beaded on the nape of her neck and trickled down her spine.

"Uh ..." She swallowed. "Can you point me toward the showers?"

Shouting came from behind the door. It burst open, and Ben shoved his way through, trailed by two Cleaners who fussed over his stunted arm. Francis trotted in behind, also harried by a pair of attendants.

"I ain't needin' no examination," Ben growled. "I toldja I ain't goin' nowhere before she gets here."

He and the others halted as they noticed the masked crowd. Ben scowled and strode onward, while the attendants hastily retreated. Francis shut the door and stood before it, arms crossed over his broad chest. Ben came up beside Dani so the hybrid huddled between them.

She whispered out of the side of her mouth. "Ben, who are these people?"

"The Board," he muttered back. "Twitchy little pricks. Figure they can just waltz in after the storm's blown over and act like they own the place."

"We hear you, Janitor Benjamin. And we do own this place."

Dani jumped as all the masked figures spoke at once. Only slight fluctuations of tone and volume provided a distinction between their voices.

"Your actions over the past few days have been noted, and Ascendant Francis has already relayed a summation to us, pending his full report. Unless further events and facts warrant, you are no longer considered threats to this company. The death-sentences on your names have been revoked."

"Ain't that a big relief," Ben said. "I'm gettin' teary-eyed over here."

"Your sarcasm is noted."

As she studied them, all at once Dani saw what she'd missed before. They didn't wear masks. Whenever they spoke, the lips moved. Cheek muscles twitched. Whatever faces the Board once possessed had been wiped clean, leaving each with the same blank features.

"What are they?" she asked.

"We are human."

"Barely," Ben said. "You're finger puppets of the Pantheon. You spend so much time tryin' to be perfect, there's hardly any room left for a bit of spit and gristle. Nothin' but logic and calculation left in your tidy little minds."

"Your insolence is also noted."

"Sure it is. Don't even pretend you get offended anymore, you twits."

"Why are you here?" Dani asked.

Their arms raised and pointed at the hybrid. *"He is to be scheduled for termination. We are here to escort him to the incinerator. Our power shall bind him so none are in danger along the way."*

As if understanding their pronouncement, the hybrid dug his fingers into Dani's arm so hard she grunted at the pain. But protectiveness overrode the urge to loosen his grip.

"He's part-human," she said. "He deserves a chance to live."

"He is saturated with Corrupt energies," the Board said. *"Even now it twists his mind and desires. He will grow up a malignancy, a disease that infects all he touches."*

"You ain't as sure of that as you want us to think," Ben said.

"The possible outcomes have been calculated. There is a ninety-eight point seven percent chance he will culminate as we have envisioned."

"He could still turn out all right," Dani said.

"We do not foresee any such factors that might allow for such developments."

"What about mercy?" Ben asked. "Why not try showin' some compassion, get him some clean clothes, a square meal, and then sittin' down and explainin' to him why it ain't in his best interest to follow in the footsteps of mommy dearest? We got a chance to salvage some good outta this mess."

"There is no Chairman present to advise us on such matters any longer."

"So get one."

"We shall. The position is offered to you, Janitor Benjamin."

Ben stuttered, and Dani could tell they'd caught him fully by surprise. His eventual laugh sounded forced. "Seein' how well you did with Destin, why would I even give it half a thought?"

Several of the Board came forward and spoke in turn.

"You have no power within you," one said.

Ben's grin faltered.

"You are nothing but flesh and blood," said another.

"You have been stripped of all potency," said a third. "Purity has abandoned you. You need us more than we need you."

To Dani's dismay, Ben's confident expression cracked and crumbled.

"Ben?"

"Well, they got me there," he said softly. "When the kid sucked the Ravishing out and my Pure energies fixed me up, it … well, it kinda burnt me out. I ain't got a drop of magic left." A swallow bobbed his Adam's apple. "I'm just a plain ol' janitor."

"We can restore you."

"If you take up the mantle."

"Of Chairman."

"Shut up," Dani shouted. "Stop trying to distract him. Give us some time to recover and think this all through. We're exhausted and starving."

"Our calculations predict your responses will not be affected by any passage of time. We do not see the necessity of such measures."

Dani looked to Ben, at a loss. He remained fixed on the Board, like a wild animal pinned by a bright light. She could almost feel the thoughts churning in his head, considering the potential he might wield.

"Ben, don't. You told me yourself what that kind of power does to people. I don't want to see that happen to you."

He licked his lips. "You don't understand, Dani. There's gotta be a Chairman. Without one, the Board ain't got nobody keepin' them connected to things like emotion or instinct. They can calculate every angle and balance the budgets of small countries without breakin' a sweat, but they can barely relate to us any more than a computer can."

"But it doesn't have to be you!"

"We offer it to none other," the Board said. *"Our choice of Destin was an error. His flaws led to his downfall."*

"Nobody's perfect," Dani said. "If you expect that, you'll always be disappointed."

"Think of it," Ben said. "If I step in, think of what I could do. Really whip things into shape. Keep you and the kid protected."

"Don't think about me here," she said. "You can't take their offer just because you want the authority to get revenge for Karen, either."

A dark cloud seemed to drop between them and she knew she'd lost him.

"Oh, I can't, huh?" He looked to the Board, hand on the teen's shoulder. "If I say yes, are you gonna give him a chance?"

Those who had moved forward now stepped back and rejoined the others. Their voices wove together again.

"So long as you accept the title of Chairman, the child shall be spared. So we swear."

"A'ight. I accept."

"Ben!"

He shrugged Dani off and approached the Board. At their gesture, Ben knelt. The Board circled him and each member laid a hand on his head. Energy sparked between their fingers and crowned Ben with a circlet of power. The room shook, and Dani hid the hybrid's face so he wouldn't see what came next.

Light poured into Ben from the Board and he glowed white-hot. For a moment, she imagined seeing his bones through his flesh. Then a flash blinded her. When the spots faded, the Board had stepped away, hands tucked once more into their sleeves.

Ben rose and a golden aura flickered into being around him. He breathed deep, as if he'd been held underwater all this time and only now came up for air.

Dani groaned. "Ben, what've you done?"

His face and eyes shone with power, and his grin had a cold edge to it that made her shiver. The teen shrank against her as well.

When he spoke, he'd lost all of the grumpy … well … charm wasn't the right word. But his voice had been comfortable, like a spongy old chair that fitted one's contours perfectly. Now his words were stamped in steel and knocked into her mind with unforgiving authority.

"Danielle Hashelheim, as Chairman of the Cleaners, with the power invested in me by the Board of Purity, I hereby state the completion of your training."

She blinked. "What?"

"Through your actions against Corruption," he said, "plus your willingness to sacrifice your own safety for the wellbeing of others, you have demonstrated the bravery, strength, and devotion to Purity the Cleaners seek to embody. You are an asset to this company, and the lucky S.O.B. who trained you oughta be given a medal of commendation." Some of Ben's old voice slipped back into this last statement, but evaporated as he continued. "Do you accept this judgment of your abilities and status?"

Dani worked saliva around until her tongue unstuck from the roof of her mouth.

"I … I do."

"Then you are to be henceforth considered a free agent of the Cleaners, with all the benefits, vacation time, and lunch breaks your position is entitled to." Another hard look, daring her to argue. "Is this acceptable?"

"It is."

Ben turned to the Board. "Satisfactory?"

The Board nodded as one. *"It is heard, recorded, and so shall be,"* they intoned. *"None will dispute her place among us."*

Ben wiped a hand over his face. "Phew. Then I figure it's about time I resign."

Their heads tilted as one. *"We do not understand."*

Glee bumped Dani's heart rate up as Ben's aura vanished. Despite his smooth face, she glimpsed an older man peering out through his eyes. While he might not have as many wrinkles and liver spots, one didn't go to the brink of death and return unchanged.

Ben walked over and slapped Francis on the back. "It's all yours, pal."

Francis looked as if he'd been punched in the gut.

"We have not offered this title to Ascendant Francis!"

Ben swung around and jabbed a finger the Board's way. "You sure got short memories. You just gave me all the rights and powers of this office. One of my duties is choosin' a successor should I deem myself unfit for further duty. And so I am, and so I'm gonna do, whether you like it or not." He smiled at Francis, who held back. "Oh, c'mon. You've been shuckin' it under Destin for years now. He did a shoddy job, so now you get to take a swing. 'Sides, I ain't ever been good at sittin' at a desk all day, signin' papers and all that other upper management dribble. You're perfect. Whaddya say?"

Francis eyed Ben sidelong. "I question this hasty decision. Shouldn't you take some time to reconsider?"

Ben thumbed over his shoulder at the Board. "Hey, they shoved it down my throat. I'm just passin' on the joy. Mebbe you oughta take some personal notes when you draw up that report and figure out some way to avoid a situation like this in the future."

Francis removed his fedora, revealing black curls. "Very well."

Ben placed his hand on the Ascendant's forehead. Both men shut their eyes. After a moment's concentration, a fiery cloud passed from Ben to Francis. The Ascendant shuddered, eyes closed as he absorbed the power.

Once the last of it flowed out, Ben staggered back and flicked the sweat from his brow. "Glad that's over with." He grinned wearily at Dani. "I woulda thought you knew to trust me by now, princess."

Francis went to one knee before the Board who collectively glared over at Ben.

"I live to serve Purity," Francis said. His voice had taken on the same steely timbre.

They waved for him to rise, and then waved at the teen.

"Schedule the hybrid for termination."

"No," Dani cried. "You promised!"

"We promised to spare it only so long as Janitor Benjamin accepted the position of Chairman. Now that he has rejected that role, we are no longer bound to that agreement."

Ben made fists. "You weasely little turds ..."

Dani shielded the hybrid with her body as Francis advanced. Out of the corner of her eye, she saw Ben move to intercept. Power sparked among the Board, and she raised a hand before anyone could ignite the brewing violence.

"Hold on. Do you want me to still work for you?"

Francis halted and looked over his shoulder at the Board. Ben held back as well, concern etched on his face. Each member of the Board went perfectly still, and Dani imagined their invisible conference, thoughts whirring between each other, metaphysical spreadsheets being drawn up, supernatural pie charts being compared and argued over.

"Your powers are desired," they said at last. *"You are strong. Young. Able to do much in the name of Purity."*

"Well you aren't going to get me unless you promise to give this kid sanctuary. That means no loopholes or caveats. He gets a chance to grow up and learn what choices he has before you send him to some oversized incinerator."

"You will not concur otherwise?"

"I'd rather clean toilets with my tongue."

Another moment of inner debate. She held her breath, as did the hybrid.

"Agreed. The child shall not be harmed so long as you remain in our employ."

"Okay then."

While their individual faces projected nothing but indifference, their collective shuffling and stances communicated petulance and wounded pride at being thwarted.

"We have remained over-long. There is business to attend."

They transformed into a swarm of glowing motes that shot through the ceiling. The room looked dowdy in their absence, despite the shining walls and tile.

Francis watched them go with a look of relief, as if he'd been afraid they would rescind his new power after all. Then he turned to the others. "As for our new guest ..."

Dani drew back, arms tight around the teen.

The Chairman reached out to her. "As Ben entrusted me with this duty, so you must trust me in seeing the Board's will carried out where the child is concerned. I understand their concerns for his future, but I'm not so far removed from compassion that I don't see the potential in him."

The hybrid looked up at Dani. She tried to see innocence in his wide eyes, but figured they were probably way past that point. Whatever road he picked, it would be a challenge, sure enough.

"Go on with Francis," she said. "It'll be okay. I'll see you later."

The teen let go and slid up beside Francis, who hesitated, then put an arm around the hybrid's bony shoulders. He replaced his fedora and tipped it to her and Ben.

"I'll be in touch with further orders. For now, I suggest you both visit the showers and cafeteria, and then rest." He guided the teen out of the room and the door shut behind them.

Dani's stomach rumbled. "I forgot this place has a cafeteria. They better have chocolate pudding."

Disappointment pinched Ben's lips and cheeks. "Dani, what about finishing school? Getting that shiny diploma and all?"

"Just because I'm on the payroll doesn't mean I have to work full-time," she said. "I'll consider it a work-study. It'll keep life interesting." She eyed the stub of his arm. "But what about you? When were you going to tell me you'd lost your powers?"

He shrugged with his good shoulder. "Figured we'd be facin' enough problems back here without heapin' another on the pile."

"Don't use that lame excuse," she said. "What's the real reason?"

Ben sighed. "I wanted to keep it quiet until things settled down, but I guess the Board let that cat out and skinned it a dozen which ways. Right now, Francis is probably figurin' the odds of sendin' a team over to scrub my memories."

"What? How could he do that to you after all you've done?"

"It'd be the most practical option. Unless my power comes back, I ain't a Cleaner no more, but I know almost everythin' about how things run here. I'm ... what's the word? A liability."

"You mean li—oh. Yeah. You got it right." She shook her head. "But I can't let them do that to you! First, you make Sydney nearly kill you. Then I thought you died from the hybrid. Now you're going to let them take you away without even putting up a fight?"

"How you gonna stop them? Take on all of HQ by yourself?" He held up a hand before she could reply. "Naw. Don't even think it. You're just now gettin' your life back. Don't be throwin' it away for me. Whatever comes, I can handle it."

Dani tried not to pout, but her lower lip pushed out despite her best effort. Ben half-smiled at her disgruntlement.

"Lookee here. I ain't givin' up. This ain't no surrender. But even if they did let me stick around, I'm just gonna be a distraction. You gotta get out on your own. Figure this bein' the next step in your career."

"But what will you do?" she asked. "Will I ever see you again?"

A grimace. "Eh. I'll figure it out. But in case I do get shoved out on the street, or wind up thinkin' my name's Edward Billings the Third, or some other fake life ... I want'cha to know somethin'."

"What?"

He took her into a swift, hard hug. Then he went to the door, which opened onto another stark hall. After looking both ways, he glanced over his shoulder.

"I'm proud of you, princess. You done good."

He strode out and the door shut behind him.

CHAPTER FORTY-ONE

After grabbing a sandwich and empty soup bowl from the cafeteria, Ben ate while registering for temporary quarters. Once assigned a room, he made his way through a series of window-portals to that section of HQ, found the proper door, and typed in the security code.

It opened and revealed a simple dresser, bathroom, and slab of padded concrete masquerading as a bed. Ben set the bowl on the dresser and then stripped down for a shower. While the water heated up, he took a few minutes to study what remained of his right arm in the mirror.

The stub was fleshy and pink, not a spot of black or gray marring the skin. It wiggled a bit when he flexed his shoulder. Ben poked and prodded, testing the sensitivity until he reassured himself that no trace of the Ravishing remained.

His attention turned to his face. A version of himself he hadn't seen in five years stared back. Firm skin, no bags under the eyes, full lips. Hair in all the right places, instead of migrating from his head to his ears and nose. His chin didn't even jiggle.

As the mirror steamed up, he abandoned the self-inspection and jumped in. Showering with one arm proved tricky until he figured out the best way to juggle lathering, rinsing, and shampooing. Once done and toweled off, he padded back into the bedroom and pulled a one-size-fits-all jumpsuit out of the dresser. It shrank to his lanky frame and faded to a dusty blue. Rubber boots from the closet fit snugly.

He sat on the bed, elbow on a knee, chin on his fist. Water swirled and foamed in the now-full soup bowl.

Ben grunted. "Ain't I a pretty sight?"

Carl blurped, making Ben glare his way.

"Whaddaya mean it ain't an improvement? Least I don't got warts under my toenails anymore."

The elemental slopped about.

"My sense of humor is just fine! Now don'tcha be givin' me that look, you—" He sighed and leaned back against the wall. "A'ight, so mebbe I fibbed a bit, huh? Gettin' kicked outta here don't sit as pretty with me as I mighta made her think. I don't wanna forget ..." He waved his arm. "All this. But what's a fella to do? What good am I now?"

The bowl wobbled as Carl almost tipped it over.

"I know you mean well, buddy, but we've always been honest with each other, ain't we?" He rubbed the stump. "It's like a second limb got chopped off along with the arm. You got any idea what that's like?" At Carl's sympathetic gurgle, he snorted. "Yeah, right. You don't even got arms. Everythin's all outta whack, inside and out. I can't even sense you anymore."

Carl shot up into a tiny fountain.

"Do I really wanna stay? What kinda question is that? Sure, things ain't been a perfect puddle of puddin', but since when did I ever expect it to be? Sure, the company's got a few iffy policies, but it's ... it's home."

The water fizzed.

"Right. Not your home. Thank you for clearin' that up." He scratched his stubble. "So, whatcha think? After they gimme the boot, you gonna head back upstream? See the family?"

Tiny waves slapped the side of the bowl.

"Well, give 'em my regards. And my thanks, yeah? Wouldn't ever have made it this long without—"

The door opened and Francis strode in. The new Chairman already held the air of command that Ben had associated with Destin. The look fit him.

"Ben." Francis nodded at the bowl of water. "Carl."

Ben stood. He winced in anticipation but his knees didn't pop. Having a fit body again would take some getting used to. Of course, once they altered his memories, he wouldn't remember ever being old in the first place, so perhaps it was a blessing in disguise.

"You're gonna take care of Dani?" he asked.

"Your proclamation during your brief stint as Chairman still stands," Francis said. "I'll make sure no one within our organization causes her any grief. Obviously, I can't watch over her every minute of the day when she's on a job."

"A'ight." Ben forced himself to stand straight. Now was not the time to be a coward. "Let's get this done."

The Chairman showed a tight smile. "Yes, let's."

He drew a manila folder out of his jacket and handed it to Ben, who took it and stared.

"What's this?"

"All the information I could dig up concerning your and Karen's final job together." Francis clasped his hands behind his back. "Unfortunately, from my cursory scan, it seems Destin only filled out a minimal account of events to satisfy the Board. Most major details seem to be missing or are blacked out. I can't make sense of what little remains, but perhaps you'll have better luck."

Ben laid the envelope on the bed. His hand trembled as he undid the string keeping the flap closed. An upside-down shake dislodged a black-and-white photograph. He dropped the envelope and snatched the photo up.

It showed Karen as he last remembered her. Curly hair down to her shoulders, a laugh about to burst from her lips, eyes alight with the joy of her work. She stared off at some unseen focus. A peek in the envelope showed a sketched map of a sewer network, a stapled report, and a handful of notes.

He looked to Francis. "Why? I figured I was gonna be scrubbed out."

"There's no guarantee your loss of powers is permanent. It'd be a waste of valuable experience if we removed you from our ranks.

That, at least, is the argument I presented to the Board. I'd like to think I possess a measure of decency the previous Chairman lacked." He made an apologetic bow. "I regret following his orders so blindly. Ever since you contracted the Ravishing, you've fought your battles alone. No Cleaner should ever be forced to work under such circumstances again. It's a blotch on our records I hope to erase."

Ben found himself speechless.

"I know our dealings in the past have been less than amicable," Francis said, "especially over the past few days. But give me a chance. I might surprise you."

"You already have." Ben slid Karen's photo back into the envelope. "Problem is, I ain't so sure I'm gonna be able to do anythin' about this, even if I dig up some leads. Without my powers, all I'm gonna be able to do is knock Scum down with some nasty coffee breath."

"I can't offer any more assistance than this," Francis said. "For now, at least. The Board is already displeased by my decision to keep you on payroll."

"Yeah, well, since when are they ever happy with anythin'?" Ben reached up to massage the loose skin of his face, then remembered he didn't have to do that anymore and dropped his hand. "What now? Where you gonna fit me in?"

"I'm sure we can work something out."

● ● ●

Dani tried to eat her meal in the cafeteria after a kindly maid showed her where it was in the first place. She sat alone with a bowl of spicy chili, sensing the stares and whispers around her. She focused on the spoon, checking for spots or films.

Salmonella. E. Coli. Diphther—

With a snort, she lowered the utensil.

Get over it, Dani. You're in the Cleaners' HQ. I'm sure they do the dishes.

She dug in, but after just a few mouthfuls, her appetite fled. Shoving the meal aside, she rose and stalked out to wander the halls of HQ, letting herself get as lost as she felt.

It wasn't fair. How could the people who ran this company, supernatural or not, be so concerned about the fate of the world and everyone in it, yet be so inhumane when it came to dealing with one of their own? It didn't make sense. In the normal world, when someone did a good job they got recognition for it. A raise. A party. Maybe a small plaque.

Here, when a guy uncovered a source of rogue manifestations and helped depose a Corrupt boss, he got wiped out as if he never existed. Could she really work for these people? Despite her promise for the sake of the hybrid, she wrestled with the impulse to run out the door the first chance she got.

Dani sighed as she turned a random corner. Underneath all her objections and fuming lay the fact that the Cleaners fascinated her. She didn't think she could ever fully cut herself off from this side of existence. And what of Sydney's prediction that all their struggles were hopeless? She refused to believe it. She had to prove him wrong somehow.

Still. It wasn't right.

"Ms. Hashelheim!"

She looked up to see Francis striding toward her. How he'd tracked her down with her aimless wandering, she couldn't guess. She waited until he stopped before her and then burst out.

"What'd you do with Ben?"

His eyes widened, and in them she saw the guilt she feared. It was too late then. They'd already removed him. He'd be as ignorant of her existence as her parents.

"Ms. Hashelheim, I—"

"Couldn't you even give me a chance to say goodbye? How can you be so heartless? I don't care what you do to me, I'm going to get him back. Where'd you send him?"

"Right here, princess."

She spun to see Ben standing behind her, a mirthful light in his eyes and a cardboard box tucked under his remaining arm.

"They didn't … you're …"

He grinned. "Yup. Francis and I had a little chat. I'm gonna be brought on as a consultant. Extra pay. Flexible hours. Expense account. All the free bagels I can stuff my yapper with. Figured I'd give it a shot."

She grabbed him into another tight hug, not caring how unprofessional it might look. He returned it for a few moments, then shuffled free and motioned for her to take the box. She did so and looked inside.

Tetris cocked his head and poked a stubby tongue out as if to say, *Where ya been?*

Dani barely suppressed a squeal of glee as she scooped the lizard out and gave him a gentle squeeze. The rows of spines along his sides pricked her palms in their comforting way.

"Stewart handed him over when Francis' team brought him in," Ben said.

"I'm still not forgiving that rat." Dani tickled the lizard's nose until Francis coughed. She returned Tetris to his box and looked to the Chairman. "Something else?"

"Just to notify you that you are free to contact your family and acquaintances again, though I'm sure you understand the necessity of keeping them ignorant of your true line of work. Also ..." Francis handed her a slip of paper.

"What's thi—" Her mouth dropped open.

"We're covering the rest of your tuition upon your return to school. Consider it payment for services rendered."

She triple-checked the amount. "Uh ... thanks. Wow."

A white smile split his face, the first of his she'd seen. "In the meantime, I believe Janitor Benjamin would like you to accompany him to the garage."

She narrowed her eyes at them. "Why?"

Ben laughed and waved for her to follow. "C'mon and see."

•　•　•

She scrutinized the white van Ben had led her to. Its front and back fenders were dinged, and a series of scratches over the back doors looked disturbingly like claw marks. Cracks laced the windshield and one of the side mirrors had been torn off. No doubt the engine sputtered and the brakes were spongy, but the van emanated a solid presence that already had her wanting to run it over the first gnash that got in her way.

Ben tossed her a set of keys. "Your first company car. Proud yet?"

"Do I get reimbursed for gas?"

"For work-related trips, yup."

"Goodie."

She slid the side door open and stuck Tetris' box on one of the empty shelves. Ben looked over her shoulder.

"You gotta visit Supplies and pick out tools and equipment. And you might wanna arrange for some lessons in handlin' different parts of your power."

"Thanks," she said. "I'll consider it."

She walked around the vehicle, noting every dent and scrape. Once she stood on the other side, where Ben couldn't hear, she patted the chassis and whispered, "I am so painting you pink."

When she finished the circuit, Ben slammed the side shut and waved for her to get in.

"Why don'tcha take her for a spin?"

With a grin and a bouncing step, she tugged open the driver's door. She and Ben froze. They looked at each other and then back at the black rose and white glove waiting on the seat. A lacy red card had been propped up against the thorny stem, reading: *A memento to keep me in your thoughts until our paths once more unite, dearest.*

Dani groaned. "Oh, for ****'s sake."

IF YOU LIKED ...

If you liked *Enter the Janitor*, you might also enjoy:

Working Stiff

Whack Job

and Coming Soon:

The Maids of Wrath

About the Author

A full-time freelance writer, Josh Vogt has been published in dozens of genre markets with work ranging from flash fiction to short stories to doorstopper novels that cover fantasy, science fiction, horror, humor, pulp, and more. He also writes for a wide variety of RPG developers such as Paizo, Modiphius, and Privateer Press. His debut fantasy novel, *Forge of Ashes*, adds to the popular Pathfinder Tales line. WordFire Press has launched his urban fantasy series, The Cleaners, with *Enter the Janitor* (2015) and *The Maids of Wrath* (2016). You can find him at JRVogt.com. He's a member of SFWA as well as the International Association of Media Tie-In Writers. He is made out of meat.

OTHER WORDFIRE PRESS TITLES

Our list of other WordFire Press authors and titles is always growing. To find out more and to see our selection of titles, visit us at

wordfirepress.com